JAKE
BUCHAN

BLIND
PURSUIT

SOMEONE ROBBED DCI JOHN STEADMAN
OF HIS SIGHT AND HIS WIFE – BUT THEY COULD
NOT KILL HIS COURAGE

JAKE
BUCHAN

BLIND
PURSUIT

SOMEONE ROBBED DCI JOHN STEADMAN
OF HIS SIGHT AND HIS WIFE – BUT THEY COULD
NOT KILL HIS COURAGE

MEREO
Cirencester

Mereo Books

1A The Wool Market Dyer Street Cirencester Gloucestershire GL7 2PR
An imprint of Memoirs Publishing www.mereobooks.com

Blind Pursuit: 978-1-86151-130-0

First published in Great Britain in 2014
by Mereo Books, an imprint of Memoirs Publishing

The address for Memoirs Publishing Group Limited can be found at
www.memoirspublishing.com

Cover Design Ray Lipscombe

The Memoirs Publishing Group Ltd Reg. No. 7834348

The Memoirs Publishing Group supports both The Forest Stewardship Council® (FSC®) and
the PEFC® leading international forest-certification organisations. Our books carrying both the
FSC label and the PEFC® and are printed on FSC®-certified paper. FSC® is the only
forest-certification scheme supported by the leading environmental organisations including
Greenpeace. Our paper procurement policy can be found at
www.memoirspublishing.com/environment

Typeset in 11.5/16pt Plantin
by Wiltshire Associates Publisher Services Ltd. Printed and bound in Great Britain by
Printondemand-Worldwide, Peterborough PE2 6XD

John ('Jake') Buchan was born in Aberdeen, Scotland and moved in 1981 to Mid Wales, where he worked as a family and hospital doctor for over thirty years. He lives with his wife, son Nick 'the blacksmith' and Robbie, a retired guide dog.

Acknowledgements

Completing any novel is a triumph of diligence over distraction, never more so than with a first attempt. Numerous people have kept me on the straight and narrow. I am particularly grateful for the help I have been given by retired Detective Sergeant Terry Parkhouse, Dr Maureen Crosby and my dear friend Nick Randall-Smith.

Robbie, undoubtedly the best guide dog ever, and his former owner have steered me gently into a world without sight; their contribution has been immeasurable.

I roped in as many of my colleagues and friends as could be pressed to read the various drafts: drinks all round and thanks to them all, especially to Nick Passmore, whose rigour may even have earned him a bar meal as well.

Thanks also to Chris Newton of Memoirs Books for his professional editing and final polish.

Above all I am indebted to my wife Trish and my children Emma, Jo and Nick for their love, encouragement and support.

To Trish

'The best thing to hold onto in life is each other.'

(Audrey Hepburn)

CHAPTER ONE

Strong hands pinned his arms firmly behind his back. Another hand pulled his hair, tugging his head back, forcing him to look at his wife. He could not scream; duct tape secured his mouth. Still on his knees, he was dragged closer. Close enough to feel the warmth of her body. He could see the terror on his wife's face. Her mouth was similarly gagged.

'Now watch, Steadman.' It was a smooth, silky voice from under a thick stocking mask. The silenced muzzle of the gun was placed on his wife's temple. She was beyond fighting now. Her eyes showed only despair. She looked directly at her husband. Just before the trigger was pulled, she shook her head very slightly; her gaze melted into tenderness, as if to say, 'It's not your fault, John. I love you.'

Detective Inspector John Steadman struggled ferociously. Handfuls of hair came out. His jaw twisted and turned as he tried to free it from the tape. His lips were torn, and they bled as a small gap appeared.

'NO!' he screamed as loud as he could.

It was too late. A muffled 'phut', like a cat sneezing; his wife's head lurched on to her shoulder. As the gun recoiled, her head lifted. The eyes were closed and a large trickle of blood crept down her cheek. Her body went completely limp. Her head flopped forward and blood dripped on to their living room carpet.

Steadman was not giving in without a fight. Now four men were on top of him trying to pin him down. The fifth still held the gun.

'Now your turn.'

He had heard that voice before. He couldn't place it, but he recognised it nonetheless. The gun was placed on his temple. He was screaming again.

'No, no – you bastards – no!'

He jerked his head as a gloved finger squeezed the trigger.

★ ★ ★

'You're all right sir, you're all right now – here let me help you.'

It was George, one of the caretakers of the safe house. Steadman was sitting up in bed, soaked in sweat, his sheets knotted and his pillows lying on the floor. His sightless eyes wandered in the direction of the comforting voice.

'Same nightmare again, sir?'

'Second time this week,' replied Steadman faintly.

'It gets more vivid every time. I just can't understand...'

'Come on, you look as though you could do with a shower. I'll change the bed. Would a scotch help?'

Steadman sighed, shaking his head as though trying to get rid of the images. 'Why not? It can't do any harm. Have one yourself.'

Steadman got to his feet and swayed slightly.

'Steady now!'

Large damp patches showed on his grey tee shirt. A bead of sweat ran down his long thin nose. He brushed it away.

'Find your own way there?' asked George.

'I'll be fine.'

He moved cautiously towards the door, his arms slightly outstretched, his fingertips probing the darkness. As he touched the door frame he felt more secure and turned left down the corridor towards the bathroom, sliding a guiding hand along the wall.

George watched the retreating figure without comment; anger and pity welled up inside him. He noticed that Steadman's hair was growing, albeit sparsely, and beginning to cover the patch of reconstructed skull. Odd how a bullet through the back of the brain could leave him almost totally blind, he thought, yet his eyes looked so normal.

Steadman had explained it simply: 'I've still got the cameras out front, it's just that nobody's in the back shop to develop the pictures.' It was a good metaphor but a gross oversimplification of his tormented world, now reduced to vague, shifting shades of grey.

He poured two large whiskies. Despite George's tough ex-paratrooper heart, in the short space of time he'd known John Steadman he'd grown fond of him. Moreover, he kept a fine selection of single malts.

Steadman returned refreshed from his shower, wearing a clean white bathrobe. He knew where all the furniture was placed. At first he had counted the steps: two paces to the right, three paces left. Now he had a mental map of his apartment and, provided nothing had been altered, he moved about with deceptive ease. He flopped down into a chair. Deliberately, George placed the whisky rather heavily on the coffee table.

'Is that mine?' Steadman inquired.

'Right in front of you, sir.'

Steadman swept his hand lightly over the table, finding the glass with his first pass.

'As ever George, you are the hero of the hour.' Steadman bowed his head in mock deference.

'I'm only here for the whisky,' replied George in tones of equal insincerity.

'I'll bet you've chosen the Talisker.'

'How did you work that out? Can you tell by the smell?'

He sniffed the glass.

'Undoubtedly. However, I know your favourite is Glenmorangie and, if my memory serves me correctly, there is only enough left in that bottle for one glass. It would be more reasonable, therefore, for you to choose your second favourite, the Talisker, which has only just been opened.' Steadman shrugged his shoulders as if to say, 'simple really.'

'You'll be a sad loss to the force. I'll wager they're missing you.'

'Not half as much as I'm missing them – or my dear Holly...' his voice trailed away and his sightless eyes filled with tears.

They sipped and savoured the peaty island whisky. Steadman brightened up. 'God bless my ancestors! I believe one of them may have come from the Isle of Skye.'

'Is that a fact?' replied George, his mind more on the whisky.

'Yes, though I suspect they would probably have been strict teetotallers.'

'I doubt it, sir.' George noted Steadman's virtually empty glass. 'Care for another?'

'One is enough at this hour. What time is it anyway?'

Looking at his watch, George replied, 'Five past three. Do you want a hand getting back into bed?'

'No, I'm fine now. I think I'll listen to the BBC World Service for a bit, thanks anyway.'

George paused and put down his empty glass. 'You know, sir, I've been thinking. Would it help to talk it through with someone? I know some of my lads witnessed terrible things, like their chums being blown up in the Middle East. It's not the same, but some of them found that it helped.'

'Not yet, George, maybe later. Maybe never.'

★ ★ ★

So, John Steadman, you survived. All my careful plans were to no avail. You have no idea how long I had waited for that one moment: no idea just how much my hatred has grown over time. It burns inside me, consuming my every waking minute. I can remember the moment of that initial hurt with such clarity that it might have occurred only a few hours ago. The passing of the years has, if anything, brought those events into sharper focus. I still feel the humiliation, the sickening pain in the pit of my stomach. Even now I can taste the bitter tears as I choked and sobbed all those years ago. I swallowed an ember of resentment that day and it stuck in my gullet. No amount of personal fame or wealth has extinguished that flame. No amount of alcohol or drugs ever dimmed its light. I had it all: the cars, the women, the big houses, the lavish lifestyle, and I laughed and grinned. I smiled for the cameras, waved to the crowds and protected myself with a carapace as tough as a dung beetle's. But inside I still writhed. One day, I thought, one day...

I followed your career – a policeman, a common copper; mundane for someone so gifted. Was it to make up for your pathetic father? Oh yes, I know all about him too. And your son; I met him, an illusionist in an 'alternative' circus. God, how that must have disappointed you, you who like everything so neat, so tidy. I toyed with the idea of making him 'disappear'; a befitting end for an illusionist! But which would hurt you more – his loss, or the constant thorn of your disappointment in him? The latter, I think.

Money is no solace, yet it can satisfy one's needs. Did I offer too much to avenge the wrong? I think not. Four greedy louts from the feral, criminal low life, willing to do my bidding, but I would hold the gun. You know what you took from me, don't you, or could you just not see it? Ironic isn't it – you now being truly blind. That wasn't how it was meant to be. That's not how it will be. I do not know how or when I will kill you. With subtlety I think, you'd appreciate that. Don't be mistaken, for one day I will kill you, John Steadman.

CHAPTER TWO

Helmsmouth sprawled out in the pale sunshine, a large coastal town split into two unequal chunks by a rocky promontory. The older part nestled round an attractive cove with a recently-built marina for the well-heeled. The crumbling waterfront had been restored and now offered a range of upmarket designer boutiques, ship's chandlers, seafood restaurants and top-end estate agents. There was money in Helmsmouth, both old and new, some honestly earned and some not so.

The old cobbled streets gave way to tree-lined boulevards. As the ground rose up from the coast, so the properties grew in size and elegance, the finest being on the top of the promontory. On the other side of the bluff was the much larger, working part of Helmsmouth. At its hub was a large deep-water harbour. The shipbuilding had all but gone; only one small yard remained, an impressive new ferry terminal had taken its place. Encroaching on the harbour were huge warehouses, container depots and a vast number of small businesses that supported the port's activities. Amongst these were grubby hotels, bars, gambling dens and a shifting tide of whorehouses; everything, in fact, to keep frustrated seafarers happy and the police busy. Backing on to all of this was a railway station and a huge new shopping mall, identical to those in every other large town.

Helmsmouth had been bombed during the war. Dotted round the harbour area in particular were concrete and glass buildings which stood incongruously next to their Victorian neighbours. Only one bomb had landed in the hinterland of old Helmsmouth. And it was here in the early 60s that the town planners had, in a fit of madness, opted to build the police headquarters.

It was a tall, ugly building that resembled the husk of a corn cob with all the kernels chewed off. The concrete was dirty beige. The windows were recessed, making them nigh on impossible to clean. Sitting on top of this, and now gently rusting, was a grey metal structure which housed the air conditioning. It bristled with redundant aerials and satellite dishes which provided excellent accommodation for a messy colony of gulls; their droppings ran down the sides like wax on a giant candle. The building was grim and forbidding. It was known by everybody as the 'Eyesore'; only those whose rank was assistant chief constable or above referred to it as Helmsmouth Police Headquarters.

Acting Detective Sergeant Alan Munro was staring through the grimy windows of the Eyesore at the sparkling sea. He had not particularly wanted to apply for promotion and was not finding his new role easy. There was something unseemly in sitting behind Steadman's desk, even if he was only an acting sergeant. Munro was the new breed of policeman; university educated and set for a fast-track career – he knew all that. He also knew of the resentment felt by some of his fellow officers. He had been working with John Steadman for barely six months before the shooting. They had become more than just colleagues. Their respective wives had been good friends and Munro's children simply adored Steadman. The murder of Holly and the attempted murder of his boss had cut short what he had hoped would be a partnership lasting for years.

Four of the five men involved had been caught; that had been easy. They were hired psychopaths, shrewd and dangerous, who would do anything if the price was right. And the price had been right; a share of one million pounds for assisting at a double murder. The four had arrived at Steadman's house by car. The fifth arrived on foot, his rucksack containing a gun, half of the money and the key to a deposit box in Helmsmouth Railway Station.

Within minutes of the attack the police had received a phone call: 'John Steadman and his wife have been shot dead. The killers are on their way to the station to collect their reward.'

That call had been traced to a public phone box not far from the Steadman house. There had been hours of questioning, at times brutal and intimidating, but it was clear that the four knew nothing of their would-be employer's identity. There had been a massive investigation. So far the only clue the police had to go on was Steadman's certainty that he had heard that voice before. It was a vague memory; he couldn't place it.

These were not the problems facing Alan Munro at this precise moment. What had started off as an 'unexpected death' was troubling him. The more he thought about it, the more he felt there was something wrong; something wasn't making sense. It was as though two jigsaw puzzles had got muddled together. It didn't help that the dead person, Alisha Gupta, was the wife of Dr Aaron Gupta, one of Helmsmouth's leading dentists and golfing partner of the Assistant Chief Constable.

To add to his worries, the first pathologist could find no cause of death and had been quite offhand with DS Munro.

'I didn't say the death was 'natural', all I'm telling you is that there is no immediately obvious cause' he had said. 'Yes, she had a small hole in the heart, but that wasn't the cause of death. I've handed it over to the Home Office for a second post mortem.' The phone had clicked down. Munro had left it all day before he called. Dr Frank Rufus the Home Office forensic pathologist had been even ruder.

'I don't bloody well know yet, and if you lot keep pestering me I'll never find out!' If you want quick answers, send me a fresh corpse with a dagger sticking out of it.' And with that, he too had put down the phone.

Detective Chief Inspector Long looked into Munro's office. He was a soft spoken man who lived up to his name by being an inch or two taller than all the other officers and was respected and feared in equal measures. He demanded high standards, even from acting sergeants.

'I detect by your furrowed brow a feeling of despair, young Munro.'

Alan Munro shifted his bulky frame in the small office chair. He was a big man, an ex-rugby player who found everything in the world, from his shirt collar to his present seat, just that bit too small.

'It's this dentist's wife. There's something not right, and I feel I'm being subtly pressured into wrapping the case up,' said Munro, running a finger round his collar in a vain attempt to stretch it.

'Ah yes! The ACC's golfing partner, and just at the start of the season. He won't like that!'

'So you've heard too – is that why you're here?'

'Partly, but I'm on your side, if it's any comfort. I don't give a damn about who or what people are. My job is to detect crimes and bring the perpetrators of those crimes to justice – straightforward, really.'

'Well, this seemed straightforward at first - a lady with a supposedly weak heart is found dead by her husband. Apart from his callous attitude, nothing was suspicious to begin with – now, I just don't know. My gut feeling is that a crime has been committed, but I've no real proof.'

'Your notes, I assume, are as detailed as ever. It must be your degree in physics. Three years studying everything from atoms to astronomy.'

'Something like that sir,' replied Munro, who didn't feel this was leading anywhere.

'Why don't you go through your notes with John Steadman? He's moved to Jamaica Mansion now. You know - the safe house about half a mile down the road - the old merchant's house behind the high wall? He's probably bored to tears and would be grateful for the company not to mention the intellectual stimulus. I can give him a call for you.'

'I know Jamaica Mansion. I didn't realise it was a safe house.'

'Oh yes - has been for some years. You will need clearance. I can sort that out for you.'

'What about confidentiality and that sort of thing?'

'No problem there. Steadman is still technically on sick leave, and you are only an acting sergeant!' There was a twinkle in Long's eye, and Munro blushed.

'I didn't mean anything,' he stammered.

'I know you didn't, that's what makes you a good officer. You know the old motto, 'once a copper, always a copper' – I'll give him a call.'

The chief inspector loped off to his office. A few minutes later he returned beaming.

'The good John Steadman will see you now,' he said.

'He says to walk down and fetch two coffees and two Danish pastries from Lloyd's café, and you can put them on his slate.'

'Are you sure it will be OK?'

'He wouldn't have offered you coffee and cakes if it wasn't.'

CHAPTER THREE

It was a lovely sunny day with the smell of summer just round the corner. Lloyd's was one of the oldest cafés in Helmsmouth and had been in the same Italian family for several generations. The original owners, the Franchettis, had arrived in Britain in the 1920s. To their disappointment they had had only one child, a daughter who had married a handsome Welshman named Owain Lloyd. They succeeded in having a large family, and it was their grandchildren who now ran the café. Although old Mr Franchetti had been upset at not passing on the family name, his daughter being a Lloyd had saved the family from being carted off to the Isle of Man during the Second World War as 'undesirable aliens'.

The café was a frequent haunt of the police, being only a few hundred yards from the Eyesore. But having a slate in Lloyd's, or being a 'Lloyd's name' as it was more affectionately called, was exceptional. As Marco Lloyd frequently pointed out, 'You police are all nice honest people, but you have short memories when it comes to paying up!'

Steadman was one of these exceptions, and Marco carefully selected the two largest pastries to go with the freshly ground coffee.

'Tell Mr Steadman I'm asking for him, wherever he's living now,' said Marco with a wink as he handed Alan Munro the small brown carrier bag.

Munro shook his head. So much for 'secret' safe houses, he thought.

★ ★ ★

Jamaica Mansion was fronted by a high, ivy-covered wall and not visible from the street. The entrance was through a door discreetly tucked into a niche in the wall. Alan pressed the button on the 'door porter' system.

'May I help you?' crackled the small speaker.

'DS Alan Munro – I'm expected.' He had been told not to mention Steadman by name.

'Would you please look closely with your right eye at the spy hole in the centre of the door?'

What appeared to be a spy hole was in fact an iris recognition monitor. Munro had been forewarned. After a few seconds the voice returned.

'That's fine sir, we'll just wait until these two pedestrians pass by and I'll open the door.'

Munro looked round and sure enough, two lovers were walking hand in hand towards him. This place must be crawling with security cameras, he thought.

The lovers passed and the wooden door slid open.

The wood was only for show; the door itself was several inches thick and made of steel. A pleasant drive wound through well-tended but slightly overgrown grounds. Jamaica Mansion was old, solid and would have been elegant had it not been for the numerous additions over the years. It was now divided up into several small apartments. Another check and he was in. He was greeted by a fit, stocky, grey-haired man.

'I'm George,' he said. 'Let me show you up to Mr Steadman's apartment. He's looking forward to seeing you.'

Realising his gaffe, George stammered, 'Not 'seeing' you as such, but …well, you know what I mean.'

John Steadman was at the door of his apartment waiting for them. He was smiling anxiously, his lean frame outlined by the sun streaming through the windows. Alan Munro grinned as he shook his colleague's outstretched hand.

'It's good to see you again, you're looking fantastic, sir,' said Munro, although his former boss appeared a good deal older than he remembered. His wavy hair was definitely streaked with more grey and his face more lined. Still, it was an improvement. The last time he had seen Steadman he had been lying in a hospital bed with his head heavily swathed in bandages.

'Less of the 'sir'. Come in. I can smell the coffee – excellent!'

The interior of the apartment was surprisingly stark and modern. There was one large public room with sunny views of old Helmsmouth and the sea beyond.

The chairs and sofa were all soft leather. Munro noticed that their places were marked on the carpet by crosses of sticky tape, like a stage set. Against one wall there was a small upright piano and on another an expensive radio/CD player with a large collection of CDs. The CDs were divided into groups by plastic spacers, each notched with a different pattern, enabling Steadman to know roughly the order they were in. The only decoration was a small display cabinet. In this was a collection of netsuke, small intricate ivory and boxwood Japanese carvings. Munro knew that Steadman had been collecting these for years. They were not only beautiful but very tactile. Munro could understand why Steadman was still so fond of them. There were no books, no photos, and no pictures – there was no need.

'I've never met anyone who has a 'Lloyd's name'' said Munro.

'A mixture of gratitude and sympathy, I fear. Someone tried to involve the Lloyds in a protection racket some years ago. That was sorted out and, of course, they now feel sorry for me.'

'How did they find out you were in Jamaica Mansion? I thought this was a safe house.'

'It is, and they're completely trustworthy. Without their provisions I reckon I would have starved to death by now.'

The two men sat with their coffee and pastries and caught up on all the gossip. One of Munro's daughters had recently been diagnosed with leukaemia and

Steadman was keen to know how she was getting on. Munro was quite upbeat. She had had a very good response to the last lot of drugs and the doctors were hopeful of a cure. Unfortunately, as a side effect, she had lost her hair.

'But I've bought her the best wig money can buy, and it won't be for that long' said Munro. His wife, Maureen, and his other daughter were both well.

John Steadman's son Ben, having helped his father settle in Jamaica Mansion, was back in France touring with his circus. Steadman's only other close relative was his sister, Linda, a professional gardener. She was in constant touch and desperate to have him visit. Munro gave him all the news from the Eyesore as Steadman drained the last of his coffee.

'Down to business – I'm dying to hear about this case. There's been no mention whatsoever in the news.'

'It may be nothing, but I have some misgivings. There is something not right. It doesn't hang together… I don't really know what's worrying me.'

'Why don't you start at the beginning and we can go through it together?' There was a faint rustle of paper as Alan Munro got out his notes.

'I'm sure you've gone over your notes a dozen times – put them away! The answer, if there is one, doesn't lie there. Why don't you make yourself as comfortable as you can? Put your feet up. If you move the furniture put it back where it was, otherwise I'll go my length. Now, how did it all start?'

Alan Munro took a deep breath.

'Monday morning, eight-thirty, I got a call from the duty desk sergeant regarding an unexpected death. A certain Dr Aaron Gupta had phoned the Coroner's Officer just before eight, but wasn't making a great deal of sense. Apparently a woman had been found dead and he, Dr Gupta that is, wasn't prepared to issue a death certificate. The Coroner's Officer had the address but had not managed to get the deceased's full name. The advice from the Coroner was to arrange a routine post mortem, inform the relatives and ask the police to get the usual information. Why the call came through to plain clothes and not to uniformed I don't know. As you're probably aware, they've made me acting sergeant. Some eyebrows have been raised at this and the last thing I wanted to do was rock the boat, so I took the address and went myself.'

Steadman nodded. 'Go on.'

'I don't know if you know Gorse Hill but there are some seriously expensive properties there. Number 47 is right at the top, with spectacular views. It has massive, ornate gates opening on to a large gravelled drive. Even the gateposts are adorned, if that's the right word, with two statues of lions painted gold. Below one of the lions are three doctors' names. Dr Gupta's is at the top. I assumed, wrongly as it turned out, that this was some sort of private medical clinic and one of his patients had dropped down dead.'

Steadman cleared his throat and was about to say something.

'I know what you're going to say: 'never assume anything'. Hindsight is marvellous' said Munro.

Steadman smiled, 'Please continue. I'm intrigued already.'

'There were only three cars parked in the drive: a Range Rover, a Porsche and a Mini. The gardens, or should I say grounds, are manicured. Next to the parking area is a fairly new building with glass doors leading to a reception area. A large Victorian house stands behind the shrubbery. A small glass corridor connects the two. I could see a woman at the reception desk shuffling notes. I suspect she's employed more for her looks than her brains. She's very easy on the eye. She seemed perplexed when I said Dr Gupta was expecting me. Dr Gupta apparently had cancelled all appointments for that day. She was even more surprised when I said that I was a policeman and that I had come about a death. She thought Dr Gupta was still at home, as his car was still there, and said she would call him. This took only a moment. Dr Gupta asked her to show me through to the house.

'I don't think I've ever seen so much luxury in my life. There were antiques, paintings, old rugs – you name it, it was there, all totally over the top. As we entered, Dr Gupta came down the stairs and shook my hand. He was impeccably dressed in a slightly shiny expensive suit, shirt and tie. I would guess that he is in his late forties and of mixed Asian origin, not particularly tall but well built with a full head of dark hair. He moved gracefully but there was not a flicker of emotion on his face. 'Thank you Jean' he said, and the woman left.'

'Do you reckon Jean was familiar with the house?' Steadman interjected.

'Almost certainly. No one could walk in and see all that luxury for the first time without staring. Anyway, she disappeared, presumably back to her lair in the clinic. I introduced myself and apologised that I did not have his patient's full name. 'It's not my patient, it's my wife,' he said – blow number one.

'I apologised again and foolishly said that I was under the impression from the Coroner's Officer that he was not able to issue a death certificate. 'That's true,' he said. 'I am not able to - no dentist can unless he is also medically qualified.' I said something like, 'I thought he *was* a doctor' – blow number two! I had forgotten that dentists can also call themselves 'doctor'. As you can imagine, I now felt totally stupid. Here I was in this man's swanky house, not knowing that it was his wife who had died and probably having also offended his profession. 'Would you like to see the body?' he asked, adding that he hadn't moved anything. He actually referred to his wife as 'the body'! His manner was so bloody matter of fact. I just couldn't warm to this man at all. Maybe it was my embarrassment, I don't know.

'Her bedroom was as sumptuous as the rest of the house - a bit more flowery perhaps. There was no disturbance - nothing obviously out of place. An alarm clock was ticking on the bedside cabinet next to an empty cup. And there she was lying flat on her back in her night dress, tucked up in bed just as though she was asleep. Her eyes were shut, but her mouth was open. Her lips and tongue were blue. She was cold and quite dead. But it was his behaviour that was most disconcerting. He was totally detached. He just stood there staring into space as though none of this was any of his concern.

'Time to take control, I thought. As no one had actually verified death I asked who the family doctor was. I contacted him and he came at once - a young nervous man by the name of Robinson. He appeared far more concerned than Dr Gupta was. He got quite flustered. He had seen her only three days before to give her a repeat prescription for her sleeping pills. He said that she had a small hole in the heart, but the experts weren't worried about it; otherwise she had a clean bill of health. After checking her pulse and looking at her eyes he confirmed what we already knew. He presumed she had had a heart attack during the night but wasn't prepared to give a certificate. I informed Dr Gupta that a routine post mortem would be arranged and that his wife's remains would be collected later that day.

'Her name is Alisha Gupta. She is 44 and as far as her husband could tell was quite well prior to going to bed. He confirmed that she took a sleeping pill occasionally but couldn't say if she had taken any the previous evening as they had separate bedrooms.'

Steadman raised a questioning eyebrow.

'Apparently he snores loudly,' Munro continued. 'She never drank nor smoked, but there is some heart disease in her family. They had been married for 17 years but had no children. Both were born somewhere in Malaysia – I've written it down but can't remember where exactly. He is a dentist and she ran some sort of cosmetics firm. Ten years ago they moved to this country, where he set up in private practice; she kept the books apparently. And certainly, looking at the house, she kept them fairly well.'

Steadman chuckled, 'Don't let your Scottish Calvinistic background prejudice you, at least not too much!'

'I'll try not to, but really, you should have seen the place! I asked if there was anybody he would like me to contact but he declined, saying he would attend to it all. And then, and I quote, he said, 'If that's all, I'm rather busy. I will ask Jean to escort you…' I must have stood there like a goldfish gasping for air. Here was a man whose wife of 17 years had died unexpectedly and I was being shown the door like a travelling salesman who had outstayed his welcome.

'Jean arrived and politely took me back to my car. Maybe Dr Gupta was afraid I would pinch something. She asked tactfully if everything was all right - I swear she didn't know what was going on. I told her Dr Gupta would come and explain. She nodded but didn't say anything.

'I don't know about you, sir, but every time I've been to a dentist on a Monday morning they're queuing out the door, so I ventured to say, 'You're very quiet today?' 'Oh, the other two dentists are on holiday,' she replied. I asked her when Dr Gupta had cancelled his Monday clinic. She thought for a minute and then said, 'Last Thursday, he said he was going to play golf today.' I asked if he often played golf on a Monday, but she became quite evasive. I don't think she liked me asking questions about her boss.'

'How long has she worked for Dr Gupta?' Steadman asked.

'I didn't think to ask.'

'Do you think they could be lovers?'

'I suspect they may be!' replied Munro with a sly grin. 'Dr Gupta must get lonely at night, snores or no snores. There are two further issues. Firstly the local pathologist could find no obvious cause of death. There was a hole in the heart – a 'patent foramen ovale' if I recall correctly - he didn't think it was significant. And so he requested the Home Office pathologist to carry out a second post mortem. I've never met Dr Rufus, but he didn't half tear a strip off me.'

At this John Steadman laughed. 'He is the rudest, most vulgar, most clever and also the kindest man you're ever likely to meet. He is a good friend and if it wasn't for his support in the last few weeks I personally would have completed the job my 'would-be assassin' tried to do. He lost his own wife many years ago. A freak wave swept her off a boat on their honeymoon. Her body was never found.'

'Jesus, that's awful,' said Munro.

'He buried himself in his work, training first as a surgeon, then as a pathologist. Latterly he has become one of Britain's most respected forensic experts. He doesn't care what people think of him. He is brutally honest - in fact the only truly honest person I know.'

'But...' stammered Munro.

Steadman held up a hand.

'I'm not saying *you* are dishonest. However, take for example when we met just now, if I recollect you said I looked 'fantastic' - polite and well-meant, but not strictly true. I know I've lost so much weight that all my clothes are too big for me, that my head is misshapen and that my hair doesn't cover where the surgery was done and that my eyes if left to their own devices wander aimlessly round in their sockets.'

'Would you rather I said those things?' inquired Munro, his cheeks turning crimson.

'No, no – you are fine just as you are. And if the world was full of people like Frank Rufus it would be completely unbearable. In fact, most people would say that outside the mortuary one Frank Rufus was one too many. But we all need a few home truths from time to time, and he's the man I'd choose to give them to me. You must meet him, I think you'd get on. Back to the case in hand - you said there were two further issues. What was the second one?'

'Well, after I got back to the Eyesore I had a phone call from Dr Gupta, who said he had discovered a broken window. He was not sure if someone hadn't entered the house, as there was some mud on the floor. I went back and took Kim Ho from forensics with me. The door to the utility room at the back of the house is half glazed, and sure enough, one of the panes had been smashed. It would have been easy to open the door and gain access to the utility room and possibly the kitchen. The main body of the house has intruder alarms. Nothing appears to have been taken. If there was any mud it had all been cleaned up along with all the broken glass. Kim couldn't find any finger prints but took away a box with the bits of glass in it. The pathways are all gravel. She may have got a shoe impression. Of course she'll have to check that it isn't from any of the staff or indeed the Guptas, both of whom, I suspect have enormous collections of shoes. Dr Gupta usually switches on the intruder alarms manually every night. He sometimes likes a stroll in the grounds before turning in. He couldn't state definitely that the alarm was on that night, he sometimes forgets. If anything he was a bit more rattled by the broken window; either that or he was a good actor. And there you have it – about as a clear as a foggy day in Dunoon.'

Steadman frowned, shifting all the bits of information round in his head. He hummed a little tune to himself; a sure sign that he was deep in thought.

'Yes, I see what you mean. It doesn't all fit together

nicely. Lots of loose ends. Let's start at the beginning. Shall we write them down?'

Alan Munro got out his pad and pen.

'Why would someone who had just found his wife dead not dial the emergency services? What are the alternatives?'

Munro smiled to himself. 'What are the alternatives?' was one of John Steadman's maxims.

'Maybe it was self-evident she was dead?' volunteered Munro.

'When did the pathologist state she had died?'

'Sometime between midnight and two a.m.'

'And he discovered her at...?'

Alan consulted his notes.

'Seven thirty.'

'She would have started to cool and stiffen a bit, I suppose. But, hell no, if you found your wife like that you would tear off the bed clothes, start mouth to mouth resuscitation or something, and at least phone for an ambulance. You said the bed was untouched?'

Munro nodded without thinking. Steadman took his silence for a 'yes'.

'If it comes to it, he needs to be grilled on exactly what he did when he found his wife. Next alternative...Suppose it was blatantly clear that she was dead, surely he would phone his family doctor?'

'Perhaps, but if it was that obvious maybe he thought it would be a waste of time,' suggested Munro.

'Maybe, maybe - but I don't like it.' Steadman

started humming again, this time tapping his long bony fingers on the side of his chair to accompany the tune.

'What about plain ignorance? He's only been ten years in the country and dental patients don't usually die,' suggested Munro.

'No – I don't buy that either. He knew all about informing the Coroner.'

'What puzzles me is why he didn't call the police,' Munro continued. 'You find a dead body - you call the police. That's how it goes, even if the dead body is your wife's.'

'Yes, but we ask awkward questions!' said Steadman mischievously.

'He certainly managed to bamboozle the Coroner's Officer, and knock me off my stride,' Munro replied, shifting his large frame to get more comfortable.

'You recovered well, though, and took control of the situation. You don't like his wealth?'

'No, you're bloody right, I don't!' exclaimed Munro. 'The ostentatious display of opulence by the *nouveau riche* when half the world's starving disgusts me.'

'Morally I cannot fault your argument, but for the moment let us leave your left wing tendencies aside and confine ourselves to the case in hand. Can he have earned enough in ten years to afford such a lavish life style? It's true that there is a lot of money to be made in private dentistry.'

'I doubt he could have made that much. Maybe it's family money, who knows? For the moment I don't have any reason or authority to investigate.'

'You said his wife kept the books?'

Munro nodded again, but this time he realised it was a pointless gesture.

'That doesn't seem right' Steadman continued. What did she do all day, and what happened to her cosmetics firm? Those might be interesting questions. What's our next worry?'

'Very convenient that no one was around on Monday other than the 'left in the dark' receptionist,' offered Munro.

'Yes, we could find out about the golf. Nobody plays golf by himself. He would have to have a tee booked and have called whoever he was playing with to say he wasn't coming.'

'Probably the Assistant Chief Constable,' replied Munro testily.

'What? He partners the ACC. Well, if you're going to get a classy alibi, look no further. Is that why there's pressure being put on you to wrap this up?'

'How did you know?'

'A 'Long' bird gave me a hint. Don't let it worry you. The ACC just wants to keep his nose clean and his epaulettes shiny. If he smells a rat he'll be out of it faster than a bishop in a brothel raid.'

'I think I should have a word with Jean the receptionist. She's naïve enough to tell the truth, especially if she thinks that it will save me from pestering the 'very busy' Dr Gupta.'

'What about the broken window?' Steadman ventured.

'I can't make head nor tail of that. There could have been an intruder, I suppose. Dr Gupta assures me that nothing has been taken. Other than dirty laundry, all that is stored in the utility room is stuff for recycling - bottles, newspapers and the like. He says he cleaned up the mess without realising what he was doing.'

'Could Dr Gupta have broken the window himself? And if so, why?' Steadman asked.

'A diversion, perhaps. But then it does end up with forensics crawling all over your house,' replied Munro.

'The problem is, we really don't know if there's actually been any foul play as yet, let alone considered what possible motives there could be. Pleasant though it is sitting here speculating, it may amount to nothing if the good Dr Rufus fails to find anything. Let's phone him.'

'Rather you than me, sir, my ears are still ringing from the last encounter.'

CHAPTER FOUR

'Unless it's important, go away!' Dr Rufus bellowed, without waiting to find out who the caller was.

'What a charming way you have with words, and what a joy it is to be greeted by an old friend in such an accommodating and affable manner.' Steadman raised his eyebrows at Munro.

'Oh, it's you is it? Have they let you out of hospital or are you still languishing, with young maidens tending to your every need?'

Dr Rufus's bearded face cracked into a wide smile. It pleased him no end to hear his friend's voice again, and sounding so much stronger. John Steadman was unaware that for three days and nights Frank Rufus had sat by his bed, only leaving when he had made sure that his friend was stable after the operation to remove the bullet from his skull.

'Yes, free as a bird, or at least as free as one that's been caged,' replied Steadman, equally pleased to hear Dr Rufus's familiar growl.

'Caged bird? - I guess they've stuffed you in a safe house, have they? Probably just as well all things considered. No news on the bastard behind the attack?'

'No - the trail is, for the moment, completely cold. DCI Long is still working on it. He's trying to get some of the recordings of my old interviews out of archives for me to listen to. I'm damned if I can place the voice - it's beginning to haunt me. I know I've heard it before.'

'Do you think he'll try again?'

'I'm fairly sure he will. He must know that I'm only winged. Yes, I reckon he'll have another pop at me.'

'Hmm...' Dr Rufus was unusually quiet.

'But that's not why I phoned. You were extremely rude to one of my officers this morning and he's gone on permanent sick leave back to his mother!'

Dr Rufus guffawed. 'Me? Rude? – It must have been my assistant. You know that I am always sweetness and light! Who is this sorely aggrieved officer?'

'DS Munro, he's sitting with me. You've never met the man but I'm sure you'd like him. He's got an able brain.'

Alan Munro blushed again.

'A policeman with a brain – well, that'd make a nice change! I don't believe he's just come to you for tea and sympathy.'

'You are as astute as ever, dear doctor. No, he's come to discuss the dentist's wife.'

'Forgive me John, but I rarely get the opportunity to take a social history from my patients. Have you got a name? That would help.'

'Alisha Gupta, 44 years old, found dead by husband, routine post mortem failed to establish cause of death,' replied Steadman.

'Got you, yes. Nothing much so far, I'm afraid. It's always a bit of a dog's dinner doing the second post mortem – organs all over the shop! I like them fresh, you know! A small patent foramen ovale – that's a hole in the heart to you - hardly life threatening and certainly not the cause of death. She'd taken a good slew of sleeping pills. We're waiting for toxicology, but I doubt it would have been enough to kill her. Did you say she was a dentist's wife?'

'Yes – do you think that's significant? How do dentists kill their spouses?'

'Bore them to death with their drills!' Dr Rufus hooted with laughter at his own joke. John Steadman merely smiled and shook his head.

'I see you've not lost your sense of timing.'

'Sorry about that,' he said regaining his composure. 'Bloody hell, John, in this job if you weren't a bit manic you wouldn't survive. Seriously, I suppose you mean other than the strangling, stabbing and the like?'

'Yes, that's exactly it. There are some odd features in this case that don't add up– any suggestions?'

'I suppose dentists could get hold of some drugs. They are allowed to prescribe, but nothing immediately springs to mind. There's not enough mercury round these days, and besides that would have been picked up already. They don't do general anaesthetics in their surgeries either but there may be some stuff kicking around if it's a very old practice.'

'No,' Steadman replied. 'It's fairly new, only been open ten years.'

'Well, that leaves injectables.'

'Have you checked for needle marks?' Steadman blurted out, then winced, for he knew what would follow.

'Oh no, being a Home Office forensic pathologist the thought never occurred to me. Thank you so much, Mr Plod, for keeping me right. By the way, when they took the bullet out of your head did they leave some brain behind, or has your anus just grown vocal cords? Of course I've bloody well checked!'

'Sorry, sorry – I was just thinking out aloud. I know the most usual place for injecting is the front of the elbow. Are there similar veins behind the knee?'

'Nothing much behind the knee. The backs of the hands and the forearms are next, but they're unmarked. Sometimes you get good veins on the foot or around the ankle. I've checked there as well as round the neck and clavicles – that's collar bones to you. The only other place would be the groin. A sample of blood for toxicology has already been taken from one of the femoral veins in her groin but that site is clearly indicated. I must say her nether regions are 'well thatched'. I suppose there might be something lurking in the undergrowth.'

'You know, Frank, you really have such a way with words. Have you ever thought of becoming a poet?'

There was silence on the other end of the phone for a second. Gruffly Dr Rufus said, 'I'll go and explore the jungle, I'll call you back.'

'Don't forget your pith helmet!' replied Steadman, but Dr Rufus had already put the phone down.

Alan Munro made to leave. 'I'd better get back to the Eyesore. As always, there's a mountain of paperwork waiting for me. This has been really helpful. I'll let you know what progress is made. And of course if anything else occurs to you please let me know. I really shouldn't be handling a case like this if it does turn out to be murder. But above all I don't want to botch it. Can I do anything for you before I go?'

'No thanks. I'm pretty well organised. Are you free this evening?' inquired Steadman.

'Yes, Maureen and the girls are visiting Maureen's parents.'

'Unless you've got anything better than beans on toast on the menu we could eat out at Capaldi's. I'll see if Frank can come; as you can imagine he's a lively companion!'

'What about..?' Munro's voice trailed off.

'Security, you mean. The truth is I'm a free agent. I've agreed reluctantly to live here for the time being and I can, if I wish have a police escort. But I don't wish it. Anyway, you and Frank will be there. He's pretty quick with a scalpel, and you used to be a rugby prop forward,' added Steadman in an attempt to lighten the situation.

'If you're OK with it all, I'm up for a meal at Capaldi's. I've always wanted to take Maureen there but can never get a table. They're booked months in advance. I assume you've thought of that?'

'What have I told you about making assumptions? In this instance you are correct. Signor Capaldi and I go back a long way, don't worry about a table. I'll give you my mobile number. Store it under a plausible pseudonym and if you call don't use my name just in case. The number changes fairly frequently. DCI Long has the list.' He paused, trying to maintain his composure. 'Thanks for coming round. You have no idea how much it's meant to me.'

Munro felt awkward. 'Look, I promise I'll keep you posted. This case may turn out to be far more complicated and it would be great to have your expertise on board. Are you sure you'll be all right? I mean, what do you do all day?'

'Don't worry about me. The challenge of the microwave lunch awaits, followed by a piano lesson, then hopefully a convivial evening out.'

'I saw the piano. I didn't know you played.'

'I don't, at least not very well, hence the lessons.'

Steadman held out his hand and Munro shook it firmly.

'It's good to be working with you again, sir.'

CHAPTER FIVE

Steadman closed the door of his apartment and walked slowly back into the living room. Ever since he had regained consciousness he had been brooding over his own situation, shifting from inconsolable grief from losing his wife to self-pity and frustration over losing his sight and to anger at not being able to seek revenge. But he was not a vengeful man. However much he despised his wife's killer, he realised that he must be a sick man – 'mad, bad and clever', a most dangerous combination. Yet the voice had been familiar. He had racked his brain to no useful purpose. Perhaps listening to some of his old interviews would jog his memory; surely there would be some clue there?

And now this, an unexpected death that stank like a sewer. Munro was right, it didn't fit neatly together. It was a welcome distraction. He went over their conversation, assimilating all the facts. His thoughts were interrupted by the telephone.

'Who's a clever detective, then?' boomed Dr Rufus.

'You've found something, Frank?'

'Yes, at least I think so. I'll have to confirm with full microscopic examination, but I believe there may be a tiny puncture wound in the groin right above the femoral vein. Did you know she had had sex the evening before she died? Not only that, her nether regions were liberally plastered with some sort of cream or jelly.'

'Spare me the anatomical details. Any idea what's going on?'

'I've got some suspicions. Forensics are running a battery of tests, as are the toxicologists. Curiously, the top of her groin has been thoroughly washed – no trace of cream and no trace of blood. I can't prove it yet, but I think she was cleaned up after she was dead.'

'You've told Munro?'

'Of course. Sadly old man, he's in the driving seat now. I gather the house has been sealed off, with DS Fairfax in place as crime scene officer.'

'The Fair Fiona Fairfax! She's absolutely solid. Is she acting as exhibits officer as well?'

'What do you think? Anything to save a bit of money.'

'Who's the lead investigating officer?' asked Steadman, trying to keep the excitement out of his voice.

'Well, that's interesting. They've let Munro lead, with DCI Long keeping a distant hand on the tiller, so to speak. I rather think they're hoping you'll keep an active interest in the case.'

'Is that why you're phoning?'

'I never could do 'subtle', could I? I said I thought you would be delighted.'

'I wondered how you got my number. Of course I would be delighted, just as long as I don't undermine young Alan. Your first solo murder is something you remember for the rest of your life.'

'John, if anyone can support him tactfully it's you.'

'I don't know about that. What are you doing tonight?'

'What had you in mind?'

'Dinner at Capaldi's with Alan Munro if he's not too bogged down.'

'Excellent! Can we make it for 9 pm, as I've still got the report to finish? I'll pick you up at eight forty five. Warn Bill or George or Daisy or whoever is manning the desk.'

'My whereabouts are meant to be a closely guarded secret! How do you know the names of the concierges?'

'Do you really think you're the first person I've had dealings with who has had the dubious pleasure of residing at Jamaica Mansion?'

★ ★ ★

John Steadman couldn't face another microwaved meal, and the pastry was still lying heavily in his stomach. He contented himself with a banana instead. The piano lesson was less than successful. Miss Elliot was as patient as always, but Steadman couldn't give it his full attention. His mind kept going back to Dr Gupta. Had he murdered his wife? If so how? And, more importantly, why? No murders are entirely motiveless. Would a murderer really have sex before killing his victim? The answer to that one was almost certainly 'yes', he thought, recalling several murdered rape victims. But surely this was different? This was his wife, for heaven's sake! What was their relationship like? Maybe it wasn't the husband who had had sex with her. What was she like? He was willing to bet that she wasn't popular. Why did he have an image of someone who was attractive yet heartless, a person with enemies? Why had she taken extra sleeping pills? God knows he would have loved to be the one interrogating Dr Gupta... so many strands, so many alternatives.

He found himself back at his piano. He had been economical with the truth to Alan Munro. He had been able to play exceedingly well earlier in his life but he had become a bit rusty, hence the lessons. His right hand was slowly retrieving its former dexterity, but his left hand remained heavy and awkward.

Inevitably he found himself playing some Bach; safe, solid, mathematically precise – a good accompaniment to logical thinking as he tried to put all the pieces of information together. But the maths was not easy; Bach never spared the performer. After some minutes he lost his place. Now everything had to be played from memory. He would have to listen to the CD again but not immediately, his mind was too busy.

A change of music and a change of thinking. He tried Nina Simone's *My Baby Just Cares for Me*. He loved the fact that Nina Simone was classically trained and had thrown in a bit of – was it also Bach? – in the middle of the piece. He wasn't sure. The music flowed; he knew this one so well.

The time for logic was over. He let his thoughts drift randomly. The broken window? That didn't tie in easily. Who had broken it, and why? Were there really muddy footprints in the house? Why would Dr Gupta phone Munro if he had smashed the glass himself? And why had he meticulously tidied up before forensics had time to do their work? No, it didn't make any sense. All Kim Ho had to go on was a vague shoe print that could be anybody's and a boxful of broken glass. If it wasn't Dr Gupta who had broken the window, who had? The murderer perhaps, if indeed it turned out that Alisha Gupta had been murdered. A killer who left no trace: now that would be highly unusual, unless someone was cleaning up after him or her.

'Alternatives, alternatives, what are the alternatives?' he mumbled to himself. Someone working for Dr Gupta perhaps – would that fit? It would be a bit elaborate, but it had possibilities. Alarms switched off, killer enters and does the deed and Dr Gupta tidies up. That would require planning and some specialist knowledge, surely. Who else knew Alisha and had access to the house? What about the buxom Jean? Was she Dr Gupta's lover? That could be a motive, but it was all based on assumption. And John Steadman disliked assumptions.

Was there one crime, two crimes or no crimes? Could the broken window simply have been a burglar whose timing was inopportune? Why was nothing taken? According to Munro there were more valuables on display than in a Christie's auction room. Had the burglar been disturbed? Had he or she heard something? Was the back door key missing? He must ask Munro. Thoughts swirled in his brain like mist in the wind.

There was something else: a niggle, another distant memory. Was it one of his early cases or had he just read about it? Something about a burglar who took nothing of value? It didn't end well, but that was all he could recall. And now he was playing Scott Joplin's *Maple Leaf Rag*. He was no longer thinking; his long fingers were running effortlessly up and down the keyboard.

Suddenly he stopped. The needle! If it was a needle that had pierced Alisha Gutpa's groin, it must be found as a matter of urgency. A wave of anxiety engulfed John Steadman. Maybe Frank Rufus is right and my brain is addled, he thought.

Should he phone? Surely Munro had already realised the importance of the needle. It was not his case, but time was of the essence. The evidence hung on the needle, and a needle is the easiest thing in the world to get rid of. What was injected was of secondary importance and could safely be left with Dr Rufus and the forensic team.

He stood up and started pacing the floor. He knew he could safely manage six paces up and down without bumping into anything. He thought hard and logically again.

'Firstly, the thief in the night - let's start with the least obvious,' he muttered. But that was hopeless, unless they were working with Dr Gupta. 'Don't make assumptions; look at the alternatives,' he said to himself. The alternatives really boiled down to Dr Gupta, with or without an accomplice, or someone not yet in the frame. If it was Dr Gupta, then where would he have disposed of the needle? Anywhere really, he thought to himself. It could be in the house, buried in the garden, out with the rubbish; he could even have driven down to the harbour and dropped it in the sea.

What about the dental surgery? Perhaps, perhaps - old habits die hard. The most logical place to dispose of it would be with the rest of the used needles, wouldn't it? What did they call it? – A 'sharps' box. What happened then? Steadman tried to recall. Wasn't there a place out on one of the industrial estates where they were incinerated at high temperature? What a perfect way of destroying evidence!

This time Steadman could not stop himself. He moved over to the coffee table where he had left his phone. Damn! In his haste he misjudged the distance, tripped and banged his forehead on the corner of the table. Instinctively he wiped his head with the back of his hand – good, no blood. He felt along the top of the table until he found his phone. It was a chunky phone with a large keypad. He orientated his fingers from the raised blip on the '5' button, and nervously dialled the number for the Eyesore.

'Smith's Bakery, can I help you?'

'Sorry, I've got the wrong number,' Steadman mumbled.

He swore under his breath. Every time he rushed, this happened. His hands were now shaking. He counted to ten and concentrated on his breathing. Slowly and carefully he re-dialled.

★ ★ ★

Sergeant Grimble was on desk duty; it was all he ever did. He was a large, rotund, bald and bespectacled officer who by rights should have retired years ago. Steadman had thought he was old when he first met him. It was a mystery how he had clung on to his job; it was rumoured that he was simply glued to his seat. He'd never been known to have a day's sick leave and never turned down the opportunity to do a bit of overtime or an extra shift. Other officers had often asked him why he didn't retire, but he would merely look puzzled at such a preposterous suggestion. 'I like it here,' was his usual reply.

He was, however, extremely good at his job. Like a large, cheerful spider sitting in the centre of the web that was Police HQ, he gathered and stored information. He knew every officer by name, memorised their shifts, their phone numbers, knew all their families' ups and downs. People confided in him. He also knew all the regular petty villains, and often their families' problems too. Even the villains trusted him. Grimble was aware of all the cases in progress as he took and relayed messages. His desk always looked deceptively untidy, but not to him. 'It's the unique Grimble filing system – I ought to patent it!' he remarked if questioned about the mess.

His phone rang.

'Police HQ, how may I help you?'

'Not been pensioned off yet, Sergeant Grimble?'

'Inspector Steadman! What a pleasure to hear your voice again,' replied a surprised Sergeant Grimble. 'I had heard you were on the mend. I was devastated to learn about your good lady wife, if I may say so. I gather the trail's gone cold. How's life in Jamaica Mansion treating you? I bet you hate being cooped up in there. Mind, better that than hospital I suppose.' If Sergeant Grimble had one fault, it was that he did like to talk. 'I guess you'll be wanting to speak to young DS Munro. Well, I can tell you he's up at Gorse Hill with DS Fairfax. Sounds like the Gupta case is warming up. I can leave a message for him to contact you. Does he have your number?'

CHAPTER SIX

Alan Munro was not sure if he was pleased to receive the call from Sergeant Grimble. Grateful though he was for his former boss's help, he was just beginning to feel that this was his case. The adrenalin was flowing. He knew that this might be his first murder. He wanted to do it his way. With mixed feelings he called the number.

Steadman was equally uneasy. The last thing he wanted was to steal Munro's thunder, but he was concerned in case his colleague's inexperience let him down. The call went well. Finding the needle had become DS Fairfax's number one priority. To that end she had recruited a dozen uniformed officers after some negotiation. Inspector Crouchley was loath to release his men for anything other than his work. In fact, he was singularly renowned for being a difficult man with an unpleasant temper. He had survived more disciplinary hearings than any other officer at the Eyesore. Sadly his attitude had never altered. Crouchley remained a 'right awkward bastard'. Like a lot of aggressive men, he was convinced that every good-looking woman fancied him. This included DS Fairfax. She winced when he said, 'This'll cost you, darling!'

Alan Munro was feeling pleased with himself. He had already thought of the surgery's sharps box. Steadman was pleased too.

'Guess when the box was collected?' asked Munro.

'Go on,' Steadman replied.

'Monday morning at ten thirty. How convenient is that? But we may have a bit of luck. I've contacted the disposal company, Carson's Recycling. Their small incinerator broke down last week and has only just been repaired. All the sharps boxes for this week are still there. The boxes are all labelled. I've asked that they go through them. I'm about to go there now. Are you up for coming with me?'

John Steadman was taken aback. Apart from a couple of hospital appointments, he had not left the grounds of Jamaica Mansion. He had been practising walking with a cane. It was quite long, with a nylon ball on the end which skittered over the bumps and hollows. It was, of course, white. To begin with he had gone round the grounds with a professional trainer. It was not easy. He had wanted to go too fast, and as a consequence had stumbled and fallen. Scuffing along and not trusting his own judgement, he had worn out two pairs of shoes already. But he was determined to gain some independence.

George or Bill or whoever was free was roped in to

take him out. Gently they had guided him by the arm until he got used to the feel of the cane. Slowly but surely he had learned to react to the slightest flick of the nylon ball, like a stylus in the groove of a record. Orientation was his biggest problem. He tended to veer to one side. Not surprising considering the injury to his brain.

He agreed to go with barely a second thought. Twenty minutes later Munro arrived in an unmarked Audi, or as he preferred to call it, a 'plain clothes' police car. Steadman was at the concierge's desk waiting for him. Munro suddenly felt very awkward. Clearly Steadman could negotiate himself indoors, but how would he manage outside? Should he hold his arm and guide him, or would that be too demeaning?

Steadman sensed his colleague's discomfort. 'I'm a bit of an amateur with the cane' he said. 'Perhaps you would be kind enough to lend me your arm, Alan, if that's OK?'

'No problem,' replied Munro with relief.

'Overhanging branches and dog shit are my biggest fears.'

'Well, you had better behave yourself when we're out or I know where I'll steer you.'

As they negotiated their way through the reinforced door, Steadman put on a pair of dark glasses. 'Some people are disconcerted by my wandering eyes' he said. 'Others simply don't believe that a man with eyes can be blind. Besides, they came free with the white cane,' he added with a wry smile.

Munro manoeuvred him into the car, gently touching the top of his head to prevent him bumping into the door frame. Steadman felt the leather seat, fingered the dashboard and gear stick.

'Is it the Audi?' he inquired.

'Yes, I rather like this car. Understated, but it can't half shift when you want it to,' replied Munro. Both men knew, though neither said it out loud, that it had bullet-proof windows and armoured doors.

After a brief fumble Steadman got the seat belt fixed.

'I expect you want to know what I've been up to?' Munro asked as he started the engine.

'Spare me no detail, no matter how small,' Steadman replied.

Munro explained that as soon as he had got the call from Dr Rufus he had spoken with DCI Long. Apart from playing hunt the needle, Dr Rufus had particularly wanted any tubes of creams or ointments they could find. They had sealed off the house, clinic and grounds. Forensics were back in as well, re-examining the broken window and the bedroom. As for Munro, he was looking for any possible motives and generally feeling his way around. There had been some interesting developments.

He had informally interviewed Jean. According to her, nobody could stand Alisha Gupta. She was stuck-up, rude to everybody and unbelievably greedy. Jean wasn't sure about the relationship between Dr Gupta and his wife, describing it as 'mutual indifference' – as long as the money kept rolling in she appeared to tolerate him, and as long as she remained painted up and pretty he tolerated her. Nobody particularly liked Dr Gupta either, she confided in Munro. He too was seen as penny-pinching, but Jean admitted she had a soft spot for him.

'It's his clinic. He's worked hard for it. Why shouldn't he take the lion's share?' she said.

When further pressed by Munro, she confessed that Dr Gupta was more than generous in her favour, paying for her rent and giving her the occasional expensive trinket. 'All for a bit of how's your father once or twice a week,' as she so eloquently had put it.

Steadman had a momentary vision of a buxom woman pouring her heart out while staring into Munro's innocent blue eyes. He really did have a knack for getting information.

Jean said she hadn't been near the house over the weekend. Dr Gupta had paid Jean a call on Sunday evening, but he had not stayed the night. She couldn't remember exactly when he had left. 'He wears me out, I sleep like a baby afterwards!' she confessed. She could provide no alibi for Dr Gupta for the early hours of Monday morning.

'Does she have keys for the clinic and the house?' Steadman asked. Apparently she had both, as she 'house-sat' for the Guptas when they went on holiday.

'What about her feelings towards Alisha Gupta?'

Steadman continued. 'Did she dislike her enough to kill her?'

'Not unless she's a very good actress,' replied Munro. 'Other than being exhausted, she has no strong alibi either.'

Steadman was silent for a moment or two.

'How long has Jean worked there and what did she do before that? She may be already known to us,' he asked.

'Five years. I'll find out a bit more about her past,' replied Munro, a little doubtfully. In truth, he had grown quite fond of Jean.

Munro had decided to keep her on at the reception desk to fend off phone calls; an unusual move, but Steadman approved.

'How has Dr Gupta taken all this?' asked Steadman

'With complete disregard really,' replied Munro. 'He did volunteer some further information that may be useful. Apparently Alisha had two separate visitors earlier on Sunday - her own sister, Reena Soraya, and her unmarried sister-in-law, Cassandra Gupta. Both encounters ended in raised voices. He says he didn't get involved as he suspects that money was at the root of both arguments. It has been in the past, but he declined to say any more. I did get their contact details and I'll be speaking to them later, if they are not on duty.'

'On duty? What do they do?' Steadman asked.

'Now that's where it gets really interesting. Alisha's sister, Reena, is a nurse and his sister, Cassandra, is a medical doctor. I did warn Aaron Gupta that I would be wanting a cosy chat with him fairly soon and not to leave the area. I asked him for a DNA sample. At first he was reluctant but I explained that it was 'routine'. Maybe I was wrong, but I did tell him that we knew his wife had had sex on Sunday night and that was why we needed his DNA. For some reason this seemed to amuse him. A smile flickered for an instant over his face, and after that he agreed. We supervised him while he packed a suitcase. His car had already been searched and he was off. Guess where to?'

'A suite at Queen Anne's,' suggested Steadman.

Queen Anne's was Helmsmouth's smartest hotel, a recently refurbished Victorian pile set on a bluff just outside the older part of the town.

'That would have been the bookies' favourite. But no, he's gone to stay with his 'good friend' Anton Lemerise.'

'Well well well... that does mean you'll have your work cut out, Alan.'

Anton Lemerise was a defence lawyer, if you could afford him. He was a squat, fat ugly man with large side-whiskers. Invariably he dressed in an antiquated three-piece suit complete with a gold watch chain and a large silk hanky protruding from his top pocket. In court he would sit with his eyes half shut, his chins resting on his chest, appearing to be asleep. But his intellect was sharp and ferocious. All he needed was the tiniest crack in the prosecution's case and he was in there, tearing it to shreds. When he did open his eyes, he would stare in a most unsettling manner. He frightened children. He was a formidable opponent.

★ ★ ★

Carson's Recycling was situated on an old disused aerodrome two miles out of Helmsmouth. The drive was pleasant and Steadman relished both the company and the freedom. He was aware of the familiar sounds and smell as they passed by the harbour, a heady mixture of seaweed and diesel. The docks were always busy. Even sealed inside the comfort of the Audi he could make out the noise from the cranes, the hoots from the boats leaving and entering and the raucous cries of the gulls.

The car rumbled over a cobbled piece of road. Steadman knew that this stretch contained sunken train tracks that led right down to the harbour's edge. For some reason he felt heartened by this small piece of familiarity.

Munro glanced over at his companion and shook his head. He thought Steadman still looked ill. His face was gaunt and drawn; the dark glasses didn't help.

'Tell me if it's too much for you, sir.'

'I'm fine,' replied Steadman. 'You have no idea what a tonic it is for me to be out and doing something.'

Munro didn't answer. Steadman sensed something was wrong. 'What is it?' he asked.

'Nothing,' replied Munro cautiously. 'There was a motorcyclist behind us. I thought maybe he was tailing us as he's been in and out of the rear view mirror since we left Jamaica Mansion... he's turned off now.'

'Any idea what sort of bike?'

'No, he was too far back...something big and black with twin headlights.'

* * *

Well, well - out for an impromptu drive with Munro the Muscle Man. I'm surprised you didn't have armed outriders to clear the streets. You really ought to be more careful, Steadman. I suppose the car is bullet proof, but even so you're making it too easy for me. No, I want you by yourself. You see I have my plans and I don't want them spoiled this time – no lucky jerks of the head. I just want there to be genuine fear in your face, see you tremble and sweat and then, of course, watch you die.

CHAPTER SEVEN

There was one question John Steadman was desperate to ask his colleague, and he could resist no longer. 'When are you going to interview Dr Gupta, Alan?'

'I was going to tell you,' replied Munro, 'because I would like you to be there. It's pencilled in for tomorrow morning at ten. I'm waiting for him to confirm. My hunch is he's waiting to see if Anton Lemerise can clear his diary.'

'You're fairly convinced Gupta's guilty?'

'I was, but I'm not so sure now. I'm trying to be open-minded. A wise policeman once advised me to 'consider the alternatives' but it's hard to see where else this case is leading.'

Steadman smiled, 'I can't think who that policeman was!'

'No, nor can I,' Munro replied, 'he also told me 'never make assumptions'! But for the sake of argument, let us assume she was murdered and that the murder involved an injection into her groin. This suggests the killer had both medical knowledge and access to hypodermic needles. Bearing in mind that the overwhelming majority of victims know their attacker, my first thoughts were that the finger surely points to Dr Gupta. Jean is an outsider but can't be ruled out. The mystery of the alleged broken window remains. And of course we now have 'the two ugly sisters' to consider.'

'I think it may all come down to motive,' Steadman said. 'Most murders are motivated by either sex or money, or both – the two great drivers of so-called civilisation. Not unless we have a random psychopath on the loose, and fortunately we have no evidence of that so far. We know that Alisha Gupta had sex before she was murdered, but we don't know who with. Maybe her husband caught her in the act. In some cultures female adultery is considered an extremely grave offence. However it could have been a jealous lover from either side.'

'I'm not with you,' said Munro, a little puzzled. He was aware that John Steadman's line of thought was at times hard to follow and that what he said was sometimes two steps behind what he was actually thinking.

'We know that Dr Gupta is having some sort of affair with Jean. What if Jean wanted something more? If Dr Gupta was not prepared to divorce his wife, then making him a widower would certainly be an option.'

'I can't see Jean in that role, she seems reasonably happy as a kept woman, though it's still a possibility, I guess,' said Munro.

'Or alternatively,' continued Steadman, 'what if Alisha had a lover, for example someone working at the clinic, who realised she was never going to leave her husband? Maybe out of spite he would be inclined to murder.'

'We're on to that,' replied Munro confidently. 'The other two dentists are happily married and have gone as a foursome on holiday to France, effectively ruling them out of the picture. The assistants, the hygienist and other receptionist can all produce reasonable alibis. Apart from their dislike of Dr Gupta and his wife, they have no possible motives.'

Steadman nodded his approval. 'You have been busy.'

Munro blushed. 'To be honest, DCI Long helped out by putting a few more constables at my disposal. I suspect even he has been leant on to wrap this case up quickly. I still can't explain the broken window.'

'Yes, that worries me too but I'm not sure exactly why,' Steadman replied. 'I'm not going to take you up on your offer of listening in to your interview with Dr Gupta. I think I would cramp your style and it will all be recorded.'

Munro was a little relieved. It was not that he didn't want Steadman's help; it was just that he wanted to prove to himself and others that he was up to the job. What John Steadman didn't tell him was that he had already made plans for tomorrow morning.

They continued the rest of the journey in reflective

silence, broken only by Steadman humming to himself and gently tapping his long fingers on his thigh in time to the tune.

★ ★ ★

A forlorn, faded orange windsock was the only reminder of the abandoned airfield's past. Half of it was given over to a go-kart track and a handful of men were laying out old tyres to mark the circuit for the first race of the season. The other half of the field was occupied by Carson's Recycling. Behind a high barbed wire fence were rows of skips full of waste and an enormous heap of old fridges, washing machines and cookers waiting to be dismantled. There were two large warehouses, and through the half-open doors of one of them Munro could glimpse a lorry being loaded with blocks of crushed metal that looked like giant ice cubes. Other buildings lay behind the warehouses, but were obscured from Munro's view. Two large chimneys broke the skyline: one silent, the other belching out clouds of pale orange smoke. The acrid smell drifted into the car.

'I presume we're here,' Steadman remarked.

They stopped at a black and yellow barrier. A grumpy, fat old man prised himself away from his newspaper and the comfort of his grubby kiosk. He looked suspiciously at the two men, especially John Steadman, who remained silent behind his dark glasses. Alan Munro flashed his ID at him; he was not impressed.

'We've come to see Matt Taylor at the small incinerator,' he said.

'Behind the big warehouse – blue door – you can't miss it,' the security guard replied grudgingly, waving a hand vaguely in the direction of the smaller chimney before returning to the dingy warmth of his cell.

'Extra marks for customer relations, do you think?' asked Steadman.

'Not quite 'aloha' and a welcoming garland of flowers was it?' replied Munro.

However, the guard was right; the blue door was behind the warehouse and couldn't be missed. Steadman cautiously tried to get out of the car. He found that he was quite stiff from sitting.

'Here, let me help you, sir.' Munro took his arm and Steadman hoisted himself out of the car, deliberately leaving his long cane folded on the seat. It was an embarrassment. Although he had practised for hours in the grounds of Jamaica Mansion, this was his first real public outing and he didn't have confidence in his own capabilities, or at least that's what he told himself. In response to Munro's knock on the door a voice from within shouted, 'Come in if you're good looking!' Munro pushed open the heavy door.

'Mind, there's a two inch ledge, sir.'

Too late; Steadman stubbed his toe and let out an oath. He realised he should have swallowed his pride and taken his cane.

The blue door led into an office dominated by a

large counter piled high with yellow sharps boxes of various shapes and sizes. On the shelf behind were some ragged and dog-eared lever arch files. The floor was scrubbed and smelt of disinfectant. Pinned to the wall was a calendar with a picture of a scantily clad lady. Apparently she was called 'April'. Next to the calendar was another door marked 'Incinerator – Authorised Staff Only'. A man with fair, spiky hair, an earring and a tattoo on his neck poked his head round the door. He looked at the two men.

'If it's religion I ain't interested – I'm a Fulham supporter,' he said in a strong London accent.

'Matt Taylor?' inquired Munro.

'Depends who's asking.'

Alan Munro showed his ID. 'DS Munro.'

Matt Taylor nodded and looked enquiringly at John Steadman.

'And Detective Inspector Steadman,' added Munro after a slight pause.

'I didn't think it was Stevie Wonder.'

Steadman nodded in the direction of the voice but said nothing.

'We spoke on the phone,' Munro continued.

'I thought it might be you,' Matt Taylor replied. 'There's a bit of a problem – funny really.'

'Problem?' Munro queried.

'Yeah – the incinerator's been fixed and fired up. As far as I know nothing ain't gone through yet. I've checked all the boxes, but I can't find the one you was looking for.'

'Are they all labelled?' Steadman asked.

'Yeah – they've gotta be, or we don't pick 'em up.'

'Do you keep a log of them as they arrive?' Steadman continued.

'Nah – not worth it. They're all contracts. The hospital sends us dozens a week. A little dental practice only sends in one or two. And then there's the vets…'

Steadman interrupted the flow; he could sense Munro getting restless beside him.

'What's the point in labelling them?' he asked.

'If the lid ain't on right and I prick my finger then the boss knows who to sue,' Taylor replied smugly.

'Are you sure the driver picked up a box from Dr Gupta on Monday?' asked Munro.

Taylor ran his fingers through his spiky hair and replied with a grin, 'Ahead of you on that one, matey.'

Munro winced at being called 'matey'.

'Spoke with the driver,' Taylor continued, now twiddling his earring, 'and he'll swear on his mother's grave that he picked up one yellow square box from Gorse Hill Clinic on Monday.'

'Did he speak with the receptionist?'

'Nah – I've done the run meself.' Taylor was now massaging the tattoo on the back of his neck. 'The box is left in a locked cupboard out the back. It's got one them combination padlocks with numbered rings, matey. Even I can remember the code, '1, 2, 3, 4' – not too hard!'

Steadman drummed his fingers on the counter.

'Is it possible the service engineer could have put the box in the incinerator when he tested it?' he asked.

'I thought of that myself, captain,' replied Taylor, grinning from ear to ear. 'Not bad, eh? I could be doing your job.'

First 'matey', now 'captain' - Munro could barely keep his patience. He gripped the edge of the counter until his knuckles turned white.

'Spoke to him less than quarter an hour ago - at least I left a message on his answering machine.' Turning to Munro, he continued, 'Of course I might've missed it, matey. You're welcome to have a dekko yourself.'

Steadman sensed the rising tension in his colleague. If he could have, he would have touched his arm in an attempt to calm him down.

'Mr Taylor, it is vital to our investigations that we find this particular sharps box. We would be obliged if you would check every box again and certainly not incinerate anything without double checking the label.'

'Right you are, captain,' replied Taylor.

'And phone me as soon as you hear from the engineer, 'matey',' added Munro as he tossed his card on to the counter. The two men stared hard into each other's eyes; Taylor was the first to look away.

'Mightn't be until tomorrow, mate... sergeant,' said Taylor, avoiding Munro's gaze.

'That'll be fine,' replied Munro.

He gently steered Steadman out of the office.

'Ledge,' he said as they approached the door.

Steadman high-stepped over the ledge and once again the two men were out in the open air. Without saying a word they got into the car and drove off.

Munro was seething. As they got to the barrier he put his hand on the horn.

'All right, keep your hat on,' muttered the guard under his breath.

Munro put his foot down. The wheels spun and screeched on the smooth concrete of the airfield.

'I don't believe it! 'Captain', 'matey'! – I'll give him 'matey'. It wouldn't surprise me if Gupta had phoned him up and told him to hide the bloody box!'

John Steadman turned his head as though to look out of the window. He was scared to say anything in case he started to laugh. Munro glanced towards Steadman. He caught his reflection in the glass and could see that Steadman was desperately trying hard to keep a straight face.

'You bastard, you're just as bad!' he said giving Steadman a friendly thump on the arm.

CHAPTER EIGHT

John Steadman was exhausted by the time they got back to Jamaica Mansion. Munro walked him safely to his apartment but declined the invitation for coffee. He could see that his colleague needed to rest; moreover he had arranged interviews with the 'two ugly sisters' later that afternoon and was already running a bit late.

'Are you sure you're up for dinner this evening?' Munro asked with a worried frown.

'I'll be fine, thanks. I'll phone Signor Capaldi and then I'll probably have a nap. You're right – I am worn out, but I've really enjoyed this afternoon.' Turning away from Munro he continued, 'My life revolved round Holly and my work. I thought I'd lost them both.'

His voice faltered. Munro put a large hand on Steadman's shoulder and gave it an affectionate squeeze. He was surprised at how little flesh there was.

'It's great to have you back. Go on - make the call and get some rest. Dr Rufus is picking me up first. We'll be here for quarter to nine.' Releasing his grip, he added, 'You could do with a bit of fattening up!'

Steadman smiled. The two men shook hands rather awkwardly and said their goodbyes.

The number for Capaldi's was a fairly easy one both to remember and to dial – 528528. Steadman found the 5 with its little raised blip. The 2 was directly above and the 8 directly below. Signor Capaldi himself answered and was delighted to hear John Steadman's voice again. Like so many of Steadman's friends and colleagues he had been charmed by Holly's love of life and easy-going manner; even in mid-life she had retained her looks. Her smile could light up a room. His grief and outrage at the murder of Holly was sincere and heartfelt.

'Is it true that you are blind?'

'Unfortunately, yes,' Steadman replied.

Signor Capaldi tutted and continued volubly in Italian. Steadman could make out some of the phrases. If he understood correctly, what Signor Capaldi had in mind involved removing the killer's eyeballs, replacing them with his testicles, then making him eat the eyeballs. It was a novel idea, thought Steadman, but not one that had occurred to him.

'Are you dining alone?'

'No, I would like a table for three if that's possible?'

'Mr Steadman, if you said thirty-three I would still make it possible.' There was a short pause, then he continued, 'Please tell me you're not bringing your friend Dr Rufus with you? He is outrageous! Let me remind you what he did the last time he was here. Paulo was leading you all to your table. As he passed Mrs Tempest he removed the buttered roll from her plate, saying, 'I'm a doctor and I'm doing this for your own good. My need is greater than yours!' I accept that Mrs Tempest is a large lady, but she is one of my best customers. It cost me a bottle of my best Valpolicella to pacify her, and all he could do was laugh!'

John Steadman remembered the occasion well. He and Holly had also found the whole incident highly entertaining.

'I'm afraid he will be with me, but I'll keep him on a tight leash. My other guest, I promise, will be well behaved. I don't think you know him, Detective Sergeant Alan Munro. He's a big, quiet, intelligent Scotsman rather prone to blushing. He's been trying to take his wife to your restaurant for some time but he can never get a table.'

'I look forward to meeting him. You can have the small private dining room to yourselves. I had a great uncle who was blinded in the war. He dreaded eating in public. It will also keep Dr Rufus away from my other customers!'

A table for three at nine o'clock in the private dining room was agreed, and Steadman put the phone down. He reflected on Signor Capaldi's thoughtfulness. Ever since he had suggested the meal out, Steadman had worried about how he would cope. He could only manage food on a plate by feeling his way round; acceptable if it was chips, but messy and undignified if there was gravy or a sauce. Cutting up meat invariably ended up with food flying in all directions. Since losing his sight, he had lived mainly on sandwiches. They were easy: he could legitimately touch them. Soup was manageable if it was in a mug; otherwise it was a complete disaster. He had already worked out what he could have that would cause the least embarrassment and would ask to sit with his back to as many of the diners as possible. The thought of a private dining room was a great relief.

He was struggling to keep awake. He thought he might listen to a CD but the effort was just too much. In the end he opted to listen to the radio. They were playing 'Golden Oldies' – a term that he always found vaguely amusing. Some of his favourite music was over three hundred years old, their so-called 'Oldies' seldom more than thirty. Nevertheless it was easy listening. He lay back on the comfortable leather chair, put his feet up on the foot stool and drifted off.

★ ★ ★

He found himself floating in mid-air as though in the middle of a cloud. It felt perfectly natural and peaceful. The mental turmoil and physical distress of the last few months seemed remote and inconsequential. He opened his eyes. Through the mist, his surroundings gradually came into focus.

Below was a brightly-lit scene of intense activity.

From his vantage point he noted that all the walls were white, sterile and devoid of any adornment, save a box emanating light on which there were some black and grey pictures. Barring some electric sockets, the only other distraction was a cluster of three or four different coloured hoses which looped gently from the wall over an iridescent floor towards the group huddled below him. Casting his gaze around, Steadman noticed in another corner a small collection of steel trolleys shrouded in green. Beside these, two people appeared to be conversing in whispers. They wore pale blue caps with matching tee shirts and baggy pants. But what struck him as most peculiar was that they were both wearing short white wellingtons very similar to those worn by a fishmonger.

His ears were now getting attuned to the surroundings. The most obvious noises were a persistent rhythmic beep and a slower mechanical wheeze followed by a metallic clunk. There was little talking, but he could pick up short, meaningless, staccato phrases.

His vision was partly obscured by a large lamp suspended from the ceiling by a series of adjustable arms. He moved down and around the lamp more by will rather than through any apparent physical effort. Underneath the light five people were huddled in a tight knot at the end of a long narrow table draped in white. Sitting close by was another person who appeared to be in charge of the wheezing, beeping machine that was fed by the multi-coloured hoses. The others were standing, capped, gloved, masked and gowned in green.

It was only then that John Steadman realised that he was in an operating theatre and that what lay under the sheet on the table was some poor soul; the focus of all their attention. The commands were now beginning to make more sense.

'Suction.'

'Artery forceps.'

The group moved like automatons in a macabre dance. His curiosity roused, he moved in a little closer. It was apparent that they were operating on the person's head, but they were in such a tight cluster a clear view was impossible. He looked behind at the box of light on the wall. The black and white pictures were x-rays. Even with his lack of medical knowledge he could see that it was a skull and that the back of it was shattered. He also recognised the shape of a small-calibre bullet; a snub-nosed piece of destruction.

Steadman moved round fascinated to see if he could recognise the victim. He caught a glimpse of exposed brain; pink, soft, oozing watery blood and more vulnerable than a new-born baby. He moved past the anaesthetist but the person's head had been shaved, the eyes padded and lightly taped, the mouth and nose distorted by tubes, valves and more tape.

'Got it!' The voice was triumphant. The surgeon was holding up in a pair of forceps a bullet from a hand gun.

'What do you do with it now?' inquired a female voice, a mixture of fear and curiosity in her dark eyes.

'Strict orders – send it by despatch rider to the forensics laboratory.'

Steadman could imagine the scene in the forensics laboratory well, for it was one of his favourite haunts.

Quite suddenly the rhythmic beeps stopped, to be replaced by a sudden silence.

'Shit – the heart's stopped – asystolic arrest! Roll the patient.'

'Large saline pack, sister. Cradle the back of the head gently. Can we externally pace the heart?'

'Doubt it – he's too chilled.'

They unwrapped the body. It was encased in a cocoon of cold packs. The temperature in the room perceptibly dropped.

'Call the cardiothoracic crash team and open a thoracoctomy pack. Time please?'

'Forty-five seconds.' It was a nervous girl's voice.

The two loiterers in the corner sped into action, one dashing out of the theatre, the other pulling off the drapes and outer wrappings from one of the steel trolleys. Stupidly Steadman felt in the way and drifted back to the wall behind the anaesthetist where the light box was situated. He noticed on the top of the light box that there was a slight smear of blood, overlooked by the cleaner, and a small key.

'One minute thirty seconds.'

He watched mesmerised. The chest was now bare. Large sticky pads had been attached and clipped to the beeping machine which refused to respond.

'Damn!'

The pads were torn off.

'Scalpel.'

A nurse frantically tried to wipe clean where the pads had been. Steadman, transfixed by what was happening, could not bear to look away. A large deep incision. Surprisingly little blood. A ghastly looking instrument like shiny steel bolt cutters.

'Two minutes thirty seconds.'

A sound like a dog eating biscuits. Ribs snapped. The time keeper neatly folded a swab and without being asked, gently wiped the sweat from the surgeon's brow. This small act of tenderness quelled the nausea that Steadman felt building up inside him. He could not resist. He moved and hovered over the surgeon's shoulder, watching closely as the surgeon slipped his hand into the chest and around the soft, purple heart, which lay as lifeless as a piece of meat on a butcher's slab. He squeezed, and instantly Steadman felt an odd rippling sensation deep within his own chest.

'Three minutes.'

'Not quite a world record, but not bad all the same!' the anaesthetist declared. 'Do you know the song with the perfect beat for getting the rhythm right?'

'No, but I bet you're going to tell me,' replied the surgeon.

'*Stayin' Alive* by the Bee Gees!'

Steadman knew that song and immediately it started up in his head: '*Whether you're a brother or whether you're a mother, you're stayin' alive, stayin' alive...*'

Something started to pump in his chest in time to the music. The room shimmered and he felt uneasy, as though he was going to fall.

'Feel the city breakin' and ev'rybody shakin', we're stayin' alive, stayin' alive...'

Pump, pump, pump, pump – he could see nothing now. He felt himself being sucked downwards, down towards the body lying on the table.

'Ah, ha, ha, ha, stayin' alive, stayin' alive...'

All he could sense now was coldness, immobility, a fading rhythmic beep and a vague ringing in his ears.

'Ah, ha, ha, ha, stayin' alive...'

The ringing got louder and louder. For a brief moment he didn't know where he was or what the sound was. He touched his chest. Even through his shirt he could feel the scar like a knotted piece of twine tethered to his skin. It was still a little tender.

It was only then that he truly woke up and realised it was the phone that was ringing. He ignored it. If it was important they would call back, or if they knew him they would let it ring. The dream, if that's what it was, remained vivid, clear and unsettling.

The caller was not giving up easily. The phone continued to ring. His hand swept over the coffee table. He found it on the second pass and picked it up. His index finger stroked the key pad, lightly searching for the right button. It was hard not to get flustered and all too easy to cut off whoever was calling.

'What kept you, or have I woken you up?' It was the unmistakable voice of Dr Rufus.

'Actually you did. I've just had the most extraordinary dream…'

Dr Rufus stopped him in mid-sentence.

'Apart from watching cricket, the most boring thing in life has to be listening to people recounting their dreams! Pin your ears back - I've got something that is far more interesting to tell you.'

Trust Frank Rufus to bring me down to earth with a bang, Steadman thought. 'Go on – you have my undivided attention.'

'Well, it's definitely a needle that's punctured her groin and it did go straight into the femoral vein. And what's more, the cream that had been applied to her nether regions did contain, as I suspected, a topical local anaesthetic.'

'Topical local anaesthetic?' queried Steadman.

'Yes – something to numb the skin. Doctors and nurses use it before giving injections to kids or adults terrified of needles. It's brilliant stuff. You can't feel a thing.'

'Any alternative uses?' Steadman asked.

'You know John, you can be infuriating sometimes. You're worse than a blooming defence lawyer. 'Alternatives, alternatives' – here I am building you up a picture of a well-constructed murder and all you can do is twist it! You'll be telling me next she had an angry run-in with an acupuncturist. And no, before you ask, it is a much bigger and longer needle that's been used.'

Dr Rufus paused for breath then continued, 'In fact

you're right, you do find a bit of topical local anaesthetic in some anti-itch preparations and in one product used by men allegedly to prolong sexual intercourse, but not in this concentration. I'd stake my reputation that this cream, or whatever it was, had been tampered with and deliberately applied to allow someone to inject her without waking her up.'

'Has DS Fairfax found anything yet?'

'About half a chemist's shop,' replied Dr Rufus. 'Most of the stuff is available in Britain, but some of the potions are from the Far East and heaven knows what they may contain. Forensics are tearing their hair out.'

John Steadman was silent.

'Are you still there or have you fallen asleep again?'

'Sorry, Frank, I was just thinking. Apparently she ran a small cosmetics firm in Malaysia. I was wondering what she dealt in and if it could be relevant, that's all. Any news from toxicology?'

'Nothing I'm afraid, but they're not done yet. Are you still up for dinner at Capaldi's?'

'The table is all booked, on condition that you are on your best behaviour. Signor Capaldi has not fully recovered from the incident of Mrs Tempest and her bread roll,' Steadman replied.

'Me? Badly behaved? Surely not! I'll call for young Munro first, then pick you up. I gather he's got a tale to tell after his encounters with the two ugly sisters.'

CHAPTER NINE

Feeling bemused and more than a little apprehensive, John Steadman prepared himself for the night ahead. Showering was no problem now that he had got used to the controls. He felt his chin; it was rough with stubble. What he really fancied was a good old-fashioned wet shave, something that would leave his skin tingling and as smooth as a baby's bottom. Up until now he had relied on an electric razor but it just wasn't the same.

He had all he needed in his toilet bag, and the bag was conveniently sitting on the shelf by the bathroom basin. Carefully he took the plastic clip off the razor head and out of habit, ran the razor under the hot tap. His face was still damp from the shower. He gave the can of shaving foam a shake, squeezed a ball of gel on to his hand and rubbed it on to his cheeks. The smell was distinctive, tea tree and mint. He did wonder what a tea tree was or if it even existed. Instantly the gel turned into a foamy lather. Picking up his razor, he muttered '*morituri te salutant*', the prelude to gladiatorial battle. He turned to look in the mirror.

'Idiot!'

He stuck his jaw out, stretching the skin on his cheeks and painstakingly started scraping off the foam. His chin and jaw were easy enough, but his moustache area was far more tricky. The last thing he wanted to do was cut himself. He gave his face a final rinse and ran his hand over his skin. It passed muster. Should he put on some aftershave? No, he thought, he was going to save that for tomorrow.

What to wear? He had been given a clever little gadget that scanned his clothes and in a mechanical monotone read out an approximation of the colour. Grey suit, white shirt, blue tie and black shoes were the order of the day. He had no idea which blue tie it was. It didn't matter, as he knew the suit was plain grey – as long as it wasn't the tie with the cartoon policeman on it that his son had given him for his last birthday, very amusing but not appropriate for dinner at Capaldi's.

He was now fully dressed and ready to go. The tinny voice of his watch told him it was only eight fifteen. He was determined not to speculate any more about the Gupta case, at least, not until he had more information. He was too restless to play the piano and he had already heard the news on the radio. The programme that was now on annoyed him: politicians arguing vehemently about something they neither cared for nor understood.

He moved over to the small display cabinet and lifted the lid. Holly had introduced him to netsuke figures. She had thought the intricate and delicate

Japanese carvings would appeal to him and she had been right. Each year on their wedding anniversary she had bought him another to add to his collection. They were all antique and quite beautiful, not just to look at but also to touch. They were like old friends to John Steadman.

He picked up one at random, a small rabbit with his ears pressed back over his head staring up at the moon. The next was an ox with heavy curved horns and his legs folded beneath him. With his finger nails, he could feel the animal's tiny cloven hooves. He put them back.

There was one he was searching for, his favourite: the first one Holly had given him. He found it in the centre of the cabinet. It was a little rat, almost curled up into a ball, with three delicate paws grasping its ringed tail. It was two hundred years old, and carved by one of the masters. His fingers picked out the rat's dainty ears and beady eyes. He vividly remembered the day Holly had given him the rat, the look of apprehension on her face, then relief as she realised her husband was enchanted.

He was about to put it back in the cabinet, but on second thoughts he slipped it into his pocket. Steadman was not superstitious, but he and Holly had always referred to this particular netsuke as the 'lucky rat' and at this present moment he felt he needed all the luck he could get.

The intercom buzzed.

'Two gentlemen to see you, Mr Steadman. They look respectable.'

'I'll be down now,' Steadman replied.

He patted his pockets: wallet, phone, keys, handkerchief, comb and of course the lucky netsuke rat. He slipped on his dark glasses, unfolded his cane and pulled the door behind him.

Dr Rufus and DS Munro were chatting amiably at the front desk. Clearly they had hit it off.

'Who's a pretty boy then?' asked Dr Rufus. 'Shame about the tie.'

'Don't tell me it's the one with the cartoon policeman on it,' replied Steadman despondently.

'No, much worse than that!'

'Take no notice of him, sir,' Munro interjected, 'it's fine – pale blue with small red diamonds. But you do have a blob of shaving foam on your right ear. Here, let me help you.'

Munro took a tissue out of his pocket and deftly wiped away the errant remains of Steadman's shave. Steadman accidently brushed his hand against Munro's jacket. The gun strapped to Munro's chest was unmistakable.

'Brought your own cutlery?' Steadman inquired.

'DCI Long's orders, I'm afraid,' came the grim reply, 'and he's insisted on me taking the Audi.'

'Pity about that, I was looking forward to my glass of mineral water' said Dr Rufus insincerely. 'I suppose I'll have to force down a glass or two of wine.'

Steadman smiled. 'Any other surprises for me?'

'Apparently there are two new temporary waitresses

– DS Fairfax and WPC Jennings.'

'I feel awful giving these people extra work,' Steadman said with a sigh.

'John, there were so many volunteers they had to draw lots,' replied Munro, blushing as he realised he had called Steadman by his first name. No-one noticed.

'They are, of course, expecting an exceedingly large tip,' said Dr Rufus. 'Come on, I'm starving!'

★ ★ ★

Signor Capaldi was waiting at the door of the restaurant to greet them. He shook Steadman's hand warmly. Steadman introduced him to Munro; Dr Rufus needed no introduction.

'My, but you're a big fellow, I'd better make sure that you get a large serving,' said Signor Capaldi, 'and of course, Dr Rufus. Please be a good boy tonight – eh, just for me? Come, Paulo will lead you to your table.'

'Take my arm, Mr Steadman,' said Paulo.

DS Munro glanced over his shoulder, but nobody appeared to be following them. Most of the tables were occupied. Munro nodded at the two new waitresses. DS Fairfax had let her hair down and looked quite stunning. WPC Jennings on the other hand looked exactly like WPC Jennings minus her black and white checked police cravat. They both shook their heads, indicating all was quiet. Paulo smiled wolf-like at DS Fairfax as they went past. A few of the diners looked up and stared at John Steadman. It was all too much for Dr Rufus.

'Guard your bread rolls!' His voice boomed out in the hushed dining room. 'Coming through, guard your rolls!'

Signor Capaldi buried his head in his hands. Munro and Steadman were grinning.

The private dining room was cosy. A log fire was burning in the grate. Only one table was laid. It was deliberately larger than necessary, with candles burning at either end, well out of harm's way. Someone had gone to a lot of effort. Paulo handed menus to Dr Rufus and DS Munro. He knelt down and in a soft voice said to Steadman, 'Signor Capaldi has arranged a special meal for you, unless there is anything you would particularly like?'

'No, no - I'll trust Signor Capaldi's judgement.'

Munro was at a loss.

'It all sounds so good. Any recommendations?'

'There's no point in asking Frank - he always has the same. Everything's good but the chef's specials are invariably exceptional.'

Paulo came back with glasses of Prosecco and took their orders.

'The wine is in front of your right hand and there is a small bowl of olives immediately in front of you,' he whispered in Steadman's ear.

The wine was biscuit-dry and chilled to perfection. Signor Capaldi himself brought in Steadman's starter.

'A little dish of fritto misto. It is customary to eat these with your fingers. I will bring you a hot towel.'

Signor Capaldi stepped back from the table and nodded to Paulo. DS Munro had ordered artichokes with prosciutto, rocket and parmesan. Dr Rufus as usual had minestrone, or at least that's what he had ordered. What Paulo put down in front of him was a bowl of dirty water.

'What the...' he spluttered.

'Dirty dishwater!' exclaimed Signor Capaldi. 'Mrs Tempest's special recipe!'

Signor Capaldi and Paulo were consumed with mirth. Munro and Steadman forced a smile but Dr Rufus roared with laughter.

'All right, you win. I promise to behave myself,' he said.

Apart from Steadman knocking over the empty Prosecco glass and losing a spoonful of tiramisu to the tablecloth, the rest of the meal passed without incident. The food was glorious; even Dr Rufus was stunned into silence. Their table was cleared and the three men retired with their coffee to comfy armchairs round the fire.

'Time, I think, for a story about two ugly sisters,' Steadman said.

'Well...' said DS Munro shifting in his chair to get more comfortable.

★ ★ ★

The two sisters had opted to be interviewed at the Eyesore rather than at home. They arrived separately, but met in the waiting area by Sergeant Grimble's desk. Cassandra Gupta, dressed expensively in black, was already sitting there when Reena Soraya entered. In total contrast, Reena looked as though she was ready to party.

It all happened very quickly. Reena scanned the room and saw Cassandra. Their eyes met. In an instant Cassandra was up on her feet, but she was not fast enough. Reena began screaming.

'You murderous bitch, I know it was you!'

She grabbed Cassandra's hair with one hand and with the other swung her handbag at Cassandra's face. It was only a glancing blow, but it caught her on the nose, which started to bleed profusely.

'Get this alcoholic slut off me!' she shrieked.

Fists and feet were flying. Both women were yelling obscenities and accusations at one another.

It was all over as quickly as it had started. At the first shout officers poured into the waiting area and prised the two women apart. Cassandra was taken away by a WPC to be cleaned up. Reena flounced into a vacant chair, looking for all the world like a sulky school child. The only person who seemed unconcerned was Sergeant Grimble, who had not moved from his seat. DS Munro had overheard the altercation - it would have been hard to avoid it - and decided to get Reena in straight away. He didn't fancy the two women facing each other again for a second round. A WPC was sent to fetch Reena and stayed throughout the interview.

Munro stood up to greet her. His massive hand dwarfed hers as though it was a doll's. Her hand was sweaty and trembling. Her breath smelt of alcohol. Munro stared at her with his innocent blue eyes and apologised for keeping her waiting. He gave her a little smile, half flirtatious, and she fell for it hook, line and sinker, like so many of the women DS Munro had interviewed. His technique was masterful.

'You don't mind if I tape our little chat, do you? It saves me an awful lot of writing,' he asked, looking warmly into her eyes.

'Oh no, not at all.' Reena averted her gaze and squirmed a little in her seat.

'Now, how do I pronounce your surname?'

'Don't bother to try. In my country we are all called by our first names.'

'Very well, Reena, I gather you don't care much for Cassandra Gupta.'

It was like opening a flood gate. No, she confided in him, they couldn't stand one another. Cassandra, she went on to say, was a total snob who maintained that her brother, Aaron, had married beneath him.

'Alisha and I were brought up in an orphanage, you see,' she explained. 'Cassandra did everything she could to stop them marrying. She didn't even turn up at their wedding!'

Reena's hands were now visibly shaking. Little beads of perspiration had formed on her top lip and over her eyebrows. She was getting restless. Munro recognised the warning signs.

'Would you like a little break?' he enquired.

She nodded and he switched off the tape recorder.

'Perhaps something to settle your nerves?' he continued, taking a small bottle of vodka from one of his pockets. Reena eyed the bottle greedily. The WPC look horrified; Munro ignored her.

'Meeting Cassandra like that must have shaken you,' he said soothingly as he poured Reena a drink. 'Oops! A bit large, but just leave what you don't want.' He handed Reena the half full tumbler. 'I'm just going to stretch my legs,' he said. 'WPC Perrin will stay with you.'

DS Munro did indeed need to stretch his legs. The chairs in the interview room were too small for him and gave him cramp. He also wanted to make sure that Cassandra Gupta wasn't badly hurt, as well as allowing a few minutes for Reena's vodka to kick in.

'How are you feeling now?' he asked on his return.

She was clearly better. He switched on the tape recorder.

'Tell me about your sister, Alisha. I thought she was a wealthy woman in her own right,' he said.

Reena assured him that she was. Alisha, after all, had a successful cosmetics firm, but when pressed, Reena couldn't name any of their products.

'Alisha made a good marriage,' she said wistfully.

'There's certainly no shortage of money. I reckon the dental practice is a positive gold mine.'

Munro continued to probe gently. Reena confirmed that she was a nurse but didn't earn a lot of money. Munro sensed that Reena was now relaxed. It was time to move into more tricky territory. Her own marriage, Reena admitted, was falling apart.

'Is that why you drink?' Munro asked, but immediately he could have kicked himself. Reena frowned and shrunk back into her seat. It was like a sea anemone withdrawing its tentacles.

'I expect Cassandra told you. It's no big deal. I don't often touch spirits, except at weekends.'

'Have you ever asked for help?' Munro asked gently.

'Only if I can't get the cork out,' she replied, with more than a hint of sarcasm.

Munro realised that if he was not careful Reena was going to stop talking.

'Tell me about the relationship between Cassandra and Alisha.'

Reena snorted, 'I've already told you Cassandra can't stand her.'

'Why does she visit her then?'

Reena looked at Munro slyly. 'Don't you know? She borrows money from her. Cassandra doesn't want her brother to know. And Alisha holds the purse strings.'

DS Munro was a little perplexed. He knew that Cassandra was a doctor and probably earning more than she needed.

'Why does she need to borrow money?'

Reena made a clicking sound and mimed holding a horse's reins.

'Cassandra keeps horses?' Munro said a little puzzled.

'No, stupid – she gambles. Horses or roulette. She's always borrowing money, or at least trying to. I'll bet she thinks it will be easier now that Alisha's dead.'

Munro let that one pass. 'What about you? Did you borrow money?'

'Occasionally.'

'Did Alisha always oblige?'

'Usually – not always.'

Munro could see Reena withdrawing into herself again, but pressed on.

'Is that what you were arguing about on Sunday?'

'Who says we were arguing?'

'You haven't answered my question.'

'You haven't answered mine!'

'Let me remind you, Reena, that I'm here to ask the questions, not you. I repeat, is that what you were arguing about on Sunday?'

Reena sighed. 'Yes. I know I shouldn't speak ill of the dead, specially not my own sister, but she could be a right mean bitch sometimes. Alisha loved seeing me beg.' There was a hint of loathing in her words. She continued, 'Maybe that painted cow Cassandra was right, Aaron Gupta was too good for her.'

'You like Aaron Gupta?' Munro asked.

'Oh yes!' She sighed again. 'Unfortunately he married the wrong sister.'

Munro paused and thought for a minute.

'What about Alisha and Aaron's marriage?'

'What marriage? It was a sham, more like a business arrangement. Aaron has always had other women.' She narrowed her eyes. 'Now it's Jean - sweet, big-bosomed, no brained Jean. And she's been round the paddock on more than one occasion. It won't last – it never does.'

'What about Alisha? Did she have lovers?'

'Why not? She tolerated Aaron's behaviour. It's only fair isn't it?'

'Do you know who her present lover is?'

After a pause she said, 'May do – but I'm not saying. She's dead now, what's the point?'

'The point is I believe your sister was murdered. I want to know who killed her.'

'Well it wasn't me, if that's what you're thinking.'

'Whoever killed her had some medical knowledge. He or she also had access to the house and saw her on Sunday. I don't think you liked your sister very much. I think you fancy her husband.'

'Christ, you're serious aren't you? You think I killed my own sister!' Reena was showing signs of becoming hysterical. 'I didn't, I bloody didn't! Go and question Cassandra, Mister Clever Policeman, before you go accusing innocent people!'

'I'm not accusing you. I'm only trying to get you to see the problem through my eyes. I will question

Cassandra, but I do need you to tell me who your sister's lover was – it's important, Reena.'

Munro stared at her with those innocent blue eyes. She melted a little.

'I'm not saying… Why don't you check her medical records?' she replied after a pause and stared back at Munro. 'Now, if you're finished with me, I want to go home.'

'Fine. Please don't leave the area without telling us.'

As she walked through the waiting area she stuck her chin in the air and pretended not to see Cassandra sitting there, still dabbing at her swollen nose.

★ ★ ★

Cassandra Gupta had caught a glimpse of DS Munro and was impressed. She liked big men. Pausing as she entered the interview room, she gave him a coquettish smile. She wiggled her way over to the chair and sat down, showing a good deal more thigh than was necessary. Munro switched on the tape recorder.

'Well,' she said, 'have you arrested her yet?'

Munro looked at her blankly. He knew her type and felt an instant dislike. She started to smile again, but on getting no response she chose to stare intently at her elegant, green nails.

'Who?' asked Munro eventually.

'Let it pass,' Cassandra replied truculently and tugged her skirt down over her thigh.

'Did Alisha Gupta lend you money last Sunday?'

The question took her unawares and appeared to unsettle her, as it was meant to. Cassandra thought for a moment.

'Oh, I get it. Your little alcoholic friend has been telling tales on me, has she? In answer to your question, no she didn't - and for the record,' she continued, addressing the tape recorder, 'I don't think she gave any to Nurse Reena the Slut either! Alisha wasn't in a generous mood.'

'Why didn't you ask your brother?'

'Because madam is the banker. My brother thinks it is vulgar to talk about money, so he leaves it to someone who lacks his inhibitions and refinement. He makes it, she spends it.'

'I thought she was wealthy in her own right with her cosmetics company?'

'Pah!' Cassandra spat out the word. 'Cosmetics company? She was nothing but a common little factory worker. My brother should have never married her. I tried to warn him but she had wormed her way into his affections. He felt sorry for her. My brother...'

Munro interrupted her; it was obvious she was lying.

'Tell me about their marriage.'

'Their marriage? I believe it was what is called 'open'. My brother is a real man, virile. He needs more than just one woman, certainly he needed more than she could offer him.'

'Has he had a lot of mistresses?'

'Mistresses? How very old-fashioned you are, Mr Munro. I'm surprised you don't call them 'sweethearts'. Listen, they're not mistresses or lovers or whatever you want to call them. They are like toys in a box to him. He takes them out when he wants to play, then puts them back and forgets about them until next time.'

'Is that true, or is that what you would like to believe?'

Cassandra didn't answer. She had found a fleck of dried blood on her skirt and was delicately picking it off.

'What about Jean?' Munro asked.

'Jean?' She had an irritating habit of starting every answer with a repeat of the question.

'You mean the blonde bombsite, all boobs and no brain!'

The WPC sniggered. Munro silenced her with a glare.

'Jean was like a convenience store, the little shop on the corner. He goes there for the everyday necessities but not for anything special.'

DS Munro was thinking to himself that he had not met a more opinionated and unpleasant person for a long time.

'Did Jean and Alisha get on together?'

'Get on? Don't make me laugh. Jean hated Alisha – we all did. Alisha was obnoxious and arrogant. You think she was murdered? Well if she was, and you find out who did it, let me know and I'll give them a medal!'

The pencil in Munro's hand snapped.

'What time did you arrive at the house?' he barked.

Cassandra was startled by his change in attitude.

'About three I think.'

'What time did you leave?'

'About four or maybe a little later.'

'Was your brother there?'

'I think so.'

'Think so? Was he there or not?'

'Yes!'

'Did he hear you argue?'

'He must have – we were screaming at each other.'

'Did you see Reena?'

'No - Alisha said Reena had been there earlier begging for money.'

'To pay for her booze?'

'And the rest…'

'What 'rest'?' inquired Munro. Had he missed something? Cassandra noticed his hesitancy.

'Reena didn't tell you? Or did you forget to ask?' she replied, trying to make the most of her slight advantage.

'Tell me what, Cassandra?' It was the first time he had used her name. It sent a frisson down her spine.

'Unlike me she's a married woman, but she wants out of it. She needs the money to buy off her husband. Then she thinks that Aaron would leave Alisha and marry her. There's a motive for you, sergeant!' she said triumphantly.

'Is that likely – that Aaron would leave his wife for Reena?'

'Not a snowball's chance in hell. Reena is even more common than her dear departed sister. Aaron is too good for the both of them.'

An unpleasant thought passed through DS Munro's mind. Who did she think was good enough for him? What was the relationship between Cassandra Gupta and Aaron Gupta?

He looked at her closely, studying her features. She was not unlike Alisha or even Reena. Surely not; the thought disgusted him. Cassandra's nose started bleeding again and a small trickle ran towards her lips.

'Your nose,' Munro said, nodding at her. He pushed a box of tissues that was lying on the desk over towards her.

'What about you? Have you a key for the house?'

'Yes, but you're not suspecting me are you?'

'Whoever killed Alisha had some medical knowledge. What sort of doctor are you?'

'A haematologist – disorders of the blood, that kind of thing.'

'I know what a haematologist is.'

Munro could feel the anger welling up inside him. His daughter with leukaemia was under the care of the haematologists. He and his wife had virtually lived in the hospital for the past few months. He didn't recognise either her or her name.

'Where do you work?' It was almost a challenge.

'At Kenworth's, the private hospital.'

That fits, thought Munro: another money-grabbing Gupta to contend with. He loosened his tie and undid the top button of his shirt. He had had just about enough of the two ugly sisters for one day.

'Interview concluded,' he said and switched off the tape recorder. He could barely keep the contempt out of his voice.

'You're free to go, but don't leave the area without telling me. The WPC will see you out and organise transport.'

Cassandra looked venomous. 'Don't bother, I'll walk.' She would have slammed the door if the constable hadn't been holding it.

CHAPTER TEN

'And there you have it,' concluded Munro, 'two ugly sisters, if not in appearance certainly in outlook – an alcoholic who fancies her brother-in-law and a gambler who's after her brother's money and possibly more. Neither of them with a shred of compassion.'

Steadman nodded. 'Are either of them capable of murder?' he asked.

'Both have motive, opportunity and the required skills - that is if it was an injection that killed Alisha Gupta, but are they killers? Your guess is as good as mine at this stage. There have been two further developments,' Munro continued, 'and I really owe you a bit of an apology.'

'Let me guess, you've found out something new about the buxom Jean?' Steadman asked.

Munro frowned, slightly annoyed at his colleague's perceptiveness.

'Yes – I took your advice and checked her records. She's never been to court, but she had two cautions for soliciting when she was a student.'

'What was she studying?'

'Drama, of all things - but if she was acting all innocent when I first met her she certainly fooled me, and missed her vocation.'

'Has she done any professional acting?'

'A few bit parts and a TV commercial. Most of the time she worked for her dad.'

'What was he – a hired assassin?' Dr Rufus mumbled. The wine was making him rather drowsy.

'No – nothing quite so glamorous, but possibly interesting nevertheless. He was a funeral director. Jean used to do the embalming.'

'She would certainly know where to stick a needle!' Dr Rufus exclaimed.

'Have you spoken with her again?' Steadman asked.

'I popped in briefly before coming here. She doesn't deny being on the game as a student. She was broke. Her father got to hear about the second caution and dragged her into the family business. The funeral work never bothered her but her father's overbearing attitude became too much so she went to night classes and got some secretarial qualifications. I did ask her if she knew Reena or Cassandra. She knew them all right, described them as 'a right pair of corkers.' Both of them had made it plain that they didn't like her. Jean put it down to jealousy.'

'Yes, I can understand that,' agreed Steadman, 'with all three of them in their own ways vying for Aaron Gupta's attention, and undoubtedly his money, Jean is by far the most successful. But you said there were two developments. What's the second?'

'Kim Ho in forensics has found a thumb print on the bottom of the cup sitting on Alisha's bedside table. The cup had been washed and wiped, but one print remained on the base of cup, and that print belongs to Aaron Gupta.'

Dr Rufus grunted.

'Sadly,' he said, 'a defence lawyer will say it proves nothing. It's his house - he can handle the cups if he wants to.'

'Possibly, but Kim reckons it could have been missed by whoever washed the cup and wiped off all the other prints' countered Munro. 'There is a smudge on the rim which could be part of an index finger print, but she can't be sure.'

'Frank, how strong is the case for murder?' asked Steadman.

'Good question. Circumstances aside, two pathologists have failed so far to identify a natural cause of death. I can only speak for one of them, but he's pretty damned good. There are some positive findings. Physically she was in good health apart from the small hole in the heart. She had taken a whacking dose of sleeping tablets and had recently had intercourse – neither of those killed her. However there are definite traces of topical local anaesthetic on her nether regions that need explaining. And lastly there is a puncture wound in her groin leading down to a large vein that I would be prepared to stand up in court and say was consistent with that caused by a hypodermic needle. It's strong but not robust – the defence would have fun tearing it to shreds!'

'I think Dr Gupta is bringing Anton Lemerise with him tomorrow,' Munro said.

Dr Rufus slammed down his cup and saucer.

'That fat turd, I can't abide the man! The number of times he has got criminals off the hook is unbelievable. Mind, he's as sharp as a tack. Be very careful, Alan – it wouldn't be the first time he's managed to turn a case on its head and land the police in the dock. The most important thing I've found is not to let him intimidate you. Any sign of weakness and he'll have you in knots!'

Being the size he was, Alan Munro was not easily intimidated, at least not physically. He also liked a good argument. It was in his Scottish blood, he declared. What he had heard about Anton Lemerise, however, caused him some concern. He didn't like being made to look stupid but, of far greater importance, he didn't want to let John Steadman down.

'Still nothing from toxicology?' Steadman inquired.

'Nothing,' replied Frank. 'They're still looking. The longer it goes on, the less likely they are to find anything.'

'How could an injection of nothing kill anyone?' Steadman asked of no one in particular.

Dr Rufus dropped his brandy glass and jumped to his feet.

'Good God, how can I be so stupid!' he exclaimed,

'Paulo, Paulo! Where the hell is he?'

Paulo appeared from the shadows at the back of the room. 'Yes, Dr Rufus, what can I do for you?'

'Damn it, you wouldn't understand. Get me a taxi immediately – sooner if you can!'

Paulo was taken aback. Munro shrugged his shoulders and shook his head at Paulo. He had no idea what was going on either.

'Very good, Dr Rufus,' replied the waiter slipping out of the room.

'What's up Frank?' asked John Steadman.

'Up? Up? Every bloody thing's 'up'. I told you I hate doing second post mortems. The body is completely mucked about. I spend as much time putting things back together as I do dissecting. The obvious is missed, then it's too late. Or at least I hope it's not too late. I must get to the mortuary! Paulo, have you ordered that taxi yet?'

'Frank, I have no idea what you're talking about, but if it's desperate I'm sure Alan could drive you. I will sit here quiet as a mouse.'

'Don't be bloody daft John, Alan's not going anywhere, are you Alan?'

'Absolutely not,' Munro replied. 'I'm under strict orders.'

'Look, I'm going to wait at the door. I may be able to flag down a passing cab.'

With that Dr Frank Rufus left the two men. At the door a couple were just about to get into a taxi. Frank barged through.

'Sorry, this is a medical emergency, Paulo will sort you out.'

The man and woman looked at the stocky, bearded doctor. It was clear that any protest would be pointless.

'No problem,' said the man.

'Not for you maybe, but by God there is for me. Driver, the police mortuary, and step on it!'

★ ★ ★

'What the heck do think that was all about?' asked Munro.

'I hope it means an answer to the riddle of how Alisha Gupta was killed,' Steadman replied.

'It's after eleven. Will he work all night?'

'If need be. When Frank gets the bit between his teeth there's no stopping him. Time becomes irrelevant. I gather he's nigh on impossible to work with. He doesn't understand that normal people have other lives to lead.'

'I admire his dedication,' said Munro.

'You're fairly dedicated yourself. What made a physics graduate join the police?'

Munro poured himself another cup of coffee.

'That's an interesting question. The glib answer is 'I looked into the past and decided there was no future in it' – at least not for me,' he answered enigmatically. 'Don't get me wrong. I love physics and for a time I thought I would pursue an academic career. However, some of the academics... I mean, Dr Rufus appears a bit unpredictable, but these people are in a different league, if not on a different planet. I couldn't see me working in that environment for long. Policing and physics are not as dissimilar as you might think. It's all about trying to uncover the truth. The origin of the universe? Who committed a crime? It's much the same. Whatever you discover, you'll never find out the absolute truth. If Alisha Gupta was murdered, I'm sure we'll find out who did it, we may even find out why. Or at least we may think we know why, but all we'll really find out is what tipped the scales. I don't think a person is often murdered for just one reason. Take Alisha Gupta. Nobody appears to have liked her, but what finally drove somebody to take her life?'

'I agree,' said Steadman. 'From the outset I believed it would come down to motives. I'm not sure yet if we've found someone with a strong enough motive. You said nobody appears to have liked her – maybe that's not true...'

'You mean her lover,' Munro interrupted. 'Apart from his DNA, the only other clue is Reena's rather cryptic comment. What did she say? 'Why don't you check her medical records?' I assume her records have been passed on to Dr Rufus. I'll take a look at them tomorrow.'

Steadman yawned. Even in the cheery glow from the fire, he had lost what little colour there had been in his cheeks.

'You're looking worn out, John. Shall we settle up and go home?'

Steadman conceded that he was getting tired. Paulo came with the bill. Munro protested, but Steadman insisted on paying. Munro noticed that he had folded down the corners of the twenty pound notes but not the tens. Steadman explained that it was remarkably difficult to tell them apart, especially if you were in a hurry. Before he came out he had sorted the notes into two piles according to size, the twenties being just that bit bigger than the tens, then folded the corners.

Dr Rufus would have been horrified at the size of the tip he left. As far as Steadman was concerned, it was not just about the service and undoubted effort Signor Capaldi and his staff had gone to, but also to mark the occasion. Before he put his wallet away he handed Alan Munro two twenty pound notes. 'Would you get DS Fairfax and WPC Jennings some flowers from me?' he said. Munro took the money and helped his former boss to his feet. Paulo took his arm and led him to the door. Much to Paulo's delight the two new waitresses accompanied them. They were the last to leave.

Once they were in the car Munro plucked up the courage to ask, 'What about you? Why did you join the police force, sir?'

Steadman shrugged his shoulders and replied, 'On account of my father.'

'Was he a policeman?' Munro had a momentary vision of an older, fatter version of John Steadman pedalling a bicycle.

'On the contrary, he was a crook of the first order.'

Munro jerked the wheel.

'What?' he said in disbelief.

'Yes – wrecked my childhood and drove my mother to make an attempt on her own life on account of the shame. He was a big man, always smiling, always generous, especially with money. What we didn't realise was that most of the notes were high-class forgeries. My father was an extremely talented artist and engraver. He could do anything from small book illustrations to full-scale reproductions of art works. I suspect that initially he saw copying bank notes as something of a challenge. I believe his biggest problem was getting the right paper, and that's when he started mixing with the less desirable elements in society. I can remember that my mother never liked my father's friends, but he would just put his arms around her, give her a big smile, and say something about rough diamonds as he slipped a few ten pound notes into her apron pocket. I was only a kid. He was my hero. I never thought about where the money came from. I had the best bike on the street. All the other kids looked up to me.

'I can remember the day my dreams were shattered. It was my tenth birthday. I had just been given a remote-controlled plane when the police arrived. My mother broke down as they took him away in handcuffs. All he could say was, 'Sorry, love, the game's up – it was fun while it lasted!'

'My sister Linda and I never saw him again. He was

convicted and given a lengthy sentence. He died of a heart attack three years later. My mother's character changed completely. We moved house. She became a recluse. It was only after he died that she told us what had been going on. She had never questioned him. Naively, she just thought he was marvellously talented. Even now I don't know the full story. My mother became depressed and took an overdose. I was in foster care for a time. She died when I was twenty-one. The doctors said it was her kidneys, but I knew she had given up the will to live. And it was on that day that I decided to become a policeman. Frank knows all about it. I don't believe it's common knowledge. I would prefer if you kept it to yourself.'

'Of course,' said Munro. He couldn't think of anything else to say.

They arrived at Jamaica Mansion and after the usual security checks Munro led Steadman up the drive to the main door. Bill was now on duty.

'I trust you have had a good night, Mr Steadman?'

'Absolutely wonderful,' replied Steadman with a weary smile.

At the door to his apartment Steadman said, 'Good luck with your interview. Don't let Anton Lemerise undermine your authority. I'm looking forward to hearing how you get on tomorrow.'

Munro didn't like to correct him; it was well past midnight.

'Don't forget to ask Dr Gupta about the broken window, and if the key has been taken.'

'That window is still bothering you, isn't it? I'll give you a call this evening. Maureen and the girls will be home by then. It will be nice not to have to cook my own food, although after tonight I don't think I'll eat for a week. I expect you're going to have a nice quiet day?'

'Probably,' said John Steadman.

But it wasn't exactly true.

CHAPTER ELEVEN

Despite his fatigue, Steadman's brain was racing. Reena, Cassandra, Jean, Alisha, Dr Gupta – the characters were tumbling about in his brain, leap-frogging over one another. God knows if they looked anything like he imagined them. And what was it about Dr Gupta that attracted all these women? Money, undoubtedly, but there had to be more. Was it his cold aloofness and suave manner? Or simply his good looks? The kaleidoscope in his mind rearranged the picture. Could Reena and Cassandra be in this together? He shook his head: not unless their performance at the Eyesore had been very well rehearsed.

He sighed. It was just not the same getting the information second hand, even from someone as capable as Alan Munro. It was often the little things that gave people away – the involuntary pause, the sudden nervous glance, the tapping of the fingers on the desk. Anger surged up inside him. Here he was, trying to work out who had killed a greedy, deceitful and by all accounts thoroughly unpleasant woman, while out there, somewhere, was a man who had killed the most innocent and kindest of creatures on God's earth and robbed him of his sight.

He paced the floor until his wrath subsided. He knew that dwelling on his wife's killer was futile. It never eased the pain.

His mind drifted relentlessly back to the Gupta case. He was after all a policeman; it was in his blood. It didn't matter how awful Alisha Gupta was. Someone had taken her life: a crime with no justification. He pondered on the phrase 'no justification'. It was true. What was also true was the absence of a real motive. It takes more than annoyance and petty squabbles to plan a murder, and that was what was bothering him. That and the broken window – why did the thought of shattered glass cause the back of his neck to prickle? And what had made Frank Rufus suddenly jump up from the table and leave? Doubtless he would find out soon enough.

It occurred to him that Alan would have turned on the lights as they had entered the apartment. Naturally he had not thought to switch them off. Steadman moved cautiously over to where the switches were located, brushing up against the arm of a chair as he passed. He reached out and touched the wall and his fingers delicately wandered up and down, almost insect-like, until he found the switches and turned them off.

Did it make a difference? Sometimes he could just

discern shadows, but it was no more than a slight increase or decrease in the intensity of the greyness. Carefully he made his way over to the window. Apart from faces, the sight he missed the most was the night sky. Alan Munro had studied astronomy as part of his physics degree. For a moment he was quite jealous, not of Munro's sight but the opportunity for studying, something that he had been denied. The heavens fascinated him. He recalled vividly walking with Holly along the sea shore. They had been young and in the first flush of love. It had been a bright, starry night and as they walked the moon had risen. Wrapped in each other's arms, they had stopped and stared out to sea as an enormous, pale golden moon heaved itself up over the horizon. There had been no sound apart from the gentle sighing of the ebb tide. He had looked at Holly and seen the moon reflected in her eyes, and he had known then that she was the one.

Was there a moon tonight? He covered one eye, then the other, and tried to peer into the gloom. Could there be one bit of the sky that was brighter than the rest? Possibly, he thought, but he could not be sure.

Finding the intercom, he called down to the concierge. Bill answered. He was a tall, silver-haired retired policeman with such a dignified bearing and manner of speaking that he had earned himself the nickname of 'The Bishop'.

'Good evening, Mr Steadman, is everything all right?'

'Fine thanks,' Steadman replied. 'A silly question really – is there a moon tonight?'

'Yes sir, a full moon tonight and not a cloud in the sky.'

Perhaps it was just the wine, but he found comfort in this tiny piece of information and went to bed feeling peaceful and content, something he had not felt for months.

CHAPTER TWELVE

It was another glorious spring morning. Sergeant Grimble had wedged the main doors of the Eyesore wide open. Although he enjoyed the birdsong, it was more to let out the stale air that pervaded the waiting room. The cleaners had been in but the room still smelt of sweat and vomit: it had been a busy night. The plastic chairs had all been scrubbed. Where they were still damp they glinted in the sunlight.

A tune had got stuck in Sergeant Grimble's head and he was happily whistling as he proceeded to tidy his desk, or at least organise the piles into what he regarded as a semblance of order. He had a cup of tea at his elbow and was just thinking how a cigarette would make his life perfect, that is, if smoking had not been banned in the Eyesore. Grimble had given up years before but still craved that 'first fag of the day'. He knew if he once yielded to temptation he would be back up to twenty a day within the week.

He closed his eyes and tried to count the years since

he had stopped smoking. Was it eleven or twelve? His sister Norah's boy had just turned twenty-one; how old would he be now?

'Excuse me, I need to speak to someone.'

Sergeant Grimble opened his eyes. 'Sorry, sir, I was miles away. How may I help you?'

Standing in front of the duty sergeant's desk stood an anxious, thin man. He was smartly dressed in a blue sports jacket, grey flannels and a shirt and tie. His shoes were light brown, highly polished and clashed abominably with the rest of his clothes. Sergeant Grimble took it all in. The man's hands were trembling and his nails bitten. He fiddled nervously with his wedding ring, and avoided the sergeant's gaze. Shuffling his feet, he tried to say something but couldn't.

Grimble smiled at the man. He was a shrewd observer. He reckoned he must be about thirty-five, educated, professional and probably self-employed, had small children and was married, but not happily. There were little sticky fingerprints on his trousers just above his left knee, and surely no wife would have let him out wearing those shoes if she had noticed them. For a moment it looked as if he might do a runner.

'You've done the hardest bit, son,' Grimble said in a reassuring voice, 'you've walked through the door. Now, who would you like to speak to?'

'I can't recall his name – a big Scottish fellow, McRae, or something like that. He came to see Alisha

Gupta. I've come to confess,' he said finishing in a whisper.

'DS Munro is the man you're looking for, and I believe he's already here. I'll try his office for you. What's your name?'

'I'd rather not say,' he replied looking around him.

'Nobody here but you and me, son, but have it your own way.'

The man went to sit down. Sergeant Grimble held up a hand.

'They're still a bit damp yet. He won't keep you if he's in… good morning, DS Munro, feeling perky like the weather, I trust? I've got a young man here with me who wants to make a confession regarding the Gupta investigation… no, he wouldn't give a name. You'll come down right away? Excellent, I'll let the gentleman know.'

The man glanced at his watch, then at the door. He took one step towards the exit.

'I wouldn't leave if I were you, Dr Robinson,' said Sergeant Grimble.

'How do you know my name?' The man looked crest fallen.

'I've just remembered where I've seen you before. You came out last Christmas Eve to my nephew Glen's little boy. He had earache and a fever. Very grateful we all were too. If I'm not mistaken here comes Detective Sergeant Munro.'

The two police officers nodded to each other.

'Dr Robinson, isn't it?' said Munro. He held out a huge hand. Dr Robinson shook it half-heartedly.

'Come this way.'

As they passed the duty sergeant's desk, Grimble winked at the doctor, who in turn gave him a look filled with a mixture of contempt and despair. Grimble shrugged, logged in the doctor's visit and finished his cup of tea.

DS Munro led Dr Robinson to one of the small interview rooms. It too had just been cleaned and smelled strongly of lavender polish. The window was wide open, and on a branch outside, a blackbird was in full song. It took flight, screeching in alarm as Munro slammed the door.

The young man started talking before he had even sat down.

'I should have come straight away and told you. I'm sorry, but it isn't that easy. I have my career to think of and my wife and my family,' he added, staring at the floor. 'I haven't slept a wink since Monday. I can barely eat. My wife knows something's up. I daren't tell her. Does she need to know?'

DS Munro raised both his massive hands. 'Whoa! Not so fast, sir. What is it you actually want to tell me?'

'Well it was me, wasn't it? I did it.' Dr Robinson lifted his eyes and faced DS Munro. He started to snivel.

'Did what exactly, sir?' asked DS Munro

'Made love to Alisha the night she died.'

'And did you kill her afterwards?'

'Good God no! We were lovers, or at least I was in love with her. It was the sex - it must have brought on her heart attack.'

Munro sat back in the chair. He looked hard at the young doctor, then closed his eyes and thought for a moment.

'Let's start at the beginning shall we, sir, and we'll tape everything just for the record.'

Dr Robinson said that he had only met Alisha Gupta six months ago. It was, at least on his part, love at first sight. It hadn't mattered to him that she was ten years older than he was. He had been mesmerised by her looks. Strong women had always attracted him. That and Alisha's haughty demeanour had bowled him over. He had two small children at home, children who wouldn't sleep, and a wife who was always exhausted. He knew it was unfair to say that his wife had 'let herself go'; it was just that she was at the bottom of her long list of priorities, and by the time she reached the bottom of that list, she was too tired to do anything about it. Dr Robinson had tried to understand, but when Alisha walked into his surgery looking glamorous and most definitely available, he was smitten.

Alisha, he explained preferred younger men, especially married men with children. It was, he thought, probably to spite her husband, as he had never managed to get her pregnant.

It was clear from the conversation that Alisha dominated the relationship. Dr Robinson had become infatuated. He was at her beck and call. He admitted that it was ruining his life.

'But what I could I do?' he asked DS Munro.

Dr Robinson's meandering explanation droned on. DS Munro was only half listening. He was doodling on the pad in front of him, writing complex equations from his student days and trying to remember the formula for the frequencies of light given out by incandescent hydrogen. He was getting bored with the man sitting opposite him, bored with his squalid tale and lame excuses. Eventually he banged the table, causing Dr Robinson to jump.

'Enough,' he said as he picked up the phone. 'Grimble, I need someone in here with me. Is there anyone about?'

'DS Fairfax is standing right beside me. I'm sure she would be delighted to join your little gathering.'

Sergeant Grimble put his hand over the mouthpiece and whispered to DS Fairfax.

'He's got young Dr Robinson, Gupta's GP, in with him. He wants to make a confession.'

DS Fairfax nodded.

'I'll ask her to go through.'

Munro swept up a chair and placed it beside him as though it was as light as his pencil. He was glad it was DS Fairfax who was joining him. A female presence would add to Dr Robinson's discomfort, he thought.

'Does it have to be a...' Dr Robinson spluttered, but Munro held up a hand.

'This is Detective Sergeant Fairfax, who is also working on the case. Now isn't that convenient?'

He could see from Robinson's face that it was

anything but. Munro recounted the story so far for DS Fairfax's benefit, then, turning to the doctor, he said, 'Right, let's talk about Sunday night. Was your meeting pre-arranged?'

'No,' replied Robinson. He had gone very pale. 'She texts me on my mobile phone when her husband has gone out.'

'Isn't your wife suspicious?' asked DS Fairfax.

Robinson swallowed. 'We have a code. She texts something like 'patient deteriorating, house call requested'.'

'Surely your wife could trace the number?' Fairfax continued.

'I have her number stored as 'district nurse',' he replied apologetically. DS Fairfax wasn't giving up that easily.

'She must have known something was going on with you running off like that, then coming back sweating, reeking of perfume and grinning like a naughty schoolboy.'

'My wife was always asleep when I got back. Sometimes I would sleep on the couch to avoid disturbing the children. That's what I did on Sunday night.'

'So how does it go? You get a bogus call, you drive round – does she leave the door open or is she standing there in her negligée waiting for you?' Munro asked.

'I have a key.'

Good grief, thought Munro, just how many people have keys to the Guptas' house?

'Go on,' he said wrinkling his forehead.

Dr Robinson was picking at the edge of the desk. He shot an embarrassed look at DS Fairfax, who appeared totally unconcerned.

'No, she's always waiting for me upstairs.'

'In bed?'

'Yes – in bed. She doesn't believe in any foreplay or anything like that or at least…'

'At least what?'

Dr Robinson looked as though he was going to faint. 'May I have a glass of water?'

DS Munro was glad of the opportunity to stretch his legs. There was a water cooler in the corner of the room. Munro handed him a paper cup. Dr Robinson's hands were shaking quite badly.

'Where were we?' said Munro. 'Oh yes, you were about to elaborate on 'at least'…'

'Do I have to? Maybe I should get a solicitor.'

'I'm sure your solicitor would instruct you to tell the complete truth.'

DS Munro couldn't believe he had said that, for it was absolute nonsense. Dr Robinson stared at the floor again and admitted that sometimes Alisha blindfolded him and tied his hands behind his back. Neither police officer passed comment.

'Back to Sunday night,' Munro continued. 'The pathologist states that her genitals were covered in some sort of jelly.'

'Yes, maybe it's to do with her age, I don't know,'

replied the doctor. He was a broken man by now, and beyond shame. 'She always used lots of lubrication.'

'And you made love as normal?'

Dr Robinson nodded.

'Anything strike you as odd?' asked DS Fairfax.

'What do you mean?'

'Forensics have told us that the jelly was laced with a large amount of lidocaine, a topical anaesthetic – something to numb the skin. No doubt you are familiar with the drug.'

Dr Robinson nodded again.

'That explains it,' he said more to himself than the two detectives.

'Explains what exactly?'

'We made love for ages. Eventually I... well you know what I mean, but I couldn't satisfy Alisha. She said she was fine, but I knew she was faking it. Then she fell asleep.'

'Is that when you injected her groin and murdered her?' asked Munro. 'You see, Dr Robinson, Alisha Gupta didn't have a heart attack.'

'What? No, no – why would I? How could I?' Dr Robinson's voice broke.

'Well, let's see,' said DS Fairfax. 'Firstly - how could you? You're a doctor. Doubtless you took in your little black bag to add to the sham of doing a house call. I presume that in your bag there are syringes, hypodermic needles and an arsenal of potentially lethal drugs.'

'I can't believe you're saying this!' cried Dr Robinson.

'And as for why would you,' continued Munro, 'your relationship with Alisha Gupta was destroying, or has destroyed, your marriage. If details of your affair come to light, your precious career is also in jeopardy. I believe your governing body takes a pretty dim view of doctors having sex with their patients. And you knew there was no way she would leave her husband for you. Let's be frank, other than sex, what had you got to offer her? You were obsessed with her, and she was ruining your life. It's more than convenient for you that she's dead. Dr Robinson, you have the motive, the opportunity and the means for murder.'

'No, it's not true, it's not true what you're saying – I didn't – I couldn't. I was in love with her. You're lying, you're lying!' He was becoming frantic.

'When did you leave?' DS Fairfax asked calmly.

'Ten thirty, quarter to eleven – no later. I swear she was sleeping soundly when I left.'

'Did you make her a drink before you left?'

Dr Robinson looked perplexed. 'No, she never touched alcohol.'

'What about a hot drink, milk or chocolate?'

'No, nothing like that, why?'

Ignoring his question DS Fairfax continued, 'Did she pay you for sex?'

'She tried but I wouldn't let her,' he replied hesitantly.

'What about gifts?'

Looking uncomfortable, he answered, 'Yes, she would buy me expensive ties – I have a thing about ties.'

DS Munro had a fleeting mental image of a naked Dr Robinson blindfolded and handcuffed with silk ties. It was not a pretty picture.

'What did your wife say to that?'

'I told her they were gifts from a wealthy patient, which was true!' Turning to DS Munro he said, 'Do you really think I killed her?'

'I haven't made up my mind yet.' Again he stared long and hard at the doctor.

'Does my wife have to be told about this?'

'It would be better coming from you,' said DS Fairfax. Dr Robinson looked aghast. 'It will come out at the inquest,' she explained.

'What was she injected with?'

His question was ignored.

'We'll need a sample of your DNA and we'll get you to sign a statement in due course. Don't even think of leaving the area without telling me,' added Munro.

'Is that absolutely necessary? I came here of my own free will, didn't I?'

'You did, but you could be bluffing. You've been deceiving your wife. You could easily be trying to deceive us. I could, if I had a mind to, arrest you on suspicion of murder.'

For the first time Dr Robinson looked DS Munro in the eyes. 'What I've told you is the truth. I thought I had caused Alisha to have a heart attack. Honestly, I swear I didn't kill her.'

Munro turned to DS Fairfax, who shook her head,

indicating that she had no further questions. What would John Steadman make of all this, he thought?

CHAPTER THIRTEEN

It really was quite easy. I knew you were lurking in your lair at Jamaica Mansion. The only time I had seen you leave was with that gorilla Munro. Oh, I could have picked you off, but where is the fun in that? I want to be there, to witness it at close quarters.

You don't have much family, do you? Parents both dead, one feckless son somewhere in France, leaving only your sweet and innocent sister, Linda. I ask you, a professional gardener; a woman with dirt permanently under her nails. Not that you would notice, at least not now. She even has her mobile number written on the side of her van. Tut tut! Security not as tight as it should be? Or is it your arrogance, Steadman? Having survived once, do you believe you're now immortal? I know your phone number keeps changing but to put a tap on your sister's phone was child's play, if one could afford it, and I can! So she's coming to collect you at 11 am precisely, to take you out for the day like a good little boy, just the two of you, such excitement. She'll call you when she's just about to arrive. Three little rings – your secret code, and you'll come out to meet her!

'It will be lovely,' she said and you agreed. We'll see, we'll see...

* * *

Linda was one of life's organisers. She had been looking forward to this day ever since her brother had regained consciousness after the operation. The weather was set fair, so she had planned a picnic in her garden. Nothing too fancy, she thought, egg and cress, smoked salmon and cream cheese sandwiches with three types of salad, a light rosé wine followed by chocolate brownies, her brother's favourite. She had borrowed her husband's car, cleaned it inside and out. She had even checked the oil. What could go wrong?

Steadman too was in high spirits. He had got up even earlier than usual. For the time being at least, the events of the previous night and the whole Gupta case were dismissed. Daisy, one of the concierges at Jamaica Mansion had at his request helped to select his clothes. She was a large, formidable lady who, Steadman suspected, had formerly worked in the prison service. She was flattered to be asked. As Steadman had pointed out, even with his sight, his taste and sense of colour coordination had been rudimentary; Holly had always sorted his clothes out.

By ten-thirty he was fully dressed and pacing the flat. He didn't like to phone, as he knew Linda would be on her way by now. He decided to splash on some aftershave; Linda would appreciate that.

The journey to Jamaica Mansion should take no more than fifty minutes. Linda had left at ten and knew the way well. The road was quiet. She checked her watch: twenty past ten, plenty of time.

The next mile was tricky. The road narrowed and twisted as it weaved through a gap in the cliffs. She noticed the van parked in the lay-by before she saw the man at the side of the road frantically waving at her to stop. He was cradling a limp bundle in his right arm. Linda could see a child's leg dangling from the bundle. Without any hesitation she stopped and wound down the window.

'My child is very sick. I need to get to a hospital. Which way please?' His accent was very thick, possibly east European, Linda thought.

'It's not that far,' she replied, 'but you're coming into Helmsmouth from the wrong side.'

She knew it was a stupid thing to say as soon as she said it. She also knew she was hopeless at giving directions.

'I have a map in the van. Could you pull in behind me and explain to my wife. She will understand better.'

Linda frowned but did as she was asked. The child, a little boy, certainly didn't look well. His face was flushed and he lay in the man's arms quite still; too still to be just sleeping.

Linda didn't notice the back door of the van opening as she climbed in beside the woman on the front seat. They produced a map, which wasn't as detailed as she would have liked.

'Hang on - I've got a better one in my car.'

'No, no it's all right. Just write on this one, there is no time.'

Patiently she wrote down the directions, marking the map carefully with little arrows. The couple insisted on going over her instructions twice. There was a loud noise from the back of the van. Before Linda could turn round the man said, 'It's only the dog, don't worry.'

She got out of their van and dusted herself down. With a toot of their horn they were off. Looking at her watch, she realised she was now going to be five minutes late. John would understand, she thought, but I'll give him a call anyway.

It was only when she went to open the driver's door that she noticed the front tyre was flat. She cursed under her breath. It was not that she was incapable of changing a wheel; it was just that she would arrive even later, grubby and sweaty. Her handbag lay on the front seat. The mobile phone was missing. She was sure she had left it on top of her bag; in fact she was absolutely certain. A feeling of trepidation welled up within her. She could feel her heart racing and her breathing becoming more rapid.

'Calm down,' she said to herself. 'First things first – let's get the wheel changed.'

Panic truly set in when she discovered that her rear nearside tyre was also completely flat. Her thoughts were now in total disarray and spinning like the wheels in a fruit machine. With a clunk, each spinning wheel stopped in turn. Realisation set in. Two tyres flat, mobile phone missing, a dog that didn't bark...

There had been no dog. Comprehension crashed over her in a tidal wave of despair. She burst into tears.

John Steadman's phone rang three times. Linda will be here any minute now, he said to himself. He pressed the button on his wrist watch. The metallic voice informed him that it was ten fifty five. He could wait no longer. Slipping on his dark glasses he unfolded his white cane and made his way down to the concierge's desk. Only at the last minute did he realise he had left his lucky rat netsuke figure in the pocket of the suit he had worn last night.

'You look very smart,' said Daisy, casting an appraising eye over him. 'You're flying a bit low though!'

'Thanks,' replied Steadman, attending to the wayward zip on his trousers. 'I'm going to wait outside. Linda will be here any minute.'

Daisy looked at the CCTV images. There was no sign of Linda.

'I really don't think you should. Why not give her another few minutes? You can wait here and keep me company.'

'Much as I hate to turn down such a tempting offer, I think I'd prefer to wait on the pavement' replied Steadman. 'She's called to say she's almost here. Linda isn't the best at parking, and when she sees me she can just pull in for a second.'

Realising that Steadman was adamant, Daisy shrugged and said, 'Your choice - I can't stop you.'

Gingerly Steadman walked down the twisting path. He was getting better with the cane, but he still had to concentrate hard. Daisy watched him on the CCTV monitor. At last he reached the electronic door in the wall. Tentatively he stretched out his hand, found the button and pressed it to let Daisy know he was there. She checked the outside monitors.

'Road clear, door opening. Have fun!' Her voice came through the small speaker. John Steadman could not help but smile. This is what it must feel like to be released from prison, he thought.

There was not much traffic passing. Steadman amused himself by trying to guess what each vehicle was. Motorbikes and trucks were fairly easy, as was the distinctive rattle of a black taxi cab. Cars and vans were far harder to tell apart. A vehicle slowed down and stopped. Steadman believed it could only be thirty or forty yards down the road. The horn gave a couple of friendly beeps. He waved and headed off in the direction of the noise. He heard a car door opening. Not far, he thought but in his haste he caught his toe on a raised pavement slab and stumbled.

'Here, let me help you.'

It was a man's voice. Steadman had not heard him approach.

'Thank you, I'm just heading for that car,' said Steadman. 'It's my sister. We're going out for the day,' he added in his excitement.

The man took his arm as they walked the remaining distance.

'Here we are,' said the man.

Steadman felt something cold and hard press into his side.

'Not one word or I shoot. Get in.'

The man holding the gun let go of Steadman's arm and with his free hand roughly pushed Steadman's head down, forcing him into the car. Another hand from inside the car grabbed his outstretched arm and pulled him on to the seat. His white stick fell from his grasp and clattered in the gutter. The man with the gun got in and slammed the door. Steadman felt himself wedged between two large men. The driver pulled off.

'Keep your hands where I can see them.'

One of the men went roughly through Steadman's pockets, found his mobile phone and switched it off.

'May I ask where we're going?'

'I said 'not one word'!' Steadman felt the gun poking harder into his side.

Daisy, who had been distracted by two phone calls that both proved to be wrong numbers, missed all of this. When she checked the outside monitors, Steadman was gone.

Not wishing to argue with a man with a gun, Steadman remained silent. His throat was dry and he felt both foolish and angry with himself. What was the point of staying in a safe house if you run out at the first available opportunity? Maybe the shot to his head had unravelled his senses?

He tried to compose himself by trying to count the bends, but that proved impossible. He noted that the traffic seemed heavier and that they stopped several times. Presumably they were going through the town. Now they speeded up. There were vehicles on either side of them.

Steadman thought hard. It must be a dual carriageway. There were only two in Helmsmouth, one leading round the docks and one running in an arc to the north of the town, acting as a bypass. He could smell nothing of the sea, suggesting they were on the latter route. In fact the only smell he could detect was the plastic odour that all new cars had.

What sort of car was it? It must be a fairly large saloon, as there was room for three men in the back seat. He didn't think there was anybody sitting in the front passenger seat or if there was he or she was sitting very still. No, he was fairly sure the front seat was empty. Would anybody notice - it must appear odd to have three people sitting in the back seat when there was room in the front? He reached down to touch the seat. The top was cloth but the facing was vinyl. He tucked both hands behind his knees and gently started picking at the plastic with his fingernails. He was almost certain they were on the north ring road for the traffic was getting lighter. No one spoke.

After about half an hour they turned off the main road. Several more minutes passed. The car turned again, sharp right then sharp left. Steadman was aware they were climbing, but had no idea where they were. If it was the hills to the north of Helmsmouth, it was an area he was not familiar with. He was also aware of the gun constantly digging into his side.

The car turned again and the surface noise changed. They were on an unmetalled road. Slowing down to avoid potholes, the car continued to climb. After a further fifteen minutes it stopped.

'Out,' said the man with the gun as he grasped Steadman's arm roughly. 'Walk, and don't try anything clever.'

The other two men got out of the car. With one man on each side of him holding an arm and one behind they set off, frog marching him up the slope.

Was one of these men his wife's killer? He didn't think so, although he had heard only one of the men speak so far. He thought he should have felt more frightened. All he felt at this moment was anger at himself for being so foolhardy.

The ground continued to rise. At first they walked on a rough path in places too narrow for three men to walk abreast. Steadman could hear the rustle of branches and feel the sun intermittently on his face. An overhanging branch caught the top of his head. Repeatedly he missed his footing. He would have fallen had it not been for the men on either side of him.

Soon the trees gave way to open grass. It was cooler here and there was a slight breeze. One of the men was panting.

'For Chrissakes, stop for a minute and let me catch my breath.' It was a different voice, but not one Steadman recognised. They paused only briefly. For a moment the gun stopped sticking into his side. Steadman felt the man move his arm as he checked his watch.

'Come on, or we'll be late.'

So, thought Steadman, we're to meet someone else. He had a sudden pain in the pit of his stomach. For a moment he considered making a run for it, but knew it would be madness. He was sure to fall within the first few steps. He clenched his fists in frustration.

The men pressed on, half carrying, half dragging the stumbling Steadman. The land flattened out, the temperature dropped and the wind rose. At last they stopped; there was someone waiting for them.

'On time, Steadman - I'm impressed!'

It was the same silky voice, familiar but unnameable. Steadman remained silent. The man moved round behind Steadman and firmly grasped his shoulders.

'Cat got your tongue, John? Let's give him a whirl, shall we?' he hissed into Steadman's ear. Sharp nails dug into the flesh at the top of his right arm and he felt the man's breath on his neck. The men pushed and jostled Steadman between them, forcing him round and round until his head was reeling.

'Stop!' ordered the voice. 'You must be tired after that,' it sneered at Steadman. 'Time for a little sleep.'

Steadman smelt the sickly stench of the chloroform just before the wadding was placed tightly over his mouth and nose. Now he was struggling, trying hard not to breathe. His efforts were futile. He felt himself spinning down into a deep, black hole. As he lost consciousness he thought he heard the voice say something about a 'poignant farewell note'.

'Pick him up and follow me.'

Two of the men grasped Steadman's legs, while the other clutched his shoulders.

'Now place him exactly on the edge with his right leg hanging over' said the silky voice.

'Christ, I hate heights,' said the man with the gun. 'Why can't we just chuck him over and be done with it?'

'I have my reasons.'

The three men looked at the man giving the orders, the man who was also paying them. It was difficult to tell under his stocking mask, but they thought he was grinning.

* * *

Yes, I had my reasons. I did think you would be frightened first time round, but oh no, fear was below the noble John Steadman. I thought I felt you tremble when we started to spin you round; maybe it was just wishful thinking on my part. This time you will know fear, real fear that wrenches your stomach just as you realise that you're falling to your death. I've imagined it countless times. You just lying there slowly wakening up, and then your right leg drops a little bit further over the precipice. Instinctively you reach out with your right hand, and that tips the balance. Immediately panic sets in. You have no time to think. You try to grasp something, anything, with your left hand, but there is nothing there. Your right arm and leg flail about in mid-air, and then over you go. Will you scream, I wonder? I would love to hear that. How long will you fall? Three seconds, four maybe, but I think it will feel a lot longer. Will your life flash before you? I hope not, or you may die of boredom before you hit the bottom. I wonder if you'll wet yourself.

I don't think they'll find the body for some time. The back of the old quarry is fairly inaccessible. I bet it's that ape Munro, bounding over the rocks like some ghastly mountain yak, who finds you. Will he feel disappointed in you when he reads the note I put in your pocket, assuming he has the wit to look in your pockets. I don't think it will be long before someone questions if it really was suicide. Was he pushed or did he jump? It will remain a mystery, for in truth it was neither. You simply tumbled off the edge, just like falling out of bed. 'Death by misadventure' I would say – subtle and clever. I'm sure that you would have appreciated it, Steadman, if you had still been alive.'

★ ★ ★

Slowly John Steadman regained consciousness. At first all he was aware of was the foul taste in his mouth. He desperately wanted to be sick. His head was swimming. A fly buzzed over his face before finally landing on his dry lips. He let it sit there, too drowsy even to attempt to brush it away. His body ached and he had developed cramp in his right calf – the leg that was teetering over the edge. Still not fully recovered from the chloroform he tried to move his leg to ease the discomfort.

Suddenly his whole body lurched and slipped. Immediately his hands shot out, clutching at anything they could find. There was only tussocky grass that slid easily through his fingers. He was more awake now but as yet without any memory of the day's events. The adrenalin was flowing. Somehow his body knew it was in a fight for survival. He tried to move his right leg back. Again he could feel himself slipping. He swore.

With an enormous effort he twisted his upper body over just far enough for him to bring his right hand over his chest. He dug his fingers as hard as he could through the grass into the gravelly soil below, scrabbling to get any grip at all. One of his fingernails tore off; he barely noticed. His left arm thrashed out wildly as far as he could stretch. It grappled with something marginally more solid, a spindly gorse branch. He clenched it tightly and twisted it round his fist, ignoring the thorns as they tore at his skin.

His chloroformed brain was frantically trying to work in overdrive. Thoughts raced through his head. He realised he had somehow to move his legs. He daren't move his right leg; most of his buttocks were resting in thin air. Very cautiously he drew up his left leg, trying desperately to find some firm ground that he could dig his heel into to get some purchase.

The sun beat down on him, making him sweat even more despite the breeze. Above him crows cawed and chucked raucously, as though laughing at his predicament. His left heel dug into the gravel, sending a small shower of stones whistling over the edge. Steadman stopped moving. Listening intently he heard the stones land after what seemed like an eternity. He swore again. He felt his left hand move a fraction; the branch was starting to give. Cautiously he drew up his left knee and dug his heel even harder into the ground. Nausea surged up inside him to the point where he could taste bile in the back of his throat.

He tried to relax and concentrate on his breathing. In, out, in, out – slow deep breaths: the sickness passed. Think, Steadman think! A slight ripping sound came from the slender branch he was clutching in his left hand and he felt his body lurch again. He dug the bleeding fingers of his right hand as deep as he could into the soil. Using what little purchase he had from his left heel and with a huge heave he swung his right leg away from the edge of the precipice, twisting over so that he now faced the ground. His right knee landed on the stony soil with a sickening crunch. For a weakened man the effort had been enormous.

He released his grip on the gorse bush and gently pushed himself up on to his elbows. He retched and vomited profusely. He patted his pockets, found his handkerchief and wiped his mouth. Something was not right. He patted his jacket pockets again. His phone was missing. That was only to be expected. A comb, some loose change and his keys were there. The little netsuke rat should be there; no – he remembered that in his haste he had left it in his other suit. But something else was there: a folded piece of paper. His immediate reaction was to take it out and look at it. Bugger, he said to himself. A vague memory came back to him. What was it that he had heard? 'A poignant farewell note' or something like that, wasn't it? Carefully he replaced the piece of paper in his pocket. Maybe, he thought, his attacker had been a little too clever this time. His head was still reeling. Out loud he shouted:

'Why Holly? Why me, you bastard? What's this all about?'

Was it his imagination or did he hear footsteps running away? He clenched his fists. There was an acute pain in the finger that had lost its nail. He sucked his finger, then wrapped it in the vomit-streaked hanky. Now he could relax a little and think.

He knew he was on a cliff edge and that the drop lay to his left. Dare he risk standing up and trying to walk? Probably not yet, he decided, as he had no idea what lay in front of him or to his right. Remembering the sounds of the stones clattering over the edge, a thought occurred to him. In between the tussocks of grass lay coarse earth. He scraped some of this up with his left hand and threw it a few feet in front of him. He heard it land. Knowing that it was safe, he cautiously moved forwards on his hands and knees away from the edge of the precipice. Apart from the crows, the only other sound he was aware of was the distant roar of a motorbike.

Progress was slow. Twice he crawled into gorse bushes, the thorns ripping at his face. He was hot, thirsty, tired, sweaty and sore. The temptation to lie down and sleep was overwhelming. He resisted and continued his tortoise-like advance. He was hoping to find a path; so far all he had felt were the same rough tufts of grass. Even if I find a path, he thought, how could I be sure it wouldn't lead me straight over the edge?

Better than a path, his head bumped into what was obviously a good, strong pig-net fence. Little by little he pulled himself upright. He ached dreadfully and his head started swimming again, but the fence offered good support. He stood there perfectly motionless until he regained his balance.

The fence was topped with barbed wire, presumably, he thought, to stop animals falling over the cliff. If he could get to the other side he could use it as a guide to lead him downhill. He tossed a few stones over the fence. They landed with a reassuring soft thud. Taking off his jacket, he draped it on the barbed wire and climbed over. If only he could have seen it, he was no more than a few yards from the gap in the fence through which his anaesthetised, limp body had been dragged only an hour previously.

He put his jacket back on and checked the pocket to make sure the piece of paper was still there. A chilly breeze sprang up. He had stopped sweating by now and had actually started to shiver. He pressed the button on his watch. The tinny voice informed him that it was one fifty seven. Only then did he remember he was supposed to have met Linda. She would be frantic, he thought. From the pit of his stomach a wave of anxiety swept over him. What if they had got her as well? She was always early for everything, but not today.

★ ★ ★

Should I have just pushed you over and finished the job? I could have, but it would have spoiled my plan and, for a fleeting second, I felt sorry for you. It didn't last. You still don't get it, do you? You stole from me the thing I wanted most in my life; that I've never stopped wanting; that I could never have – Holly! With Holly by my side I would still be a success. I've watched, I've dreamed and planned. But I know what I've become and it's too late. She would have been no use to me now, old and spent like an empty shotgun cartridge. The Holly that I wanted was still sixteen, vibrant and innocent. That's probably how you still saw her. Oh, how I wanted you to feel my loss, even if only for a moment. And you've lost more, but you have not suffered as I have, and so, John Steadman, I'm afraid I am not finished with you yet...

CHAPTER FOURTEEN

Sergeant Grimble cupped his hand over the receiver.

'They're here.'

Alan Munro put down the phone, stretched, scratched the back of his head and made his way down to the interview rooms. He had been uneasy about meeting Anton Lemerise for some time. Everybody he had spoken to had either warned him or smiled and said, 'Rather you than me' before giving him a less than reassuring pat on the back. Now that the moment had arrived, he had to admit he was more curious than anxious.

DS Fairfax poked her head round the door.

'Sorry, Alan, something important has cropped up. I must dash. Speak with you later - good luck!'

Munro had no time to reply. This was a blow, and it left him with a bit of a problem. He had been relying on DS Fairfax to be with him during the interview. She was not easily fazed, either by hardened criminals or clever solicitors.

He went back upstairs. Most of the rooms were

empty. In those that were occupied, the officers all appeared to be busy writing reports or staring gloomily at flickering computer screens. Standing next to the coffee machine with a faraway look in his eyes was Detective Constable Will Lofthouse. He was shorter and slighter than the other officers, but, with jet black hair and pale green eyes he was not lacking female admirers. Inspector Crouchley had described him as a waste of space with his head permanently in the clouds and had been glad to get rid of him from the uniformed team. Alan Munro liked him. Lofthouse certainly brought an unusual perspective to every investigation. His brain appeared to be wired differently from anyone else Munro had ever met.

'If you're not too busy, Will, would you sit in with me for the interview with Dr Gupta?'

'Sure – no problem. I gather he's bringing the solicitor from hell with him.'

'They're both downstairs waiting. Have you met Lemerise?'

'No, but I've heard all about him. This will be a lot of fun,' he said, rubbing his hands in anticipation.

Munro shook his head; DC Lofthouse certainly viewed the world from an odd angle.

★ ★ ★

Neither Aaron Gupta nor Anton Lemerise took up Sergeant Grimble's offer of a seat. They stood a little way off from the reception desk and tried to ignore their surroundings.

Footsteps could be heard coming down the stairs. 'I expect that's DS Munro now,' Grimble said to them.

Lemerise took out a gold fob watch from his waistcoat pocket and was deliberately staring at it when Munro pushed open the door. It was ten thirty three. Lemerise looked at Munro, and with an exaggerated sigh slowly closed his watch and stowed it back into his pocket. He ignored Munro's outstretched hand, as did Dr Gupta. Munro started to blush. 'Calm down,' he said to himself as he pushed open the swing door.

'This way, gentlemen, please.'

He led them into the interview room he had used earlier with Dr Robinson. The blackbird was back, singing for all it was worth just outside the window. This appeared to annoy Anton Lemerise, much to Munro's satisfaction.

He introduced DC Lofthouse, who appeared so at ease that Alan Munro would not have been surprised if he had slackened off his tie and put his feet up on the desk.

'Is this likely to take long?' asked Lemerise.

'It may do,' replied Munro, who, having regained his composure stared intently at Lemerise. But the solicitor's eyes were half shut and it was impossible to gauge what he was thinking.

'What is the status of my client?' he asked.

'From our point of view, Dr Gupta is here as a witness helping with police enquiries.'

Lemerise sighed again, as though bored with the proceedings already. Slowly he took some papers out of his briefcase, shuffled them and laid them on the desk. Munro knew that Lemerise was deliberately trying to unsettle him; it didn't stop his cheeks turning red again. He could see out of the corner of his eye Dr Gupta trying hard not to smirk. The blackbird, which had paused for breath, struck up its song again even louder than before.

Lemerise turned to look out of the window. As he moved in his chair Munro noticed a large, brown gobbet of wax dangling on a tuft of hair protruding from his ear. Dr Gupta noticed it too. In the sterile atmosphere of the interview room it appeared all the more disgusting. Dr Gupta frowned; now it was Munro's turn to suppress a grin. From that moment on he knew the interview was going to be a piece of cake. How could anyone be intimidated by a solicitor with half a dirty candle hanging out of his ear?

'I'll shut the window, sir,' said Lofthouse. 'We might get a bit of peace and quiet.'

Munro nodded. 'To begin with,' he said, 'I owe you two apologies Dr Gupta. When I arrived at your house I did not realise the deceased was your wife. I had assumed that she was one of your patients, but there was no excuse – I should have known.' He paused, then continued, 'And then I had completely forgotten that dentists now called themselves 'doctors' and wrongly assumed that yours was a medical clinic, not a dental clinic. I trust you will forgive both lapses.'

Munro spread out his enormous hands and smiled as innocently as a child. Dr Gupta was lost for words. DC Lofthouse looked bemused. Anton Lemerise brushed some imaginary fluff off his sleeves. He didn't say anything, but he was more than a little perplexed by Munro's candid and unorthodox start to the interview.

'Let me put the police findings to you so far,' Munro began. 'Alisha Gupta, we believe, died in the early hours of Monday morning. Death was confirmed by her GP, Dr Robinson. He was aware that she had a heart problem and possibly a family history of heart disease, but the death was quite unexpected and under the circumstances he did not feel he could issue a death certificate. Initially there appeared to be nothing suspicious and the coroner requested a routine post mortem examination. However, this failed to establish a cause of death and so the coroner instructed a second post mortem to be carried out by Dr Frank Rufus, the Home Office pathologist.

'We now know several things for certain. We know that Alisha Gupta had sexual intercourse the night before she died, but not with you, Dr Gupta. The DNA does not match. We know that she had taken a large dose of sleeping pills – not enough to kill her but enough to make her very drowsy, if not unconscious, for a time. We know that lubricating jelly heavily laced with local anaesthetic was smeared on her groin and genital area. Finally, there is evidence that a needle had been carefully inserted into the large vein in her groin. It is a distinct possibility that your wife died as a result of an injection of a noxious substance. In other words we have reason to believe that Alisha Gupta was probably murdered.'

Dr Gupta sat silent and stony faced, betraying not a flicker of emotion. Lemerise had written four words on the sheet of paper in front of him. He tapped the desk with the end of his pen.

'What 'noxious substance'?' he asked.

'That still has to be ascertained,' Munro replied.

Lemerise clicked his tongue and ticked off one of the words on his list. 'Have you found the alleged needle?'

'No.' Munro concentrated hard on the mental image of the wax in Lemerise's hairy ear.

'And this 'laced lubricating jelly', as you so eloquently put it, has that been found?'

'No.'

'Oh dear,' Lemerise continued, raising his eyebrows and shaking his head. 'What about the mysterious lover? Please don't tell me he has not been found either.' He ticked off the last of the words on his list.

'I was hoping your client could enlighten us,' responded Munro.

'I am sure the suggestion that his wife had a lover, as well as the far-fetched notion that she could have been murdered, has come as a great shock to Dr Gupta.'

Alan Munro glanced at the dentist. If he was shocked, there was no sign of it on his face. Lemerise sat back in his chair with his hands clasped over his paunch. There was a just a flicker of a triumph on his face. The blackbird burst into song again. As Lemerise turned to the window, Munro again noticed the ghastly lump of wax hanging out of his ear. It was truly awful, but in its own way, quite mesmerising.

'I would like to conduct the interview in three sections. Firstly, I would like to know more about your relationship with your wife,' Munro said, turning to Dr Gupta. 'Secondly, I would like you to recall the events of Sunday. And finally, I would like you to describe in detail what you did on Monday morning.'

Dr Gupta gave an almost imperceptible nod of his head. His solicitor dragged a fresh sheet of paper out of his briefcase.

'Again I will be honest with you. I have interviewed three women so far in this investigation, namely your receptionist Jean, your sister-in-law Reena and your own sister Cassandra. All have shed some light on your wife's character, but theirs is a very one-sided view. I would like to form my own opinion. Let's start at the beginning. Can you tell me how and when you met?'

Dr Gupta looked at his solicitor, who gave a small shrug.

'We met 18 years ago. I had built up a small but thriving dental practice in Malaysia. Alisha came to see me complaining of toothache. There was nothing wrong with her teeth. In fact, she later confessed that the whole thing had been a ruse to meet me. She was young, pretty and lively. On Thursdays I always ate at the same small restaurant. Alisha found out and, after bribing the waiter, arranged to sit at the table next to me. Feigning surprise when I arrived at the restaurant, she persuaded me to join her at her table. The rest, as they say, is history. We married a year later. Cassandra was set against it. Alisha came from a humble background. My sister was, and still is, convinced she only married me for the money.'

Lemerise cleared his throat and Dr Gupta stopped talking.

'Do you believe she married you just for the money?'

'No, I don't. But in Malaysia, just as here in Britain, any woman who marries a professional is always regarded as having made a good 'catch' for herself.'

'Were you happily married?'

Lemerise raised an eyebrow.

'To begin with yes, but she wanted a child – the one thing I couldn't give her' Dr Gupta continued. 'If she couldn't have children she was determined to have everything money could buy. She threw herself into her business and became quite successful. She was shrewd and intelligent.'

'What exactly was her business?'

'It started off making cheap toiletries. Alisha worked out that more money was to be made in skin bleaching products, and she was right. They are not that difficult to manufacture and the mark-up is considerable.'

'How did she sell the products?'

'Local wholesalers in Malaysia initially, but now the

vast majority is done on-line. She had her own website.'

Munro scratched his head. He remembered seeing a laptop computer in Dr Gupta's car but nothing else in the house. He must speak with DS Fairfax. He took out a very small notepad from his pocket and scribbled 'computer???' on it.

'So why the move to Britain?'

'Purely financial. Alisha's company virtually runs itself. She would go over three or four times a year to check things herself and to see her friends.'

Was there something just a little too well rehearsed about all of this, thought Munro? It all sounded too easy, too simple to be true.

'But some of your family came as well?'

'Only my sister Cassandra – and Reena. They came more recently.'

'What about yourself?'

'I was specialising more and more in restorative dentistry…'

'Restorative?' queried Munro.

'Cosmetic, if you like. The market for this type of work is in the West. It was much easier to set up in Britain than in the States.'

'And it pays well?'

Lemerise gave a small cough.

'Let's just say that I am comfortable,' replied Dr Gupta.

'What about Alisha's money – how did that work?'

Lemerise interrupted, 'I do not believe it is relevant

to your enquiry. I advise my client not to answer.'

Munro added another query to his notepad, 'bank statements'. He would need to go to the magistrate's court to get authorisation. Blast it, he thought, more paperwork. He looked at Dr Gupta. Was he really telling the truth? He recalled the house, the furnishings and the art works. Could Dr Gupta be bluffing? Was he really that wealthy, or was he up to his ears in debt? Were all the possessions really his wife's choice? He doubted it.

'You said you were happily married to begin with – I take it that this was not now the case?'

'I wouldn't say we were unhappily married, if that's what you're implying.'

'How would you describe it then?'

'You wouldn't understand.'

'Try me!' replied Munro. He pushed himself back on the chair, trying to get more comfortable. Dr Gupta paused and gathered his thoughts.

'As you wish. To begin with, we were very much physically attracted to one another. Shortly after we came to Britain we lost interest in that side of the marriage. Perhaps it was because I couldn't give her a child. However it was financially convenient to stay together...'

Lemerise touched his arm.

'We decided not to separate,' he continued, 'but to have – shall we say – an 'open' marriage. If I wanted to see someone else I could, and vice versa. Does that offend your British sense of morals, Mr Munro?'

It did, but he refused to rise to the bait.

'So, you've had a string of lovers, with Jean your present fancy? You don't have to answer – Jean has told us everything. What about Reena? Has she been one of your conquests?'

He laughed, 'She wishes – but no, I fear not!'

'Cassandra approves, though, of your affairs, does she not?'

The smile disappeared from his face and he uncrossed and crossed his legs. Somehow the subject of his sister appeared to unsettle him.

'Cassandra never liked my wife. Possibly because our father died young and I had to assume the role of head of the household. I am older than she is. I'm not sure if Cassandra regards me as her brother or a substitute father or what. In her eyes I am something of a hero. I can do no wrong and no woman is good enough for me.'

Munro was tempted to say 'bar herself', but kept quiet.

'Yes, Cassandra approved of my affairs,' he continued. 'She appears to think they make me more of a 'man'.'

'Your wife had affairs too, I presume?'

'I believe so.'

'How did that make you feel?'

'I told you, we decided to have an open marriage.'

'You say 'we' – do you really mean that? Or was it you or her who actually decided?'

'I knew you wouldn't understand,' he replied with a

sniff.

'What did Cassandra make of your wife having affairs?'

'She thought Alisha was a whore.'

'How much would you say Cassandra disliked your wife?'

'She hated her with a vengeance!'

'Enough to kill her?'

Lemerise interrupted: 'It is not an established fact, Sergeant Munro, that Alisha Gupta was murdered.' Munro ignored him.

The interruption had given Dr Gupta time to think.

'How much would you say is enough? I doubt that Cassandra would kill her - she relied on her too much.'

'For money?'

'Precisely,' replied Dr Gupta.

There was a knock on the door. A young policeman whom DS Munro didn't recognise stuck his head round the door.

'Sorry to interrupt, sir, there's an urgent call from a Dr Rufus, at least I think that's what he said.'

'OK,' said Munro looking at his watch, 'we'll have a ten minute break. DC Lofthouse will get you a coffee and show you where the toilets are.'

CHAPTER FIFTEEN

Dr Rufus had been unusually quiet in the back of the taxi. He liked taxi drivers, with their unfounded prejudices and half-baked political notions. He loved nothing more than getting into a heated argument. The size of the tip, if any, more often than not reflected the quality of the debate. It had been a truly enjoyable evening right up until something John Steadman had said that brought him back to earth with a resounding crash.

'How could an injection of nothing kill someone?'

Suddenly it all made sense. Toxicology had found nothing because there was nothing to find. He had tried to console himself with the thought that he might have picked it up if he had done the first post mortem. That was cold comfort. He felt he should have thought of the possibility before now; it was no use blaming someone else. He only hoped he had not left it too late to prove conclusively that Alisha Gupta had been murdered: murdered by something as simple as a large and rapid injection of air. And in someone who was already heavily drugged with sleeping pills a big enough injection of air would cause the heart to stop beating. It might have been obvious when the heart or even one of the large blood vessels was opened, if you were looking for it. These of course had already been dissected by the first pathologist and any evidence washed down the drain.

Dr Rufus thought he had better start by re-reading the first pathology report: maybe there was a comment or footnote he had missed. It wouldn't be a bad idea to have a chat with the pathologist in question in case he or she could recall something that might be helpful. Doubtless the pathologist would have done another half dozen post mortems by now and had probably completely forgotten ever doing the examination on Alisha Gupta. Even so, he thought, it had to be worth a try.

What he had to do now was both tricky and unpleasant, for it involved removing and dissecting at least one of Alisha Gupta's eyeballs. It was an awfully long shot; he only hoped he had not left it too late.

Dr Rufus shut his eyes. His chin slipped on to his chest and within seconds he was fast asleep. Sleep and Dr Rufus had been uneasy bedfellows for most of his adult life. Recurring nightmares are the bane of many forensic pathologists and Frank Rufus was no exception. The dream was always the same: he was doing a post mortem on a small boy and for some obscure reason was removing the child's arm. Half way through the procedure the child turned to him and said, 'Please don't hurt me any more.' At this point he always woke with a start, his pulse racing and sweating profusely. Sometimes large tears would be rolling down his cheeks. He had never mentioned his dream to anyone, not even John Steadman.

'Front or side entrance, Dr Rufus?' The taxi driver had recognised his passenger.

'Been here before, have you?' asked the doctor.

'Taken you twice. Both times you had a right go at me! First time, if I remember rightly was about kids hanging round the streets and the second time was about prostitutes.'

Dr Rufus grunted with pleasure, 'Did I give you much of a tip?'

'You did the second time. You said you liked a good ding-dong!'

'Not tonight though. Side entrance will do nicely.'

'Here we are then.'

Dr Rufus got out of the taxi, paid and tipped, but slightly less than last time.

There was no one in the police mortuary, at least no one alive. This never bothered him, dreams or no dreams. He switched on the lights and changed out of his clothes into theatre scrubs. The Gupta file was still on his desk. He sat down and started to read. It was quite warm in his office. The words on the page drifted in and out of focus. Twice he nodded off and woke with a jerk. The third time he drifted off into a deep and dreamless sleep.

At half past seven two cleaners arrived and it was

their chattering that woke him. His mouth was like an ashtray and his head was pounding.

'You're in early, Dr Rufus. Can I make you a cup of tea? Marge and I were just about to have one.'

A cup of tea sounded like bliss. Dr Rufus nodded, then regretted it.

'You wouldn't have a couple of paracetamol on you?' he asked.

The cleaner looked at him wistfully and replied, 'I'm sure I've got some in my bag.'

She was about to say something else but thought better of it. She had witnessed Dr Rufus in full flight on more than one occasion.

He swallowed the paracetamol, sipped his tea and re-read the first pathologist's report. There was nothing of note there; he didn't think there would be. The hole in the heart had been recorded but was not thought to be of much significance, certainly not the cause of death. But it was that hole, thought Dr Rufus, that small broken window between the two sides of the heart, a trivial defect that Alisha Gupta had been born with, that could hold the key to proving that she was murdered. He knew that a large injection of air would reach the heart as frothy blood. The heart would try to pump this foam into the lungs. It wouldn't last long; three beats, six at most, then the heart would stop. But it was just possible that in those dying beats some of the froth would have been pushed through the hole in her heart, and if you knew where to look you might find tiny air bubbles still trapped in some of the small blood vessels. Dr Rufus knew exactly where to look; in the retina at the back of the eye.

He would need a steady hand and a clear head. The police mortuary was equipped with showers. The water was piping hot and came out with such force that it stung his skin. Dr Rufus lathered himself all over. Never had a shower felt so refreshing. He even started singing. He hadn't a bad voice and it was certainly loud enough. For some reason he had chosen to sing 'Mack the Knife' except that he had substituted 'Frank' for 'Mack'.

The two cleaners couldn't help but hear him. They looked at each other, raised their eyebrows and shook their heads.

'Sad isn't it,' said Marge.

'At least he's happy at his work,' her friend replied.

★ ★ ★

He wheeled Alisha Gupta's body out of the fridge. The heavy door closed with a soft clunk. Automatically he switched on the overhead lights and the extractor fan. He half undid the plastic zip on the body bag; there was no need to expose the whole body. Carefully he pulled back the sheet that covered the head. He was devoid of any emotion other than curiosity. This was what he did; this was who Frank Rufus was.

Delicately he prised open one of the eyelids. The white of the eye was discoloured; the pupil was large and as lifeless as a dead fish. He moistened the front of the eye with a little water and, using a sophisticated magnifying light, peered into the murky depths.

'Well, well, well Alisha Gupta, the hole in your heart didn't kill you right enough but it's given the game away as to how you were killed,' he said to himself with some satisfaction, for there at the back of the eye were the unmistakable bubbles that could only have been caused by one thing. There was now no doubt that she had been murdered by a large and deliberate injection of nothing more toxic than air.

He would need photographs. That wasn't a problem; the police photographers had all the equipment. He gave them a call. Fortunately they had just arrived in work and agreed to come round straight away. In the meantime he tried to get hold of the first pathologist but met with no luck. Apparently he had been a locum who had now gone to Australia.

Dr Rufus was very pleased with himself. He whistled a little tune as he added to his report. The photographers arrived and duly set about their task. Once they were finished, Dr Rufus knew that to have absolute proof, he would have to remove one of the eyes, fix it in formalin and prepare microscope slides. Preparing the slides would take another forty-eight hours, but it had to be done.

In contrast to his brusque, gauche manner, Dr Rufus was extremely dextrous. Slowly, meticulously and with a skill equal to, if not better than the vast majority of surgeons, he carefully eased the eyeball out of the socket. One by one he cut the muscles that move the eyeball and finally severed the big nerve behind the eye. It came away from the socket with a soft sucking noise like a jelly coming out of a mould. He placed the eye in a small jar of formalin.

'Here's looking at you kid!' he said as he labelled the specimen.

He noticed the time on the big clock that hung on the wall in the dissecting room and was surprised to find that it was almost eleven. Other staff were now in. He handed the specimen to one of the technicians before going off for a second shower and a change of clothes. He always kept spare clothes at the mortuary, for obvious reasons. This afternoon he had to go to London to give evidence in another murder investigation.

'Can you get Detective Sergeant Alan Munro on the phone?' he asked his secretary. 'He'll be at the Eyesore – tell them it's urgent. How do I look?'

'Honestly? Like an upper class tramp,' she replied. 'Why don't you at least let me press your suit? If you appear in court like that you're likely to get sent down yourself!'

Dr Rufus shook his head. It had been an ongoing battle between the two of them for some time.

'Thanks, I'll take the risk,' he said with a smile as she passed him the phone.

'Is that you, Alan? Good, don't interrupt, I've got to go to London and I'm already late. It's definitely murder.'

'Has toxicology come up with something?' asked Munro.

'Toxicology be damned – no it was me! I would have found out earlier if you and John Steadman hadn't forced me so full of food and drink last night that I fell asleep in the chair when I got here!'

Dr Rufus was in full flow now and there was no stopping him. He explained as patiently as he could about the injection of air. The technicalities were lost on Alan Munro, especially the bit about the hole in the heart. At last Dr Rufus finished.

'One quick question – how much air would be needed to kill a person?' Munro asked.

'It all depends on how quickly the air was injected. The books say at least one millilitre of air per kilogram body weight is required but probably more – say two or three hundred in total. If I was intent on murder I wouldn't hang around. I would use a big needle and whack in as much as I could in one go. As to what it was injected with – you're the detective, I can't be expected to do all your work. A bloody big syringe would do but whatever it was, it required a steady hand. Remember there was no bruising at the injection site. Somebody knew what they were doing. I must go. Will you let Steadman know? Good luck!'

Alan Munro put the phone down. Will Lofthouse was standing at his elbow.

'Did you hear all that?' Munro asked.

'Hard not to miss it - I wonder why he bothers with the phone. Are you going to spring this on Dr Gupta?'

'No, not yet. Let's string him along for a bit and see where it gets us.'

CHAPTER SIXTEEN

Alan Munro had second thoughts as he walked back to the interview room. This was new evidence and the rules were clear. Up until this moment he had been completely open with Dr Gupta. Why should he compromise his integrity now? Frank Rufus had got his proof and was adamant that it was murder. No lawyer, no matter how clever, would be able to refute the word of Dr Rufus.

'Go back to the interview room Will and see if 'Laurel and Hardy' are OK. I want to run this past DCI Long.'

'Sure,' replied Lofthouse with the same dreamy, unquestioning look in his eyes.

Munro took the stairs two at a time and almost knocked over DCI Long, who was coming in the opposite direction.

'Terribly sorry, sir, I was hoping I could have a quick word with you.'

'Sorry Alan, it will have to wait – major problem – can't stop.'

Munro watched the balding head of DCI Long bobbing down the stairs and wondered what on earth could be so important as to drag the chief out of his office and in such a hurry.

A few of the desks were occupied, but nobody looked up from their work as he made his way to his own desk. He noticed John Steadman's name was still on the door. His hand hovered over the phone. Should he call him? Dr Rufus had asked him to tell Steadman of the developments and he desperately needed advice from someone more senior. In his own heart he knew what he ought to do, but it would be extremely helpful to have some support. He lifted the receiver and was about to dial.

'Lemerise got you over a barrel already?' Detective Sergeant Gregg, who Munro only knew as a nodding acquaintance, stood gloating in the door frame. Munro bristled and put down the receiver.

'No, not in the slightest. I left him whimpering and begging for mercy.' Munro stood up. 'If you'll excuse me, I must get back to deliver the final *coup de grâce*.'

DS Gregg forced a laugh and moved aside to let the big man through. Munro barged past him. With his head down and deep in thought he made his way back to the interview room. He still hadn't fully made his mind up.

The door was ajar. Dr Gupta was recounting a golfing anecdote to Anton Lemerise, who was clearly finding it highly amusing. Something inside Alan

Munro snapped. He pushed the door open with more force than was actually necessary. The conversation ceased abruptly.

'Aaron Gupta, I am arresting you on suspicion of the murder of your wife Alisha Gupta…'

There was a deathly hush; even the blackbird stopped singing. Munro continued with the all too familiar statement of his rights. Gupta said nothing. It was DC Lofthouse who broke the silence.

'I'll take him along to the Custody Officer,' he said in a totally matter of fact tone, as though he had been expecting this turn of events all along.

Anton Lemerise levered himself up from his chair. For once he looked directly at DS Alan Munro. Despite his puffy face, it was a cold, hard, steely gaze. He beckoned to Munro.

'A word in private,' he said putting his hand on the sergeant's shoulder. The touch was delicate but uncomfortable. Munro felt himself being steered out of the room more by the solicitor's formidable presence than by anything else. They reached the corridor. Lemerise gently pulled the door behind him.

'Mr Munro, you are young, bright and intelligent, however I fear you are in need of some advice.'

Munro felt his cheeks start to redden.

'I know you are only an acting sergeant and that your promotion was precipitous following the tragic accident. I refer, of course, to the shooting of John Steadman and his wife. I can understand that you are keen to prove yourself, but I believe you are making a grave error of judgement. Dr Gupta is a man of some standing in Helmsmouth, with friends in the highest quarters. I do not know what tale Dr Rufus related to you but, be warned, young man - he is a loose cannon who one day will blow himself up, consumed as he is with his own self confidence. Today may well be that day.'

Lemerise patted Munro's shoulder. Munro felt his muscles tense and not for the first time that day his collar seemed too tight. He remained silent.

'Now I am prepared to ignore your little outburst, and I am sure that I can persuade my client to have, shall we say, a small memory lapse.'

The solicitor gave a watery smile and even winked at Munro. He got no response. All attempts at humour drained from Lemerise's face.

'Call off the visit to the Custody Officer and drop this preposterous charge or I'll make sure that you'll still be a constable when you collect your pension.' His voice was cold and utterly ruthless.

Munro stared at him blankly. He lifted his huge right hand and not so gently placed it on Lemerise's shoulder. The solicitor staggered slightly.

'Let me in my turn give you a wee bit of friendly advice,' said Munro, who had now regained his composure. 'You have a large, dirty brown piece of wax hanging out of your right ear. We're all finding it most off-putting, even your client.'

He almost patted Lemerise's shoulder, but thought

better of it. He strode off with DC Lofthouse and Dr Gupta to meet the Custody Officer. At the corner of the corridor, he cast a glance back at Anton Lemerise. He had pulled out the handkerchief from his top pocket and, having wiped his ear, was now carefully examining its contents.

★ ★ ★

It did not take long to complete the formalities. The detention was authorised and a custody sheet opened. Dr Gupta appeared aloof throughout. Was there a slight tremor in his hand? Munro could not be sure. The three men made their way back to the interview room. Fortunately, Anton Lemerise had buried his hanky back in his pocket. Munro switched on the tape recorder.

'The witness, Dr Aaron Gupta, has now been arrested on suspicion of murder. He has been cautioned. He remains in the interview room with his solicitor, Anton Lemerise, and I am accompanied by DC Lofthouse…

'Now where were we, gentlemen? I believe, Dr Gupta, you were going to tell me all about Sunday.'

There was little that was new to Munro. The Guptas had got up separately but had breakfasted together. He had read the Sunday papers and she had busied herself with some embroidery until lunchtime.

'Which paper did you read?' asked Munro.

'The Sunday Telegraph.'

'What did you do with it afterwards?'

Dr Gupta looked puzzled.

'After lunch my wife wanted to read the supplements. I put the rest of the newspaper in the recycle bin in the utility room. Why?'

Munro didn't answer. He closed his eyes and tried hard to recall the stack of newspapers in the utility room. He was almost certain that the paper at the top of pile was Saturday's. All the papers that day had had the same picture of a train crash that had killed over twenty people. He scribbled 'Sunday Telegraph???' in his little notebook. A thought occurred to him.

'Are you quite sure you didn't use the newspaper to tidy up the glass from the broken window?'

'No, I used a small cardboard box and paper towels from my clinic.'

That was true; Munro remembered Kim Ho from forensics taking it away.

'Go on.'

'My wife prepared lunch and we ate it together.'

'What did you talk about?'

'The usual things.'

'Would you care to elaborate?'

'No – can you remember what you talked about with your wife on Sunday?' Dr Gupta retorted caustically.

Munro clearly remembered Sunday lunch; cold baked beans straight out of the tin in front of the television watching the rugby. Maureen would have disapproved. As it was she was safely at her parents.

'Did you argue?'

'Not that I recall.'

'Tell me about the visitors.'

'Reena was the first to arrive. She doesn't knock on the door or ring the bell. She has her own key. She has the annoying habit of shouting 'coo-ee!' when she comes in. I immediately retreated to my study. Reena must have stayed thirty or forty minutes. I only heard the latter part of their conversation. Reena appeared to be hysterical and was screaming abuse at Alisha, accusing her of being greedy and uncaring. As I'm sure you've gathered Reena has a drink problem but refuses to go for help - she frequently has to borrow money. They did not part on good terms.'

'And Cassandra?'

'My sister arrived shortly after Reena left. She rings the bell twice before she lets herself in.'

Munro was aware of a slight hesitancy in Dr Gupta's reply.

'Did you speak to her?'

'No. I knew that Cassandra's Sunday afternoon calls are always to see Alisha. I prefer not to get involved. Almost certainly Cassandra also wanted to borrow money. She has a lavish life style and her outgoings often exceed her income.'

'She gambles, does she not?' Munro interjected.

Lemerise seemed to waken up again and touched Dr Gupta's arm. They exchanged glances.

'I could not possibly comment. Suffice to say that their conversation too became heated. I distinctly heard my sister say that Alisha had only married me for my money. This is a frequent charge that she laid at Alisha's feet, especially if my wife did not accede to her request.'

Why was it, Munro wondered, that Dr Gupta was happy to recount these conversations but not any conversation he and his wife had had that day? Could it really be that these were two people who simply lived parallel lives under one roof? Could Dr Gupta have murdered his wife out of boredom? No, he thought, recalling John Steadman's words, 'it may all come down to motives'; and so far no good motive had been established.

'Why was Alisha in such a parsimonious mood?'

'I couldn't possibly say.'

'I put it to you that it was because the two of you had been arguing.'

Lemerise interrupted once more:

'My client has already stated that he cannot recall arguing with his wife.'

'Well then, Dr Gupta, what did you and your wife talk about all day?'

'The usual things.'

Munro could see this was going nowhere. He clenched his hands and tapped his big fists gently on the table.

'What were you doing in your study all afternoon?'

'Catching up on paperwork, reading journals and...' Dr Gupta was about to add 'and the usual things' but on seeing the dark look on Munro's face thought better of it.

'When did you leave the house?'

'I fancied a walk and a breath of fresh air. It was still light so it must have been around six. I can't be more precise.'

'And you arrived at Jean's apartment when?'

Lemerise went to touch his client's arm again.

'There is no point in denying it,' Munro said testily. 'I have spoken with Jean and she assures me that you went to her flat for a 'bit of how's your father' as she so eloquently put it.'

'I am not familiar with the phrase,' Dr Gupta replied.

'Sex, carnal knowledge, nooky, oats, shagging...' DC Lofthouse interjected.

'Yes, thank you, Will. I'm sure Dr Gupta now fully understands the meaning of the expression.' Munro could have sworn that DC Lofthouse had been miles away daydreaming.

'If you must know, I arrived at Jean's at six forty-five.'

'Was she expecting you?'

'Yes, I had called to say I would pick up some food and that I was on my way,' Dr Gupta said with a shrug.

There was an arrogance about the man that was starting to rile DS Munro. It was clear that he never asked Jean if it was convenient and probably never even asked her what food she liked. Munro tapped his teeth with the end of his pen. It was important that he did not let his emotions interfere with the interview.

'And you had sex?'

'No, sergeant, we played snakes and ladders!'

'May I remind you, Dr Gupta, you are under caution. Did you have sex?'

'No comment.'

'When did you leave?'

'I can't remember - quite late I think.'

'You'll have to try harder than that. Was it ten, eleven, midnight or when?'

'Around eleven.'

'Did you walk home or take a taxi?'

'I walked home.'

'Did you see anybody on your way home or when you arrived at your house?'

He shook his head.

'You know, of course, that your wife had company that evening. 'When the cat's away the mice will play' – another phrase you may be unfamiliar with but I'm sure you get its meaning!'

Dr Gupta looked nonplussed. 'That would be her choice. I have repeatedly explained that we had an open marriage.'

'So what did you and your wife speak about when you got home?'

'Who said we spoke? I went upstairs straight to bed.'

'You didn't make your wife a drink?'

Dr Gupta's eyes darted towards his solicitor. Was there just a chink of self-doubt appearing?

'My client has already informed you that he went straight to bed.'

'Then perhaps your client would be good enough to explain how his thumb print came to be on the base of a cup on the deceased's bedside table. A cup that had been thoroughly washed, dried and wiped clean - like this.' Munro lifted his own plastic cup and demonstrated.

'I think my client has every right to handle any article of crockery in his own house. In fact I would go so far as to state categorically there is no law that states how you should or should not wash and dry a cup. I do hope, for your sake, DS Munro, that you have not arrested my client on the basis of a thumb print on the bottom of one of his own cups.'

Anton Lemerise sat back in his chair with a look of smug defiance. Munro tried to ignore him.

'Can you explain why your wife's fingerprints were not on the cup and why it had been rinsed out?'

'I have no idea.'

'Could it be that you prepared a night time drink for your wife, say hot milk or cocoa and then spiked the drink with a few extra sleeping pills, knowing full well that she would also take the prescribed dose?'

'No comment.'

'Do you deny it?'

'Look here, Sergeant Munro, you have no evidence to back this outrageous claim. This is all fantasy and supposition based on a clean cup allegedly with my client's thumb print on it,' interjected Lemerise.

Munro banged his fist down on the table.

'Listen carefully. Fact – Alisha Gupta swallowed an excessive dose of sleeping tablets. Fact – those pills were kept in her bedside cabinet. Fact – there is no other cup or glass either in her bedroom or her bathroom. Fact – the only print on the cup was your client's. These need explaining. If Alisha Gupta had taken an overdose herself then the cup would have her prints on it. It does not seem remotely likely that she swallowed the pills then carefully washed and wiped the cup clean, leaving only her husband's intact thumb print on the base. Does your client still deny handling the cup on Sunday evening?'

Lemerise scribbled something on the sheet of paper in front of him and passed it to Dr Gupta.

'I have nothing further to add,' he read.

The blackbird, which had remained quiet since Dr Gupta's arrest, as if noticing the deafening silence in the interview room, took this as a cue to burst into song. Even Munro was starting to find it irritating.

'I need to stretch my legs – five-minute break,' he said switching off the tape recorder.

CHAPTER SEVENTEEN

Munro strode out of the interview room. His back was sore from being cramped in the little chair and his legs were stiff. The strain of the interview was beginning to get to him. Had he been right to arrest the stony-faced dentist? The circumstantial evidence was strong, but he would need something a bit more convincing to actually charge the man with murder rather than simply arrest him 'on suspicion'. Perhaps he should have waited and spoken with one of his superiors, or at least run it past John Steadman. Too late, he thought: the die was cast.

There appeared to be a lot of commotion in the corridors of the Eyesore, far more than usual. He could distinctly hear the rasping voice of Inspector Crouchley swearing at a group of constables. There was only one person to ask, the redoubtable Sergeant Grimble, who as usual, was sitting at his desk effortlessly answering the phone, writing down messages and moving round pieces of paper in the infamous Grimble filing system. It was as though he had an extra pair of hands. He was the only officer who was apparently not in a hurry; however Munro noticed that his usual affable expression had been replaced by a worried frown.

'What's going on?' Munro asked.

'Ah! The robust figure of DS Munro looms over me!' he said, looking up from his paperwork. 'How's the interview going?'

'I've arrested him on suspicion. Dr Rufus has irrefutable evidence that his wife was murdered.'

Sergeant Grimble nodded; of course he knew all of this already.

'I saw DCI Long briefly. He said there's a major problem and Crouchley is along the corridor bellowing at a load of constables and half of them look as though they've been dragged out of their beds. You must know!'

Sergeant Grimble hesitated, then put down his pen.

'DCI Long asked me not to tell you until after your interview.'

'Tell me what?' Munro closed his eyes; he knew it was not going to be good news.

'John Steadman's been abducted.'

'No! - How? When? Who by..?'

'Calm down and grab a chair. He had planned to go out with his sister today. It was a secret. None of us knew, not even me. Well, it appeared that somebody knew. Linda, his sister, was flagged down by a man with an apparently sick child. While she was giving directions to the wife on how to get to the hospital somebody let down two of her tyres and pinched her mobile phone.

Meanwhile Steadman went out on to the pavement to meet her. The concierge got distracted and Steadman was bundled off in a car. They found his white stick lying in the gutter. There is some CCTV footage but it's fairly murky. The car is probably hired and the latest information I have is that they think it headed inland. The Air Sea Rescue and police helicopters are on standby, but no news so far. Do you know Linda?'

'I've met her a couple of times. I'll bet she's beside herself with worry.'

'That's putting it mildly,' Sergeant Grimble replied. 'She's upstairs in DCI Long's office with her husband and WPC Jennings, who is trying to calm her down. Naturally she blames herself.'

Munro stood up, but before he could say anything Sergeant Grimble put up his hand.

'I know what you're thinking, but I have strict orders not to let you out of the building until you've finished - properly finished - your little *tête-à-tête* with Dr Gupta and the charming Anton Lemerise,' he added, giving Munro a stern, fatherly look. 'There's nothing you can do, and I promise I'll keep you informed of any developments. Now, bugger off before you discover the secrets of the Grimble filing system!'

The sergeant's phone rang. Munro took one last look at the shambles on Grimble's desk and with even greater reluctance returned to the interview room. Gupta, Lemerise and DC Lofthouse were all nursing cups of coffee. The fact that he had forgotten to get one for himself only added to his exasperation.

'Monday morning – when did you waken, what did you do? You've had plenty time to think about it. I want a minute-by-minute account with no interruptions.' He gave Lemerise a filthy look, but it was wasted. The solicitor's fat chin was resting on his chest and his eyes were closed but he was no more asleep than Dr Gupta, who was clearly less comfortable with Munro's changed attitude.

It was another well-rehearsed story. Dr Gupta had got up at his usual time of seven despite the fact that he had taken the day off to play golf. He had showered and dressed before going to see if his wife wanted a cup of tea. It was obvious, he said, that she was quite dead.

'How was it obvious?' Munro inquired.

'She didn't rouse when I called her name. I touched her cheek - it was cold. She was not breathing.'

'So you calmly phoned the coroner's officer – not a doctor, not an ambulance. You didn't scream or shout or try mouth-to-mouth resuscitation?'

'Your culture is different from mine. I have seen a lot of death. It was quite obvious to me that she had been dead for hours, so tell me Sergeant Munro, exactly what good would calling a doctor or an ambulance, let alone screaming or shouting, have done?'

Munro was taken aback at the man's callousness.

'I just don't get you! This is your wife, for God's sake, even if it is some sort of crazy 'open' marriage that you have. You must have some feelings?'

'Of course I have feelings but, unlike you, I can keep my emotions in check.'

Anton Lemerise grunted with pleasure, half opened his eyes and gave Munro a mocking glance. Not for the first time that day he started to blush.

'How do you know all about coroners?'

'My client is clearly a highly intelligent man. Why shouldn't he know about coronial procedure?'

'That's not an answer to my question.'

Dr Gupta made no reply.

'Moving on then – why did you deliberately mislead the coroner's officer?'

'This is outrageous! What evidence do you have that the coroner's officer was misled?' said Lemerise.

'Your client told the officer he was a doctor who was concerned about an unexpected death and that he was not in a position to issue a death certificate. He didn't say he was a dentist and, more to the point, didn't say that it was his wife who had died. In fact he managed somehow or other to avoid giving the deceased's full name before hanging up. I call that misleading.'

'My client denies the allegation.'

'How did you think your wife died, Dr Gupta?'

'I knew she had a weak heart, I presumed she had a heart attack during the night.'

'Presumed, or hoped that's what everyone else would think?'

'No comment.'

Munro sighed and ran his fingers through his hair.

'Who were you going to play golf with?'

'The Assistant Chief Constable - he and I are regular

partners. I called him after I spoke with the coroner's officer. He offered to cancel the tee. We were due to play at Saint Cecilia's.'

Munro was not surprised. Saint Cecilia's was the snootiest golf course for miles around. As a boy, Munro had been used to playing on the municipal links courses in Scotland. Golf there was a sport to be enjoyed by all. Here it was a business opportunity, a chance to rub shoulders with the great and the good: the golf was almost irrelevant. He scribbled 'Saint Cecilia's' and 'ACC' in his notebook.

'What did you do while you were waiting for the police to arrive?'

'I can't remember.'

'Let me jog your memory. I put it to you that you carefully washed out the cup that you had laced with extra sleeping pills the night before and wiped the packet of pills and the knob on the drawer of the bedside cabinet to remove all traces of your fingerprints.'

'Oh dear, Sergeant Munro – you're not back to that dreary piece of crockery,' Lemerise answered.

It was a clever game that the two of them were playing. Every time Munro asked a difficult question the solicitor butted in with a glib reply, hoping to derail the sergeant's train of thought. It also gave his client a chance to think of a more plausible answer, if pressed.

'Why were there no fingerprints on the knob of the drawer?'

'You're the detective!'

'You're right there, Dr Gupta, I am the detective. The reason there are no prints is because somebody wiped them off; somebody who was in your house on Sunday or in the wee small hours of Monday morning. Now there are only a handful of people who could possibly have done that. Jean, Reena and Cassandra all have keys to your house and they all disliked your wife, though possibly not enough to kill her. Her lover perhaps?' Munro shook his head. 'I can't see that. I think you would agree that it would be a most odd thing to do. Your wife maybe wiped them all off in a fit of spring cleaning before she went to sleep? I don't think so somehow. And that leaves you.'

'What possible motive could I have? And you're forgetting that someone broke into my house.'

'As for motive, I think it relates to what you and your wife were speaking about before you went for your breath of fresh air. You know – 'the usual things' – would you care to elaborate?'

The solicitor twitched. Dr Gupta's eyes flicked in his direction.

'No comment.'

'You see, Dr Gupta, I don't believe you have been entirely honest with me. Something about all of this stinks to high heaven, like a side of Scottish salmon left out in the sun for a fortnight. But don't worry - I'll find out, no matter what cock and bull story you and Mr Lemerise have concocted between you – I'll find out.'

'Sergeant Munro, I'd be very careful if I were you, those are serious allegations,' Lemerise said, taking his handkerchief out to blow his nose. Munro noticed the greasy, brown streak where the solicitor had previously cleaned his ear.

'Oh I'm known for my carefulness in the force. Isn't that right, DC Lofthouse?'

Will Lofthouse, who was thoroughly enjoying himself, nodded in agreement.

'Let's talk about the broken window.'

It was almost impossible to read Dr Gupta's expression. Was he relieved by the change of subject or was he more concerned? It was difficult to tell. Lemerise appeared to have fallen asleep again.

'When did you discover the broken window?' continued Munro.

'When I went down to clear away the breakfast dishes. I didn't notice it earlier. Between the kitchen and the utility room there is also a half glazed door. But there is a net curtain over the glass. When I was putting my cup and plate in the dishwasher the curtain moved. I thought the outside door must be open and that a draught had caused the curtain to move. It was only when I opened the adjoining door that I noticed the glass on the outside door had been broken.'

Munro noticed that Lemerise was content to let Dr Gupta prattle on about the door without interruption. Was it all irrelevant or a deliberate red herring? Munro couldn't be sure.

'Without thinking, I tidied up the mess,' Dr Gupta continued. 'I am a very tidy person by nature.'

That was true, thought Munro, but he still wasn't satisfied.

'Why did you call me?'

'I thought you ought to know.'

'Was the key taken?'

Dr Gupta paused and thought for a moment.

'Yes – I think it was. I had to use the spare key to lock the door.'

Damn, thought Munro, another person with a key to the Gupta property.

'You said there were footprints on the floor. What were they like?'

'Smallish – certainly smaller than mine. Possibly from a trainer.'

Munro was tempted to say that it was remarkable how he could recollect these details but not any of the conversation he had had with his wife the previous day. He let it pass.

'Why would anyone break into your house?'

'I have a lot of valuable antiques and paintings. You may have noticed them but not appreciated their worth.'

The sergeant's face began to redden again.

'Besides, you have already worked out that my wife was a difficult lady and not very popular. Maybe she had offended someone once too often.'

'Oh, I see!' Munro replied. 'The random killer who breaks into your house, presumably takes off his shoes so as not to leave dirty prints in the kitchen, then tiptoes up to your wife's bedroom and murders her? Convenient that your wife was drugged. Convenient that your alarm system was switched off. Convenient that this stranger managed to find his way to your wife's room in the dark, then fatally injected her without waking her up. Way too convenient, I think, Dr Gupta! No, I don't know who broke the window or why. It could have been you who did it, just to muddy the waters.'

Munro gave Dr Gupta a questioning look, but he remained totally impassive. Munro scribbled 'broken window???' in his little book and underlined it three times.

'So you've nothing more to tell me?'

'No – nothing.'

'I presume you will release my client on bail? You have no reason to hold him,' said Lemerise.

Munro drummed the desk with his fingers and leant back in his chair.

'DC Lofthouse, have you any questions?' he asked.

'Only one – why did you bring your solicitor when you were only being interviewed as a witness?'

Out of the mouths of babes and sucklings, thought Munro.

'My f-f-friend Anton Lemerise thought it advisable, given the circumstances,' he replied, giving his solicitor a worried look. It was the first time he had stammered.

'He is within his rights,' Lemerise responded.

'Oh yes, I know all that,' said DC Lofthouse. 'It just struck me as very odd, that's all.'

Munro stood up and without looking at Lemerise, informed Dr Gupta that he would be bailed by the Custody Officer.

'You will then be released to re-appear in this station in two days' time at ten am. Do not under any circumstances even think about leaving the area without notifying me.'

'When may I return home?' Dr Gupta asked.

'I'll check with DS Fairfax. It may be that you will be able to return tonight or tomorrow. I'll let you know.'

Munro switched off the tape recorder and asked DC Lofthouse to sort out the remaining paper work with the Custody Officer. He was desperate for news of John Steadman.

CHAPTER EIGHTEEN

It was by no means the first abduction case DCI Long had dealt with in his career, but it was, without a doubt, the one with the most urgency. He was fully aware, as was every other officer involved, that this was not a simple case of ransom. Unless he was very fortunate, DCI Long knew that by the end of the day he would be leading another murder investigation.

Linda had been near hysterical. Gently but quite firmly DCI Long had got her to realise that time was of the essence. All he wanted was the bare facts. Haltingly, she told her story between sobs of self-recrimination. It was evident that the whole thing had been meticulously planned. DCI Long's priority had to be to trace the car; he would leave pursuing those involved in Linda's roadside charade to others.

Jamaica Mansion was not that far from the Eyesore and within minutes an officer on the beat had retrieved John Steadman's white cane from the gutter. A finger-tip search of the pavement and road outside Jamaica

Mansion had found nothing of any use, not even a tyre print. DCI Long had gone himself to the safe house to look at the CCTV footage. At the edge of the range of the surveillance camera the car was just visible. A man had got out of the back of the car and walked slowly down to meet with John Steadman. He had kept close to the wall with his head down. He was a heavily built man with a short thick neck. DCI Long recognised him instantly. He was a doorman at one of Helmsmouth's less salubrious night clubs and had long been suspected of dealing in drugs. His name was Philip Aintree, but he was better known as 'the Shed'. Inspector Eric Crouchley had joined DCI Long in Jamaica Mansion. He too knew the Shed and immediately detailed some officers to go to his house and pick him up if he was there.

DCI Long was re-running the footage frame by frame. He paused just as Steadman was being forced into the car.

'Eric, you'd better get the lads armed and have back-up,' he said. The image on the screen revealed a gun in the Shed's hand. Inspector Crouchley swore; he was a man who swore a lot.

The car was a large light-coloured Ford, probably silver. Sunlight reflected off the rear number plate and only the last letter could be deciphered.

'If it is Philip Aintree's friends that are in on this,' said DCI Long, 'none of them are very bright. It's probably a locally hired car.'

Without being asked, one of the detective constables said, 'I'm on to it.'

Crouchley got on to the traffic division. There weren't many traffic cameras in Helmsmouth and most of these were concentrated round the harbour area. After an agonising twenty minutes a report came in of a possible sighting in the centre of Helmsmouth. It was definitely the same make and model of car. The footage showed the driver and, just visible, the dark shapes of three people in the back seat. The features of the driver were not distinguishable, but what was clear was the car's number plate. The direction of the car suggested it was possibly heading for the north circular road rather than the harbour, but it could just as easily have taken a detour on any number of side streets.

'Call Grimble and put out an alert to all officers,' barked Crouchley to no one in particular. Seeing that no one was listening he swore again and phoned Sergeant Grimble himself.

DCI Long noticed that Daisy was standing by the window. She had largely been ignored after the first few minutes and big tears were softly rolling down her cheeks. Long touched her gently on the shoulder.

'Those two phone calls...' he said.

Before he could finish, Daisy replied:

'Both male, both English, both from withheld numbers.'

It was routine practice at Jamaica Mansion to identify all in-coming calls. DCI Long nodded.

'Could you get me the number for Radio Helmsmouth please?'

Delighted to be able to do something to redeem her position, Daisy produced the number in less than thirty seconds.

'Good heavens, Daisy, you're efficient! You don't have any spare hours? I could do with someone like you at Police HQ.'

Daisy beamed. DCI Long really was a gentleman.

The local radio station was only too happy to help. Long had asked that they broadcast the request for information about the car every fifteen minutes until further notice.

'Tell them there's a substantial reward.'

There wasn't, but if need be DCI Long was prepared to pay out of his own pocket if it meant finding his friend and colleague.

A young constable spoke up:

'Traced the car, sir. Hired this morning from Frenchley's Auto Hire by a Mr John Smith.'

'For God's sake, they can't even think of a decent alias,' Crouchley remarked.

'I think we should return to the Eyesore. No point in drawing too much attention to Jamaica Mansion,' said DCI Long.

★ ★ ★

Sergeant Grimble looked up from his desk as the two

inspectors entered. Before he could ask, DCI Long shook his head.

'We've traced the car and are fairly sure it was heading north. Phil the Shed is involved, and he's armed. Are the Air Sea Rescue and police helicopters on standby?'

The Shed had not been at home, but his girlfriend was and had been brought in for questioning. She was no stranger to the Eyesore and her language was even more choice than that of Inspector Crouchley.

'I don't effing well know where the eff he is, and if I effing well did I wouldn't effing well tell you!' she said before Sergeant Grimble had even written down her name.

'The problem,' said DCI Long as he pored over a large map of the area, 'is the time factor. If they've just kept driving they could be halfway to London by now. We have only presumed they've headed north. They could equally as well have turned back on themselves and headed for the ferry terminal.'

'They've not boarded the ferry,' Crouchley replied. 'There's only one sailing today. That was at twelve, and the car's not on board.'

The phone rang. It was Sergeant Grimble.

'Important information, sir, I'll put him straight through.'

It was a Mr Peters, who had been on the north circular road with a mobile speed camera. He was having his lunch in the back of his van and had been listening to Radio Helmsmouth when the call went out. He vaguely remembered a large silver Ford going past. What had struck him as odd was that it was going quite slowly, as if looking for a turn off. He had looked back at the recording and sure enough there was the car. The driver's features were quite visible but not the passengers in the back seat. The time then was eleven twenty-eight.

Crouchley sent out an officer to retrieve the recording. It was likely, he thought, that the driver would be well known to them and would definitely not be a 'Mr John Smith'.

DCI Long looked at his watch. That was well over an hour ago.

'Eric, I think we should scramble the helicopters. The land to the north of the circular route rises steeply. If you look at the map there's about half a dozen farms but the rest is forest and moorland. We could check the farms, but a manned search would be nigh on impossible if we're hoping to…'

He didn't have to say 'find Steadman alive'. Inspector Crouchley agreed. There were two helicopters; the small police surveillance helicopter and the large Air Sea Rescue 'Sea King'.

'I'll get on to it. They'll need to liaise and divide up the area, but they won't need me to tell them.'

The minutes ticked by. DCI Long went to see Linda and her husband to update them on progress so far.

'Do you think they've killed him?' Linda asked.

DCI Long looked at her tear-stained face.

'I haven't given up hope yet,' he said, 'but I am gravely concerned. Does his son know?'

'Yes – he's just outside Paris and is trying to get a flight back.'

'If he does, will you let me know and I'll arrange a car to pick him up from the airport.'

'Thanks,' replied Linda in a quiet voice before burying her face in her husband's shoulder.

DCI Long's phone was ringing. It was Sergeant Grimble again.

'They've found the car.'

'Where?'

'Abandoned in a cul-de-sac by the railway station. The wheels are covered in mud. Two officers are there now. I expect you'll want forensics to collect it?'

'Any witnesses?'

'None so far. If I remember rightly there are no houses around there, only some storage depots.'

Inspector Crouchley had overheard the conversation.

'Once the car is picked up I'll get some men to sniff around, but I know the area. I doubt if anyone will have seen anything and I'd be even more surprised if anyone admitted to it – especially if Phil The Shed and a couple of other heavies are involved.'

'If the wheels are muddy it does suggest they turned off the north circular and went up into the hills. Whether they left Steadman there or what they've done with him is anybody's guess. If I was a betting man,' DCI Long continued, 'I think they've taken him to meet someone. I only hope we're not too late, but I fear the worse.'

Inspector Crouchley grimaced and scratched an ear.

'I've just remembered something - one of my new recruits comes from a farm on the north side of town. He probably knows everybody that lives round there. I'll get him to ring all the farms. Lunchtime will be as good a time as any and if need be he can always go out. At least he won't get lost.'

But all that came from that line of investigation was that one of the farmers thought he had heard a motorbike at around eleven thirty and again before he returned home for lunch.

There was nothing to do now but wait. Crouchley managed some sandwiches, but DCI Long had no appetite.

Two sightings from the Air Sea Rescue helicopter initially raised hopes, only for them to be dashed. The first turned out to be an irate farmer and the second a lone rambler.

Kim Ho from forensics was the first to come up with anything substantial. Fingerprints from the vinyl panel below the back seat confirmed that John Steadman had been in the car.

'He also scratched the panel,' she said, 'but more interestingly, we think we know where the car has been. We have a rough idea from the mileage. The mud is not helpful as the land around the top of the north circular is all the same – however, the car is covered in pollen. It must have been parked under some birch trees. There aren't many birches in Helmsmouth. There are none round the railway station and none at Frenchley's Auto Hire, I've checked. I do a bit of rambling and the only birches I can think of are at the foot of a path that leads up Quarry Hill. There's a nice view from the top on a sunny day.'

DCI long traced a finger over the map and found Quarry Hill. His stomach lurched when he saw that one half of the hill appeared to be a sheer drop.

'Kim, is there a cliff or something up there?'

'The south side of the hill was blasted away. There is a fence to prevent you getting too near to the edge...'

She stopped in mid-sentence.

'You don't think that...' but she couldn't go on.

'I'll get one of the choppers there immediately,' Long interjected.

CHAPTER NINETEEN

The distant throbbing of an engine broke into John Steadman's troubled deliberations. If Linda had been abducted there was nothing he could do about it. As long as she's not been hurt, he thought. He was not able to contemplate the possibility of anything worse.

The sound got louder. His first impression was that it could be the motorbike returning. He ducked down. It was a futile gesture, and he knew it. There was no cover. He was exposed and completely vulnerable, and until whatever it was got nearer he had no idea of its direction.

Grabbing hold of the fence, he pulled himself up and listened intently. The throbbing was definitely closer. He concentrated hard, moving his head from side to side trying to locate the sound. It was too coarse to be a motorbike.

He tilted his head back. The noise seemed to be above him. Could it be a tractor? No, that couldn't be right unless it was coming downhill. The beat of the engine was much louder and appeared to be moving from side to side.

All at once he realised it was a helicopter. He raised both hands in the air and waved frantically. In his excitement, he stepped forward, lost his footing and tumbled over. On his hands and knees, he crawled back towards the fence. His scalp brushed the wire netting. The helicopter was now directly overhead. Steadman could feel the down draught. Cautiously he turned round and sat with his back leaning up against the fence. His body ached all over, especially the hand that had lost the fingernail, but that didn't stop him from shouting and waving.

The helicopter flew off as quickly as it had come, leaving Steadman bewildered and desolate. Surely they saw me, he thought. Again he pulled himself to his feet. His sleeve snagged and tore on the barbed wire: he was past caring. As well as the pain he was exhausted and thirsty, and he suddenly felt very cold. The chloroform wasn't fully out of his system. He started to shiver. Small beads of sweat appeared on his brow and trickled down his temples leaving dirty streaks.

There was a rushing sound in his ears and he felt faint. At first he thought the wind had picked up. The rushing got louder and was accompanied by an ominous pounding in his head. Slowly his knees gave way as he sank back to the ground. He put his hands over his ears, but the noise was deafening. He was drenched in sweat and his whole body was shaking.

'My God, the train's come to get me!' he shouted as he passed out on the grass.

The train that so troubled John Steadman had been a recurring nightmare since early childhood. As a boy, he had always loved to look at the pictures in his father's art books, especially those by the surrealist painters. In amongst the melting clocks of Salvador Dali was a black and white illustration of a painting by Magritte. It showed a small perfectly ordinary steam train coming out of a fireplace with its smoke billowing up the chimney. The image had haunted him, possibly because the fireplace with its clock and candle sticks was so like the one in their own living room. In the night that train would come trackless, hissing and snarling down the chimney and he would wake screaming and shaking.

It must have been years since he had had that particular dream, but now in his blind delirium he was convinced that the train had returned. He saw it clearly in his mind's eye. No longer was it shades of grey but vivid green, blue and yellow, with great white clouds of smoke belching out of its stack. Red sparks flew from its wheels as it drew closer. And there were voices too, muffled at first but now more distinct.

'Yes, it's Steadman all right, I worked with him once.'

He lay paralysed on the ground in that awful gap between sleep and wakefulness, unable to move and unable to speak.

'Roll him gently. Have you got the shoulders?'

'Mind his head, for goodness sake!'

There were other voices, barely audible over the roar

of the engine, all unrecognisable. He felt something soft and warm being tucked under him.

'Now the other way.'

The warmth enveloped him, and once more he drifted off into unconsciousness.

A loud click brought him partially to his senses. Something cold and hard had been slipped underneath him. He tried to move his legs but found that he couldn't.

'One more strap round his chest ought to do it.'

He sat bolt upright.

'You're not bloody well taking me on that train!' he said flailing his arms around.

'Whoa, tiger! Take it easy!'

Someone ran forward and knelt down beside him.

'Inspector Steadman – Inspector Steadman, sir. You're OK – you're safe now. It's PC Timms. Do you remember me? I was a cadet with you a couple of years ago.'

The young constable had got hold of one of John Steadman's hands and was holding it gently in his own.

'Do you remember, sir, you used to make fun of my moustache because it was black and I've got ginger hair. You used to tell me to take it back to lost property!'

Steadman lay back with a groan.

'Yes, I remember you. What's happening?'

'It looks like you've had a lucky escape. The lads here are from the Air Sea Rescue. I was up in the small police chopper. It was us who spotted you and now they're going to fly you down to Helmsmouth General for a check over. Is that OK?'

Steadman nodded. The pieces of the puzzle were falling into place.

'I understand now. Have they got the big Sea King?'

'Yes sir.'

'Not a steam train, then?'

'No sir. I don't know why you thought that, but it's definitely a helicopter.'

He lay back on the stretcher and they carried him gently towards the open door of the Sea King.

Steadman had always wanted to fly in a helicopter. He wanted to fly in towards Helmsmouth from the sea; fly over the old port, up and over the bluff and then to gaze on the new Helmsmouth sprawling from the docks into the countryside like some sleeping mechanical monster. At least that is how he imagined it. Did it really look like that? He was all too aware that he would never know.

The helicopter journey was short and unpleasant. The noise was unbearable and even with the blanket, he was bitterly cold. It was a mixture of relief and apprehension to be wheeled out of the helicopter into the warmth of Helmsmouth General Accident and Emergency Department. The smell of the place brought back so many memories, most of them unpleasant. It was hard to pinpoint that particular hospital smell: a mixture of alcohol, cleanliness with a whiff of steamed cabbage, perhaps? But here in the accident and emergency department even in the afternoon there was the distinct aroma of humanity – so many nurses and doctors rushing around in a hot environment trying to help too many patients brought here in a hurry, unprepared and unwashed.

Thinking of this, John Steadman became acutely aware of his own condition. He knew he must be dirty and his shirt was still clinging to him soaked with cold sweat.

'What's the name?'

Before he could answer one of the Sea King crew responded, 'John Steadman.'

'Any middle names?' the receptionist continued.

'Have you any middle names?' the crewman relayed slowly and unnecessarily to Steadman. His voice suggested either that he thought he was still in the helicopter or that Steadman was now both deaf and stupid. Steadman shook his head.

'What's the address?'

Steadman butted in, before anyone could reply on his behalf, and gave his old address. No point, he thought, in advertising Jamaica Mansion.

Someone was whispering into the receptionist's ear. All Steadman could hear was indistinct voices. He had no idea what was going on and no one thought to enlighten him. He could feel the anger forming a knot in his stomach. He felt like shouting, 'Speak to me!'

'He's to go straight through to room 2. The porter will fetch him now.'

Steadman clenched his fists. 'Typical!' he muttered to himself. 'Five minutes in an institution and I'm reduced to the third person.'

They took him off the stretcher and placed him in a wheelchair.

'We'll be off then,' said the man from the Sea King. 'Good luck!'

John Steadman tried to say something but the words wouldn't come out. He nodded and raised a hand.

'I'll take him through and bring you back the blanket,' said the porter.

It was as though Steadman as a person in his own right had ceased to exist. If he could have, he would have stood up and walked straight out of the hospital. Getting ever more cross, he sat mute and sullen as he was wheeled through another two sets of doors.

'Can you stand?' asked the porter.

'Yes, I can stand and walk perfectly well, my only problem is that I can't see,' he replied struggling to keep the bitterness out of his voice.

In all fairness the porter proved to be exceedingly kind and with an experienced hand, skilfully manoeuvred him on to the bed.

'Are you warm enough? Can I take away the blanket?'

Steadman nodded.

'I'm glad about that,' said the porter. 'It says on it 'Property of Helmsmouth Air Sea Rescue'. He was a big fellow that brought you in. I wouldn't like to get on the wrong side of him. I expect the nurse will be along in a minute. All right if I leave you?'

It wasn't 'all right'. Steadman felt quite lost; it would have been nice to have some company. However he wasn't alone for long.

'Hello, I'm Sally. I'm one of the nurses who will be looking after you. I just want to do a set of obs.'

Fortunately John Steadman knew what 'doing a set of obs' entailed and dutifully took his uninjured arm out of his jacket and rolled up his shirt sleeve.

'Your blood pressure is a bit low – does it always run low?' asked the nurse.

'I really have no idea,' he replied.

A thermometer was placed under his tongue. It was uncomfortable: his mouth was very dry.

'All your other obs are fine. Can I get you anything?'

'I'm very thirsty.'

'I'll get you some water,' she replied and slipped through the door. Within seconds she was back.

'There – I've put a jug and a glass on the locker.'

'I'm sorry, but I'm blind,' Steadman said. It was the bit he hated most – telling someone he was blind. Why oh why did he always feel the need to apologise?

'Oh! – I didn't realise. I'll get a sign for above the bed.'

She slipped out of the room again returning some minutes later.

'There,' she said triumphantly, 'I've pinned a sign above your bed so everyone will know. I think the houseman is coming to see you now.'

She was off before Steadman could point out that a sign above the bed wouldn't help him find the jug or pour a glass of water.

A junior doctor came and asked him if he had any serious pain. Steadman was disappointed to find out that a torn-off fingernail didn't count as 'serious pain', no matter how uncomfortable it was. Obligingly he moved all four limbs for the doctor, said 'aah!' and stuck his tongue out. The doctor confirmed that his heart was still beating and that he was still breathing. With surprisingly cold hands he prodded Steadman's stomach to his own satisfaction.

'Can you look at my fingers and follow them round with your eyes?'

'No, I'm sorry but I'm blind.' Steadman's cheeks flushed as he found himself apologising again.

'Well in that case can you tell me how many fingers I'm holding up?'

It was the end of a dismal consultation.

Another stranger entered the room and asked him to sign a disclaimer for any property that he had brought in with him. He was damned if he was going to apologise again. The clipboard was placed in his outstretched hand. He could feel the sheet of paper with his thumb. A pen was attached to the clipboard with a piece of string. It rolled down the board and after a fumble he found it with his injured hand. He had no idea what he was signing or even if he was signing in the right place. What did it matter? In a spidery hand he slowly wrote

'Mickey Mouse' as best he could. The stranger relieved Steadman of the clipboard and without looking at it, thanked him. In return Steadman assured her that the pleasure had been all his. He still hadn't had a glass of water. He lay back on the bed and groaned.

'Would you like a cup of tea, love?'

Steadman thought he had heard the familiar clink and rattle of the tea trolley.

'Heaven must have sent you, I'm dying for a drink,' he replied.

'Has the doctor said you can have a cup of tea?'

Foolishly Steadman hesitated.

'I better not give you one until you've had the all clear. There's some water on your locker. I'll come back later.'

Steadman cursed.

'Don't get nasty with me, young man – I'm only doing my job!'

Under any other circumstance John Steadman would have said something, but there just didn't seem to be any point. Through the half open door he heard a familiar voice.

'Where's John Steadman?'

'Who are you?'

'I'm his sister Linda, I must see him.'

'I think the doctors are with him. If you would just take a seat.'

Dominic touched his wife's arm and pointed to the white board behind the nurse. Written in block capitals for all to see was 'Room 2 JOHN STEADMAN'. Linda took one look at the board and was off. The nurse was about to say something. Dominic raised a hand and shook his head.

'She's a woman on a mission. I wouldn't try to stop her. Give her a minute or two. Once she knows that her brother is safe she'll calm down and I'll take her away for a coffee.'

The nurse behind the desk looked rather sulky and sniffed. She mumbled something about 'rules,' but didn't elaborate. Dominic tried a conciliatory smile; it was a wasted effort.

'Oh John, John, it's all my fault! Are you all right? Did they hurt you? I blame myself – I'm so stupid. What happened? Was it him again?'

'Linda – you're safe! Come here and give me a hug. I'm fine – a bit sore and exhausted - wounded pride more than anything. It's me that's foolish and it's not your fault at all. I expect, however, DCI Long is going to tear a strip off me. As to what happened, you probably know more than I do. And yes, it was him again and no, I still don't know who he is. I'm not sure where they took me. They gave me a whiff of chloroform, and I think I was left on the edge of a cliff in the anticipation that when I came round I would tumble off. As you can see it didn't work. But what about you, are you hurt?'

Linda told her story. Steadman listened attentively.

'I'm so sorry to have put you through all that. I feel so guilty.'

Dominic had followed his wife into the room and was now shaking his head.

'Would you two stop blaming yourselves? Self-recrimination is not helpful. This was all carefully planned by someone who is both wicked and clever. I don't know about you, Linda, but if I don't get a coffee and a bite to eat soon I think I'll pass out. John, I'll bring you back a coffee. If memory serves me right what passes for hot beverages in hospital are unidentifiable and full of putrid chemicals to stop you molesting the nurses. Come on Linda, leave him alone.'

'Would you pass me a glass of water before you go? I'm pretty certain they left a jug close by but I don't want to upset anyone by knocking it over.'

'They do realise you're blind do they?' Linda asked.

'I have told them and I believe they've put a sign somewhere.'

Sure enough, pinned on the wall behind his bed was a tatty piece of card that read 'IMPAIRED VISION'.

'Of course that didn't stop someone asking me to sign something,' continued Steadman. 'And, bless him, a young doctor asked if I could tell how many fingers he was holding up. I said 'two' as that is rather how I feel about the world just now. I did point out to him that even if he was standing naked doing a belly dance, I wouldn't have a clue.'

Linda looked at her brother as she poured him some water. He was bedraggled and filthy. His face was covered in scratches. His hand was still wrapped in a dirty hanky and there was sick down his shirt and tie.

'I wish they would let me clean you up.'

'I'm fine, honestly. I expect the police surgeon as well as the consultant will want to look me over. Then I'll have to face the wrath of DCI Long. Does Alan Munro know about today's fun and games?'

Linda said she hadn't seen him.

'No, I suspect he's been too busy,' Steadman mused. 'He was interviewing a witness who was bringing with him the less than lovable Anton Lemerise. I would have liked to listen in. It would certainly have been a lot more productive and a lot less trouble than being bundled off in a car and nearly toppling over the edge of a cliff.'

The door opened and two doctors entered.

'Time for us to leave, I think,' said Dominic.

CHAPTER TWENTY

Munro was glad to get out of the stuffy interview room. He had had about as much as he could stomach of Gupta and Lemerise. The corridor leading to the waiting area had already lost its newly-cleaned, lavender-polished smell. There were photos of former policemen all along the wall. Munro hadn't taken much notice of them before; it had never occurred to him that all these officers were dead. The hairs prickled on the back of his neck. Would they be putting a picture of John Steadman up there next?

He pushed open the doors into the waiting area. Sergeant Grimble looked up from his desk. On seeing Munro he gave him the 'thumbs up'.

'Found him at the top of Quarry Hill – dazed and a bit knocked around, but alive. They've airlifted him down to Helmsmouth General. Linda and her husband have gone to meet him. DCI Long and Inspector Crouchley are upstairs and will give you all the details. I rather think that our Chief Inspector is waiting for you before going to the hospital himself.'

Munro breathed a sigh of relief. He turned on his heel, almost knocked down an old lady who had come to report her lost cat, and bounded up the stairs. DCI Long's door was open. He didn't bother to knock.

'I gather he's safe.'

DCI Long reassured him.

'I'll tell you all about it on the way to the hospital. I thought you would like to come with me. I suspect John will want to know about your morning as much as I want to know about his. I'd also like a witness with me, and I need a strong man to carry that lot.' He pointed to a cardboard box in the corner. Munro gave him a questioning look.

'A little light penitence for the headstrong Inspector Steadman. Those are the recordings of previous interviews. He can listen to them while he's nursing his wounded pride.'

'But he's all right otherwise, isn't he, sir?'

'Let's go and find out.' Long replied.

Alan Munro lifted the box as though it were empty.

'Oh, Eric,' Long continued, 'I think we had better have an armed officer keeping a beady eye on Steadman until we can get him back to the safety of Jamaica Mansion. Can you detail one of your men?'

Crouchley, who had been largely ignored during the exchange between the two detectives, scowled at them. Any trace of cooperation and good humour evaporated from his face. He stared long and hard at the Chief Inspector. The colour drained from his face, bar two bright red splashes below his eyes.

'Oh, that's how is, is it?' he spat the words out. 'Call in the uniformed boys to do all the hard work while you lot go take all the credit. Planned the interview on the hospital steps in front of the TV cameras, have we?'

'Eric, that's not what I...' pleaded DCI Long, but it was no use. Once Crouchley was in this frame of mind all reasoning was useless.

'I know exactly what you meant,' Crouchley continued. 'We're no longer necessary – surplus to requirement – go back to football hooligans and litter louts! Oh, I forgot,' his voice was heavy with sarcasm, 'I forgot you need a *uniformed* armed officer.' He stressed the word uniformed, drawing it out slowly and letting it hang in the air. 'I suppose it would be so unprofessional, so unreasonable for one of your grey-suited dandies to be seen toting a weapon. Oh no, it has to be one of my men!'

'But Eric, you know the regulations...'

'Don't bloody well quote the regulations at me, Long. I know them better than any other man in the force.'

This was undoubtedly the case. Crouchley not only knew all the regulations but also how far he could bend them and where all the loopholes were.

'OK, OK – I'll tell you what I'll do. I'll send down an armed officer but that's one you owe me - and don't bother to thank me for the help today.'

'I was just about to say...' The door slammed and Crouchley was gone. '...thank you for all your help.'

DCI Long finished the sentence and shook his head. 'An interesting character is our Inspector Crouchley.'

Munro was livid.

'I don't know how you put up with that, sir. I would have punched him on the nose!'

'That would be against regulations, even I know that. Alan you're the physicist – how does it go? 'For every force there is an equal and opposite force.' Which means, I think, you might have ended up hurting your fist.'

'I would have taken the chance,' replied Munro.

★ ★ ★

The two men squeezed into one of the police cars. DCI Long had to stoop to prevent his head from brushing the roof of the car. DS Munro was just too big all round. Even with the seat pushed right back, his knees still touched the steering wheel. The Chief Inspector gave a very brief account of the morning's events.

'I'd rather hear the full story from Steadman,' he explained.

He listened carefully to Munro's encounter with Dr Gupta and Anton Lemerise.

'I did want to have a word with you before I arrested him on suspicion, sir. I hope I did the right thing.'

'I don't think you had a lot of choice, Alan. The whole case is still rather messy. And I don't like Lemerise's involvement. He's smart and slippery – no, I don't like that at all,' Long mused. 'You don't think Dr Robinson is bluffing?'

'He could be, but I rather fancy that Gupta took advantage of him being there.'

'What about a motive? And what about...' DCI Long was about to mention the window when something out of the corner of his eye caught his attention. It was an advertising board outside a newsagent's shop. It read: 'BLIND DETECTIVE CALLED IN TO SOLVE MYSTERY OF BROKEN WINDOW'.

'Pull in, would you, Alan. I won't be a moment.'

DCI Long got out of the car and headed off towards the shop. He came back clutching a copy of the Helmsmouth Echo. He was muttering under his breath and obviously very angry.

'It would seem that, regardless of our efforts, the Eyesore remains as leaky as a sieve.'

Munro noticed the headlines and turned ashen.

'Carry on driving and I'll read it out to you.

'A reliable source has informed the Helmsmouth Echo' – doubtless for a large bribe - *'that our local police force has requested the assistance of retired Detective Inspector John Steadman to solve a case that has so far baffled them. Inspector Steadman, who was blinded in a brutal attack that left his wife dead, is believed to be living in hiding somewhere in the Helmsmouth area. He has been seen in the company of the detective investigating the sudden death of Alisha Gupta, wife of one of Helmsmouth's most eminent dentists. The only clue the police have to go on is a broken window at the rear of the Gupta's lavish residence. Our source states*

that the police remain completely mystified and have brought in the blind detective out of sheer desperation. The Echo notes that the murder of Holly Steadman remains unsolved. It is not known if the two cases are linked. Alisha Gupta's husband was too distressed to comment. His solicitor Mr Anton Lemerise informed the Echo that Dr Gupta was helping the police in every way possible but was frustrated at the lack of progress made by the detective leading the case. No one from Helmsmouth Police HQ was available for comment.''

A fly was buzzing around in the car. Munro swatted it with the back of his hand and wiped the remains on the corner of his seat.

'It could have been worse,' Long said in a conciliatory voice.

'Yes, they could have named me.'

'That too – I was thinking more that at least they didn't give out Steadman's address.'

Munro blushed. DCI Long continued:

'I will have to lean on the editor of the Echo again, though I doubt it will do much good. The Chief Constable is forever encouraging us to foster good relationships with the press.'

'Do you have any idea who could have leaked that story, sir?'

'No, not really. Certainly Lemerise has given it a nice spin. You know, Alan, it's an odd game we're in. We pay people to inform on criminals. Criminals pay people to shut up. And the press pay anyone to tell them a story that will help them sell their newspapers. Maybe we all have a price. All I can say for certain is that the Helmsmouth Echo couldn't afford me.'

A police car screamed passed them with its blue lights flashing and its siren blaring.

'Do you reckon that's our armed officer?' asked Munro.

'I guess so,' replied DCI Long. 'Doubtless with strict instructions to beat us to the hospital.'

The two detectives arrived at the Accident and Emergency Department of Helmsmouth General. They struggled to find a parking space. One police car was already there, parked in a disabled bay next to the main entrance. Munro sighed and shrugged his massive shoulders in disbelief.

'Thoughtless git! And to think we've trusted him with a firearm! I'll get the keys and move it later.'

They showed their IDs to a startled receptionist who looked as though she had just left school. The waiting room was shabby. The notice board was crowded with out-of-date information and dire warnings of the consequences of abusing any member of staff. A half-hearted attempt had been made to lighten the atmosphere by putting Renoir and Monet prints on one wall: they looked self-conscious and out of place. There were no magazines or children's toys.

'Probably too unhygienic,' Long remarked.

Despite it being the middle of the afternoon the place was crowded. Munro, uncomfortable as always in any normal-sized chair, looked round the room. The people appeared poor, careworn and dejected. The dingy magnolia paint didn't help. Munro thought they all looked sickly, as if they had not been out in the fresh air for some time. Nobody seemed especially ill, apart from one baby who wouldn't stop crying. None of them met his gaze. Even out of uniform, it was obvious that the two men were police officers.

A porter came into the waiting room and, after a brief word with the receptionist, signalled to the two detectives to follow him.

'They've taken your chum up to a side ward on the admissions unit. Darth Vader is standing guard at the door.'

Sure enough there was an armed officer wearing full protective gear including a bullet proof helmet.

'Expecting a riot, are we?' asked Munro.

The officer, who felt as stupid as he looked, replied in a surly voice, 'Only obeying orders, sir.'

A slip of an Indian lady doctor came out of the room and proffered a tiny hand to DCI Long. He shook it gently as though she were a little child.

'DCI Long, I presume - pleased to meet you. I'm Dr Patel, one of the new police surgeons. Shall we go in and I will tell you my findings?'

'This is DS Munro,' replied Long, nodding his head.

'Oh, I've heard all about you from Mr Steadman. He speaks very highly of you.' Needless to say Alan Munro turned bright crimson.

She opened the door and led the way.

'Oi! I'm meant to check your IDs,' interrupted the armed officer.

'Bugger off,' said Munro, 'and take that stupid helmet off. You look a right pillock!'

John Steadman was lying in bed. He looked pale and worn out. One hand was swathed in fresh bandages and his face, although now clean, was scratched and grazed. His sightless eyes tried in vain to see who had come into his room. There was no mistaking the low, rumbling voice of DCI Long.

'Hello, John, how do you feel?'

Immediately Steadman sat up in the bed. 'Before I answer that, may I apologise for my stupidity and all the trouble I've caused. I'm truly sorry.'

There was a moment's hesitation before DCI Long replied.

'I've been trying to put myself in your shoes, John, and to tell you the truth I couldn't. To lose your wife and your sight – no, I can't imagine it. And until we catch whoever is behind this, you remain effectively a prisoner. I don't condone what you did, but I perfectly understand why you just wanted a bit of freedom with your sister. A day out is not too much to ask after what you've been through. I would have probably done the same. Sergeant Munro, on the other hand, thinks you should be keelhauled at the very least!'

'Alan! I didn't hear you creeping in. How did you get on with Gupta and Lemerise? Have there been any new developments?'

'Later, later,' said DCI Long, 'Dr Patel is first going to tell us her findings. Then you are going to relate in precise detail exactly what happened to you. Then, and only then, will I allow Munro to tell his story.'

Dr Patel confirmed that she and the accident and emergency consultant had examined John Steadman. Other than the lost fingernail, all his injuries were superficial.

'But there is one very interesting finding,' she continued. 'Mr Steadman, may I show these gentlemen your shoulders?'

Her delicate fingers swiftly undid the buttons on his shirt. Steadman didn't mind the intrusion. Dr Patel knew her job; more than that, she cared and made no presumptions. That was it, he thought, she was someone who cared.

'There – do you see?' she said pointing at some barely perceptible marks on Steadman's right shoulder. 'There are three small elliptical marks on the anterior aspect of the shoulder and one similar but larger one on the posterior aspect.'

Munro wondered why she just didn't say 'back' and 'front', but presumed it was simply the way doctors talked.

'These are consistent with being grabbed from the back like this.'

She moved behind John Steadman and placed her tiny hand over his shoulder.

'Clearly,' she continued flashing a smile at the two

detectives, 'whoever did this had much bigger hands than mine. But if you look closely at the other shoulder – there,' she said as she exposed Steadman's left shoulder. 'No nail marks - only the fingertip bruises from a strong grip.'

'Maybe he had a glove on his left hand,' Munro suggested.

'That would be a possibility, but Mr Steadman doesn't think so.'

John Steadman nodded in agreement. Munro thought for a moment.

'Perhaps he just bites the nails on his left hand.'

Dr Patel laughed. It was a tinkling, pleasant sound that lifted the otherwise sombre atmosphere.

'That would be most unusual. I think fingernails taste the same on both hands. I'll leave the mystery with you. I'm only the doctor.'

'Thank you, Dr Patel, you have been exceedingly helpful. When may I have your report?' asked DCI Long.

'I'll have it ready by the end of the afternoon.'

Deftly she did up the buttons on John Steadman's shirt.

'There,' she said placing the call buzzer in his unbandaged hand. 'If you need anything, just press the button. I'll leave you gentlemen to yourselves.'

CHAPTER TWENTY ONE

The door closed behind Dr Patel with a soft click. This was the moment John Steadman had been dreading since his rescue. The room was silent and it was impossible for him to read that silence. He couldn't tell if DCI Long was angry or pleased: he thought the former more likely. Alan Munro must surely be glad, but this was the most frustrating part of being blind, the impossibility of having full social interaction. The smile, the nod, the raise of an eyebrow, the averted gaze, the pursed lips, the shrug of the shoulders, even the wag of a finger: all of these were lost to him. Steadman sat there with two of his closest colleagues, and in that brief moment he felt very alone. It was as if he was in solitary confinement, locked in a prison or stuck on some desert island.

In point of fact Long and Munro were neither angry nor pleased. Both simply looked at Steadman, then at each other. DCI Long shook his head wearily and Munro held out both his open hands as if to say 'what can we do?' The man who sat before them was just a shadow of his former self: weak, scrawny, bruised and scratched, and now recovering from another attempt on his frail life. It was almost impossible to believe that only a few months before John Steadman had been Helmsmouth's most dashing and capable detective, happy in his work and happy with his life.

DCI Long spoke first.

'John, we're so relieved that you survived. I promise I'll find the person that's behind this if it's the last thing I do, so help me. Are you up for going over today's events? You know I'll have to ask you to make a statement.'

'It's just that I feel so...'

'Don't go there, John,' DCI Long interrupted. 'There is no need to apologise further. Let's see if the three of us can get something positive from today. Why don't you start from the beginning and I'll tell you what we know as we go along.'

Steadman was, regardless of his blindness, a good witness. He was a little surprised that the man with the gun was Phil the Shed.

'I know of him, of course, but I've never met him,' he said. 'I thought drugs were his little sideline, not abduction.'

'He's gone to ground,' added Munro, 'but we've got a picture of the driver. It may lead us somewhere, although I doubt it somehow. I'm willing to bet it will be the same scenario as last time – written instructions, no questions and large sums of money.'

Steadman told them of the drive and of how he had picked at the vinyl under the seat.

'Yes, we found the car,' said Long. 'Locally hired job, and got your prints, but why scratch the vinyl?'

'Simple really,' Steadman replied. 'I thought it might help identify the car. They could clean it out and get rid of any prints, but they would be hard pushed to repair a little damage and in all probability might even overlook it.'

'I wouldn't have thought of that,' said Munro.

'Until you're put in that situation, Alan, you really don't know what you would think. I suspect you're far too intelligent to be taken for the fool that I was and end up being snatched in the first place.'

'We were fortunate in finding the car,' Long interjected, 'and if you owe anybody gratitude it's Kim Ho in forensics. She identified some tree pollen from the car and gave us a possible location. But go on.'

'The three of them frog-marched me up the hill. It wasn't easy as I kept tripping up. One of them wasn't very fit. I remember he asked for a rest. I did think of doing a runner – crazy idea really. They pushed on. It was clear they had a deadline to meet. Eventually we stopped, somewhere near the top I guess, and there he was.'

'You're absolutely positive that it was the same man?'

'I'd recognise that voice anywhere – yes, I'm certain. It's odd about the marks on my shoulders. I remember at the time feeling his nails dig into my right shoulder but not the left. I know my jacket wasn't in the way as he had pulled that down over my back to stop me lashing out. They spun me round before putting the chloroform soaked pad over my face. There is one thing that may give us a clue. Is my jacket lying about?'

'Yes, it's behind my chair,' said Munro.

'I can remember just as I was losing consciousness he slipped a piece of paper into my pocket. I suspect it's a fake suicide note. Can you find it?'

Munro slipped on a pair of plastic gloves and carefully retrieved the slip of paper.

'What does it say?' asked Steadman.

Alan unfolded the piece of paper.

'I can't give any more. I can't live if living is without you',' he read

'Is it written or typed?'

'Typed – do you think he handled it?'

'Hard to tell,' replied Steadman. 'He must have, because he slipped it into my pocket. He could have used a paper tissue or something, I'm not sure. I wasn't fully with it, so I took it out of my pocket to try and read it – I couldn't help myself. '

'We'll get forensics to go over it,' said DCI Long. 'Unusual choice of words. I'm sure I've heard them somewhere before.'

All three men agreed that the words were vaguely familiar but they couldn't place them.

Steadman skimmed briefly over his time at the top of the cliff.

'I think I may have lost my dark glasses there. Pity, I had grown quite attached to them.'

'There are some men up there combing the area,' Long reassured him.

'We've got your white cane,' Munro added. 'I'll bring it back this evening with your glasses, if they've been found.'

'Anything else that might be of interest?' Long asked.

'I'm sure he was watching me struggle,' Steadman replied, 'and I'm fairly certain he went off on a motorbike. I doubt if you'll find any tracks. The ground at the top was bone dry and hard packed.' He paused for a moment. 'That's enough about me. What I really want to know is how Alan's been getting on with the Gupta case.'

Tactfully DCI Long excused himself on the pretext of having to make a phone call. He knew that Munro would be self-conscious if he stayed.

'There certainly have been some developments,' Munro said. He continued by telling Steadman of the extraordinary confessions of Dr Robinson.

'Very interesting,' said Steadman nodding his head. 'It would account for his nervousness at having to confirm her death. Yet he vigorously denies that he murdered her. Do you believe him?'

'I think so. It's a shame you weren't there.'

Steadman didn't like to say that since he had lost his sight it was almost impossible for him to tell if someone was lying. You need eyes to see through the mask of deception.

'How did you cope with Anton Lemerise?'

Munro explained about the gobbet of ear wax and the blackbird singing outside the window. He recounted the interview in detail; the odd relationship, the visits of Reena and Cassandra, Jean, the thumb print on the cup and finally the phone call from Dr Rufus.

'An injection of air! That's novel,' Steadman remarked. 'And five people with the ability and opportunity,' he continued, counting them off on his fingers.

'Six,' Munro corrected him. 'The key to the back door is missing, taken at the time the window was broken.'

Steadman frowned.

'The broken window is still bothering me - I'm not sure why.'

'There are a couple of other things worrying me,' Munro continued. 'I need to double check, but I think the Guptas' Sunday paper is missing. It may be nothing. The other is the lack of a computer. If Alisha is running this on-line business she's going to need more than a little laptop. I wouldn't mind looking at the bank statements.'

'Did you arrest him on suspicion?'

'I did. I would have liked to discuss it with DCI Long, but…'

'He was far too busy looking for me,' Steadman interjected. 'Lemerise wouldn't have liked that.'

'No, he threatened me with all sorts of things, but you can't be intimidated by a man with a greasy, brown candle dangling out his ear. Gupta's been released on bail.'

'Not an easy case for your first murder, I'm afraid,' Steadman remarked. 'There remains the question of motive. I'm not convinced that we really know why Alisha Gupta was murdered. It's not a criticism. Considering the speed of events not to mention the distractions, you're doing very well. I'm sure DCI Long…'

'Is satisfied with DS Munro's handling of the case,' said the Chief Inspector, finishing off John Steadman's sentence as he re-entered the room. 'More than satisfied, in fact.'

Poor Munro! With the heat in the room and the lavish praise from his superior officers, his face was burning like some great beacon.

The door opened again and Linda and Dominic burst in.

'Oh! Sorry, are we disturbing you?' Linda asked.

'No, come in. It would be useful if you could go over your story with John and I'll listen in, if I may?' said DCI Long. Turning to Munro, he continued, 'Blast, we forgot the box – would you mind fetching it?'

'I'll go now and I'll move Darth Vader's car out of the disabled bay.'

Munro got up and stretched. The plastic chair shot out from under him as though trying get away. He pulled open the door.

'Give us your car keys,' he said to the armed officer.

'Why?'

'Because you're parked in the disabled bay and you're not disabled – though I could arrange it for you!'

Grudgingly the officer handed over the keys. Munro sauntered down the corridor whistling. He returned twenty minutes later with a large cardboard box under his arm. He tossed the car keys back to the armed officer who, not surprisingly, couldn't catch them.

'Oops! Sorry about that,' Munro said without a trace of sincerity.

The contents of the box were explained to John Steadman who nodded.

'If Linda or Dominic would set it up, I'm sure you'll remember which buttons to press.'

Steadman was not looking forward to listening to the tapes. He had mentally played them all back in his head repeatedly. He also didn't want to hear himself as he once was. He knew he would sound confident, sure of who he was and what he was doing.

The tapes would bring back other memories. Always at the end of a difficult investigation he would take Holly away for the weekend, somewhere quiet and romantic, never the same place twice. These were always magical times. He couldn't bring himself to relive these yet; they were too painful.

'John, I'm going to take your jacket as well as the note back with me to give to forensics. I doubt they'll find anything but it's worth a try. Alan, if you're coming back this evening, will you call in past Jamaica Mansion? I'll ask Daisy if she could look out a change of clothes. Is there anything else that you need?' said DCI Long.

'Only my soap bag – and a large cake of dark chocolate.'

The two detectives left Dominic and Linda to set up the tape recorder. Steadman would wait until he was alone before donning the headphones. He remained apprehensive and moreover, was struggling to keep awake.

DCI Long nodded to the armed officer.

'Oi! Munro – where did you leave my car?'

'Oh sorry, didn't I tell you? – Car park 8, the main car parks were full. It must be visiting time.'

Neither officer spoke as they made their way back to their own vehicle. DCI Long paused as he fastened his seat belt.

'There isn't a car park 8, is there?' he asked.

'Did I say car park 8?' replied Munro trying to look all innocent. 'I meant to say car park 4.'

Car park 4 was the most awkward to reach being, tucked behind the nurses' residence.

'If I didn't know better,' said Long, 'I would say that under that gentle Scottish exterior there lurks a malicious, vindictive streak.'

'You're just saying that, sir, to make me feel better.' Munro replied.

They drove back slowly through the evening traffic. A new billboard was placed outside the newsagent. This time it read: 'BLIND DETECTIVE KIDNAPPED'.

'Pull in would you, Alan? We'd better find out what they have to say. Do you want a copy?'

'No thanks, sir, I get the Helmsmouth Evening News delivered to the house.'

★ ★ ★

Well, well, well – two big policemen returning from the hospital. What little clues did they find? A folded piece of paper with some words on it. That won't get them far. And how was the wounded hero, I wonder? Doubtless loving all the attention; the man of the moment no less, even made the evening papers. I did enjoy seeing you struggle – so close, so close. If only those louts weren't so scared of heights they would have put you an inch nearer the edge, and Steadman, your efforts would have been in vain. Maybe I'm trying to be too artistic. Maybe I'm relying on others too much. Less subtlety and the direct approach next time, I think. What do they say? Third time lucky.

CHAPTER TWENTY TWO

DCI Long glanced at the newspaper article in silence. There was nothing he didn't know already. On page 2 there was however another piece that caught his attention. 'Alan, you might be interested in this' he said. He cleared his throat and read:

'*More broken windows mystify police. Two more instances of unexplained broken windows are baffling Helmsmouth police. The crimes appear motiveless, as nothing of value was taken. Mr Tedders of Beaumont Green said he only noticed that his kitchen window was broken this morning. A gardening magazine that he had been reading while drinking a mug of cocoa in the kitchen before going to bed is apparently missing. The other victim, who does not wish to be named, said the window in her back door had been broken. She reports that the only item taken was yesterday's copy of the Helmsmouth Evening News which she had placed under her cat's food bowl. 'I always change the paper every night but this morning it was gone,' she said. Tiddles the cat was unharmed. As reported in our sister paper, the*

Helmsmouth Echo, police are still investigating the mystery of the broken window and the death of Mrs Alisha Gupta, wife of Helmsmouth's leading dentist, Dr Aaron Gupta. DS Alan Munro, the investigating officer, was unavailable for comment. However a police spokesman stated that there is no obvious link and that Helmsmouth residents have no need to panic. But the Evening News is not so sure. Are these copycat crimes? Are we to expect more mysterious deaths? Could there be a potential serial killer on the loose?'

Munro groaned as DCI Long folded up his newspaper. 'That's just what I don't need! They can't be copycat crimes. That's just bollocks – if you pardon the expression, sir. The Echo only printed their story this morning. Not unless it's someone from the paper who got an early edition last night. But sure as hell, there'll be a spate of copycat crimes now. Maybe we should issue a police warning advising people to lock up their newspapers and...' He stopped in mid-sentence.

'What's bothering you?' Long asked.

'It's just... Dr Gupta said he had spent part of Sunday reading the *Sunday Telegraph*, but I don't remember seeing it anywhere in the house. I'm sure the paper on the top of the stack for recycling was from Saturday as it had the picture of the train crash. It's in my notebook to double check. I'll have a word with DS Fairfax in the morning. I wonder who these other people are.'

'Leave that one with me,' said DCI Long. 'I'll find out who the investigating officers are and see what they've got so far. I think I have a busy evening ahead of me.'

'You don't really think there's a serial killer out there do you sir?'

'I don't know what to think. I do feel a vague sense of unease, that's all.'

Munro was not convinced. It was bad enough having John Steadman with a bee in his bonnet, worrying about the broken window, and now DCI Long putting in some over-time. It didn't make sense. There was no logical explanation for the crimes to be related and Alan Munro liked logical explanations.

'Should I mention the newspaper reports to John Steadman this evening?' he asked.

'Better he learns from us than second hand from someone else,' replied Long.

Munro dropped DCI Long at the Eyesore. He retrieved Steadman's white cane and the dark glasses, which had been found at the edge of the cliff. Daisy had a small case already packed with Steadman's clothes and toiletries. She was still distraught. Munro reassured her as best he could. 'He'll be back tomorrow. I'll fetch him as soon as the doctors have done their rounds.'

The evening traffic had cleared, and in no time Munro arrived home. He opened the door and shouted, 'Hello – anybody in?' Two very excited little girls stampeded towards him with loud squeals of 'Daddy!' He scooped them up in his massive arms and kissed them. They clung tightly to his neck and in return peppered his cheeks with childlike kisses of their own.

'Steady on you two! Let's look at my princesses.'

Gently he stood them down on the floor. Melanie, the older of the two said, 'Do you like Annie's new hair?'

Annie pirouetted unsteadily, holding her arms out to balance her delicate body. Munro was astounded. The wig was so near the colour and style of Annie's hair before it fell out that it took him a second to realise the point of Melanie's question.

'You are absolutely beautiful. Both of you are!' He scooped up the children again. 'Let's find Mummy.'

Maureen came out of the kitchen, drying her hands on her apron. 'I thought I heard a noise,' she said with a big grin. 'Would you girls mind if I kiss your father?'

'OK,' said Annie, 'but only one.'

The smell of cooking wafted out of the kitchen. Other than the meal at Capaldi's, Munro's diet for the last few days had been anything cold from a tin or police canteen food. He was about to ask what was for dinner but in the nick of time stopped himself and asked how Maureen's parents were instead.

'Much the same - older, more set in their ways, worried about you and the children, you know, the usual. I expect you're hungry.'

'I'm always hungry,' Munro pleaded as his wife rushed back to the kitchen to attend to a boiling pan.

'Mummy says that if we're not careful you'll turn into a big fatty,' said Melanie. Both girls giggled uncontrollably.

'Oh she did, did she?' Munro said in mock anger. 'We'll have to see about that! Maureen, who have you been calling a big fatty? I'm fading away to nothing.'

'Well you're certainly turning into the same shape as a big round nothing,' she replied, placing a large roast chicken on the centre of the table.

'You would be offended if I didn't appreciate your cooking. A man just can't win!'

The exchange was good humoured. Despite his meal at Capaldi's Maureen secretly thought that he had lost a few pounds over the last week.

Alan explained that he had to go back to the hospital that evening.

'Is John all right?' Maureen asked.

Not wanting to upset the children, Munro merely stated that he'd had a nasty tumble.

'Was it that bad man that pushed him?' Annie asked.

You couldn't hide anything from children, Munro thought.

'The girls have been making chocolate brownies. Why don't you take him some?'

The girls leapt down from the table, racing each other to the cupboard where all the plastic storage boxes, old ice cream containers and baking trays were kept. They tumbled out on to the floor with a sound like distant thunder. Having selected an unnecessarily large one, they dutifully stacked the rest back in the cupboard.

'They're good kids,' Munro commented.

'And very fond of their Uncle John,' added Maureen.

The girls had opted for the title 'uncle' themselves. 'John' was considered too familiar and 'Mr Steadman' too formal. Being called 'uncle' had pleased Steadman no end. Munro took the box of brownies, put his jacket back on and kissed Maureen and the girls.

'I don't expect I'll be late,' he said as he picked up the car keys. He knew that there was something else he should take. A cake of chocolate, that was it; no doubt the brownies would do instead.

As he approached Steadman's hospital room he could hear the sound of laughter. Munro looked quizzically at the armed constable standing by the door.

'His son, Ben, and Dr Rufus have arrived,' she explained.

Darth Vader's replacement was a young female officer who somehow made Munro feel uncomfortable. 'I'll get you a chair,' he said. He stomped off down the corridor and returned brandishing a seat, looking very pleased with himself.

'There, that's better.'

Doubtless the WPC would not have agreed.

'Evening John, I see you've got company.'

'You remember my son, don't you?'

Munro shook Ben's hand. He was tall and lean like his father. His hair was long and pulled back in a ponytail. He had high cheekbones and looked as though he laughed a lot. Munro reckoned he probably took after his mother.

'You made it here quickly, in fact you both have,' Munro observed.

Ben explained. 'I was showing some card tricks to a boy on the plane and naturally got chatting with his parents. They were going into London and gave me a lift to Waterloo Station. Who should I meet on the platform but my godfather. Frank promptly bumped me up to first class, and here we are.'

'I didn't know Dr Rufus was your godfather.'

'He probably wants to keep it secret. I'm not sure how good a spiritual influence he's been, but financially... what can I say?'

Dr Rufus mumbled something about what's the point in having money.

'So, how's the invalid?' Munro asked covering up Dr Rufus's embarrassment.

'I'm fine. I'm not sure why they're keeping me in overnight.'

'I'll collect you in the morning as soon as you're given the all clear,' Munro reassured him.

'Now for a little magic,' Ben announced. 'I've been working on something that Dad would appreciate. It's been blooming difficult, let me tell you. Virtually every trick out there depends on deceiving the eye. But the great Ben Steadman, illusionist extraordinaire, has devised some magic that would impress even the sighted in a darkened room.'

He was quite masterful. Dr Rufus and DS Munro looked at him with rapt attention. John Steadman lay back smiling, filled with a mixture of curiosity and pride.

'Give me your right hand. Let us call it the Grasping Right Hand of Greed.' There was often a strong political element to Ben's act. 'Now tell me what I've placed in your right hand.'

Steadman felt the objects between his thumb and fingertips. 'I would say three pound coins.'

'Correct!' shouted Dr Rufus, who was quite carried away.

'Now tell me what I have put in your left hand. Let us call it the Poor Impoverished Left Hand of Need.'

This time it was a single object. Steadman had a little more difficulty in placing it.

'It's some sort of ring. Is it a napkin ring?'

'To you, dear father, it may seem like an innocent napkin ring, but in truth it is the Magical Siphon of Poverty! Turn your left hand over and if the Grasping Hand of Greed allows, place all three coins on the back of your left hand. That's it, one on top of the other. Now very carefully take the Magical Siphon of Poverty, which you dismissed as a mere napkin ring, in your right hand and place it over the stack of coins. Perfect! I will assist by holding them in place with the blunt end of this pencil. It works better with a pen but I can't afford one.'

Ben took a pencil out of his inside pocket. It was one with an eraser on the end.

'Let the fingers of your left hand dangle down in despair,' he continued. 'Good, now touch the fingers of your left hand with those of your right hand to form a cage. I'll keep the coins balanced with the end of my pencil. We shall call this cage the Unacceptable Cage of Capitalism! You can hold your hands a little higher like this,' he said gently, raising his father's hands.

'Now, all I have to say is the magic words 'hedge fund managers' and with a gentle prod of the pencil...'

There was a chinking sound as all three coins somehow fell into Steadman's right hand.

'And there you have it. Greed once again triumphs over need!'

'I say, how in the name did you do that?' exclaimed Dr Rufus. 'I don't think much of all the political guff, but the trick was amazing.'

'Dad, what did you think? Did it work for you?'

John Steadman was touched. He had always liked conjuring and card tricks but hadn't given them a thought since losing his sight. He had been a keen bridge player and had even persuaded Holly to learn. She was charmingly hopeless, would frown if she got a bad hand and be all smiles if it was good and bid recklessly. It all came back to him in a flash. He missed her dreadfully.

'Excellent, Ben. I never felt the coins leave the back of my left hand – or even pass straight through. I hope there's no blood! Alan, what did you think?'

Munro was a shrewd observer. He had glimpsed the switch as Ben adjusted the position of his father's hands.

'Very impressive - I liked the rhetoric too.'

'Oh ho! – I detect someone I can have a good argument with. I like that. Steadman's too wishy-washy and never rises to the challenge.'

Munro pretended not to hear Dr Rufus's comment.

'Talking of mysteries, have you shown Frank the marks on your shoulders?'

'I haven't had a chance yet,' Steadman replied.

He struggled with the buttons of his hospital issue pyjama jacket. Munro was itching to help but knew it would not have been appreciated.

'Wow! Serious scar, Dad,' Ben exclaimed as the ugly, purple suture line on Steadman's chest was revealed.

Munro reiterated Dr Patel's findings. Dr Rufus nodded in agreement.

'Yes, I see. Four clear nail imprints, one from the thumb and the others from the first three fingers of the right hand, but only matching bruises on the left. You say he grabbed you from behind. He wasn't wearing a glove on his left hand?'

'I'm certain that he wasn't,' Steadman replied.

'He plays the guitar.'

'What was that, Ben?'

'He's a guitarist, like me. Look,' he said holding out his hands. Sure enough the nails on his left hand were very short, whereas those on his right thumb, index, middle and ring fingers were long and thick.

'You don't finger pick a guitar with your little finger.'

He placed his hands over his father's shoulders. The marks were almost a perfect match.

'I don't think I've encountered any murderous musicians. How bizarre!' Steadman furrowed his brows. 'He also left a note in my pocket. Can you remember exactly what it said, Alan?'

'Sure, it said, *'I can't give any more. I can't live if living is without you'.*'

'Harry Nilsson – 'Without You'. It's the chorus, except he's got the phrase round the wrong way,' said Ben. He sang it as it should be.

'I knew the words were familiar. You're firing on all cylinders, Ben. You wouldn't like a job in the police?' Munro remarked.

Ben stroked his pony tail.

'Somehow I think not.'

'Have you managed to listen to any of the interview tapes?' Alan asked turning towards Steadman.

Before he could answer, Ben interrupted:

'That's a waste of time. I'm sure Dad's gone over them a hundred times or more in his head.'

'Ben's right. There isn't a list in the box is there? If so, Alan, you could just read them out to me in case there's any that I've forgotten. I just don't think the voice is one that I heard as a police officer.'

There was a typed list in the box. Realising the sensitive nature of the information, Dr Rufus took his godson away for a coffee. Steadman listened attentively, shaking his head as Munro read each name. There were only two on the list that he had forgotten about; neither was remotely similar to the voice on the top of the cliff.

'How are Maureen and the girls?'

'They're all well. Annie was wearing her new hairpiece and it wasn't until Melanie pointed it that I noticed - it's that good.'

'That'll make her feel better,' Steadman said, trying hard to picture the little girl.

'There's another couple of things I should tell you. Firstly, you've made the papers. Damn, I meant to bring in my copy to read out to you. I knew there was something else I had to remember. I can give you the gist.'

Munro recounted the stories from the morning and evening papers.

'Very difficult to keep anything secret in the Eyesore,' Steadman commented.

'Secondly, there have been another two people who have reported that they've been broken into and nothing taken except an old newspaper and a magazine. The press are really stirring it all up. I think I told you that I didn't recall seeing Dr Gupta's copy of the *Sunday Telegraph*.'

'Were windows broken in both cases?'

'Yes.'

'Do you know if any of the glass was missing?'

Munro puffed his cheeks.

'I doubt if anybody checked. What's bothering you?'

'A vague shadow of a case I read about as a cadet. I'm struggling to recall all the details. Hopefully it will come back to me.'

Munro noticed that Steadman suddenly looked very gaunt and tired. All the animation that had been in his face when Ben was doing his magic trick had disappeared.

'I forgot the cake of chocolate, but Maureen and the girls have sent a box of homemade brownies. Should I hide them in your locker before Frank and Ben get back?'

Too late: the door swung open. 'Did I hear you say that you've brought some chocolate brownies? I'm starving,' said Ben.

'And I had better check one - just to make sure they're not poisoned' Dr Rufus added.

CHAPTER TWENTY THREE

Relief spread over Steadman's face as the bell signalling the end of visiting clanged in the corridor. Munro confirmed that he would call for him as soon as permitted. Ben suggested that he organise lunch: Ben was not a morning person. Steadman was desperate for some peace and quiet in order to gather his thoughts. There was so much to mull over, so much new information to sift through and assimilate.

It was at times like these that he recalled taking Ben fishing as a little boy. Always he would get his line tangled. It was rather like that, Steadman thought. He needed to tease out each strand of information, undo every knot, then slowly reel it all back in so that it made sense. There was something very callous in the elaborate plot to kill him. And also something slightly mad. This reassured Steadman; mad men make mistakes. His assailant played guitar and left garbled song lyrics as a would-be suicide note. It wasn't much to go on, but it was something; a faint glimmer of light. He was also certain that he had been right all along in believing that the voice was not that of a known criminal. He would have to think elsewhere.

Then there was the surprising revelation from Dr Robinson. No wonder he was edgy when he was called to verify Alisha Gupta's death. Was he a lover and a murderer? Munro didn't think so, but he only had his word for it. What would he have given to be at that encounter and to stare into Dr Robinson's eyes!

And the evidence against Aaron Gupta? It was circumstantial: no jury would convict on the strength of it, certainly not if Lemerise was acting for the defence. DC Lofthouse was right. What was Lemerise doing there anyway if Gupta had nothing to hide? But why would he kill his wife? Surely not for the sake of his sister and definitely not to marry Reena. Steadman was certain that a man like Aaron Gupta didn't have enough romance in his soul to run away with Jean. There was no motive. Without a motive the case made little sense.

The broken window – why couldn't he get that out of his mind? Munro was convinced it was irrelevant. Maybe he was right, but it was there and it wouldn't go away. And now two more similar instances seemingly unrelated. Why had he asked if all the glass was accounted for? It just came out for no reason. There was something lurking in the deepest recesses of his memory, something unpleasant, but he was too tired to go looking for it.

He tried to imagine Munro's two little girls clinging

to their father's neck. He loved those children as though they were his own. Quite suddenly it occurred to him that he would never see them grow up, at least not literally. For him they would always be frozen in time. As would, he thought, his entire world. Ben would always be tall and lean and in his twenties. Munro would always look as though he had just come off the rugby pitch. Even Frank Rufus's beard would always remain red with just a few flecks of grey. What would he see if he looked in the mirror? He shuddered at the thought. And Holly? For him she had never changed since the day they married. However, there was another image of Holly, a dreadful image; an image of her with blood oozing down her temple which he knew would haunt him for the rest of his days.

'Would you like a warm drink? Milk? Cocoa? Horlicks?'

Steadman came out of his daydream with a start. 'Oh - warm milk, please, but not too full.'

'I'll leave it on your locker.'

'I'd rather have it in my hands. I'm blind, I might knock it over.'

'Your locker's not that far away!'

To this, Steadman decided, there was no reply.

The milk was awful. Steadman gingerly groped with his outstretched right hand. Sure enough there was a locker and a space on top to put the mug down safely.

The door opened once more. 'It's only me again,' said a cheery voice, although Steadman had no idea who the 'me' in question actually was.

'I've come to do one last set of obs.'

Dutifully Steadman rolled up his sleeve and opened his mouth. His temperature and blood pressure were normal.

'Anything I can do for you?' the cheery nurse inquired.

'Yes, I'd like to go for a pee and clean my teeth.'

'Come on then. I'll take your soap bag.'

Arm in arm they shuffled out of the room.

'Where are you going?' It was the poor armed officer who had ultimately swallowed her pride, sat down in Munro's chair and in the heat of the hospital, fallen asleep.

'Off to the bathroom,' the cheery voice responded. 'You're welcome to join us!'

'Do you know I've never had an armed escort to take me to the toilet,' said Steadman.

'First time for everything,' the nurse replied.

Gently she steered him there and back.

'You look exhausted, Mr Steadman. I'll switch off the light and let you sleep.'

He was about to make a comment. However the nurse was more perceptive than he had given her credit for.

'I know it won't make any difference to you, but the light attracts moths and other unwanted visitors. I think you need to rest.'

She switched off the light. Whether he was just tired or whether it was a reflex reaction to the click of the switch, he felt his body relaxing, his shoulders sagged and his head nestled back in the pillow. The voices in the corridor grew more distant, his breathing became slower and deeper.

Quite suddenly, it was daylight and he was opening the door of the Eyesore. Sergeant Grimble looked up from his desk, which was overflowing with documents.

'Thank goodness you've come back, sir. They're breaking windows all the time and stealing our papers. No one can see them, that's why we thought you could help, seeing as how you're blind anyway.'

'But I can see you,' Steadman replied.

'That's what they all say, sir, but never mind.'

'Where are DS Munro and DCI Long?'

'Haven't you heard, sir? Both in the morgue, and no-one to do the post mortem, seeing as Dr Rufus is lying on the slab between them. You'd better get along to your interview. I expect you remember the way.'

Steadman pushed open the swing doors but the familiar corridor with the photos of former police officers was gone. The corridor was now full of brambles that caught on his hands and whipped across his face. The smell was terrible. He looked down to find the floor was covered in dog excrement. No matter where he stepped his foot fell right on top of another offensive pile. And he could hear laughter: nasty, mocking laughter coming from interview room one. He pushed open the door. There was Anton Lemerise with tears rolling down his toad-like face, holding his fat belly, which was shaking with mirth. He appeared oblivious to the brown wax oozing out of both his ears and forming greasy epaulettes on his crumpled suit. Beside him sat a man who Steadman didn't recognise. He was olive skinned, suave and superficially sophisticated. He too was laughing. Opposite them and sitting in Steadman's place, and here Steadman's heart missed a beat, was his double, wearing only pyjamas and dark glasses. But this John Steadman was mute and immobile, as though he was a tailor's dummy.

'You'll like this one – watch!' Anton Lemerise could barely contain himself as he scribbled something on the paper in front of him. He passed it over to his companion who slapped his thigh and chortled.

'Go on, show him,' he said encouragingly to the solicitor.

Lemerise held up the paper to the Steadman sat opposite them. On it he had written in a childish scrawl, 'YOU SMELL LIKE DOG POO'. Both men fell about. The wax spurting from Lemerise's ears spattered on to the floor like a guttering candle.

There was an almighty crash from outside the room as another window was smashed in. He could hear Grimble's voice shouting, 'They're at it again. Where's John Steadman?'

Steadman fled from the room. He blinked. Wherever he was now was much brighter. A figure working at a desk looked up. It was Kim Ho. In front of her was an incomplete pane of glass made up from jigsaw puzzle pieces. To her right was a box half full of similar shaped pieces of glass. Kim Ho looked him straight in the face.

'Some of the bits are missing,' she said, 'and no one is safe to bring in newspapers any more.'

'Why?' Steadman replied.

'I don't know – you're the blind detective.'

'Yes, you're the blind detective,' chimed in Lemerise and his companion who had now joined Kim Ho.

'I'm afraid it's true, sir, there's no getting away from it,' added Sergeant Grimble, 'you *are* the blind detective.'

'But I'm not,' pleaded Steadman. 'Grimble, you'll back me up. What about all the cases I did before the shooting?'

And in an instant the scene changed. Snapshots of interviews played before his eyes, starting from his most recent case working backwards in rapid succession. Sometimes there was dialogue, sometimes a phrase, sometimes only a word. With each one Steadman could hear himself shouting out 'that's not him,' 'no, that's not him,' 'nor him,' 'nor him'. The scenes shot past, flickering in and out of view like the lit-up windows of a railway carriage passing in the night.

He was a police cadet now, at the passing out parade. 'You've got sharp eyes, Steadman, keep them that way,' said the Commissioner as he shook his hand.

'I will, sir.'

'Good man!'

And now he was back at school. Here was Holly

rushing to meet him, hot and pink from playing hockey. His heart missed a beat. He went to touch her hand but it was as insubstantial as smoke. A familiar voice behind him shouted:

'I hate you. I hate you and I always will hate you!'

Steadman turned around. A boy was running away from him. He tried to see who it was.

'Stop!' he yelled.

The boy faltered. He halted and turned his head. But already Steadman's vision was failing. Where the boy's face should have been there was a scorch mark. Other marks appeared. It was as if the image was on a sheet of paper being held over a flame. Little by little the picture faded, turned brown, then black, then disappeared altogether. Once again John Steadman was plunged into a world of shadows.

There was another crash, but this time it was for real and came from outside his door.

'Tea, coffee, cereal, porridge, toast – what would you like for breakfast?'

Half awake, Steadman replied:

'Oh… coffee and toast please.'

He lay back on his pillows, desperately trying to remember the dream. All that he could recall was Kim Ho doing a glass jigsaw puzzle and Anton Lemerise with wax dribbling out of his ears; that and a vague feeling of apprehension.

'I'll just pull over the bed table. There – it's right in front of you.'

Steadman gently stretched out his hands until they touched the solid surface. There was a clunk as the mug was placed on the table.

'Coffee is on your right. Will I spread your toast for you, seeing as you've got a bandaged finger?' she tactfully continued. 'These little pots of marmalade are a devil to open.

'Actually, Mr Steadman, I was wanting to have a quiet word with you. Is it true that you're the blind detective mentioned in the newspaper?'

'Yes – go on,' replied Steadman somewhat intrigued. 'First, though, tell me your name.'

'Of course, I was forgetting that you can't see my name badge. I'm Ruby – Ruby Connell. I work here as a domestic.'

'I'm not holding you back?' Steadman asked between mouthfuls of toast.

'Not at all, I arranged it so that you would be my last breakfast. What I wanted to say was that I worked for the Guptas until fairly recently. I was a hospital domestic, but they offered me voluntary redundancy ten years ago. At my age it was too good an offer to turn down. The Guptas hadn't been in Helmsmouth long. They had bought the house on Gorse Hill and had just opened the clinic. From the start there was never any shortage of money, though where it all came from was a mystery to me - wealthy parents, I suspect. Mind, they were not generous employers and liked their pound of flesh. I've never been afraid of hard work. No – it was

247

how they lived their lives that bothered me. They never shared the same bedroom, at least not with each other. They hadn't been long in the area before the parties started. Maybe I'm old-fashioned, but when me and Bert got married that was it, and the only time I slept in a different bed was when he had lumbago! Let me tell you, after those parties I had to change every bed in the house. And worse – I had to pick up things – oh, Mr Steadman, they were disgusting. I didn't know what half of them were, but I could guess! Well, I said to his lordship, Dr Gupta that is, he and his wife could behave as they liked, but if they expected me to clean up after them I would need something extra. Do you know what he gave me?'

John Steadman shook his head.

'A box of rubber gloves from his dental surgery, that's what!' Ruby paused to draw breath.

'Was there any violence at these parties, do you know?' Steadman asked.

'Not violence as such, but there were things like uniforms and handcuffs and horrible masks.' She shuddered.

'I gather the house is full of antiques.'

'Oh yes, every week glossy catalogues would arrive from the London showrooms. He would go through them, tick the pieces he fancied and write down what he was willing to pay.'

'Did Mrs Gupta ever look through the catalogues?'

'I'm sure she must have, but the antiques were

mostly his choice. Manly things you know – like weapons and hunting trophies and pictures of half-naked ladies cavorting about. I think she chose the decorations for the house - curtains, wallpaper and the like. Everything was the best. She could spend as well as him. Yes indeed, the Guptas knew how to spend – at least on themselves,' she added.

'Anything else odd that you think I should know about?'

'There is one thing. They didn't ever want me to clean the study. His lordship said that all his papers were kept spread out there for his research and he didn't want them disturbed. He said Mrs Gupta would clean the study.' Ruby sniffed. 'It took Mrs Gupta all her strength to keep herself clean. That's what got me dismissed. One day he'd left the door open – he usually locked it – and I could see it was filthy. I swear all I did was do a bit of dusting and vacuum the floor. When he found out I was straight out the door. The hospital was expanding again so I got my old job back. I don't know if that's any help but I thought you ought to know.'

'May I ask you some questions?'

'Fire away - I've got plenty of time?'

'Did you read any of the papers on Dr Gupta's desk?'

'Some of them were in a foreign language, but I could see that others were just old bills or bank statements.'

'Was anybody else allowed in the study?'

'Only Mrs Gupta. Reena never went there – mind she wouldn't go in as there was no booze in the study. I never saw Dr Gupta's sister, Cassandra, in there either. I think she liked the idea of her brother having a secret study and doing grand research. She's an odd lady, that Cassandra.'

'What about Mrs Gupta's business? She's meant to own a company selling beauty products or something?'

'I never saw her doing any work. Probably a tax dodge, if you ask me.'

'That's been really helpful, thank you. Detective Sergeant Munro is leading the investigation; he may want to ask you some questions.'

'Well you know where to find me. I'd better be off, here's the ward round coming.'

With a clatter of her trolley she was gone. John Steadman munched on his cold toast. Unlike the Guptas' private lives, the toast was quite pleasant.

CHAPTER TWENTY FOUR

Before he could reflect on all that Ruby had told him, the door opened yet again. Steadman could discern from the shuffling of feet and the muffled whispering that quite a gaggle had entered his room.

'How are we today? Fully recovered, I trust?' It was a patronising, upper class voice which instantly raised Steadman's hackles.

'That, of course, all depends on who's asking,' he replied peevishly. He could hear a sharp intake of breath.

'*This* is our consultant,' said a female voice laced with suppressed outrage.

'Ah! – And does 'our consultant' have a name? And while you're at it, perhaps you would kindly introduce yourself. I believe there is a sign above my bed reminding you of my lack of sight, although of course I can't see it.'

Someone at the back of the room sniggered.

'*I* am Sister Watson,' she declared in tones that

suggested he ought to have known already, 'and *this* is Dr Goodbody.'

It was Steadman's turn to try and keep a straight face. 'Goodbody', he thought, what a name, I bet he's short, fat and balding.

'Well, Dr Goodbody, in answer to your questions, 'we' are fine and apart from some bizarre dreams, have had a restful night. As far as being fully recovered, if you mean the loss of a fingernail and a few scratches, I am physically better than expected. If, on the other hand, you mean have I recovered from the second attempt on my life by the man who murdered my wife and deprived me of my sight, then sadly, no. Excellent though the care has been, it will take more than a night's rest in your hospital for me to be 'fully recovered', as you put it.' Steadman could feel his cheeks flush. It was hard not to get angry.

Dr Goodbody turned and asked the sister:

'Has he been up today?'

'Doctor, it is only my sight that has been lost. I can hear perfectly well!'

The consultant almost apologised, but the words got stuck somewhere in his throat.

'I suppose if he can manage to wash and dress himself and doesn't feel too unsteady on his feet, we could let him go,' Dr Goodbody replied.

'What about the dressing on his finger?' Sister Watson interjected.

'If you supply me with the necessary, I'm sure I'll be

able to make arrangements for the dressing to be changed,' Steadman replied. Daisy, Bill or George back at Jamaica mansion would be more than capable, he thought.

'That seems all in order, Sister. Mr Steadman can be discharged with no follow-up.'

Dr Goodbody turned and without saying another word left the room, trailing his entourage behind him. Steadman was seething. If there had been the remotest possibility of him hitting the target, he would have thrown something at the retreating figure.

'Just ignore him, he's an arrogant pig and always has been. I'm Dave by the way, one of the nursing assistants. If you tell me what to do I'll help you get washed and dressed.'

Steadman calmed down. 'What about Sister Watson?'

'Oh, Goodbody's been shagging her for years. It's no secret. The only person that doesn't know is Goodbody's wife. She's still under the delusion that her husband is the most dedicated consultant in Helmsmouth General. Mind, it's no wonder he comes home tired every night.'

Steadman was warming to Dave.

'First things first,' he said. 'Would you phone the Eyesore and ask for Detective Sergeant Alan Munro? Tell him I'm being released - he'll come and fetch me.'

'Hold your horses, boss! Let's make sure you're steady on your pins. If you behave yourself in the bathroom, I'll call him while you're getting dressed – agreed?'

'Agreed,' Steadman conceded.

Bar stubbing his toe and walking into the door jamb, Steadman's ablutions went off without a hitch.

'You've got a choice of a blue or white shirt and a grey stripy or red spotted tie.'

'A white shirt and the grey tie, I think,' said Steadman. 'I'm sure one can always face the world with a braver face wearing a white shirt.'

Dave laid out the clothes as John Steadman instructed, then went off to phone DS Munro. When he got back Steadman was fully dressed. Dave packed his case while a young nurse changed the bandage on his finger.

'Here, your collar's up at the back,' said Dave as he deftly adjusted Steadman's jacket. 'I've left a message for Sergeant Munro. Do you want your dark glasses and white stick?'

'Yes please, and thanks for your help.'

'No problem, that's what I'm here for.'

'Is an armed officer still at the door?'

'They've just swapped over guard duty. Would you like a word with him?' asked Dave.

Steadman was desperate for some news. Unfortunately the armed officer was new to the job. He hadn't heard anything and was so in awe of John Steadman all he could do was stammer 'yes sir', 'no sir', and 'sorry, sir, I don't know'.

★ ★ ★

An anguished howl escaped DS Munro's lips as he trod on something sharp. He had been trying to make an early morning cup of tea without opening his eyes, imagining what it was like to be in John Steadman's blanked out world. He had already 'cheated' once trying to find the milk and had spilled sugar all over the table. Cursing, he opened his eyes, expecting to find one of the girl's toys on the floor.

To his surprise, it was a piece of broken glass. His first thought was that Melanie or Annie had dropped a tumbler getting a midnight drink. He switched on the light. Only then did he notice that one of the panes of glass in the back door had been broken. 'I knew something like this would happen,' he muttered to himself, 'virtually guaranteed after that article in the paper.'

By now he was dripping blood on the tiled floor. He grabbed some kitchen roll and wrapped it round his foot before getting the dustpan and brush. Maureen came in, tying the belt on her dressing gown and pushing sleepy hair off her face.

'What's up?' she asked.

'Blooming kids,' replied Munro. 'Thought it would be a bit of fun, after reading last night's paper, to heave a brick through the window.'

'I can't see any brick.'

'You know what I mean. Copycats, stupid bloody copycats – can't even think of an original bit of mischief. It'll be the kids from the estate, mark my words.'

'Sit down, love, you're bleeding everywhere,' Maureen said in a soothing voice.

Munro did as he was told.

'Ouch! - that hurt.'

'For goodness sake, you're worse than the children. There, that's got it. There was a sliver of glass in your foot…'

'Alan, you're sure…' her voice trailed off.

'About it being some kids? Bound to be – what have we got in common with the Guptas, let alone those other two people? I can't even remember their names. One of them had a cat, hadn't she? We don't have a cat, let alone one called Tiddles!'

'I'm surprised you didn't notice the broken window as soon as you came in and switched the light on.'

'I didn't switch the light on immediately. I was pretending to be blind,' confessed Munro. 'I was trying to make a cup of tea without opening my eyes. I couldn't do it without peeping. Damn, I've spilled milk and sugar everywhere. I don't know how he manages without going mad,' he added pensively.

'You're very fond of John Steadman, aren't you?'

'More than that, I respect him. In some ways he's taught me more in the last year than all the time I was at university. At least – he's taught me different things and a different way of thinking.'

'If he gets out of hospital today, do you think he would like to stay here for a couple nights?' asked Maureen. 'He knows the house, and the spare room is next to the bathroom. The girls adore him.'

Munro thought that would be a good idea, if he could get Steadman to agree. Maureen bit her lip.

'I'm not doubting you about the window, Alan, but what if it wasn't kids? What if there really is a madman out there? I'm frightened. It's all right when you're here, but I would be no use on my own. We would never forgive ourselves if something happened to the girls. Couldn't we call somebody, you know, just to double check?'

'No. I'm telling you it's some kids – probably the same lot that sprayed PIG on the garage door last year,' Munro replied obstinately. He didn't like arguing with his wife, but the thought of Inspector Crouchley nosing around his house with a sarcastic sneer on his face was intolerable.

'Trust me, it'll be fine. I'll finish sweeping up and stick a bit of board over the broken window if you would make some toast. And I could do with a fresh cup of tea. There's too much milk in this one.'

They didn't speak over breakfast. Twice Maureen started but stopped when she saw the look on Alan's face. Like most wives, she knew her husband better than he did himself. She could tell that he was worried too. Eventually she broke the silence.

'Has anything been taken?'

Alan spread out his massive hands and shrugged.

'Nothing obvious. There isn't anything of value in our kitchen, unless you count the girls' paintings.'

He frowned.

'What is it?'

Munro pushed back his chair, heaved his bulk up from the table which groaned under the extra load.

'Damn and blast it,' he said, 'they've nicked the key.'

'Are you sure?' asked Maureen.

'Yes, positive. It was in the lock last night. Besides,' he continued grasping the handle, 'the door's not locked.'

Maureen visibly blanched.

'Don't worry love, I'll send the locksmith round this morning. Sergeant Grimble has the phone number, and I promise it will be the first thing I do when I get into work.'

He finished his tea and toast.

'That's better. I'll get the rest of the glass swept up.'

'I'll fetch an old newspaper to wrap up the pieces,' Maureen added.

Between them they tidied up the mess. Maureen still looked anxious.

'I promise I'll get a locksmith round this morning,' Alan said as he gave his wife a kiss on the cheek.

Maureen said nothing. Alan picked up his car keys. For the briefest of moments he paused. He was fairly certain that he had left the keys lying on top of yesterday's newspaper. He was about to ask Maureen if she had used that particular paper to wrap up the broken glass but he thought it best not to stress her further.

★ ★ ★

The door of the Eyesore was already wedged open to let in the fresh spring air.

'Good morning, Detective Sergeant Munro,' said Grimble, looking up from the mess of papers on his desk. 'I perceive from the careworn features and lack of that sunny, Scottish smile, all is not well. Come and confess to 'Father Grimble', that I might grant you absolution!'

Munro was not in the mood for fooling around.

'Have you got the phone number of the locksmith?' he asked.

'Indeed I have not one but two, both reputable and registered with the police.'

'Would you be a pal and get one to go round to my house and change the lock on the back door? Some kids smashed a window in the door and nicked the key last night.'

'Indeed, is that so?' said Grimble raising his eyebrows.

'Don't you start. I've had enough grief from Maureen already. Do me a favour – once you've got a locksmith organised, give her a call and say something reassuring – please?'

If it hadn't been for that last 'please' Grimble would have been sorely tempted to tell him to do it himself.

'It would be my pleasure to converse with your

delightful wife,' he replied carefully. 'There are two messages for you before you dash off.' Grimble shuffled through his papers. 'Number one - DS Fairfax says the forensic team are finished at Gorse Hill. Dr Gupta can have his house back, if you're happy with that. Number two, the hospital has rung and Detective Inspector Steadman is ready to be picked up at your convenience.'

Alan Munro brightened up at the second bit of news.

'You wouldn't phone…'

Before he could finish his sentence Sergeant Grimble interrupted.

'I'll arrange a locksmith and I'll phone your wife for you, but I will not speak with the obnoxious Anton Lemerise. Unless you want me to say to him: 'I'm arresting you for years of underhand, duplicitous criminality'. I'm sorry, but I refuse point blank to communicate with him.'

'I take it that's a 'no', then,' said Munro. 'I don't blame you – I'll go upstairs and do it myself.'

In a matter of minutes he returned.

'Of course the fat slug of a solicitor is still in his bed. His secretary is none too polite either. I'll be off to collect Steadman.'

Grimble nodded as he picked up the phone.

'Yes… He's here. May I have your name? Very good, sir, just hold the line.' Grimble put his hand over the receiver. 'A Mr Matt Taylor for you, he says it's urgent.'

Alan Munro took the phone.

'DS Munro here.'

'How's it going at your end?' said a chirpy voice. Munro instantly recognised the cockney accent.

'It's me, Matt Taylor - you know, from Carson's Recycling. You'll never guess what's turned up!'

'Tell me.'

'The blooming missing sharps box from Gorse Hill surgery, that's what. It's on the desk right in front of me. Want to know where it's been?'

The story could wait, thought Munro. 'Don't touch it. Don't let it out of your sight. I'll pick it up myself within the next couple of hours.'

'OK matey. I'll put the kettle on. Bring your blind chum with you, it might cheer him up.'

CHAPTER TWENTY FIVE

Alan Munro turned to leave the Eyesore and almost knocked DS Fairfax over.

'Oh, I am sorry, I didn't hear you come up behind me,' Munro said apologetically. 'Are you all right?'

'No damage done – is it OK for me to hand back the house to Dr Gupta?'

'I think so,' Munro replied. 'Just let me check my notes.'

He fished in his pocket and retrieved his tiny notebook. It looked ridiculous in his spade-sized hands. He could sense Fiona Fairfax staring at it.

'My girls gave me it last Christmas,' he said going bright red. 'I think it came out of a cracker.' He flicked through the pages. 'Here we are – did you find a computer other than Dr Gupta's laptop?'

'No, just that one. Do you want me to impound it and go through the hard drive?'

'No no. We'd need to get a further warrant and I'm not sure if it's worth the candle. Somehow I can't see

Alisha running her business from it, that's all. There's only one other thing. Did you find Dr Gupta's copy of the *Sunday Telegraph*?'

'No, only the magazine,' she replied. 'We went through the papers that were left for recycling and the most recent was Saturday's. It had the picture of the train crash on the front. Why do you want to find the newspaper?'

Munro explained about the other two broken windows. Grimble cleared his throat rather loudly; Munro took no notice.

'How's Inspector Steadman?' asked DS Fairfax.

'I'm going to the hospital now and...' he paused, 'we think the missing sharps box has turned up. I'm going to collect it as soon as I've picked up the boss.'

Grimble coughed again.

'I may even bring our desk sergeant some lozenges back to help with his throat.'

Fiona looked puzzled. Alan merely shrugged his shoulders and stepped out into the sunlight.

★ ★ ★

The hospital car park was full. It took Munro two circuits before a space became available. John Steadman was waiting in the small café by the main door. It was a drab, draughty space. The floors and walls were differing shades of beige. Black and white pictures of long-forgotten physicians and surgeons had been hung carelessly and were about as interesting as a washing line of nappies left out in the rain. Even the morning sunlight doing its best to stream through the steamed up windows did little to relieve the gloom.

Oblivious to his surroundings, Steadman sat silently nursing a mug of coffee and nibbling on one of his chocolate brownies.

'Morning sir, you're looking very dapper. How do you feel?'

'Quite ready to face the world, thank you. What news have you got?'

'Nothing much on your assailant, I'm afraid. Someone saw a man on a big motorbike on Quarry Hill and that's about it. We've found the driver but – surprise, surprise – he knows nothing. Phil the Shed has gone to ground in London and the third bloke is probably his cousin. If it is, he's another ne'er-do-well with a string of convictions. Once you've finished your coffee we'll go out to the car and I'll tell you the rest of my news.'

Steadman put one hand on the table and gently placed his mug beside it. He was still quite stiff and needed help to stand. Munro took his arm and slowly they walked out of the hospital.

'Have you thought about getting a guide dog? You know if you got something like a Rottweiler or a Doberman you might be a bit safer.'

'I think you'll find that all guide dogs have a remarkably even temperament. I believe it is a prerequisite for the job. But yes, I have wondered about a dog, maybe when I'm out of Jamaica Mansion. It's a thought, though – a guide dog with attitude.'

Steadman stumbled on a loose paving stone. 'You know we must look ridiculous,' he said regaining his balance.

'It's all right. I just tell people you're my uncle and you're over fond of the bottle.'

They reached the car without further incident. Steadman nestled into the soft leather of the seat.

'My, my, we are privileged – the armoured Audi again! Where to now?'

'Back to Carson's Recycling. The cockney git phoned half an hour ago to say the Gorse Hill Surgery sharps box has turned up. Talking of boxes, what did you do with all the tapes?'

'The armed officer has taken them back to the Eyesore. It will make Sergeant Grimble jump when he marches in brandishing a rifle.'

Munro didn't respond: Sergeant Grimble was not his most favourite person at the moment.

'What has Matt Taylor – that was his name, wasn't it - got to say for himself?'

'He said, 'Bring your blind chum, it might cheer him up.' I'm sure he'll give us the full story when we get there.

'Come on, move it!' Munro pressed the horn. 'There's a car double parked. I don't believe it - he's coming out of the shop with a packet of fags!' He pressed the horn again.

A burly man with three days' growth on his face came up to Munro's car and rapped on the window. Munro eased it down and without even looking at him held up his ID.

'Move it, or you're booked.'

'OK, OK - I'm going.'

Steadman shook his head. 'I think you enjoyed that.'

'Beats holding up a physics degree.'

They continued their drive. Steadman told him about his encounter with Ruby the domestic and the unusual happenings at the Gupta household.

'You know, Gupta was right when he said I wouldn't understand his 'open' marriage – I don't. Romping around in a mask with someone else's wife while your own wife is in the next room having it off with someone she doesn't know from Adam. No, it makes me sick,' Munro said pulling a face. 'I didn't think there was a swinger scene in Helmsmouth.'

'There is a dark underbelly of debauchery in every city, and I suspect Helmsmouth is no different,' Steadman replied.

'Before I forget, Maureen has asked if you would like to stay for a couple of nights. The girls would love it, and you would be doing me a favour. We had words this morning.'

Munro explained that the window in his back door had been smashed during the night and the key and his newspaper were missing. He didn't say anything about pretending to be blind.

'I told her it was just some kids from the estate hell-bent on mischief but she doesn't believe me.'

'Neither do I. Pull in.'

Munro was taken aback.

'Are you serious?'

'I've never been more serious in my life. What have I told you about making assumptions? I confess I don't know what it's about, but the safety of our officers and their families is paramount. It may well be some prank - I doubt it. Kids having a lark throw a stone through your window, then scarper. Whoever did this went on to take your key and your newspaper – doesn't sound like kids to me, Alan.'

Munro bit his lip.

'I know, I know – you're right. I just get pig-headed sometimes. What'll I do?'

'Start by phoning Maureen to see if she's all right. Once you've done that...' He paused, then continued, 'Blame me, if you like – tell her I insist that someone comes round to the house and takes a look.'

Alan, bright red with embarrassment, pulled over and took out his mobile phone. He swallowed hard as he heard the familiar voice of his wife.

'Hi, it's only me. I just wanted to...'

Before he could finish Maureen interrupted him.

'Oh Alan, you really are the most thoughtful and kind person! Sergeant Grimble explained how worried you were about me and that just to put my mind at rest, arranged for the forensics team to come and check the house over. They're here now. Kim Ho is in charge of things. She's lovely. Do you want a word with her?'

Munro didn't know how to reply. Steadman, who had overheard all of this, indicated he would like to speak.

'Hang on, Maureen - I think Inspector Steadman would like a word with her.'

'Hello Kim. We're certainly keeping you busy! DCI Long reckons you saved my life yesterday.'

'I wouldn't say that, sir. It was more luck than anything that they parked under the only birch trees for miles around.'

'You are too modest by far, Kim. I truly am grateful, luck or no luck. What about Munro's house, is it the same pattern as the others?'

'Exactly, sir.'

'Thought it might be. Can you do me a favour? Can you check if any of the glass is missing?'

'I doubt it, sir - there must be several hundred pieces.'

'Hmm, I wondered if that might be the case. What if we weigh all the pieces against the weight of the new pane? Provided the glass is the same thickness it should give us a rough estimate as to whether any of it has been taken.'

'What are you thinking, sir?'

'Just a hunch and the fragment of a memory…' He didn't mention his dreams. 'Keep in touch.' He handed the phone back to Munro.

'Well I'll be … Wait until I see Sergeant Grimble!'

'I doubt if he did it off his own bat. I suspect he had a discreet word with DCI Long. Grimble doesn't have the authority to send in the forensics team. Cheer up, Alan, it's all for the best. We coppers have to look after each other, even if some of us don't think we need it. Look where my foolhardiness landed me yesterday. A police badge doesn't stop us being human.'

Munro pulled back into the traffic.

'Have you thought about coming to stay with us for a couple of nights?'

'You know, Alan, I think I would like that very much. It would be lovely to see Maureen and the girls.'

Alan looked across at his colleague. The one thing he'll never do is 'see' Maureen and the girls again, he thought sadly.

★ ★ ★

They made good time to the old airfield where Carson's was situated. The tattered orange windsock was flapping in the breeze. The grumpy security guard barely looked up from his paper. 'You know the way,' was all he said. Matt Taylor opened the blue door before Sergeant Munro had time to knock.

'I thought it was you. I heard the car. Here, mind your step guv'nor, there's a bit of ledge. I've put the kettle on and I've bought a packet of Hobnobs.' He glanced up and down at Munro. 'I forgot how big you was – maybe I should've bought two! Tea or coffee? – I'm afraid the coffee's only instant.'

'A cup of tea and a biscuit sounds good to me,' said Steadman.

'I'll have tea as well,' Munro added.

'Here, have a seat.'

Matt Taylor had put a small patio table and three mismatched chairs in the corner of his office. Munro looked at the chairs dubiously before selecting the most sturdy. Steadman gently fingered his way over and with a little assistance from Munro eased himself into a seat.

'I brought them from home,' Matt Taylor continued. 'On a nice day me and the lads sit outside and have a bit of lunch – very civilised! Do either of you take sugar?'

Steadman shook his head. Munro shovelled a few spoonfuls into his mug.

'Tea's right in front of you and the Hobnobs are on your left,' Matt Taylor said helpfully. 'Now I expect you gents want to hear the story of the disappearing sharps box.'

'Go on,' said Munro. 'Blooming good cup of tea, by the way.'

'Thanks. Well, it's no great mystery really. You know I told you the engineer was out here fixing the incinerator. It's always a bit windy up here. He's got the instruction manual open in the back of his van, but the pages keep blowing over. So what does he do? He takes one of the sharps boxes to act as a paperweight. Here, have another biscuit. You ain't into double figures yet,' he said to Munro pushing the packet of Hobnobs in his direction. 'Where was I? Yeah, he used the box to hold down the pages, and when he was finished, instead of putting the box back with the rest of them like he should've, he shoves it into the van then puts his tool box in front of it. He had the following day off as it was his wedding anniversary. I reckon he was just tired from the night before if you get my meaning – lucky devil! Anyway he eventually picks up the message on his answer phone, checks his van and legs it up here double quick time. Fancy another cuppa?'

Both men declined.

'Is that the sharps box on the counter?'

'Signed, sealed and dated. That's it right enough. The handwriting's the same too, you can always tell Jean's scrawl.'

Munro took a large plastic evidence bag from his pocket and eased the box into it.

'We'll need to take your fingerprints, those of the engineer and the man who picked up the box on Monday morning. If you could give me their details.'

Matt Taylor beamed from ear to ear.

'Always like to be one step ahead, I do. I've written them all out with their addresses and phone numbers.'

'You've got an able brain, Mr Taylor,' said Steadman. 'May I ask what you're doing in a job like this?'

'I ask myself that sometimes. The pay is better than you think and all the management are knocking on pension age.' He gave Steadman a pointless wink. 'I may apply for a bit of promotion.'

'I'm sure we could write a letter commending your assistance with our investigation, couldn't we, Alan?'

Munro grunted his approval.

'That would be real kind. I thought you was a gent when I first saw you. Look,' he said, turning to Munro, 'no hard feelings about the other day. I mean, some days I don't speak to anyone from dawn to dusk. You get out of the way of being polite, not to mention being a bit lonely.'

Steadman could fully empathise with the latter sentiment. They shook hands, and the two police officers got back into the car.

'Yes! You beauty!' said Munro triumphantly as he fastened his seat belt. 'I'll nail the arrogant git and his so-called 'open' marriage!'

'Don't count your chickens,' Steadman cautioned, 'but I confess I'm optimistic too. The one thing Aaron Gupta did not expect was for us to retrieve his sharps box. Let's hope it doesn't disappoint.'

Munro tooted the horn gaily as they approached the barrier. Without looking up, the guard raised the barrier. In the rear-view mirror Munro saw him gesticulating from the safety of his kiosk.

'Charming,' said Munro, 'he's just given us a two-fingered salute!'

Nothing could dent his spirits, not even the motorcyclist who cut him up on the way back to the Eyesore.

★ ★ ★

Out of hospital so soon! I thought you would enjoy playing the sick role, at least for a few days. Your Scottish chauffeur seems very pleased with himself. What grubby bit of filth has he unearthed? It will give me great pleasure to wipe the smile off his face. And believe me, John Steadman, when I'm finished with you no-one will be smiling – apart from me, of course.

CHAPTER TWENTY SIX

The two men drove back into Helmsmouth, both deep in their own thoughts. Munro was as excited as a child on Christmas Eve, desperate to open the sharps box to see what treasures it might hold. His good humour was almost tangible. Munro was a difficult man not to like; what you saw was what you got. If he was happy, he smiled; if he was angry, look out! He wore his heart not so much on his sleeve as stuck to his forehead. Steadman liked that.

They had decided as a priority to deliver the box to Kim Ho and her team. Hopefully she would have finished at Munro's house, or at least have been able to deputise any remaining work. The forensic laboratory was next to the police mortuary in a shapeless grey building. DS Munro delivered the box and filled in the required forms. His protests were ignored and he was not allowed into the lab, nor could he persuade anyone to open the box there and then.

'Spoilsports, the lot of them,' he said as he got back into the car.

Munro didn't notice Steadman's increasing anxiety as they drove on to the Eyesore. Steadman had not set foot in the building since the shooting. Would his colleagues gush with sympathy, patronise him or ignore him? All of these prospects filled him with dread. Maybe I'm becoming paranoid, he thought. He tried to put himself in their place but failed. He realised that it would be his own behaviour that ultimately determined their reactions. It couldn't be like it was before; he had lost his sight and his wife. How should he act? For a man who usually managed to control his emotions he was not finding this easy. No doubt he would welcome the familiar sounds and smells of the place. Heaven knows how much of his life he had spent there. But he was no longer a part of it, no longer part of the fabric of the building and the team of people that worked there. It was going to be difficult.

'I'll bet you're looking forward to being back at the Eyesore, sir.'

'Yes, on balance I probably am,' Steadman replied with some trepidation.

'You'll be fine. Everybody will be dying to see you.'

'That's probably what I'm most afraid of – that and the fact that I'll feel like an unwelcome intruder.'

'Get away with you! Wasn't it you who said 'we coppers always look after each other'? Trust me on this one, sir, it'll be great.'

Munro stopped the car outside a mini-market.

'Won't be a moment, sir, there's a wee something I need to buy.'

Steadman's thoughts went back to the sharps box. If it contained nothing but surgery waste, where did that leave the investigation? Dr Robinson, Reena, Cassandra, Jean? The case began to look untidy again and as if it might unravel. What would be the best possible scenario? A large needle covered in Alisha's blood and a big syringe with Dr Gupta's bloodstained finger prints, perhaps? That would be too much to hope for. If Gupta was the murderer he would surely have been more careful. And if it was Gupta, it still left the question 'why'? A pre-meditated murder has to have a motive. And what about the broken window?

'Sorry about that, sir, there was a queue at the till,' said Munro as he shut the car door.

'Got what you were after?' inquired Steadman.

'I hope so,' replied Munro.

They arrived at the Eyesore and managed to find a parking place close to the main door.

'Do you want to go solo or take my arm, sir?'

'I think the ignominy of falling is worse than the embarrassment of holding on to you, but I'll take my cane as well. It may be useful to fend off the crowds!'

Steadman got out of the car and stood for a minute. He took a deep breath, checked his tie and patted his hair down at the back.

'Let's go.'

He tried to remember how many steps there were up to the door. Was it seven or eight? He could visualise in his mind's eye the polished brass hand rail with its curved end – a too-convenient hook for revellers to hang the remains of their weekend take-aways on. Munro pushed open the door and went in first. Sergeant Grimble barely glanced up before bending down and retrieving from under his desk a Second World War helmet with 'ARP Warden' written on it. He donned his helmet, adjusted the chin strap and looked Munro straight in the eye.

'Just in case you were a bit upset at my intervention,' he said tapping the edge of the helmet.

'You daft bugger! Here, I've brought you a peace offering.' He handed over the tin of Scottish shortbread that he had just bought.

'Absolutely unnecessary,' Grimble replied, 'but I'm pleased to see the other gift that you've brought with you.'

Grimble got out of his seat and waddled round to the other side of his desk; a notably rare occurrence. He clasped Steadman's hand.

'That's twice now I never thought I would see you again. Don't make it a third, my heart won't stand the strain.'

Steadman shook Grimble's hand. He struggled to reply.

'You're not the only one who thought I'd never be back here.'

'C'mon, before you two get maudlin. Let's go and find DCI Long.'

The next hour was an emotional roller coaster for

John Steadman. Word had got round that he was in the building. He shook hands, said the same things over and over again. Yes, it was nice to meet his old colleagues, but he knew he was now an outsider. He could feel his own despair and resentment suffocating him from the inside. Why should he feel guilty? He hadn't asked to be shot and blinded, but he felt it nonetheless.

DCI Long could see that he was tiring and called a halt to the gathering. Under the pretext of wanting a private word with DS Munro he shooed the other officers away.

'Come in both of you. I hear you've found the sharps box.'

Munro was happy to recount the tale of the missing sharps box, but far less so when it came to the break-in at his own house.

'I presume that Inspector Steadman has given you a sufficient dressing-down, so I won't add to your misery other than to say, don't let your enthusiasm get in the way of common sense. I could in fact address that remark to both of you.'

It was a close call as to who between Steadman and Munro had the reddest face.

'John,' he continued, 'you're looking worn out. What are your plans for the rest of the day?'

'Ben was supposed to be organising lunch. I haven't heard from him yet'. He pressed the button on the side of his watch; 'twelve fifteen' said the tinny voice.

'I'll go and call him,' said Munro, leaving the other two alone in DCI Long's office.

'How are you really, John?'

'Confused, angry, despondent, sore, tired - but otherwise well.'

'Thank you for looking after Munro – he's doing a good enough job. It's not a straightforward case.'

'I agree. I don't believe in premonitions.' He paused. 'It's that blasted window that's irking me. I can't get it out of my mind.'

Before he could elaborate Munro returned.

'That's all sorted. Maureen's made soup and chicken sandwiches for you. I reckon Ben was still asleep when I called. He'll meet us back at my place. I offered to pick him up, but he said he'd rather walk.'

'That doesn't surprise me. The last couple of times Ben was in a police car he had been arrested at anti-capitalist protests.'

'Good for him!' exclaimed Munro. 'I mean for protesting,' he stammered, 'not for being arrested.'

'I think we ought to go,' said Steadman.

The sky had clouded over and a fine rain was falling. Steadman struggled to keep awake in the car. Munro's two daughters had not seen their 'Uncle' John since the shooting. They stood at the window waiting patiently with suppressed excitement. As soon as the car pulled into the drive they could contain themselves no longer and ran out to greet him.

'Steady, you two! Uncle John's a bit tired.'

'We're going to look after him,' they replied.

Taking a hand each, they dragged him towards the

door like two eager puppies out for a walk. Fortunately Maureen came and intervened. She gave him a kiss, told him to mind the step and steered him into a comfortable chair.

'I'll be off – loads of paperwork,' said Munro as he got back into the car. 'See you this evening. You girls be good!'

'Why are you wearing dark glasses? The sun's gone away and it's started to rain,' asked Annie.

Her mother tried to hush her, but Steadman held up a hand.

'No, it's a fair question,' he said. 'I wear them to let people know I'm blind.'

'Can you not see anything?' Melanie chipped in.

'Only very bright lights, and they're just a dim blur. I still know that the two of you are just as beautiful as ever.'

'How do you know, Uncle John?'

'Magic! And talking of magic I think I hear someone at the door and unless I'm mistaken, it is my son Ben.'

The girls were quite unsure what to make of the tall young man that entered. They were so used to seeing their father with short hair, wearing a suit and tie. And here was Ben, his hair in a pony tail, a short goatee beard, faded jeans, a leather jerkin and a checked neckerchief tied loosely round his neck. The contrast was sharp; little wonder that the two girls tried to hide behind their mother.

'Don't be silly, you two, come and shake hands with Ben.'

'Let me see – you must be Melanie.'

He shook her hand very formally. She was amazed to find that when she let go she was holding a large golden chocolate coin.

'And you, therefore, must be Annie.'

She was greeted with the same sleight of hand.

'You can eat those after lunch!' Maureen added in a not quite stern tone.

The ice was broken. Maureen served the soup in mugs along with the chicken sandwiches. Steadman excused himself after lunch and, with his son's help, lay down for a rest. He fell into a dreamless sleep almost immediately.

Ben entertained the girls for the rest of the afternoon to Maureen's relief as it was now raining too heavily for them to play outside. Ben did card tricks, guessing games and produced a torrent of sugar mice and chocolate coins from their ears, noses, pockets and, in one remarkable feat of dexterity, their shoes. At four o'clock he tapped gently on his father's door.

'Sorry to wake you, Dad, but I'm off.'

'Going so soon, Ben?'

'Yep – I've managed to get a cheap flight at midnight. The circus is due to open again in two days' time. Apart from anything else, Melanie and Annie have virtually cleaned me out of treats!'

'It was good of you to come. Pass me my wallet – at least allow me to pay for your tickets.'

'There's no need, Frank has been more than generous. However if you insist…'

Steadman knew his son lived pretty much from hand to mouth. He never complained. As he said, 'It's my choice'. Ben helped his father get up and dressed.

'Are you sure you're going to be safe?' he asked. 'This nutter's really got it in for you.'

'No, I'm not safe, but I'm damned if I'm going to let him spoil what's left of my life. He'll try again. I know he will, because his pride is wounded. But I think he's getting careless – either that or desperate. And I'll take my chances, just as you do, Ben. Like father like son, I'm afraid.'

The rain was now pouring down.

'Won't you wait until Alan gets home?' pleaded Maureen, 'I'm sure he would run you down to the station.'

Ben pulled a large black leather hat and some waterproof leggings out of his rucksack.

'No no – I like walking in the rain.'

He thanked Maureen profusely for the lunch, hugged his father, tweaked both the girls' noses, magically producing two lollipops, and strode off into the rainstorm. There was a low rumble of thunder in the distance.

The sky was inky black and it was almost dark when Alan Munro came home. The heavy rain did little to dampen his spirits. Seeing that he was keen to talk to Steadman, Maureen ushered the girls into the kitchen on the pretext of getting them to help prepare the evening meal.

'Well – what has Kim Ho found in the box of delights?' Steadman asked.

'Among all the dental needles and syringes there was one much larger hypodermic needle.'

'Interesting,' Steadman said, trying to keep the anticipation out of his voice.

'Wait, it gets better. Kim found a fleck of blood in the bore of the needle. It's the same group as Alisha Gupta's. And...' he continued, 'there's a tube of lubricating jelly, completely wiped of fingerprints of course, but definitely laced with some local anaesthetic. Kim put a spot on the crook of my elbow and within a few minutes the skin was quite numb.'

'No big syringe?'

'Alas no, but it's not looking too rosy for Dr Gupta.'

Steadman frowned, and bit his thumb nail.

'No – but we've got no direct proof yet. Lemerise would argue that Jean for example, was equally placed to dispose of a needle and a tube of jelly in the sharps box. We've got to think of all the possibilities.'

'True' replied Munro, 'but I know who my money is on. Oh, and for what it's worth Kim said to tell you that the new pane of glass for my door was ten percent heavier than the old one.'

Steadman tried to calculate what size ten per cent might be. Perhaps because he was tired or because he was not yet fully recovered, he kept getting confused between square inches and inches squared. Apart from sending the cruet set flying, their evening meal passed uneventfully.

'Uncle John, will you read us a bedtime story?' asked Melanie.

'I can't read you one, but I can certainly tell you one.'

The girls dragged him off to their bedroom and plonked him in a chair.

'Are you ready? Good. Well, this is a story that happened long ago.'

'Uncle John, I hope this story has a happy ending.'

'Hush, Annie, let Uncle John go on.'

Steadman told his tale, complete with happy ending. Melanie sighed.

'That was a lovely story,' she said in a sleepy voice. Annie was already gently snoring. Maureen was standing by the door

'My – you're quite the story teller. I think we should get you round here every night. Did you make it up?' she asked as she helped him back to the sitting room. Steadman was a bit embarrassed.

'Yes, Ben used to love me telling him stories.'

'We should write them down.'

'I hate to interrupt,' said Alan, 'but there's a bottle of Glenfiddich that is crying out for some attention. Do you fancy a nightcap?'

They chatted for a little while. Steadman could barely keep his eyes open. Maureen took him up to his room and helped him get his bearings. Thoughtfully she had cleared plenty of space for him.

'Can you remember the layout of the bathroom?' she asked.

'I think so,' he replied. 'Bath on the left, wash basin directly in front of you and the loo in the corner.'

'That's it. I'll leave you to it. Shout if you want anything.'

It wasn't long before he was in bed and soundly asleep.

'I'll lock up, I think I could do with an early night myself,' said Munro. His wife agreed.

The new pane of glass still had grubby fingerprints on it. He turned the key in the replacement lock. It was a bit stiff. The shiny key looked vaguely familiar. Munro frowned and retrieved the old spare key from the hook on the wall. He tried the old key, and the door unlocked. Swearing softly under his breath, he replaced both keys. Should he tell Maureen? When he got to the bedroom he could tell by her breathing that she too was already fast asleep.

A little past midnight, the phone rang. Steadman rolled over and stretched out an arm before remembering where he was. He could hear Munro's voice.

'What? I don't believe it, are you sure..? I'm on my way!'

Seconds later he burst into Steadman's room.

'Are you awake, John? That was the Eyesore. They've had a call from Jean. She's round at Dr Gupta's house. He's dead – his throat's been cut! We'd better get round there.'

There was an almighty crash of thunder and all the

lights went out. Without thinking, Munro asked, 'Will you manage to get dressed in the dark?'

CHAPTER TWENTY SEVEN

It was on his lips. In the darkness he almost said, 'Welcome to my world', but it wouldn't be fair. There was no welcome in this world of perpetual shadow.

'I'm sorry..., I wasn't thinking,' stammered Munro.

'That's all right,' Steadman responded in a conciliatory tone. 'I reckon I'll manage better than you. I've had a bit more practice.'

Steadman had meticulously laid out his next day's clothes and was dressed well before Munro who had gone to look for a flashlight. The ever-resourceful Maureen was already in the kitchen wearing a head-torch and boiling a kettle on a camping stove.

'Coffee before you go – sorry, it's only instant.'

The two men sipped a few scalding mouthfuls.

'I suppose you'll be gone all night,' said Maureen.

'More than likely,' her husband replied. He was getting agitated.

There was another rumble and flash. In that brief, stark moment of illumination Munro glimpsed the scrawny outline of his colleague, hunched and clutching his mug with both hands. I should have let him sleep, he thought. But he was also dreading what the night would bring. Another body, another violent death – he was going to need all the help he could get.

Between the flashes of lightning the two men got into the car. Both were soaked through. Even with the wipers on at double speed it was barely possible to drive. The lack of street lights didn't help.

'It's my fault, I should have kept him in custody,' Munro blurted out.

'That's nonsense. Lemerise would have had him bounced out in no time. The real question is, did he cut his own throat or did somebody do it for him?'

'I only got the briefest of messages. I can't see Dr Gupta as a throat-slasher. If he killed his wife and thought we could prove it and believed suicide was the only way out, he would have chosen something a lot less messy. For one thing his suits are too expensive. My God, but I can hardly see a thing in front of me!'

The car crawled along. The noise from the rain and now hail pelting on the roof was deafening.

'There was certainly no shortage of potential weapons in his house,' Munro continued. 'He had a fine collection of daggers and swords on the wall going up the stairs.'

Steadman said nothing. It was good to let his young colleague go over the possibilities. Besides he had thoughts of his own. Munro continued:

'If he didn't do it himself, who out of our little gang could have? Jean was too much in love with him and I can't see her as a murderer. Reena if she was drunk enough, I suppose - she certainly caught Cassandra Gupta a beauty with her handbag in the waiting room at the Eyesore. I can't make Cassandra out at all. She's cold-blooded, but why would she want to kill her brother? That only leaves Dr Robinson. Poor little trembling Dr Robinson – he's lost his mistress. If he thinks Dr Gupta's guilty he might just have a poke at him!'

Steadman was only half listening.

'I don't think I've heard of any doctor turned killer who's despatched his victim by brute force, have you?' he asked.

'There's got to be a first time,' Munro said hopefully. 'What do you think?'

'All sorts of things, but they keep getting jumbled. Maybe once I get the feel of the place I'll understand better. Didn't you say right at the start of this investigation it seemed like two jigsaw puzzles that have got the pieces muddled?'

Steadman began to hum a little tune, a minuet by Bach. His long fingers tapped out the rhythm on his thigh. The sound was barely discernible but in his head a harpsichord was playing, the notes weaving in and out, up and down in their complicated progression. The music was but a background. In his mind's eye the characters that Munro had painted were acting out each possible scenario. Every so often he would stop drumming his fingers. Under his breath he would mutter, 'That can't be right' or 'That's a possibility but only if...' then the minuet would pick up from where it had left off and the drumming of his fingers would resume.

They came to a crossroads normally controlled by traffic signals. Munro braked and skidded to avoid a lorry that had no intention of stopping.

'Better put on the flashing lights, though it seems ludicrous if I can't go faster than ten miles per hour.'

Steadman didn't hear him. He was lost in his own thoughts and music. Munro looked across at him. Even by the faint glow of the dashboard light he could see that pursuing a conversation was pointless.

No matter how often Steadman re-arranged the facts, he kept coming to the same conclusion. Could it be that the two murders, a husband and wife, killed within days of each other in the same house, were not related? It was an uncomfortable conclusion. Was it just coincidence? He didn't like coincidences. But taken together, they didn't add up. However, if you teased them apart then they started to make sense. The first crime, premeditated and cleverly constructed so as not to look like murder. The second, and here he agreed with Munro, Dr Gupta did not seem the sort of person to cut his own throat, a violent crime, a desperate act filled to the brim and overflowing with emotion. Retaliation for the death of Alisha Gupta? Surely not: as a motive that only put the feeble Dr Robinson in the frame. He shook his head. What about a rejected Reena or a disillusioned Cassandra? How could he judge? Everything he knew about this case was second hand. He clenched his fists in exasperation. The music in his head stopped, but he could have sworn that somewhere in the distance he heard the sound of breaking glass.

'We're almost there, sir,' said Munro as he swerved the Audi into the Guptas' drive, narrowly missing a motorcyclist.

A bedraggled uniformed officer waved them in.

'The gang's all here by the looks of things, sir. There must be half a dozen police cars – even a mobile incident unit and a generator. There's some light in the house.' Munro gave the wipers a final flick. 'Good grief, they've even managed to get a pop-up tent over the front door. And somebody has driven a decrepit old Volvo estate on to the lawn!'

'That would be Dr Rufus. It's not that he's a bad driver, it's just that his mind is always on other things,' Steadman explained.

The rain and hail had stopped. The air remained moist, charged with electricity and smelling of sulphur. In the distance thunder continued to rumble and groan. Munro led Steadman into the bright warmth of the mobile incident unit. DS Fairfax was there, comforting a sobbing woman. Munro felt torn. He bit his lip and exchanged glances with Fairfax.

'Look, I really must get into the house and see what's going on. Would you mind, sir, if I left you here with DS Fairfax?'

'Not at all,' replied Steadman. 'Is that Jean?' he asked Munro in a whisper.

'Yes.'

'Would you mind if I had a chat with her?'

'No, by all means go ahead.'

DS Fairfax brought Steadman a chair and introduced him to Jean. She looked up with bloodshot eyes.

'Are you the blind detective?'

'I gather that's what the papers are calling me. Do you think you're up to answering a few questions?'

She sobbed again, but nodded her head. DS Fairfax sat beside her and squeezed her hand.

'Go ahead, sir - she's indicated it will be OK.'

'Jean, I'm aware of your relationship with Dr Gupta and the events around Alisha's death. However I know very little of what's occurred tonight. Can you tell me exactly what happened and how you came to be here?'

Jean blew her nose and began.

'He sent me a text saying that he was allowed back into his house. He was having dinner with that solicitor friend of his, but he wanted to meet me after. I assumed that he would come round to my flat. I texted him back to say that would be fine. I heard nothing more. At ten I texted him, and again at ten thirty. By eleven I was getting worried so I rang him, first on his mobile then on his home number. I didn't want to ring Lemerise, he gives me the creeps. I thought I would go round to the house to see if he was OK. The lights were on upstairs.

No-one answered the door. I have a key and let myself in. He didn't answer when I called his name. There was a red streak on the wall but I didn't think anything of it. His feet were sticking out of the bathroom door...' Her voice trailed off.

'Take your time,' said Fairfax.

'He was lying face down in a pool of blood,' Jean continued. 'In fact there was blood everywhere. I tried to lift his head...it was only then...it was awful.'

Jean broke down. Steadman knew that it was best to not to say anything. Eventually she regained enough composure to continue.

'I've never seen anything like it. It was horrible – all the muscles and sinews, even his windpipe had been slashed open. Inspector Steadman, my father was a funeral director and I worked with him for a time. I've seen lots of dead bodies, but they were all sort of peaceful, if you know what I mean. But this... how could someone have done that to him? I know he could be difficult but he was kind to me. I think I was the only person that understood him.'

'What did you do then?'

'I screamed and ran out of the room. I sat at the bottom of stairs for – I don't know – maybe five minutes, just trying to think straight. Then I phoned 999.' She finished with a sigh and a sniff.

'That's how we found her, sir,' Fairfax added.

Steadman could imagine her sitting there on the stairs with her arms clasped round her knees gently rocking and weeping.

'May I ask you two further questions? Did you see any possible weapon?'

'No, but there was so much blood, and I didn't like to roll him over or even touch him again.'

'Final question – do you think Dr Gupta could have committed suicide?'

'No, no – he wasn't like that. I know Alisha's dead, but he didn't love her. He told me that. He had me – he cared for me. I loved him…' She burst into tears.

In his mind's eye Steadman tried to picture Jean: a woman just past her prime but still attractive, and now desperately trying to hold herself together. Like Munro, he could not visualise her as a cold-blooded killer. She wasn't acting; if anything she was being unashamedly honest.

'Can I go home?' she asked.

'I'm not sure,' replied DS Fairfax. 'I'll have to check. You know that there's still no electricity?'

'I've got some candles. I just want to go to bed.'

'I'll take full responsibility,' Steadman interjected. 'Jean, don't leave your flat. I'm sure Sergeant Munro will want to speak with you again.'

WPC Jennings was on driver's duty. Gently she helped Jean into her coat and took her out to the waiting police car.

'Would you like a cup of tea, sir?' asked DS Fairfax.

'No, I'm all right for the moment thank you. What the heck is that noise outside?'

Two women could be heard shouting and one of them was swearing at the top of her voice.

'Unless I'm mistaken it sounds like Cassandra and Reena, Dr Gupta's sister and sister-in-law.'

'Ah! The two ugly sisters, as Munro calls them, although I'll have to take his word for it.'

The door banged open.

'Sorry, sarge, I couldn't stop them,' said the soaking constable who was on duty at the gates.

'That's OK. Sergeant Fairfax, would you be kind enough to get these ladies a couple of seats?'

'Who the hell are you?' asked Reena.

'I am Detective Inspector John Steadman. Now, please both of you sit down.'

There was a calm authority in his voice that both women recognised. Reluctantly they sat down.

'I presume that you are Cassandra Gupta and Reena Soraya?'

'What the fuck is this – a game of blind man's buff?'

'An unworthy comment I think, Reena.'

'How do you know I'm Reena?'

'Let's just say that's why I'm a detective.' He didn't like to say that it was her breath, which reeked of stale alcohol.

'What's happened to my brother-in-law?'

'All in good time. Tell me exactly where you were and what you were doing between nine o'clock and midnight?'

The two women exchanged anxious looks. The situation was unnerving and slightly surreal. The whole town was in complete darkness apart from the odd building like the Eyesore and Helmsmouth General, which had their own generators. And of course 47 Gorse Hill, where half a dozen police cars with their flashing blue lights and a portable generator made Dr Gupta's clinic stand out like a freak light show. Both women lived not far away and had been drawn to the scene by the wailing sirens and the lights. They had arrived flustered and hostile. Now they sat in silence, facing an ill-looking, thin man wearing dark glasses. But this was Steadman's domain and the two women both felt it would be futile, even dangerous, to cross him.

'I was out drinking at Hennessey's Night Club with some friends, if you must know. I can give you their names. I was no sooner in the house when there was an enormous clap of thunder and the lights went out. I watched the storm and saw all the cop cars racing about. When the rain stopped I could see they were here. Do you want my friends' names now?'

Reena twisted her bright red stiletto heels on the floor. Her coat fell open, and DS Fairfax glimpsed a dress that was too short and a neckline that was too low.

'Later,' Steadman replied. 'Now your turn Cassandra – same question.'

Cassandra hesitated. 'I was at home by myself.'

'What were you doing?'

'Watching television.'

'What was on?'

'I can't remember – some sort of nature programme.'

'You'll have to do better than that, 'some sort of nature programme' is on every night.'

'I watched the news.'

'What was the headline?'

There was no answer.

'Why don't you tell me the truth? I can assure you, Cassandra, that it will be a lot easier for you.'

'I want my solicitor.'

'Alas, I am informed that all the phone lines are down as well the electricity. Don't you want to know what's happened to your brother?'

Cassandra looked at the floor and bit her thumb.

'Something awful has happened, hasn't it?'

'Yes,' said Steadman in a flat voice, 'that's precisely why I need to know where you were late this evening.'

'What's happened to Aaron?' shrieked Reena.

Steadman held up his hand. 'In a moment – be patient please! Let Cassandra speak.'

In a very small voice Cassandra said:

'I was sitting in my car in the rain outside Jean's house just watching and waiting. I thought he would come, he always does. I often just sit there – watching.'

There was something sad and pathetic in her voice. Steadman knew there was no point in asking her why.

'When did Jean leave?' he asked softly.

'At two minutes past eleven. I followed her here then went home. I can see the house from my apartment. I went to bed but couldn't read. Then the lights went out. I sat staring out of my window at the rain and the lightning. I could see the blue flashing lights, but without the street lamps and with all the rain it was difficult to work out where they were. When the storm passed I knew. I was certain that something had happened to my brother.'

'Aaron Gupta is dead,' said John Steadman. 'I'm sorry.'

'That bitch killed him – first my sister, now him!' Reena yelled as she tried to stand up. DS Fairfax put a firm hand on her shoulder.

'Not that simple, I'm afraid,' said Steadman.

'I'll kill her myself, God help me I will!' Reena screamed.

'For goodness sake can't someone give her some more booze and shut her up?' Cassandra muttered.

'He should have married me – none of this would have happened!' Reena staggered to her feet. DS Fairfax caught her and sat her down again.

'How did he die?' Cassandra asked.

'He was murdered. Someone cut his throat. Brutal and violent, but death was probably instantaneous.'

Reena and Cassandra sat there ashen-faced, silent, not daring to look at one another.

'Reena, your alibi will be checked and someone will take a formal statement later in the day.'

'I'll get someone to drive you home,' DS Fairfax added.

'I can manage perfectly well,' said Reena.

'Not unless you want to be arrested for drunk

driving,' replied DS Fairfax steering her out of the incident unit.

'Cassandra, there is no way your alibi can be corroborated unless someone saw your car. However I have no reason to disbelieve you. I expect you'll want to see your brother's body, but that won't be possible until after the post mortem. We'll let you know as soon as possible.'

Cassandra was moaning softly. She had screwed up her scarf into a tight ball, biting on it, trying very hard not to cry out loud.

'Can I go?' she asked eventually.

'Is Sergeant Fairfax here?' asked Steadman.

'Just back,' said Fiona closing the door behind her. 'Do you want me to arrange transport?'

'I'll manage – unlike Reena, I'm stone cold sober. Inspector Steadman, do you think the same person that killed Alisha also killed my brother?'

Steadman shrugged. 'Too early to say, but off the record I think it unlikely. I'm not even sure the two crimes are related.'

CHAPTER TWENTY EIGHT

Alone in the incident unit, Steadman stood up and carefully started pacing the floor trying to get his bearings. There was not a lot of room and he held his white cane close in front of him. He could conjure up from memory a vague image of what the inside of the van was like. Very slowly he moved forwards until he bumped into the opposite wall, then turned round and moved backwards, counting each step. He repeated the process from side to side. He located the door, the chairs and the desk. An upturned waste paper bin nearly sent him sprawling.

'What would you like to do now, sir?' asked DS Fairfax as she re-entered the van.

'I would very much like to go inside Dr Gupta's house, if that's possible. I know it sounds odd, but I would just like to get a feel of the place, soak up some of the atmosphere. There's something not right here and I can't place it. None of them stand to benefit from either of the deaths. It doesn't make sense.'

DS Fairfax guided Steadman towards the house. Inside the pop-up tent she helped him into the plastic over-shoes and white overalls.

'Probably best if you don't go upstairs. There's cables, photographers and forensics crawling over everything. I can explain the layout downstairs if you like but remember there's no lights.' It was out before she realised what she had said.

The large oak front door opened into a vestibule, then on to a long corridor. On either side were two evenly proportioned rooms. One was Dr Gupta's study, the other the dining room. Behind the study, running at right angles to the main corridor another passage had been formed, linking the house to the clinic, and continued on behind the dining room to a conservatory. Beyond these lay further rooms and, at the rear of the house, the kitchen and utility room.

Hard quarry tiles by the front door soon gave way to carpet. Even through the plastic over-shoes Steadman could feel the deep pile. The corridor was broad and the strip of carpet didn't fully extend from side to side. The nylon ball on the end of his cane slid on the wooden floorboards until it hit the skirting board. Steadman gripped the cane more tightly so as not to lose control. He could hear voices upstairs, but there was no sign of DS Munro. Halfway up the corridor were two heavy doors directly opposite each other. Neither was locked. Gently he pushed open the door on his right. He was greeted by a draught of cold air laced with the smell of candle wax and apples. Probably the dining room, he thought. This was soon confirmed as his cane rattled between the legs of a dining chair. Slowly he paced round the table. It was long with rounded ends. He counted twelve chairs.

Very cautiously he paced up and down the room, his cane delicately weaving from side to side. In the bay window he stumbled into a single large winged chair. It felt cold, almost damp. At the far end of the room were two glass cabinets. Without opening them, he couldn't tell if they were for drinks or display. Opposite the door there appeared to be a large fireplace. Steadman sensed that the fire had never been lit and that the chimney was probably blocked. He didn't touch the mantle shelf for fearing of disturbing any ornaments. There were several sideboards. He bumped heavily into one, causing the cutlery inside to jangle. The room felt unfriendly and Steadman suspected that it was seldom used.

The room opposite was quite different. It smelt of leather, wood ash and coffee. The back wall, as well as the one in front of him, seemed to be covered in books. Steadman pulled one out. The binding felt expensive, but the pages were thin and of poor quality. He thought it might be a bound journal.

Slowly he progressed round the room. There was a very large desk with an equally large office chair. His fingers lightly caressed the top of the desk. It was covered in papers. Again Steadman paced back and forth and up and down, counting each step. In the bay window was a soft leather chair, its arms and back worn smooth with constant use. In front of the chair there was a footstool. Steadman was sorely tempted to settle down and have a nap. He liked this room: it was very masculine. But something in the room was troubling him. He began to retrace his steps.

* * *

'You said John Steadman's in the house?' It was the deep booming voice of DCI Long.

'He's downstairs somewhere,' replied Fiona Fairfax, shining her torch down the length of the corridor. The light picked out the gilt frames of numerous oil paintings and glinted off a large crystal chandelier hanging from the high ceiling.

'See what I mean about him having expensive tastes?' chipped in Munro.

'I'm in the study,' Steadman said loudly.

'Nice room, lovely books. I wonder if he bought them by the yard or actually read them?' said DCI Long as he shone his torch round the laden shelves. DS Fairfax wasn't so sure about the room; Munro thought the whole place reeked of decadence.

'What has Dr Rufus made of the body?' Steadman asked.

'It's definitely Dr Gupta, although it was difficult to see his face at first with all the blood,' Munro replied. 'Dr Rufus reckons it was just one determined slash delivered from behind, cutting Gupta's throat from left to right. Jesus – it was revolting. I've never seen a severed windpipe. It looked like the hose from a vacuum cleaner, except full of blood clots. Rufus was in his element! I'm afraid I was a bit of big girl's blouse and had to get some fresh air. By the way Fiona, the vomit on the lawn is mine, if anybody's wondering.'

'What about a weapon?' inquired Steadman.

'They found it lying under the body. It probably won't surprise you that it was a piece of broken glass,' Munro replied.

'And I guess that it was wrapped in some newspaper – in this case the front page of Dr Gupta's Sunday Telegraph with his name scribbled in the corner. Am I right?' Steadman asked.

'It's a blood-soaked bit of newspaper right enough. Forensics have taken it away.'

'You look worried, John. What's bothering you?' asked DCI Long.

'There's got to be something else – something's missing,' he replied.

'Dr Gupta's wig is missing, if that's any help. He's as bald as a coot!' Munro added.

Steadman raised his head sharply. 'Did you say that Dr Gupta was wearing a wig?'

'Not now he isn't, but he must have been when he was attacked. There's no blood on his scalp and I've never seen him with anything but a full head of hair. It would appear that whoever slashed his throat took his wig, for some reason. A trophy, perhaps?'

'Is all the power still off?'

'Yes, why...'

'Alan, get in the car – now! Grab an officer on your way and go home before someone tries to kill your daughter!'

'My daughter? Murdered? You're joking, aren't you?'

'It's Annie's life, for God's sake – it's the wig and the broken window. Don't just stand there. Explanations can wait – GO!'

Munro let out a terrible oath and ran as fast as he could out of the house. He grabbed Fiona Fairfax on the way, almost lifting her off her feet as he went past. The car doors slammed. The gears crunched and gravel scattered in all directions as Munro booted the Audi out of the drive.

'Hubert,' said Steadman. DCI Long's ears pricked up; only very rarely was he ever addressed by his first name. 'Can you send squad cars round to the other two houses that reported their windows broken?'

DCI Long didn't question why. He knew John Steadman too well.

'Stay here, John - I'll be back for you in a minute.'

All thoughts of what had been troubling him in the study vanished. He could only think about Annie. Poor little Annie, so brave during all her treatment and now so proud of her new hair. An expensive wig that could cost her her life, if his theory was right. Steadman prayed that Munro would not be too late.

Two cars raced out of the drive with their sirens

wailing and lights flashing. DCI Long came back into the study.

'You're shaking, John. Let's get you back into the warmth of the incident unit and you can explain. Here, take my arm.'

WPC Rosie Jennings was in the van doing what all good police officers do best with time on their hands – making tea. Steadman and Long sat down at the small table, grateful for the steaming mugs.

'I don't really know where to begin,' said Steadman. 'From the outset it didn't seem plain sailing. The broken window wouldn't go away, and neither would the vague recollection of a case I studied as a cadet. Here we have a husband and wife murdered in the same house, but the only way I could make sense of the two crimes was to tease them apart, picture them as two entirely separate events. We don't have a motive for Alisha's death, but...' He stopped and furrowed his brow. 'No matter,' he continued. 'The stolen newspaper also bothered me. Why would someone steal an old newspaper? Only yesterday did it occur to me that whoever smashed the window may have taken a piece of the broken glass and wrapped it in the paper. It still didn't add up. Why not take your own paper with you? What would you do with a broken piece of glass? No, there had to be a reason. And there had to be something linking the four break-ins. I hope I'm wrong, but I think it's the wigs.'

'Still not fully with you, John,' said DCI Long.

'I'm sorry, I'm not making myself clear. I'm not that sure myself, but in Dr Gupta's study I suddenly remembered a case I read about all those years ago. It happened in the 1950s in Glasgow. A man with a rare blood group kept being called in to donate blood. When he was involved in an accident they couldn't find a suitable donor and he bled to death. His wife managed to trace and murder three of the recipients of her husband's blood before she was finally caught. The similarity was that she had broken into each house some days beforehand and had stolen only a kitchen knife…'

Steadman broke off and started drumming on the table with his fingers. His feet were fidgeting.

'Do you really think someone will have a go at Annie tonight?' Long asked.

'The blood-lust is up – why not? Tonight's the perfect night, with no electricity. And, but I can't tell you why, I reckon it will be her first - from the strongest victim to the weakest. Are the blasted phones not working yet?'

DCI Long could see that his colleague was getting increasingly agitated.

'John, would you feel any easier if Rosie ran you over to Munro's house?'

Steadman stood up and nodded. He didn't have to say anything.

CHAPTER TWENTY NINE

Rosie Jennings put down her mug of tea. She took Steadman by the arm over to the car and helped him in. Possibly because he was becoming ever more anxious, he struggled to get the seat belt fastened.

'Let me do it, sir,' said Rosie, turning round in her seat.

Steadman caught the faintest whiff of stale perfume and sweat. It had been a long night for all of them.

'It's still very dark, sir. Do you mind if we go on the south circular past the harbour? I know it's a bit longer, but I'm more familiar with that road.'

Steadman waved a hand as if to say 'OK'. He was lost in his own thoughts again. Was his hunch right? It had to be; it was the only plausible explanation. Could he have prevented Dr Gupta's death if he had recalled the crime in Glasgow earlier? He chewed his lower lip – possibly, possibly. And Annie – at the thought of something happening to the Munros' younger daughter he felt physically ill. He was about to ask WPC Jennings if she could go a bit faster, but what was the point? What could a blind detective do, other than get in the way? And besides Rosie appeared to be going quite fast as it was. Self-pity never helped, and he knew, blind or not, he was in the thick of a double murder investigation.

So who killed Dr Gupta? 'Think, think!' he mumbled to himself. It must be to do with the wig. He remembered Munro's pride in buying his daughter the best, and his surprise at not noticing the wig when he first saw Annie wearing it. Was it made of human hair? Almost certainly Aaron Gupta wouldn't have settled for anything less. What about the two other properties with their broken windows? Did the cat lady or the gardening Mr Tedders wear wigs? He would have to find out later. What sort of person grows his or her hair, then sells it? He'd never thought about it before: a woman, presumably. Why would she kill to get it back? No, that made no sense. A jealous husband or lover, perhaps? Surely not. All that Kim Ho had found at the Gupta's house was one small shoe print that really could have been anybody's.

He started humming Mozart's *Rondo Alla Turca*; it was always Mozart when he was wrestling with a difficult problem. He never really knew if he liked Mozart's work or not. It troubled him in its complexity. What was so special about these wigs? He drummed his fingers impatiently. 'If I knew that,' he said to himself, 'I would be a good way to solving the mystery.'

'Sir – sir!'

'Sorry, Rosie, I was miles away. What is it?'

'I think we're being followed.'

'Followed? What by?'

'Someone on a motorbike - no lights on, but when I brake I'm sure I can see a reflection in a visor.' She touched the brakes again. 'Yes, definitely somebody on a large motorbike!'

'Can you get through to the Eyesore on the car radio?' Steadman asked. He couldn't keep the note of urgency out of his voice. 'Ask for immediate assistance with armed back-up!'

Rosie didn't question his request.

'Where are we now?'

'Just approaching the docks. Do you think it's the man who attacked you, sir?'

'More than likely – and I suspect he's got a gun with him.' He sighed. 'Rosie, I'm truly sorry.'

'Back-up will be here soon, sir, and I'm not giving in without a fight. I know this area really well. I was a bobby on the beat here for two years – first name terms with every pimp and prostitute. Hold tight!'

Without signalling, she took a sharp left. The tail of the car skidded, but she tucked its nose in, straightened out and accelerated away. For a moment she thought she had lost their pursuer; but no, in the rear view mirror she could see the bike clearly.

'He's put on his headlights, sir. Damn, he's gaining on us.'

She threw the car round a sharp right then a left.

Steadman could tell by the sudden rumbling of the tyres that they were now in the cobbled labyrinth of roads and alleyways round the old warehouses.

'Is it worth putting on the siren and lights, if only to draw attention to ourselves..?'

The noise echoed eerily in the lonely dark streets. Rosie weaved in and out of the buildings, throwing John Steadman from side to side. He felt nauseous. Was it just the motion of the car, or was it because memories of the fateful night when he lost his wife and his sight were flooding back?

'There's a handle you can hang on to above the door.'

He grappled with his left hand, found the strap and clung on tightly. They turned another corner, only to find their way blocked by road works. Rosie swore.

'Sorry, sir,' she said, 'I'm going to have to do a handbrake turn. With any luck I might hit your chum on the motorbike. Hold tight again!'

The tyres screeched. There was a smell of burning rubber. The car lurched round in a sharp loop. They narrowly missed the motorcyclist, who had slowed right down. There was a brief flash of light, then a very loud crack as one of the side windows exploded in a thousand fragments.

'Are you all right, sir?'

Steadman nodded. Rosie contacted the Eyesore again.

'Pursuer armed and has fired at the car. Nobody injured – how long before we get back-up?'

There was a brief pause.

'Three minutes. Where are you exactly?'

'Sugarhouse Lane turning on to Drakes Quay. I can see some of the boats are lit up. Maybe that will scare him off.'

'Can you see him?' asked Steadman.

'He's behind us again. I don't think he can fire and ride the bike at the same time. If only I can keep some distance between him and us until help arrives.'

Rosie Jennings put her foot flat on the accelerator and shot on to Drakes Quay. There were a handful of boats lit up, but everything else was dark, silent and deserted.

'I'm going to do a wide figure of eight round Pinkerton's Yard, back along the waterfront, then round the old fish market.'

Steadman knew Pinkerton's Yard; he had led a successful drug raid there some years ago.

'He may switch off his lights and just wait for us,' Steadman said.

'I know, but on the straight he can catch up with us in seconds. The cobbles are greasy and treacherous especially if you've only got two wheels. I think it's our best chance, sir.'

The car skidded round the back of Pinkerton's Yard, coming back on to Drakes Quay almost sideways. They bumped over the sunken railway lines. The back wing clipped a plastic traffic cone, sending it spinning down the street behind them.

'I can see blue flashing lights coming down the hill,' Rosie exclaimed. 'And the power is back on!' In an instant the docks were brightly illuminated in the industrial orange glow of neon.

They never reached the fish market. As the streetlights went on the man on the motorbike killed his own headlights and wound up the throttle. The rear windscreen caved in with a deafening bang. Automatically Steadman and Rosie ducked.

It was the smallest of screams. Rosie's body twisted sideways and forwards out of her seat belt. Her head bounced off the dashboard as the car spun round, hitting first a concrete bollard before ripping along the harbour's perimeter fence. With a final crunch the car came to a halt up against a tall street light. The limp body of Rosie Jennings slipped off the dashboard and her head came to rest in Steadman's lap. Dazed, he put a hand underneath her shoulder. He could feel the soft warmth of blood as it oozed through her tattered uniform. She was still breathing, but each breath was hard, laboured and rattling. He held her head as gently as he could. Tears rolled down from his sightless eyes.

'Oh Rosie, Rosie – not you as well.'

CHAPTER THIRTY

Munro sat tight lipped. His big hands clenched the steering wheel with a grip like a mole wrench. He had thrown off the blue vinyl gloves but was still wearing the white overalls. A thin bead of sweat trickled down his temple. He trusted John Steadman's judgement. He had never known him to be wrong; only this time he prayed he was mistaken

There was no traffic. Helmsmouth remained ghostly, black and empty. Munro shot the Audi across road junctions. The tyres squealed as he pushed the car round the bends and roundabouts. DS Fairfax clutched the edges of her seat. A quick glance at Munro and she knew she should keep quiet. What could she say anyway? All murders are appalling, but to take a child's life...

Munro hit the brakes. An old man out walking his dog had stepped on to the road without looking.

'Get out of the bloody way! It's the middle of the night - you've got all day to exercise your damned pooch!' Munro shouted.

Despite the siren and the flashing lights, the old man angrily waved his stick in defiance at the car as it raced past.

To Munro it seemed an eternity until they screeched to a halt in his drive. The two officers leapt out of the car.

'I'll take the front door – you go round the back,' ordered Munro.

DS Fairfax was, in fact, the senior officer, but this was not the time to pull rank. Munro unlocked the front door and was in, hardly breaking his step. He could hear Maureen's voice in the kitchen and rushed down the corridor. The back door was unlocked. DS Fairfax and Munro entered the kitchen at the same time.

There were two candles on the table and a third on the work surface. In the soft half-light Munro saw his wife sitting at the table gently rocking a bundle on her lap. She was talking in little more than a whisper in a sing-song voice, as if comforting a distressed child. She put a finger to her lips and nodded in the direction of two chairs. Munro and Fairfax sat down. In answer to Munro's unasked question Maureen said:

'Annie and Melanie are fine. They're fast asleep upstairs.'

Munro heaved an enormous sigh of relief. DS Fairfax couldn't help herself. She grasped hold of Munro's hand and gave it a squeeze. He was about to say something, but again Maureen put her finger to her lips.

'This is Abigail,' she said. 'Abi, this is my husband

Alan, the one I was telling you about. And this is his colleague Fiona Fairfax. They're both police officers.'

Munro and Fairfax looked at the bundle of rags in Maureen's lap. In the candle light they could just make out an emaciated figure wearing a blood-spattered, grey hooded sweatshirt and denim jeans. Both items of clothing appeared much too large for her. A small claw-like hand was clutching on to the lapel of Maureen's dressing gown. Munro could not be sure, but he thought the other little hand was holding one of the lollipops that Ben had magically produced the previous afternoon. His heart gave a leap as he noticed at the far end of the table a large sliver of glass. A piece of newspaper was wrapped round one end to form a handle. Munro didn't have to look too closely to know that it would be the front page of his copy of the *Helmsmouth Evening News*.

'Abi, I think it's for the best if I tell Alan and Fiona how we met and what we've been chatting about, don't you?'

There was a slight incline of the hooded head. Fiona caught a glimpse of a pointed chin and a sunken cheek.

'Alan, you had just left. I checked the back door and had got half way upstairs to bed. I couldn't remember if I had turned off the camping stove so I thought I'd better make sure. I was still wearing my head torch. The back door was wide open. Abi was standing in the kitchen holding that piece of glass. She was shaking and simply stared at me like a frightened animal caught in a car's headlights.'

The bundle on Maureen's lap moaned.

'So much for your locksmith! Our old key fitted the new lock perfectly well.'

Alan pushed his chair back into the shadows, hoping that Maureen wouldn't notice his embarrassment.

'You didn't know what to say, did you?' she said looking down at the small figure that was clinging on to her. 'And neither did I. After a moment I think I said something silly like 'you look really cold, would you like a cup of tea?' Abi looked at me and started to cry. I took the glass from her and just held her. I noticed she was covered in blood and I asked her if she had cut herself.' Maureen continued to rock Abi in her arms. 'She said she hadn't, but that she had killed Dr Gupta. I thought it best if we sat down and we've been chatting ever since.'

The kitchen suddenly seemed very cold.

'Shall I make everyone a cup of something hot?' asked Munro. He got up and put a pan of water on the camping stove.

'Would you like a hot drink, Abi?' asked Maureen.

The bundle shook its head. Munro noticed that the lollipop was untouched.

'Abi doesn't eat or drink very much, as you can see,' Maureen continued. 'Can I tell Alan and Fiona your story?'

Again there was the slightest movement of Abi's head.

'Abi lived with her older sister Elizabeth. They've been in and out of care most of their lives, but when

Elizabeth was old enough she set up home and took Abi with her. They did everything they could to make money. It was Elizabeth who grew and sold her hair. Did you know that there's still one traditional wig maker in Helmsmouth?'

Alan shook his head. He couldn't take his eyes off the quivering figure huddled up so close to his wife.

'Elizabeth took ill last year. Sadly all her hair fell out.' The bundle let out a quiet sob. 'She died three months ago. I don't think Abi has eaten much since then, other than the odd bag of crisps.'

Fiona's eyes had grown accustomed to the light. It was difficult to tell, but she reckoned Abi could only weigh four or five stone.

'Abi thought that if she got all of Elizabeth's hair back she might also get her sister back. It wasn't hard to find who the wigs belonged to – she simply broke into the wig maker's workshop and went through her books.'

Alan looked puzzled. 'Why the broken glass and the newspaper and…?' He drew a finger across his throat.

Maureen gave him a withering look and pulled Abi closer to her.

'Alan, I don't think there is an awful lot of logic going on here. She's obviously unwell,' she hissed at him.

Munro blushed again. 'Of course, of course – I was just wondering if there was any significance, that's all…'

Maureen shook her head.

'Do you know how old Abi is, Maureen?' asked Fiona.

'She'll be seventeen in May.'

Quite unexpectedly the power came back on and the kitchen filled with light. Everybody blinked. The three adults stared at Abi. Her clothes were caked with dry blood. She was woefully thin. Her hood fell back, but she didn't open her eyes, at least not immediately. The sallow skin on her face seemed to be pulled taut over her cheekbones and was covered in fine down, like a new-born baby. She had a little upturned nose and would have been quite pretty if she hadn't been so wasted. Munro was speechless.

DS Fairfax stood up. 'May I?' she said, in an enquiring voice which the other woman recognised instantly.

'Of course,' replied Maureen, 'first door on the left by the front door.'

There was a phone on a table by the front door. DS Fairfax flushed the toilet, leaving the door open. Hoping that the sound would mask her voice, she called the Eyesore, requesting a car and two female officers.

Maureen looked at her husband. The man was a wreck. As though mesmerised, he sat with his eyes now fixed on the piece of broken glass.

'Why don't you take off your overalls? You look like a golf caddy from the Masters at Augusta! And what about that cup of tea you promised?'

Munro got up and dutifully took off his overalls. The camping stove had eventually given up the struggle to heat the water. Munro switched on the electric kettle.

DS Fairfax poked her head round the door and signalled for Alan to join her. Quickly she told him about her phone call.

'I'll have to take her back to the Eyesore with me,' she explained.

Munro, still bewildered, just nodded. He made them all tea. As he placed the mugs on the table, Fiona slipped on a pair of gloves and carefully placed the large sliver of glass in an evidence bag. He was hardly aware of what DS Fairfax was saying. She had taken charge of the situation. In as a kind a voice as was possible she formally arrested Abi, cautioned her and explained her rights. Maureen looked aghast. She clung on to Abi and said, 'Don't worry it'll be all right', but she knew it wouldn't be. DS Fairfax tried to set her mind at rest her by explaining that they would get Abi cleaned up as soon as possible and have an officer with her at all times.

'We'll also get the medics to see her first thing in the morning,' she said reassuringly.

Alan left the room and went upstairs to see his two sleeping children. Annie's wig was lying by her bed. It could all have been so different, he thought.

A car pulled up in the drive and the banging of the doors brought him back to his senses. The kitchen seemed crowded now with the two extra officers. One of them produced a pair of handcuffs. Before Maureen could object, DS Fairfax intervened.

'Those won't be necessary - besides they wouldn't fit,' she added under her breath.

DS Fairfax took Abi's arm and she stood up. She was still clutching her lollipop. It was hard to believe that somebody who looked so fragile could have inflicted such a dreadful blow to Dr Gupta. Munro shook his head in disbelief. Abi turned to Maureen and quite unexpectedly asked her in a hoarse whisper, 'Will you come and visit me in prison? I would like that.'

'Of course I will, Abi, but promise me you will try and eat a little more!'

Munro looked at his wife in disbelief. Here was a person who had already killed someone in cold blood that night and, if it hadn't been for Maureen worrying about a camping stove, would have undoubtedly cut their own daughter's throat. And now Maureen was offering to visit her!

'Maureen, I'll give you a call later. I'll need a formal statement,' said DS Fairfax as she led Abi out of the house.

★ ★ ★

'I know what you're thinking Alan. You think I'm mad, don't you? But I bet that not one person has ever shown that girl any love or affection in her life. You can surely guess how else she and her sister made money! She's mentally and physically very ill and I just feel so, so sorry for her...' The emotion of the night finally caught up with her and she crumpled into her husband's arms.

'There, there, pet – you're right of course. It's just that... Oh, I don't know what I'm trying to say...

Maureen, you're all in all a much better person than I am. Let me run you a bath and get you some clean clothes.'

'Alan, how did you know to come back?'

'Steadman worked it out – don't ask me how. He knew Annie's life was in danger.'

'Will you promise me one thing?' Maureen asked.

'Anything.'

'Can you change the lock on the back door?'

Before Alan Munro could answer the phone rang. It was DCI Long.

'Relieved to hear about Annie, but we have another problem on our hands. Can you get yourself down to Drakes Quay? Steadman's been shot at again. He's all right, but Rosie Jennings' been seriously injured. I think she's still alive. I'll meet you down there.'

Maureen had slipped to the bathroom, washed her face and hands and was now wearing one of her husband's dressing gowns. She fetched the tin of chocolate brownies from the cupboard.

'More work, I suppose? Eat something before you go, and don't worry about me. I'll be fine.'

'That was DCI Long. Someone's had another go at John Steadman. They missed, but hit Rosie Jennings. I'll bet you anything he was on his way over here. I don't know how badly injured Rosie is…' He let out another great sigh. 'Sometimes I hate this bloody job!'

Maureen put her hands on her husband's beefy shoulders and gave them a rub.

'Go on, Alan, see what you can do. Try and persuade John to come back here – it's the least we can do.'

CHAPTER THIRTY ONE

'Are you all right, sir?'

'Who are you?' asked John Steadman warily.

'Sorry, sir, I'm PC Crammond,' replied the young officer sheepishly as he shone his torch into the car.

'I'm OK, but Rosie Jennings has been shot in the left shoulder. I think her lungs must be damaged. She can hardly breathe.'

The beam from PC Crammond's torch flitted across Rosie's pale face cradled in Steadman's hands. The warm blood oozing from her shoulder was beginning to congeal in his lap. Her breathing was shallow and erratic.

'The ambulance is almost here, sir,' said Crammond, waving his torch in the air to attract the driver's attention.

Steadman already knew. The sound of the siren was quite distinct from that of a police car or a fire engine. The wailing stopped. One of the paramedics pulled open the buckled door and glanced briefly at Rosie.

'Are you able to support her head for a little bit

longer?' asked the paramedic. Her tone was reassuringly brisk and authoritative.

She slashed Rosie's seat belt and carefully moved her legs round to make it easier to get her out on to the stretcher. An oxygen mask was slipped over her face by the other paramedic who had climbed in behind Rosie and had dropped the back of her seat. With the help of PC Crammond they lifted Rosie on to the stretcher.

'Is she badly hurt?' asked Steadman. He knew it was a foolish question. Rosie was unconscious, and he was soaked in her blood. Nobody appeared to hear him, or at least no one answered. He undid his seat belt. There should be a stash of paper towels in the glove box, if he could find it. He groped the dashboard and found the lock. It opened with a soft click. Sure enough there was a pile of paper towels. He did his best to clean himself up. The door on his side wouldn't open. The glass had shattered, and a cool breeze blew in through the gaping hole. It brought with it the familiar dockside smell of seaweed, diesel and decay. He could hear voices and more cars arriving. Eventually he heard the plaintive wail of the ambulance as it set off for Helmsmouth General. He felt both angry and guilty. 'Pray God she survives,' he muttered to himself.

'Is he still in the car?'

Steadman instantly recognised the deep voice of DCI Long.

'Are you hurt at all, John?' he asked.

'No – the blood is all from Rosie, though I would rather it had been mine. Is she still alive?'

'She appeared to be regaining consciousness in the ambulance, but she's not looking too good,' DCI Long replied honestly. 'Let's get you out of here. Damn, the door's jammed! John, the fire crew has just arrived. I'll get a couple of their men to force the door.'

'Hubert, just a minute – is Annie safe?'

It had only that second come back to Steadman that the whole reason for him being in the car was to get to Munro's house. He clutched his forehead dreading what DCI Long was going to say.

'Yes, she's safe and we've caught Dr Gupta's killer. I don't have the full story. Munro is on his way and will fill us both in.'

Steadman nodded. At least something positive had come out of tonight.

'Any idea of what became of the person on the motorbike?' he asked.

'I'm only just here myself. There's some commotion down by the harbour's edge. I'll go and investigate while these chaps wrench your door open.'

Two burly firemen approached the car with a massive crowbar. There was an ear splitting crunch. Slowly the door creaked open on its bent hinges. The firemen helped Steadman to his feet.

'There should be a white cane folded up in there somewhere – probably under the seat. Can you find it for me?'

One of the firemen looked in the car and retrieved the cane.

'Here you are, sir. You don't mind me asking, but are you the blind detective that was mentioned in the papers?'

Fortunately the arrival of Alan Munro saved him from having to reply.

'You realise that your nickname is going to stick,' he said when the two men were alone at last.

'It could be worse,' Steadman replied. 'It could be the blind ex-detective. But tell me about Annie. I know she's safe.'

Munro outlined the events of the last couple of hours and Maureen's extraordinary display of courage and understanding.

'The anorexic, grieving, dysfunctional sibling – that makes sense,' said Steadman.

'Not to me it doesn't,' replied Munro. 'What was it that put you on to it?'

'It was the broken window – the break-in with no obvious purpose. I couldn't get it out of my head. When you mentioned that Dr Gupta's toupee was missing, I immediately thought of Annie, and it suddenly made sense.'

'What about you?' asked Munro. 'I presume you were heading in my direction.'

Steadman told his story as best he could.

'I feel really awful about Rosie. Will you let me know how she is?'

Arm in arm, the two men picked their way across the cobbles towards the harbour edge, where a group of people were standing in a huddle. There were no kerbs or walls, just the wide open space of the empty dockside. Even with Munro's support Steadman felt disorientated and quite sick.

'Can we slow down a bit?' he asked. His grip on Munro's arm tightened.

Twice Steadman lost his footing on the greasy stones. He resorted to scuffing his way along the ground much as he had done when he first started to walk after losing his sight. They came to the customs barrier in the perimeter fence.

'It's completely smashed in,' Munro explained. 'I wonder if it was your biker pal that went through it.'

The huddle at the water's edge broke up. The tall, gangly figure of DCI Long loped over to meet them.

'It's a large motorbike right enough. I'm not sure what make as somebody has taken the trouble to spray the whole machine matt black. It looks like it hit the barrier at speed before colliding with that large steel bollard. The front of the bike is mangled. There's no sign of the rider, I'm afraid. The customs officer was asleep and only woke up when he heard a loud bang. I've detailed some officers to search the harbour wall, and there are some officers on the big container ship that's tied up here. Hopefully a crew member will have seen something despite the dark.'

Steadman thought for a moment then said:

'I'm fairly certain that Rosie said the power was back on before we were shot at.'

Munro was about to say something, but just then there was a small explosion at the quayside and a large ball of flame shot into the night sky.

'Hell and damnation!' exclaimed DCI Long. 'The bike is on fire. I thought I could smell petrol.'

The fire crew were there within seconds and quickly doused the flames.

'There goes any chance of forensic evidence,' Munro commented ruefully.

An officer sidled up to DCI Long. 'The number plate you asked me to check, sir, is licensed to a double-decker bus in London.'

A small disturbance had broken out at the edge of the police cordon. The voice of Dr Frank Rufus could be clearly heard.

'Blast your eyes, officer - don't you know who I am? I am the Home Office pathologist. I even get a Christmas card from the Chief Constable. Let me through!'

DCI Long galloped over to the scene. 'That's OK, officer, he can come through. Why don't you carry your ID with you, Frank?'

'Oh, it's in my desk somewhere. What in the name has been happening? I've just finished with Helmsmouth's answer to Anne Boleyn. They've taken his body to the mortuary and I'll do a full post mortem later, not that it is likely to add much!'

Briefly DCI Long filled him in.

'So a quiet night by all accounts,' Dr Rufus

responded dryly. 'Good grief, John, you look dreadful,' he said turning to a shivering Steadman. 'Would you like me to take you home?'

Steadman tried to reply airily that he just felt cold.

'Let's commandeer the customs shed. There are bound to be some chairs in there, and it will be warmer than standing out here.'

The first pale rays of dawn were starting to break through the leaden sky. The four men sat huddled round a small paraffin stove that gave out a meagre amount of heat.

'It reminds me of my father's greenhouse,' Munro remarked.

From the quayside they could hear wolf whistles and cheering. A flushed faced female officer knocked on the door and came in, accompanied by a tall, blonde seaman.

'Sorry about that, sir' said the officer. 'It's impossible to make a ladylike exit up a vertical ladder with six sailors staring up your skirt. This is Hans. He's Dutch, but speaks perfect English. He was on the bridge when the motorbike crashed into the bollard.'

Another chair was found for Hans. Steadman recognised the smell of cannabis immediately.

'I heard the siren and saw the police car going up one side of the harbour, then back down again. I thought I saw a motorbike chasing the car.' Although Hans spoke good English, he still had a strong Dutch accent. 'It's funny – no? Usually the police chase the guys on the motorbike!' Nobody laughed. 'As I say, first they went up, then I lose sight of them. Then down they come again. Wah, wah, wah, and the blue light flashing! I'm still smiling, then boof! – all the lights come on and I think, man, this place is like Vegas! Then I hear this gunshot – bang! Just like that! This motorbike comes crashing through the barrier. If it hadn't been for the bollard he would have landed on the deck – maybe better for him! But no, he hits the bollard – another bang! Then - hey, I think I'm seeing things - all legs and arms going in every direction.'

Hans broke off and made a whistling noise as his hand, with wiggling fingers, carved out a wide arc in the air. In his mind's eye Steadman could clearly see the figure flailing about in the air. It gave him no satisfaction.

'I've never seen anything like it. He flew straight over the boat and disappeared on the other side. Odd - I never heard a splash. I ran over to the end of the bridge, but it was all dark in the water.'

'Why didn't you report this to your captain?' asked DCI Long angrily.

'Hey, you don't know the boss! Nobody disturbs the captain at night unless the boat's sinking, know what I mean?'

Hans hesitated, and then continued:

'Truth is I was smoking myself a 'J' and I said to myself, 'Hans, this dope has got one hell of a kick!' I didn't believe what I saw and when you start thinking things like that, then I reckon it's time to call it a day.

So I went to my bunk.'

Steadman was trying hard to picture the scene.

'Did you notice if he was holding a gun?'

Hans thought long and hard. He did the same whistling half circle with his hand.

'No,' he said at last, 'I can't say for sure either way. I was completely stoned!'

DCI Long stood up.

'Right, Alan, can you get on to the coastguard and call out the police divers. I'm sorry, constable, I don't know your name.'

'Sue Oliver, sir.'

'Thanks. Can you take a full written statement from Hans? We'll need to tell the officers round the harbour to look for the body in the water. At least it's getting lighter. I'll go on board and have a word with the captain. John, you're looking unwell...'

'Maureen says I've to persuade you to go back to our house,' said Munro.

'I can't go there in this state,' Steadman replied.

'I know just the place for you,' said Dr Rufus. 'The police mortuary!'

'I'm not dead yet!'

'I know, but the mortuary has the most wonderful hot showers in the whole of Helmsmouth. We'll get you cleaned up, and you can catch a bit of shut-eye at my place. I don't suppose you'll mind sleeping in Ben's bed. I haven't changed the sheets yet.'

CHAPTER THIRTY TWO

There was a furious knocking at the door. 'There's something floating in the middle of the harbour,' gasped a rather fat constable.

DCI Long and DS Munro were out of their seats before the officer had drawn another breath. John Steadman almost rose to follow them. It was only natural. Could this mark the end of his ordeal? Would it be an overwhelming relief or a deeply depressing anticlimax? Dr Rufus gave a small cough.

'Do you want to go and see what it's all about, Frank?' Steadman asked.

'Not really - don't get me wrong, I'm never happier than when I'm visiting the scene of a crime, but I'm too old to start walking on water. I'm good John, just not that good. Anyway it's a damn sight warmer in here than out there. I would give a week's wages for a decent cup of coffee right now. We'll know what's happening soon enough.'

He looked at his companion, who was drumming his

long fingers on his thighs. It was difficult to read the expression on his face. Steadman's dark glasses appeared even more impenetrable in the gloom of the customs shed.

'Penny for your thoughts, John?'

'Difficult to put into words as they're so jumbled. Partly I'm exhausted, and that doesn't help. Mainly I'm worried about other people's expectations. If it is him floating in the water then no doubt there will be a big celebration, not only in the Eyesore but also in the local press. I can visualise the headlines – 'HELMSMOUTH KILLER DROWNS IN HARBOUR'. People will think it is an end and that life will go back to normal. But it won't for me, Frank, it never will. You know what it's like to lose a wife, and without wishing to wallow too much in self-pity, I've lost more than that. It's horrible to say, but there was a time tonight when all the power was down that I felt, only for a moment, that some equality had returned to my world. It was only very briefly – I wouldn't wish blindness on anyone.'

'I can understand that. I guess you will feel some relief, if not release, surely?'

'Knowing is always better than not knowing, granted. But even if I understood what sick motivation this bastard had, don't expect forgiveness from me. I'm no saint, Frank. Release? Sure, I won't need a minder with me every time I go anywhere, and I'll be able to leave Jamaica Mansion – just as I'm getting used to the place.'

'Come on, your allotted time for self-pity is over. Let's go and see what they've fished out.'

In the feeble early morning light a small group of officers were chattering noisily on the quayside. Dr Rufus and John Steadman shuffled slowly towards them. The sun was not yet high enough to fully illuminate the blackness of the water in the harbour. It wasn't immediately apparent what all the excitement was about until they got much closer. Where the water lapped the quayside there was an unsavoury mix of detritus being picked over by squawking gulls. In the middle of the harbour, in a slick of iridescent diesel something round and head shaped was bobbing gently up and down.

'Could be a harbour seal,' Dr Rufus suggested.

'Would you care to put some money on that, sir? I could give you very good odds – say twenty to one?' The constable licked his pen and opened a fresh page of his notepad.

'Are you running a book on this?' asked Dr Rufus.

'Just a bit of harmless fun for the lads and lasses. It's evens for it being the bloke off the bike, two to one it being some drunken sailor, five to one it's one of the local hookers and three to two that it is just a load of rubbish. A harbour seal at twenty to one must be worth a flutter.'

'I doubt if a seal would be bobbing about in a pool of diesel unless it was dead,' remarked Dr Rufus.

A worried look came over the bookie's face.

'Fifty to one for a live seal, seven to two for a dead seal – how about that then?'

Dr Rufus's wallet stayed firmly in his pocket. The sound of the in-shore rescue boat put paid to the betting. The beam of its searchlight swept across the water. Was it a body? It still wasn't clear. The engines were cut. Silently the little boat circled the pool of diesel until it came to a halt. One of the crew took a boat hook, leaned over the side and pulled out something round, shiny and black.

'What is it?' asked Steadman.

'A motorcycle helmet,' replied a young constable, 'that's all.'

'Does that count as 'just rubbish'?' asked another.

'Afraid not,' replied the officer who was running the book. He moved hurriedly to the back of the group. 'That's valuable evidence and as none of you put money on that…'

'You jammy bugger, you've just made thirty-five quid!'

'And would you have felt sorry for me if you lot of miserable punters had skinned me alive?'

It was a reasonable defence but not to everyone's satisfaction. The group started to disperse.

'Shall we go?' asked Dr Rufus.

The two men walked slowly over the damp cobbles to the edge of the police cordon. The officer who had tried to bar Dr Rufus's entry remained on duty.

'I'll bring that Christmas card to show you next

time. It had a picture of Santa Claus on it wearing a policeman's helmet – quite droll,' remarked Dr Rufus. The officer gave him a blank stare. 'Oh well, suit yourself!'

Dr Rufus shifted a pile of notes off the passenger seat and guided Steadman safely in.

'Dear God, Frank, it stinks in here!'

'Does it? After all these years my nose has grown accustomed to almost anything that's thrown its way.'

He reached into the large pocket on the door and pulled out a half-drunk carton of lumpy milk. He sniffed at it delicately.

'Found the culprit!'

Without a second thought he wound down the window and shouted at the officer.

'Here, hold this a minute, would you?'

As soon as the man had taken the offensive carton, Frank Rufus put his foot on the accelerator and drove off.

'I hate people without a sense of humour,' he said.

The car soon warmed up, but Steadman was unable to relax. He felt tired and dirty. It had been an awful night.

'You know, Frank, I would have liked to have met Abi. Our society can be so cruel and uncaring. I wonder at what point she was written off. Aren't we meant to look after the most vulnerable? The media will love it - 'Teenage psycho on the rampage', or something like that. And then there will be the endless investigations and blame games. I suppose some would say the writing was on the wall the day she and her sister were put into care, or even the day they were born. It shouldn't have been like that, and it makes me so angry. How long will she be held in a secure hospital – fifteen, twenty years at a vast cost to the taxpayer? Yet if only a fraction of that had been used wisely years ago there's a good chance she wouldn't be in the mess she's in now.'

Dr Rufus grunted, 'I don't think Munro can comprehend how somebody so scrawny could have inflicted such a dreadful blow to Aaron Gupta. She probably can't recall a thing about it.'

'I remember Holly and I rented a cottage once and a squirrel got down the chimney. It can't have been there for more than an hour but it had frantically gnawed almost completely through the door. I made a grab for it and the damned creature took a lump out of my arm that required a dozen stitches. No, I don't think you can always equate size to destructive force.'

'I agree – the smallest kidney stone can cause unbelievable pain, whereas you can be riddled with cancer and not notice a thing.'

Steadman smiled. No matter what the conversation was about, Frank Rufus always turned it to something medical.

The sun was now up and the weather looked promising. The Volvo came to a halt at the side entrance of the police mortuary. The air under the trees was damp and the earth had a lovely, musty aroma. Birds were singing lustily.

'I love the smell of the ground after it's been raining,' Steadman remarked. 'That, and the dawn chorus.'

'All very well, but they crap all over my car. I'm with the fellow who was all for baking four and twenty of them in a pie.'

'I think, Frank, you'll find that these are not all blackbirds.'

'Probably not, but I bet they all taste the same. Let's get you in and cleaned up.'

Dr Rufus opened the door and manoeuvred Steadman through to the changing room.

'Don't mind me, I'm a doctor' he said as he helped Steadman undress.

The suit, shirt, tie and underwear were ruined. Blood had even congealed in the belt buckle. Dr Rufus noticed that two extra holes had been added to the belt. He was appalled to see how thin his friend had become. The purple scar on his chest looked angry and painful. Steadman took off his dark glasses and his unseeing eyes wandered aimlessly round, staring at nothing in particular. Dr Rufus had turned on the shower, and the water was now piping hot.

'There's shower gel on the wall on your left … that's it, you've got it. I've put a nailbrush in the corner nearest your right foot. Give a shout when you're done. I'll go and see what I can do about your clothes.'

Frank Rufus took one last look at his friend. His hair was now wet and plastered down on his scalp. It was obvious where he had lost a bit of his skull.

Only Steadman's shoes and socks could be salvaged. Dr Rufus went through all the pockets and put Steadman's possessions in a plastic bag. He was intrigued to find the little netsuke rat.

'The carving really is exquisite,' he remarked as he handed Steadman a towel. 'Sorry, but other than your shoes and socks everything else is only fit for the bin. There are some theatre scrubs that are your size and an old raincoat of mine. I've phoned Maureen and she's going to drop off your spare clothes later this morning.'

'Have you phoned...'

Before he could finish Dr Rufus replied:

'Yes – Rosie is in theatre. I have to phone again in two hours.'

On the way back to his house Dr Rufus stopped and picked up some croissants and a newspaper.

'They've only managed to print two pages because of the power cut, and it is all about last night's storm.'

The croissants were still warm. Dr Rufus insisted on having them drenched in honey.

'Come on, John, before you fall asleep at the table let's get you into bed.'

'One last question – do you think the man who shot Rosie could have survived?'

'I've been wondering about that. He would have to have been quick and a strong swimmer. Full biking leathers and boots must weigh about seven or eight kilos. He managed to get his helmet off though. There are plenty of ladders that reach into the water. It was high tide and with all the rain he wouldn't have left much trace. The divers will be there by now. They hate working in the docks – the visibility underwater is poor, and there are always clumps of raw sewage floating about. Invariably they end up with stomach upsets. They are more likely to find the gun. Assuming he dropped it, it would sink straight down.'

'And the body, if he didn't survive?' queried Steadman.

'It would sink, but be washed about by the tide and currents. I would guess that it would get wedged under one of the jetties. After a few days it would fill up with gas and bob up to the surface. They're never a pretty sight, all bloated with no nose or ears.'

'You're going to tell me why, I presume?' Steadman said as an unpleasant vision conjured up in his mind's eye.

'Crabs' said Dr Rufus. 'They nibble off the soft bits.'

Even with that dreadful image, Steadman slept soundly until half past twelve. Maureen had not only brought round spare clothes but had thoughtfully bought sandwiches for the two men to have for lunch. Frank Rufus had dozed in a chair. Before waking Steadman he had phoned the hospital. Rosie was out of theatre and in the intensive care unit. The hospital described her condition as critical.

'What does that mean?' asked Steadman.

'Fifty-fifty chance of survival,' Dr Rufus replied. 'And in case you were contemplating saying anything about wishing it was you, it wasn't, and that's an end to it.'

The phone rang before Steadman could reply.

'Hang on, I'll ask him. DCI Long wants to know if you're up for giving a statement this afternoon?'

Steadman nodded.

'The divers haven't found the body, I suppose? No, but they've found the gun… Yes, I'll tell him.' Dr Rufus put the phone down. 'You heard all that?'

'It won't be the same gun. The one that shot Holly was a small calibre pistol. This one was something much bigger. Big enough to blow out the car windows and maim at some distance. And have a kick that knocked the biker off balance.' Steadman paused, lost in his own thoughts. 'We know the killer is right handed. He must have taken his hand off the throttle to fire the gun. With only one hand on the handlebars, the bike would lurch to one side with the kick back. I guess he would make a frantic attempt to grab the bike with his right hand. He didn't drop the gun - maybe it got stuck in the throttle - certainly he wouldn't be able to apply the front brakes. At least that's how I read it.'

The inside of the Volvo still smelt rancid. Dr Rufus didn't notice.

'Do you like Louis Armstrong?' he asked. 'I've just bought a CD of his greatest hits.'

The first track that played was *La Vie en Rose*. A quizzical look came over Steadman's face as the final trumpet solo played.

'Tell me, Frank, what's the volume of a man's lungs?'

'It depends on the size of the man's chest and how

fit he is. Louis Armstrong had a huge chest. The most useful measure is how much you can blow out after taking a big breath in, something we doctors call 'vital capacity'.'

'What would mine be – roughly?'

'About five litres – why? Are you thinking of taking up the trumpet?'

The Eyesore stood tall and ugly in the afternoon sunlight. Sergeant Grimble had wedged the door open yet again and was shuffling round pieces of paper with a far-away look on his face.

'Good afternoon gentlemen,' he said politely. 'Kim Ho in forensics is desperate to speak with you, Dr Rufus. You can use my phone and man the barricades while I take DI Steadman up to meet the boss.'

CHAPTER THIRTY THREE

'Shall we take the lift?' Grimble suggested. Without a second thought he took Steadman's arm and led him through the swing doors along the corridor lined with the photos of long gone officers. Even here the smell of disinfectant hung in the air. The lift was small and stuffy; it was seldom used. Sergeant Grimble turned round awkwardly and pressed the button for the second floor. The numbers were also marked in Braille.

'I've never noticed that before,' he remarked. 'Can you read Braille?'

'I've had a few lessons but I found it nigh on impossible. I think if you learnt it as a child or were born blind it would be easier. Go on, try it yourself. Close your eyes and see if you can tell the difference between the four and the six. You're right handed, aren't you? You may find the fingertips on your left hand more sensitive as the skin isn't so thick.'

'It's blooming difficult, and these are probably much bigger than in Braille books, I would have thought.'

The lift clanked to a standstill, and the doors opened with a groan. It was much warmer on this floor, and noisier too. Steadman could hear the murmur of voices and the tapping of numerous keyboards typing out the endless reports that no one would probably ever read. DCI Long's office was immaculate; a total contrast to the 'Grimble Filing System'. Everything was neatly stacked in small piles, and his in-tray was empty. A clock on the wall told the correct time. Apart from a year planner the only other adornments were some pictures of his family and a small vase of spring flowers on his desk. Hubert Long was a keen gardener.

The interview was not very lengthy. Steadman could recall vividly his feeling of nausea and the rush of adrenalin when Rosie announced that they were being followed. He remembered the car twisting and turning, and the deafening blast of the first gunshot as it took out one of the side windows; the rumble of the wheels as it skidded over the cobbles, and then the second shot. Now everything appeared to be happening in slow motion; the car scraping along the perimeter fence, before coming to a halt with a bang and a jolt. And then Rosie's head landing in his lap; her blood oozing through her uniform. In truth, however, all he could report to DCI Long was what Rosie had said to him on that wretched journey.

'You are quite certain Rosie saw only one person on the motorbike?' asked DCI Long.

'Definitely – I know we had to double back on

ourselves and at one point pass very close to him. That's when he fired the first shot.' He paused for a moment. In his head he could hear the window exploding and the echo of the gunshot in the deserted street. 'She would have noticed if there was an accomplice,' Steadman continued.

'It certainly looks like he was acting on his own. The Dutchman, regardless of being high on cannabis, would surely have seen a second person,' said DCI Long.

'I don't suppose there is any sign of a body?'

'No – the divers are still there. The tide has gone out, and it's possible that the body has been washed out to sea.'

'Provided he didn't clamber out before you all arrived,' Steadman added.

'That's a possibility that is worrying me. In the immediate aftermath it wouldn't have been difficult for somebody dressed in black to slip through the broken barrier and disappear into the night.'

'I'm sorry I can't be more helpful,' said Steadman. 'Changing the subject, what has happened to Abi? She intrigues me.'

'Sadly, she made a half-hearted attempt on her own life shortly after coming in. She tried to drown herself in the toilet! Anyway, the psychiatrists came and she's now in a secure hospital. I spoke with Munro's wife earlier. I gather she wants to visit her, despite everything.'

'Maureen is a truly remarkable woman – she'll probably do Abi more good than a hospital full of psychiatrists.'

DCI Long looked at his watch.

'Time for a cup of tea. By the way, Linda has been on the phone. Rumours are rife apparently. I've done my best to reassure her that you're OK. I'm sure she would like to speak with you herself.'

Steadman nodded; he knew his sister only too well. No matter how much she cared for him she would give him an awful dressing down.

Tea duly arrived and brought with it DS Alan Munro.

'Is there anything to eat, I'm starving?' he asked.

DCI Long produced a packet of chocolate biscuits from his desk.

'Work hard, Munro, and one day you too may have your own personal supply of biscuits,' he said, handing Munro the packet, a move he was later to regret as he watched most of its contents disappear.

'You were right about the wigs,' said Munro in between mouthfuls. 'The cat woman is an old orthodox Jewish lady who has worn a wig for years and treated herself to a new one last month. Mr Tedders bought one as a New Year's resolution, thinking it would improve his matrimonial chances. We found shards of glass all neatly wrapped at Abi's flat. It was pathetic - the whole place was a shrine to her sister.'

Steadman was not surprised. He had seen something like this before and knew how easy a trap it was to fall into. Linda had helped him dispose of most of Holly's possessions. Ben only wanted a photograph and one of the paintings she had done as a student. Steadman too had kept a photograph. Even if he couldn't see it he knew it intimately: a picture of the two of them on their honeymoon. It was in the drawer by his bed.

'Have you spoken with anyone else today?' Steadman asked.

'Only briefly,' replied Munro. 'Jean is fairly stoical but very withdrawn. The more I look at Reena and Cassandra the more similar they appear, especially without their war paint. Maybe I'm indulging in racial stereo-typing, I hope not, but their eyes are almost identical. Reena had a hangover from hell and Cassandra had lost her high and mighty attitude. Both of them wanted to bring back the death penalty. Only Jean showed any compassion towards Abi. Unless anything new crops up, I'm going to leave Dr Robinson to stew in his own juice for the meantime.'

'Which brings us back to the question of who killed Alisha Gupta,' Steadman said.

At that point the door opened and a bemused Dr Rufus, accompanied by Kim Ho, entered the room.

'Well, we've found something that's interesting, but I'm not sure how it helps,' boomed Dr Rufus. 'Kim can explain.'

Kim Ho pushed her silky black hair off her face and tucked it behind her ears. She was naturally a shy person and gave a small nervous giggle.

'The blood in the bore of the needle is definitely that

of Alisha Gupta, but when I examined the plastic sleeve I noticed a tiny blob of something sticky on the inside. At first I thought it might be some of the lubricating jelly that had been smeared on her groin...'

'But it wasn't!' interrupted Dr Rufus. 'You'll never guess what it was.'

In a quiet voice John Steadman replied:

'Dr Aaron Gupta's saliva.'

'How the hell did you work that out?' said Dr Rufus in a voice that was both disappointed and astonished.

'Louis Armstrong – the CD you were playing in the car on the way here gave me the clue. And I think I know how Dr Gupta killed his wife. I believe you commented right from the start, Frank, how neat and tidy the needle puncture site was. The mark was barely visible; there was no bruising; no multiple attempts; so clearly somebody knew what they were doing – somebody with a very steady hand. From Alan's description of Reena and Dr Robinson, I doubt if either of them would have been capable of giving an injection without leaving an obvious mark, especially when we were later told by our esteemed Home Office pathologist that she had been injected with a large volume of air. Jean has experience of embalming, but that is quite a different art. And, having met her, I didn't get the impression that she's a killer, not that you should go on impressions. Both Cassandra and Aaron Gupta, I reckon, would have the skills. As a haematologist Cassandra would be regularly taking blood samples and injecting medicines, I presume.'

'Tell me about it,' Munro said with a sigh.

'But who has more steady hands than a dentist?' Steadman continued. 'Only here was the problem – how do you inject a large volume of air through a needle swiftly with only one pair of hands? Dr Gupta didn't appear to have an accomplice. I thought about bicycle pumps, aerosol cans – in fact you name it, I've considered it! My best guess was using a toy balloon tied tightly to the needle but…it just seemed too clumsy. Then Frank played me some Louis Armstrong, and it suddenly struck me.

'Dr Gupta waits until Robinson leaves, then makes sure his wife has had an extra dose of sleeping pills. Once she's asleep he peels back the bedcovers. He knows her groin is going to be numb as he had previously laced the lubricating jelly with anaesthetic. With one hand he feels where the vein should be. He is already holding the hypodermic needle between his teeth. With his tongue and the other hand he steadies the needle and plunges it in. He takes a deep breath and then blows through the needle as fast as he dares. One big, long puff - out comes the needle, and he presses firmly with a tissue until he is certain there is no bleeding. During which time, of course, he watches his wife die.'

The room was silent. Eventually Munro looked up and said:

'You know if Abi hadn't cut his throat I might have been tempted to do it myself.'

DCI Long raised an eyebrow, but Dr Rufus was in total agreement.

'Hear, hear,' he said. 'A baptism of fire for your first murder case, Alan, but well done!'

'It's not completed yet,' interrupted Steadman. 'We know the 'who' and the 'how', but not the 'why', and with Dr Gupta dead, that is going to require a bit more detective work.'

The phone on DCI Long's desk rang.

'Hello... Yes... Are you sure? Thanks.' He put the phone down. 'The hospital has called in Rosie Jennings' family.'

Nobody spoke. Eventually Kim Ho stood up, made her apologies and silently slipped from the room.

'Why couldn't it have been me?' Steadman said.

'Because it wasn't, John. If anybody should feel guilty, it should be me. I was in charge and I suggested she drive you over and sanctioned her actions. It's my head on the block, not yours, although I doubt if that will make you feel any better. I have also been to see her parents. Naturally they are very upset, but they are also very proud of their daughter. They don't hold you responsible at all. Her father is a vicar.'

Steadman was not sure if that last bit of information made him feel worse or better.

'I would like to go and meet her family,' he said. 'Could you spare somebody to drive me to the hospital?'

'I'll take you,' Munro volunteered. 'That's if...'

'Of course, take the Audi,' DCI Long replied.

'I have a couple of post mortems to perform. Do you want to spend the night at my place?'

'No – I think I will go back to Jamaica Mansion. It will be safer for all concerned.' Steadman screwed up his face. 'There was something important that I was going to say before the phone rang, but it has completely slipped my mind.'

* * *

Steadman had confused memories of the intensive care unit at Helmsmouth General. He could recall the constant beeping of the machines, the pain, the realisation that he was blind and the day he remembered his wife's final minutes. They were not happy memories.

Fortunately the nurse who met him was new and didn't recognise him. This was not the moment for a reunion.

Rosie's father stood up. His face was lined and there were dark circles under his eyes. Steadman held out a hand, and it was warmly grasped by the Reverend Jennings.

'I'm very pleased to meet you. Rosie has spoken a lot about you.'

'How is she?' Steadman asked.

'Stable again, thank God. There was a blood clot or something in her wind pipe, I didn't fully understand but it's gone now. She is still on the ventilator. Her mother is with her.'

'I am truly sorry for what happened. I feel personally responsible.'

'Why? You weren't the one with the gun.'

'No, but the shot was intended for me.'

'I'm not so sure about that – let me explain. Both of us have spent our working lives dealing with criminals. You probably don't know, but I have been a prison chaplain for many years. I spend hours every day talking with, and trying to understand, the people that our society deems are our most evil. Do you believe in God, Inspector?'

'The tenuous hold I had on religion has been tested to the limit and now barely hangs on by a thread. It is easier to believe in the devil sometimes.'

'That doesn't surprise me, and it is precisely the point I am trying to make. I have followed your case with, shall we say, a 'professional interest'. The man who blinded you after killing your wife is undeniably evil. He is perhaps even more than that. DCI Long told me of your travails on Quarry Hill. What struck me was that if he had wanted to kill you, why didn't he just push you over? Last night you were followed by a motorbike – a big, powerful machine that could easily overtake a car, but didn't. No, he enjoyed the chase and the fear he was generating. I gather Rosie had to double back due to road works, and he shot out a back seat window at close range – deliberate or accidental? And then later when he has you within his sights he has a choice – he could kill you or further torment you by shooting your companion, knowing that the latter would consume you with guilt. I think that is the choice he made. You are not the one responsible for my daughter's injuries.'

'But…'

'There are no 'buts'. My daughter was doing the job she loved, and we would not expect her to have done anything less.' He paused. 'Would you like to see her?' As if for the first time he noted Steadman's dark glasses and white cane, and then added, 'I'm sorry - forgive me, I forgot for the moment.'

'That's all right. I would like to go to her bedside and meet your wife.'

Mrs Jennings was too distraught to say very much. She gave Steadman her chair and he sat down awkwardly. His knees touched the edge of the bed. Slowly and gently he reached out and found Rosie's hand. It was cold and limp. He took her hand in his.

'We'll get the man that did this to you, Rosie,' he said in a whisper.

Was it his imagination, or did he feel a barely perceptible tightening of Rosie's grip?

CHAPTER THIRTY FOUR

The steel reinforced door closed with a dull clunk. Beyond the walls of Jamaica Mansion, Steadman heard Munro turning the Audi and roaring back to the Eyesore. The grounds were deathly quiet, almost claustrophobic. He had thought he would feel a sense of security, perhaps even elation at being back. Instead, to his surprise, he felt confined and resentful. His mood did not improve as he stumbled and shuffled up the path. George was waiting for him and held the door open.

'How's Rosie Jennings?' he asked.

Dear God, thought Steadman, does the whole world know about my misadventure already?

'She's critical but stable,' he replied. 'I've just come from the hospital. I've spoken with her parents.'

'They must be terribly upset.'

Steadman was getting irritated and struggled to prevent himself from snapping at George.

'It wouldn't be natural if they weren't,' he said rather more abruptly than he intended.

'Of course, of course,' George replied, sensing that Steadman was not keen to talk. 'I gather you spent the night with Dr Rufus. I'll bet you are exhausted.'

'Is there anything about my activities that is not public knowledge? How do you know all this? Is everyone keeping tabs on me?'

'It must seem like that,' George said, thoughtfully. 'This is a safe house. We have a duty of care towards you, Mr Steadman, and we feel we have let you down once. We don't want to make the same mistake twice. DCI Long's office has kept Jamaica Mansion informed, that's all.'

'I'm sorry, George, I didn't mean to lose my rag. I'm not physically exhausted but I am emotionally drained - and I can't help but feeling that it is all my fault. Poor Rosie...'

There was an awkward pause.

'Well, here's something to take your mind off things - your sister Linda is coming over to make you some food.'

'And probably tear a strip off me,' Steadman added. 'If you hear breaking glass, come and rescue me.'

The air in the apartment was stale. The first thing Steadman did was open a window. A limp sun was trying to peer through the clouds. Its light touched Steadman's face as he struggled with the window latch. The warm glow lifted his spirits ever so slightly. Steadman hated sitting at home wearing a jacket. A jacket indoors meant work, interviews or executive meetings. On point of principle he always removed it and put on a jumper, the scruffier the better. His favourite was a blue woollen one that was frayed at the welt and thin at the elbows. Linda would not approve. He patted the pockets of his jacket and found the little netsuke good luck rat. 'I wonder if you're to blame,' he muttered to himself, carefully putting it back in the display cabinet. 'From now I'll take my own chances.'

Linda arrived. She hugged him, she laughed, she wept, pummelling his back half-heartedly with her fists.

'What am I to do with you? I don't suppose there is any point in me saying anything?'

'None whatsoever.'

'Can you tell me what happened? The evening paper and the local radio are full of the story. It can't all be true!'

Linda seldom had time to watch television, especially at this time of year when there was so much to do in her greenhouses and potting shed. Steadman told his story. There was no point in concealing anything from his sister; she could spot a half-truth a mile away. Like her brother she was disturbed and distressed by Abi. And exactly like her brother, at the end of the narrative all she could say was, 'Poor Rosie.'

'Do you really think the vicar is right and he wasn't shooting at you after all?'

'It could be,' Steadman mused. 'If it is true, it makes him all the more evil.'

'Do you think he drowned?'

'I wish I knew for certain. Until we find a body…'

'You think he's still alive, don't you?' Linda interjected.

Steadman couldn't lie. 'Yes, I do actually. I've been thinking about it. Regardless of the extra weight of his protective gear, I reckon a motorcyclist would be quite buoyant, at least for a short time. I don't know if you've noticed, but somebody on a motorbike always looks larger than normal.'

Linda confessed that she hadn't.

'Well,' continued Steadman, 'that's because the wind whistles into every seam when they're riding, blowing them up like a Michelin man. Until water replaces the air he would bob about like a cork. I gather he went in just the other side of the container ship. It wouldn't take much to swim round and shin up a ladder. In the immediate aftermath he could have easily slipped out.'

'Doesn't that worry you, John?'

He shrugged his shoulders by way of reply.

As Linda couldn't think of anything else to say she decided to make them both something to eat. She took the opportunity of going through her brother's fridge and threw out all the food that was mouldy or past its sell-by date. She cleaned all the work surfaces and changed the tea towels.

'Don't worry,' she shouted through to her brother, 'I've put everything back in the same place.'

Steadman knew what she'd be up to and didn't really mind. He had put on a Billie Holiday CD and, as the smell of cooking wafted from the kitchen, he suddenly realised he was famished.

The food was simple and wholesome. Linda had not only emptied the fridge but stocked it up with prepared meals. She had put each in a different shaped container and made her brother recite what was in each one and how it was to be heated up until she was satisfied that he had memorised them all correctly. They spent a pleasant evening chatting about this and that. Steadman told her that he was feeling smothered living in Jamaica Mansion and that he would like to move out. Ever the cautious one, Linda voiced her concerns but she knew her brother only too well. He'll be out of here in under a month, she thought to herself. Steadman tactfully moved the topic of conversation on to Linda's garden.

'Everything's coming on splendidly, despite the storm. I do love the spring. And I'm working on something for you. I'm hoping it will be ready for your birthday!'

Steadman had completely forgotten that it would be his birthday soon. When he was younger he couldn't wait for them to come round; now they seemed to sneak up on him with increasing and unwelcome regularity.

'What have you been up to?' he asked.

'If I told you it would spoil the surprise. You'll just have to wait.'

Steadman's sightless eyes felt heavy, and more than once he found himself nodding off as Linda finished tidying up.

'Do you want a hand getting into bed?'

'No, I'll be fine. Thanks for everything.'

She gave him a hug and a peck on the cheek and rushed off before he could notice that she was crying again.

Steadman was perplexed as to what Linda was planning for his birthday surprise. As he drifted off to sleep he found himself wandering down through her garden, his vision returning with each dreaming step. The sky was a vivid ultramarine and the wet grass shone like emeralds. The only bird in the garden was a large white peacock with an enormous tail sitting on a branch. The tail tumbled down to the ground like a vast bridal train. The bird flew past him, brushing its tail across his face. He couldn't see his sister and thought she must be in the potting shed. Inside the shed it was quite dark. The windows were dusty and covered in cobwebs. There were mounds of moist compost, and the place smelt of damp and growth. Linda's tools were neatly arranged on the wall, all clean and gleaming but there was no sign of his sister.

Steadman turned to leave. The door had vanished. Confused, he looked round the shed. In the darkest corner was another door he had never noticed before. It led into a much smaller room illuminated only by a grimy skylight. Here were the toys of their childhood: bikes, dolls, guns, comics, even their old rocking horse. Steadman turned to shout through the door; Linda just had to see what he had found. But again the door had disappeared. In its place were heavy thick drapes decorated with a coat of arms. Steadman pushed the curtains aside. Behind them was a much more solid door with an ornate brass handle. The room beyond, and this time it was a proper room, was laid out like a large study. Two of the walls were covered in books, and in the centre of the room was a very grand desk covered in a mass of papers. A high-backed leather winged chair sat in the bay window. The chair was quite worn and there was a footstool in front of it. The room felt vaguely familiar. From the doorway he could even read the titles of the books. They were mainly scientific, but in amongst them were antiquarian books bound in leather with faded gilt titles in Latin and French. On the wall behind him hung two portraits of men in military regalia, neither of whom he recognised. Something creaked. He turned round. The walls with the books seemed a little closer. Another creak – this time he could see the walls move. Some of the books tumbled off the top shelves landing on the desk, sending the papers flying like over-sized confetti. The walls moved again. Steadman turned to go out. The door was gone. Hanging in its place was another picture, this time a full-length portrait of a man in uniform. He had a sarcastic grin on his face and as Steadman watched he started to clap slowly and rhythmically. The men in the other two pictures joined in with the clapping. They too were grinning. The clapping got progressively faster and with each clap the books inched forward, now pushing the desk in front of them. Steadman made for the bay window, but the white peacock was there sitting on the curtain pole with his tail fanning down, all but obscuring the window. The feathers stiffened, pressing on to Steadman's face. Something hard poked him in the back. Was it a book or the edge of the desk? The clapping got louder, harsher and more incessant. And as quickly as he had fallen asleep he was awake.

He was lying at an angle on the side of the bed. His head was jammed up against the headboard underneath the pillow, and the corner of the bedside cabinet was sticking into his back. There was somebody knocking loudly at the door. The last vestiges of the dream flickered and died. He pushed the pillow off his face, rolled over and sat up, swinging his legs over the edge of the bed. The door of his apartment opened and a deep, gentle voice said:

'Mr Steadman, are you all right?'

It was Bill, who had taken over from George.

'It is almost eleven, sir, and we were getting quite concerned. Please forgive the intrusion, but you did not respond to the intercom, and I have been knocking for several minutes.'

Steadman was still slightly dazed.

'I do apologise, Bill, I was sound asleep. I think I was dreaming.'

'Nothing too unpleasant, I hope?'

But all Steadman could recall was a large white peacock with an extraordinarily lavish tail. He got up, and Bill handed him his dressing gown that was lying in a heap on the floor.

'You have some mail. Do you wish me to read it for you? I have taken the liberty of bringing it with me.'

Bill really would have suited the church, thought Steadman. It was as though each of his statements should end with a solemn 'amen'.

The first letter was from Lloyd's café. In addition to an account, there was a hand-written note. Bill read it out:

"Dear Mr Steadman, we have heard that you may be able to leave your present accommodation and wonder if the following might be of interest. We have two flats above the café. My parents live in the first floor but the second floor flat is empty. It is quite spacious and has just been refitted and decorated. Although there is a kitchen, the café would, of course, provide you with any refreshments you require. As you are only too aware being so close to the Eyesore, the majority of our clientele are police officers, so you would not be short of company. You need not worry about rent. Our family will always be in your debt. I look forward to hearing from you. Yours sincerely, Marco Lloyd."

Steadman was taken aback.

'I couldn't live there for nothing, but it's a thought,' he said.

'Do you think it's wise to leave us so soon?' asked Bill.

'I don't know, but I can't stay here forever. What's the other letter?'

'Forgive me for smiling, sir,' said Bill. 'It's a circular from a book club offering, and I quote, "A unique opportunity to collect leather-bound classics that will be the envy of your friends as you build up your own personal library". Shall I bin it?'

In a flash, Steadman's dream came back to him. He knew why the study felt familiar, and what it was that had been troubling him in Dr Gupta's house.

CHAPTER THIRTY FIVE

'Alan, have you got the keys for the Guptas' house?'

The line was still crackly after the storm, and Steadman had difficulty in catching all the words.

'No, but DS Fairfax has. I'm sorry, I can barely hear you… Why? There's something I want to check up on. It may be nothing, but it could be important. It would be easier to explain if we were there. Have you got a long tape measure? Good, I'll be ready in half an hour.'

Steadman hung up. He was acutely aware that he might be about to make a fool of himself. There could be a perfectly logical explanation for the apparent discrepancy in the lengths of the two rooms, but he was sure that there was one. He would not tell DS Munro about his dream. Some things, he thought, are best kept private.

Although he had eaten well with his sister the previous evening, Steadman realised he had missed breakfast and would probably miss his lunch. He still had to wash and dress; there was no time to prepare any food if he was to be ready in half an hour. Without his sight, everything took so much longer. There was nothing left for it but to raid the biscuit tin.

Munro arrived right on time and informed him that DS Fairfax was waiting in the car.

'Am I presentable?' Steadman asked.

Munro looked him over. His shoes could have done with a polish; other than that everything seemed in order. Steadman slipped on his dark glasses and unfolded his cane. Arm in arm the two men made their way to the car.

'I'm thinking I will try and get a guide dog once life has regained some semblance of order' said Steadman.

'I'm sure it would give you a bit more freedom as well as some company,' replied Munro.

Steadman told him about the offer of a flat over Lloyd's café and about Linda's anxiety. 'Don't get me wrong, I'm very grateful for being in Jamaica Mansion, but it will never be home. Would you come and look at the flat with me and give me your opinion?'

Munro went bright red.

'Of course, I'd be delighted,' he stammered.

DS Fairfax got out of the car and greeted him warmly.

'I hope I'm not leading you on a wild goose chase. If you remember, you were kind enough to let me prowl round the ground floor on the night of Dr Gupta's murder,' he explained. 'I might be quite wrong, but when I paced out the rooms and the corridor there appeared to be about two or three feet unaccounted for in Gupta's study. Sorry, I should have said something earlier. Until this morning the fact had gone completely out of my mind.'

'You mean between the back wall and the corridor?' DS Fairfax asked.

'Exactly. By the way, the desk was covered in papers, wasn't it? Was there anything relevant?'

'I was just about to mention that,' Fairfax replied. 'They were mainly utility bills, subscriptions and some foreign correspondence. What was odd was that some of them were quite old. They were scattered about in no particular order.'

'So anyone peeking into his study would get the impression he was hard at work,' Steadman said as he pursed his lips.

'It also doesn't really fit in with his character,' added Munro. 'I would guess that he was a man whose life was well ordered – a place for everything and everything in its place. I was wondering why you wanted me to bring a tape measure.'

There was a policeman standing by the gate. He looked at Munro's ID, opened the gate and flagged them in. The house stood looking forlorn, alone and deserted. It was as if it knew something awful had happened inside it and that it would never be inhabited again.

The tyre marks from Dr Rufus's car were clearly visible on the lawn. Fortunately the rain had washed away Munro's vomit. The mobile incident unit still sat in the drive. Some of the plastic ribbon that had been used to cordon off the house had been blown loose in the storm and was now entangled in the bushes by the front door. DS Fairfax brushed it aside.

'What do you think will happen to the place?' she asked as she unlocked the front door.

'Difficult to say,' Steadman replied. 'They may try to sell it in a few years' time or pull it down and build something in its place.'

'I wouldn't fancy living in it,' Fairfax said, shuddering. 'Already it gives me the creeps.'

'Oh, I don't know,' Munro chipped in. 'If the price was right, I could live with its history. I don't believe in ghosts.'

Steadman was willing to bet that wild horses wouldn't drag Maureen and the girls here, even if the house was given to Munro for nothing.

The silence in the house was broken only by the ticking of a long-case clock by the stairwell. There was a slightly unpleasant smell reminiscent of a butcher's shop on a hot day.

'I don't suppose it has been cleaned yet,' Steadman commented.

'What would you like us to do first?' asked DS Fairfax.

'Measure the room on the right, which I believe is the dining room.'

DS Fairfax guided him in and led him to a chair. She and Munro measured the length and the width.

'Correct me if I'm wrong - the corridor behind these two rooms is perfectly straight,' said Steadman.

Munro checked. The corridor was indeed perfectly straight, running from the clinic at one end to the conservatory at the other.

Initially neither Munro nor Fairfax noticed anything amiss with the study. The wall facing them was covered in books, as was the back wall.

'Is there a leather chair in the bay window?' asked Steadman.

Munro confirmed that there was and helped Steadman into it. 'There's a footstool, if you like,' he said.

'You'll be offering me a coffee and a brandy next,' Steadman replied.

Fairfax had removed some books from the bottom shelves on both walls. They measured, then re-measured. Munro was still sceptical and insisted on measuring the outside of the room. There was no doubt about it; the study was two and a half feet shorter than it should have been.

Fairfax and Munro examined the corridor thoroughly. There was no sign of a concealed door, nor was there anything immediately obvious in the wall of books. Munro pulled out volumes at random every eighteen inches along the wall, hoping to find some dummy books. All of them were genuine.

'What about the architrave?' asked Steadman. 'Can you see any breaks?'

'Nothing that I can see, but it is carved with overlapping shells and scrolls,' answered Munro.

'What about the carpet? Are there any marks to suggest a door opening?'

It was Fairfax who responded this time.

'I know what you mean, sir, like an arc where the door has rubbed.' She looked at the carpet from several angles, then got down on her hands and knees. 'Wait a minute. Alan, can you remove that chair?'

There was another winged chair in the corner. Munro picked it up with ease and deposited it by the fireplace.

'If you look closely at the carpet pile behind the chair it's flattened and slightly grubby,' she said.

'Fiona's right,' added Munro. 'Somebody has spent a bit of time standing here. I can't see anything of particular interest. The books here are all bound journals on dentistry.'

'Are any of the spines more worn than the others?' Steadman asked.

'Volume 38 looks a bit more battered than the rest, and it won't come out,' said Munro giving the book a tug.

'Try pushing it in,' Steadman suggested.

There was a muffled click as a whole section of books receded into the wall and slipped behind the neighbouring shelves.

'Well I'll be damned!' exclaimed Munro. 'It's like opening the sliding door on a van!'

But the gap proved disappointing. Fiona produced a small pocket torch and handed it to Munro, who was already standing in the hidden space. It was narrow, clean and completely empty.

'At least it proves you were right, sir,' said Munro, unable to keep the disappointment out of his voice.

Steadman remained silent. He couldn't accept that someone had gone to the trouble of building a secret door without a good reason. It was only when Munro stepped back into the room that Fairfax noticed that his large feet had been covering the latch of a trapdoor.

'Of course,' said Steadman, 'I should have thought of it earlier. A house of this age would undoubtedly have a cellar.'

Munro lifted the trapdoor. A light came on automatically, revealing a low room about half the size of the study. There was another desk, modern and more business-like with a computer on it. A bookcase and a filing cabinet sat in front of the desk. Apart from a solitary chair, the room was otherwise bare.

'Here, let me go down,' suggested Fairfax. 'I doubt if that ladder would take your weight.'

Nimbly she descended into Gupta's lair. Munro repositioned the second easy chair and guided Steadman round so he could hear what Fiona was saying.

'Where shall I start?' she asked, slipping on a pair of vinyl gloves.

'Why don't you see if you can open the computer?'

'Blast!' said Fiona. 'It needs a password – any suggestions?'

Munro looked at his watch, 'Excuse me – back in a moment.'

'Most people write their passwords down somewhere. Has the desk got any drawers?' Steadman asked.

DS Fairfax rifled through the drawers. There were computer manuals, telephone directories, foreign directories and a small pocket notebook. On the inside cover in neat writing was 'GUPTA888'.

'I think I may have found it, sir.'

'I bet it has his name in block capitals.'

'How did you guess?'

'He just sounds that sort of person.'

It took a little time for the computer to load. DS Fairfax started to flick through some of the files in the bookcase. The first few seemed to be accounts related to his dental practice. Others contained bank statements showing occasional large sums of money being transferred from a foreign drug manufacturer, probably Alisha's company, Fairfax presumed.

The study door banged open and Munro came in carrying a cardboard drinks tray and a large brown paper bag.

'Bacon rolls, coffee and flapjack,' he announced.

Fiona re-appeared and wrinkled her nose.

'I'm vegetarian.'

'No problem – I'll swap you my piece of flapjack for your bacon roll,' Munro replied.

As it was, the portions of flapjack were the size of small paving slabs. Munro managed to eat not only two bacon rolls but also his own piece of flapjack, which Fairfax had declined, and the half left by Steadman.

'Waste not, want not – as my mother used to say. Just think of all the starving children in Africa,' quoted Munro. 'Are you all right up here by yourself? I'm going to risk the ladder.'

It didn't take the two of them long to get a sense of what Dr Gupta had been up to. The first clue came in a file full of pictures of young Malaysian women. Some of these pictures were marked with a red cross and a date. Each date corresponded with a large sum of money coming into his UK bank account via Alisha's drug company.

'I think he is running a marriage agency, finding brides for wealthy clients,' said DS Fairfax. 'Is that legal?'

'It all depends on the arrangements and whether coercion was used. A lot of work for the Vice Squad, I think,' said Steadman. 'It could explain his lavish lifestyle, but not why he murdered his wife. Have you found anything on the computer?'

'An awful lot of it seems to be financial transactions. By the looks of things he dabbled in the stock market, and both he and his wife had offshore bank accounts.'

'And I bet they avoided paying tax,' added Munro.

'The only other thing on the computer is that he seemed to be obsessed with genealogy.'

She opened a document named 'Fruits of the Family Tree'. It was not easy to decipher. There were lots of names and dates. Some of the names were highlighted in green, some in yellow and some in red, rather like traffic lights. Fairfax studied the screen intently. Only the female names were highlighted. Age also appeared to be important. The younger ones were all in amber and the older ones in either red or green. One name highlighted in red seemed familiar.

'Alan,' she asked, 'have you got the file with all the photos?'

He nodded.

'Is this name in the book?' she said as she pointed to the screen.

Munro flicked through the photos. Sure enough the name was there along with a red cross and a date.

'It seems, sir, that he was marrying off his cousins, second cousins and any other female relatives he could find,' Fairfax shouted up to Steadman.

'Has he actually done a family history, or does the 'tree' only show who is alive?' he asked.

Fiona clicked back on to the document and tried to trace it back. It stopped at Aaron Gupta, his sister Cassandra and their parents, who were both dead.

'Is there a similar tree for Alisha, or is it all merged into one?' asked Steadman.

Fiona scrolled back and forth. Alisha's tree was very short.

'It appears she was brought up in an orphanage with her sister Reena - parents both unknown.'

Munro had been rummaging in the filing cabinet, having opened it surreptitiously with an illegal set of lock-picks that he just happened to find in his pocket.

He was now delicately flicking through a small book.

'Not according to Aaron Gupta's diary, they're not!' he exclaimed. 'Or should I say he found out exactly who Alisha's mother was two weeks ago. Oh, my God...'

'What is it?' said Steadman and Fairfax in unison.

'Alisha was not just his wife. According to his diary he discovered that she was also his half-sister, as was Reena! He found out that they were the offspring of mother Gupta's first marriage. They were abandoned when she met the man who was to become husband number two, the father of Cassandra and Aaron. No wonder I thought they all looked vaguely alike!'

'It could explain why they never had children,' added DS Fairfax.

'Far more importantly, it explains why he murdered his wife,' said Steadman. 'Not only is it illegal to marry your half-sister, but for a man like Aaron Gupta if that had become public knowledge it would have ruined him utterly and completely.'

CHAPTER THIRTY SIX

It was another sunny day. Munro had planned to walk to Jamaica Mansion: DCI Long had insisted that he take the Audi.

'I can't make Inspector Steadman stay in the safe house. Until a body turns up or his assailant is captured, the least we can do is try to protect him on the streets,' he explained.

Munro was early. He passed through the security gate and wandered slowly up towards the main entrance. The walled grounds were gloomy, despite the sun and the first flush of green. A second security check and he was in. Even Munro could feel the ever-pressing sense of confinement in Jamaica Mansion. He understood why Steadman was keen to leave.

'Cometh the man, cometh the hour,' said Bill.

'I'm sorry?' Munro frowned as he tried to figure out what Bill was talking about.

'Mr Steadman will explain,' Bill replied enigmatically.

Munro climbed the stairs and knocked on the door.
'Come in, it's not locked,' Steadman shouted.

Munro pushed the door open. He had never really looked at the corridor before. It was stark. There were no pictures on the wall. There was no mirror by the door. The only break in the magnolia was a grimy streak at waist height where Steadman had slid a guiding hand along the wall.

'Ah, the man everyone's talking about!' Steadman exclaimed.

'You're as bad as Bill – what are you on about?'

'Haven't you seen the papers? Whoever is on duty always reads me the interesting bits. What did it say in yesterday's evening paper? 'A brilliant piece of crime-solving work by detectives Alan Munro and Fiona Fairfax has uncovered a secret den in the Gupta House. The detectives discovered that Dr Gupta and his wife had been running an illegal money-for-brides ring. The Helmsmouth Evening News believes this could account for their wealth and lavish lifestyle'.'

Munro grunted. His face was vermilion.

'And in this morning's paper,' Steadman continued, 'I think it said something like, 'The Helmsmouth Echo has found out that more detailed work by DS Munro and DS Fairfax has led to a startling breakthrough. They now know the reason why Dr Gupta brutally murdered his wife, although our source was not able to elaborate.'

'Odd, isn't it, how the press always put the words

'brutal' and 'murder' together? In the case of Alisha Gupta it was anything but brutal. It was cold and calculated and he almost got away with it,' Steadman added.

'I notice there is no mention of the 'blind detective' in any of this,' Munro remarked.

'Thank God for that,' Steadman replied. What he didn't tell Munro was that the 'blind detective' being left out was part of the deal Steadman had struck with the two editors when he had spoken with them earlier.

Munro was beaming. 'Amazing how quickly they change their tune,' he remarked. 'Guess what's happened to Gupta's golfing partner, the Assistant Chief Constable?'

'Done a runner, I'll bet!'

'Right in one. He's taken a month's unpaid leave and gone to the Algarve with his golf clubs.'

'Why does that not surprise me?' Steadman replied. 'Shall we go?'

The two men ambled off to the car.

'I'm flattered that you've asked me to look at the Lloyds' flat with you. Won't Linda mind?'

'My sister has a heart of gold. If she had her way I would be wrapped in cotton wool and put in a bullet-proof box. I don't want her to feel in any way responsible if something happens to me when I leave Jamaica Mansion. And neither should you,' Steadman added as an afterthought.

'What am I supposed to be looking out for?'

'Oh, I don't know – things like loose rugs and unnecessary furniture. More importantly, just get a feel for the place – is it clean and comfortable? Will I be able to fit my piano in? That sort of thing.'

'It can't be less homely than your apartment in Jamaica Mansion.'

'Don't you start as well! Linda is always on at me to get some things put on the walls to cheer the place up a bit. I have tried to argue that they won't do anything for me other than when I knock them off the wall and cut myself on the broken glass, but she won't have it.'

Munro pulled up outside Lloyd's café. Marco was waiting for them. He led them to a solid Victorian maroon door next to the café. Munro couldn't recall having seen it before, and it was only a vague memory for John Steadman.

'Are there stained glass panels on either side?' he asked.

There were, and they cast pretty coloured shadows in the vestibule beyond.

'Mind the doormat, sir,' said Munro.

Marco explained, as he opened the vestibule door, that the corridor on the left continued back and opened into the staff area between the counter and the kitchens. On the right were the stairs that led to the two flats. Out of habit Steadman counted the steps: seven to the first landing, then seven more until he was outside the door of the first flat. Mr and Mrs Lloyd senior were standing at the door, waiting to greet him.

'It is so good to see you again, Mr Steadman. We hope you will be very happy here.'

'Papa, he's only come to look at the flat – he might not like it.'

'What's not to like?' replied Mr Lloyd senior.

'The nosy neighbours in the flat below, for one thing!' Marco responded, shaking his head.

'Just ignore him, Mr Steadman. Come in for a coffee after your visit and bring...aren't you DS Munro? I recognise you from your picture in the morning paper.'

Munro wished the ground would swallow him.

'You never told me my picture was in the paper as well,' he muttered to Steadman once they were inside the vacant flat.

'How would I know?' he responded as innocently as he could.

The flat was very light and airy and not too dissimilar in layout to the one in Jamaica Mansion.

'You should see the view,' said Marco, before realising his blunder. 'I'm sorry, I didn't...'

'Don't worry about it,' Steadman reassured him. 'Tell me what you see.'

'It really is cracking,' answered Munro. 'I can see right down the hill to the marina.'

'Can you see the Eyesore?'

'Thankfully no, it must be just tucked out of view and I don't think you can see it from the back either.' He strode through to the kitchen. 'No, only treetops, gardens and a few roofs.'

Marco was very proud of the kitchen.

'It's brand new,' he said. 'There's a fitted fridge freezer and a washing machine with a built in tumble dryer.' He turned on the tap with a flourish. There was a low growl and a gurgle. 'It's even got a built-in waste disposal unit under the sink,' he said grandly.

Munro was not so impressed. He had visions of Steadman putting his hand in and getting his fingers chewed off.

'Is there space for my piano?' Steadman asked.

There was plenty of room. Marco had deliberately kept the furniture to a minimum. There were no obvious trip hazards and nothing with sharp corners. He had even put an intercom down to the bar so that Steadman could order food and drinks or ask for help.

'I think I will be very happy here,' he said, 'once we have settled the rent.'

Steadman eventually won the argument, and they shook hands.

'Now I promised to have coffee with your parents.'

'You don't mind, do you?' asked Marco. 'It will mean a lot to them.'

'I'm very fond of your parents. I suspect it may become a pleasant habit.'

'You know, I've never seen or heard any of your neighbours in Jamaica Mansion,' Munro remarked.

'They have brushed passed me at the concierge's desk. Not one has knocked on my door or ever spoken with me. It may be a safe house but it reeks of paranoia.'

★ ★ ★

So, John Steadman, you are planning your escape from Jamaica Mansion. Is it arrogance, or do you just feel out of harm's way following our last encounter? Your sister won't like it. I can't believe you're considering moving to a poky flat above Lloyd's café. Why, you'll end up smelling like last night's takeaway! I must confess I am enjoying your decline. But I have had enough now. A blind man moving into a newly refurbished flat...The possibilities are endless! I am spoilt for choice. Let me think. Let me think...

CHAPTER THIRTY SEVEN

Steadman woke bright and early to the aroma of freshly roasted coffee, one of the joys of living above the café. He couldn't resist. For the first few days, and with some trepidation, he had asked via the intercom for a cup to be sent up. The coffee had been wonderful. Fearing that he might be making a nuisance of himself, he had desisted for two days in a row. Marco and his brother had taken this as a personal affront, so it was now established as a daily routine. Although he could also have a breakfast sent up, he had deliberately chosen not do so. Some degree of independence was vital, he felt. Breakfast was not a grand affair: fruit juice followed by toast or cereal, and of course a steaming cup of fine Italian coffee. Today was an exception: it was his birthday. As well as his coffee, he asked for bacon in a warm croissant.

This year his birthday fell on a Sunday. As the weather had stayed sunny Linda had organised a lunchtime party in her garden. Dominic, her husband, prided himself in his skills at the barbecue. At noon Alan Munro arrived in the Audi to pick him up. Maureen and the two girls were sitting in the back.

'We've got a present for you, Uncle John. Can you guess what it is?' said Annie.

Judging by the chocolatey smell Steadman deduced it was a fresh supply of brownies. Rather than spoil the girls' surprise he suggested several highly improbable items, including a toilet brush and a hamster, which had them both in a fit of the giggles.

He had specifically asked Linda to write 'no presents' on the invitations. Nobody had taken any notice of it. Dominic had found him a netsuke figure of a tiny frog sitting on a lily pad carved out of mammoth tusk. It was just the sort of gift Holly would have given him. Dr Frank Rufus gave him a CD of bawdy sea shanties. DCI Long too had got him a CD; Glenn Gould playing Bach. It was a replacement for the one Steadman had dropped and subsequently stood on during the move. DS Fairfax gave him some aftershave. George and Daisy brought him a bottle of Tullibardine malt whisky. Bill the 'Bishop' had contributed, but was on duty as seemed fitting, it being a Sunday. Even Rosie's parents had come along, and, as Steadman said to them quietly, his best present was the news that Rosie was making a good recovery.

While everybody was eating, Linda led him away to a more secluded part of the garden. She sat him in a comfortable swinging chair. The air was heavy with perfume.

'This is my surprise for you, John. I've made you your own scented garden. The plants I've chosen are all highly fragrant, and there will be something in flower for ten months of the year. You can touch all of them. Some, like the lemon balm, only release their scent if you brush your hands through the leaves.'

They spent the next quarter of an hour going round the individual plants.

'To really appreciate the garden you need to visit it as often as possible. Dominic and I would like you to come for Sunday lunch, every week if you are able. We will sit out here afterwards, weather permitting.'

John Steadman struggled to find the correct words to say; it was so kind and thoughtful.

'Here they are!' exclaimed Munro through a mouthful of hot dog.

'We thought you'd been kidnapped again,' added Dr Rufus. 'Come on, the boss wants to make a speech.'

DCI Long tapped the side of his glass with a fork. 'I would just like to say a few words...'

'Not too many, I hope!' heckled Dr Rufus.

DCI Long ignored him. He thanked Linda and Dominic, welcomed Rosie's parents and shared the news of her progress. He said how delighted he had been to have John Steadman working with him again. There was a murmur of 'hear, hear' from everybody. He remembered Holly Steadman and reiterated his determination to close the case.

'I would like to finish by making two

announcements,' he said. 'Firstly, in recognition of the excellent work Alan Munro has put into the Gupta investigation, I am pleased to announce that he is to be made a full detective sergeant.'

There was a round of applause. Munro blushed like a schoolgirl.

'And secondly, I have been instructed by the Chief Constable, no less, that I have the authority to employ Detective Inspector John Steadman as a consultant in any future investigation that I deem appropriate.'

There was an even louder round of applause and it was Steadman's turn to go pink. They all raised their glasses to toast his birthday and future success.

Nobody noticed the man in the motorcycle helmet peering through the hedge and listening to every word.

CHAPTER THIRTY EIGHT

The move to the flat above Lloyd's café had been less traumatic than Steadman had feared. As the weeks had gone by he had become more relaxed. There was always company in the café if he wished. He had even ventured out by himself on several occasions, much to Linda's despair. The distances were very short to begin with, but nonetheless intimidating. He counted his steps, familiarised himself with the pavements, the walls and the kerbs, noted where hedges stopped and started and where trees had been planted at the edge of the road. Progress was painfully slow. Not for the first time he thought about getting a guide dog.

He had thrown himself wholeheartedly into re-learning the piano and fortified with a second cup of fine Italian coffee, was practising his scales. Miss Elliot, the piano tutor, had set him a formidable piece of homework designed to test and improve his left hand. Mr and Mrs Lloyd senior made no objection to his playing. As Mrs Lloyd remarked, 'It makes a nice change from listening to the radio.'

The exercises were proving tiresome, so he gave them up. Instead he lost himself in something of Jacques Loussier's – Bach with a twist: late night jazz. All he needed was a drummer, a bass player, a packet of Gauloises and, in his mind's eye, he could be in a Parisian night club.

Someone was knocking on his door. The noise was loud and urgent. Alan Munro had said he would call in sometime after eleven; surely it was too early. The small metallic voice of his watch confirmed that it was only ten twenty. There was no point in rushing to answer the door. Although his mental map of the flat was complete, he knew that if he hurried he would end up bumping into something or falling over. The knocking persisted. He fiddled with the lock and dislodged the security chain.

'Mr Steadman? I'm Mike Howard, plumber. There's water coming through the ceiling in the flat below. Mr Lloyd sent me up. We think it's coming from your kitchen.'

The man had a high-pitched voice and spoke with a stutter, pausing before the words 'plumber' and 'water', which he eventually articulated with a spittle flecked explosion.

'I can't hear anything, but I've been playing the piano. The kitchen's this way,' Steadman replied.

The man stepped ahead of him.

'I'd better take a look.'

Steadman knew that he should have made some sort of attempt to have the man's ID checked. Faced with the prospect of his elderly neighbours' ceiling falling down, he let him pass. There was a smell of something familiar about the man.

'It's the w-waste disposal unit under the sink,' he stammered, 'b-bloody useless things – always going wrong. I'll need to switch off the electricity.'

'The fuses are behind the front...'

Before Steadman could finish he had brushed past him and was already opening the box. His footsteps were light and almost silent. He must be wearing trainers or crepe sole shoes; odd for a tradesman, Steadman mused.

'Shall I call Mr and Mrs Lloyd and tell them not to worry?' he offered.

'No – don't bother, I'll have it fixed up in no time.' There was no stammer in his reply.

Steadman went back into his living room and sat down at the piano. Maybe I should check with Marco, he thought, his fingers drumming on the edge of the piano. There was a loud click as the electricity went off. 'Damn, the cordless phone and the intercom won't work now,' Steadman muttered to himself, realising also that his mobile phone was charging in the bedroom.

A clatter came from the kitchen as the plumber dropped a tool. Had he had a tool box with him? Surely not – he had moved too quickly. Perhaps he just had some essentials in his pocket.

The hair on the back of Steadman's neck prickled. He pressed the button on the side of his watch again: 'ten thirty', chirped the little voice.

'That's a handy gadget you've got there, John.'

Steadman made no reply. He felt uncomfortable with the plumber's over-familiar tone.

'Yes,' the plumber squeaked, 'it's the out flow from the w-waste disposal unit. They shake themselves loose in no time if they've not been fitted p-properly and then continue to d-dribble away even when they're not working.'

Why did John Steadman not believe him? His stammer seemed to come and go and the pitch of his voice seemed absurdly high.

'Would you like a coffee sent up?' Steadman asked.

'No! – I mean no thank you, I'm almost finished.'

Steadman tried to figure out what he was doing. Judging by the grunting, the man was lying on his back fiddling with something. The minutes ticked by.

'There, that's it done. I'll put the electricity back on.'

Steadman heard him open the fuse box by the door. The fridge freezer immediately whirred back to life.

'I would leave it an hour so that it can fill up with water.' The plumber hesitated. 'Maybe I should just check...'

He brushed past Steadman on his way back to the kitchen. Again there was a vague suggestion of something familiar. The plumber was muttering to himself, but Steadman couldn't make out what he was saying. All he could hear was the faintest of creaks as the taps were turned on.

It was more like a bellow than a scream: the sound

a bull might make being dragged to the slaughterhouse, a horrifying roar of pain and shock.

'Are you OK?' Steadman called out. The bellow had been replaced by a ghastly hiss. He could hear the man's legs banging repeatedly on the cabinet doors. Christ, he's having a fit, thought Steadman.

The bellowing started again, even louder, incessant and terrifying. Steadman made for the intercom. 'Help! Someone – anyone, come as quick as you can!' he shouted.

The banging continued as the man in Steadman's kitchen continued to twitch and jerk. Now the acrid stench of burning flesh filled the room. The smoke alarm was going off. Above the din Steadman heard footsteps thundering up the stairs. Marco Lloyd, accompanied by Alan Munro, burst into the flat. Steadman flung out his arm.

'Don't touch him! Switch off the electricity first.'

Marco flicked the switch. The banging stopped.

Munro surveyed the devastation. The plumber lay lifeless on the floor, his blackened hands still clenched tight. Munro opened the window to let out the smoke and the smell. In the nick of time he caught John Steadman as his legs gave way beneath him. Munro lifted him as though he were a child and placed him on the sofa.

'I'm fine,' Steadman protested.

'No you're not. Lie still. Marco, could you get him a coffee, maybe with a shot of grappa in it and some sugar – in fact make that two.'

'Is he dead?' Steadman asked.

'Dead and half cremated,' Munro replied.

'What's happening? And what's that awful smell?'

Mr and Mrs Lloyd senior had appeared in Steadman's flat.

'I'm afraid your plumber has electrocuted himself,' said Steadman.

'Plumber? Why would we need a plumber?' said Mr Lloyd senior.

Steadman let out a soft moan. 'So who's the man lying on the floor of my kitchen?'

'Marco, I think it would be best if your parents didn't see,' Alan Munro said as he peered at the body. 'I don't recognise him.'

Marco Lloyd joined him and stared at the corpse with the smouldering hands.

'I recognise him,' he said. 'He came from the Blind People's Housing Association to check over the flat before you moved in.'

'There's no such organisation,' replied Steadman.

'You don't think...'

Before Munro could finish Steadman said, 'Check his fingernails.'

Marco looked puzzled, but Alan Munro knew exactly what he meant. He slipped on a pair of vinyl gloves and prised open the charred remains of the man's hands.

'You're right, sir. Neatly-trimmed nails on the left, but thick long nails on the right.'

Marco Lloyd seemed even more perplexed.

'He played guitar,' Munro explained, 'and so did the man who attempted to kill DI Steadman. I'm sorry, Marco, we'll have to seal off the flat. I wouldn't mind that coffee, and maybe a slice of cake,' he added as he took out his phone and called the Eyesore.

★ ★ ★

'How did he get in?' asked DCI Long.

Munro explained that one of the waiters recalled serving him that morning and saw him go to the toilet. Someone in the main kitchen stated that a man in workman's overalls had strolled through at a quarter past ten. Apparently he had even said, 'Good morning', and had given a friendly wave.

Dr Frank Rufus arrived.

'What's cooking?' he asked. 'You haven't burnt the Sunday joint again, have you, John?'

Steadman gave him a weak smile.

'Do either of you recognise him?' he asked.

DCI Long and Dr Rufus traipsed through to Steadman's kitchen. The flat seemed very small and crowded as more of the forensic team arrived.

'Come on, drink up your coffee. Would you like some of my cake?' said Munro.

Steadman shook his head.

'Marco Lloyd is in a terrible state,' he continued.

'That's understandable. It's not his fault – I'll speak with him later.'

The sweet, grappa-laced coffee tasted good. Steadman held the cup tightly. He was still shaking.

DCI Long and Dr Rufus were deliberating in the kitchen.

'Are you sure?'

'Oh yes, it's him all right. He's dyed his hair, but I'm quite certain.'

'We'll have to confirm with DNA testing. I don't think there's enough left to get decent fingerprints.'

'We had better tell John.'

'So, who is he?' Steadman asked when the two men re-entered the living room.

'We think he's the singer Jerry Machismo, although for the life of me I can't remember his real name,' said DCI Long.

Alan Munro looked blank.

'He was famous for a time, about twenty years ago,' Long added.

'But then,' Dr Rufus continued, 'he made a complete arse of himself at the Eurovision Song Contest. He muddled up the words of the song, something he was notorious for. The press never forgave him. His career nosedived, but he had already made a fortune. I think he was questioned on several occasions for minor drug offences and kerb crawling, wasn't he?'

'That's right, but he was never charged,' DCI Long confirmed. 'Does he mean anything to you, John?'

'Sadly yes,' he replied, shaking his head. 'We were at the same school. He was two years below me as I recall, and was obsessed with Holly at the time.' Steadman's dream came back to him: a voice shouting, a boy running away. 'I remember now – he vowed he would hate me for the rest of his life... for heaven's sake, he was only a kid. I can't believe a grown man would still bear a childhood grudge.'

'Quite possible,' said Dr Rufus. 'First love and all that. Failure in later life – a brain addled with drugs and alcohol. He's got to blame somebody for his predicament. Only natural, in a perverse sort of way that he should hold to account the person who stole his true love.'

'But why kill Holly?' asked Munro

'Oh, there's no sound logic, only petty childish reasoning,' explained Dr Rufus. 'A case of 'if I can't have her then nobody can'. I suspect it was as simple as that.'

'What happened today?' asked Steadman.

'He set up a simple but ingenious booby trap for you,' DCI Long explained. 'Firstly, he switched off the electricity and replaced the fuse with a piece of solid metal that wouldn't blow. Then he rewired the waste disposal unit so that when you turned on both taps you would electrocute yourself. Only problem was that he doesn't appear to have resisted the temptation to test it himself. Maybe he thought his bowling shoes would insulate him – who knows?'

'How soon can you get rid of the body?' Steadman asked.

'They're coming now,' DCI Long reassured him.

$\star\ \star\ \star$

Steadman had stayed with Linda and Dominic until his colleagues had finished their grisly task. He had become restless, resentful at losing his hard won independence and moreover, his sister did not have a piano. After what had seemed an eternity, but in reality was only a few days, he was allowed to return. Alan Munro had collected him and Linda had insisted that she accompany her brother.

The late afternoon sun streamed through the windows of Steadman's flat. The air was once again infused with the aroma of coffee and appetising home cooking from the café below.

'It's beautiful,' said Linda. She was standing looking out of the window.

'Describe what you see,' replied her brother, coming to stand beside her. Where should she start?

'Well, there are some wispy clouds on the horizon, so it will be a gorgeous sunset. The sea goes from dark blue to green and even brown. It is flecked with gold where the sun's rays are bouncing off the water.'

Steadman nodded, drinking in every word.

'Go on.'

'I can see the tips of the masts in the marina, and they too are catching the light. There must have been a shower earlier – the cobbles by the harbour are glinting. It looks like something out of the Wizard of Oz – you know, the 'yellow brick road'. The only buildings visible from here are the very old ones. It is enchanting – no two are alike.'

Steadman slipped off his dark glasses and covered each eye in turn. He could just discern the patch of brightness where the sun was; his imagination painted the rest of the picture.

'And even better,' added Munro as he joined them after parking the Audi, 'you can't see the Eyesore.'

'I can't believe it's all over,' said Linda as she put an arm round her brother.

'All bar getting the last bit of plumbing sorted out,' Munro replied.

As if on cue Mr Price, a genuine plumber this time, clumped into the room. I bet he's wearing stout working shoes, thought Steadman.

'Have you got a bucket to catch the water?'

Linda almost ran through to the kitchen. She was itching to put on her rubber gloves and scrub the place thoroughly.

'You've got that piece of metal and the old fuse, have you, sergeant?' asked Mr Price.

Munro patted his pocket.

'Right ho – I won't be long.'

In no time Mr Price had removed the waste disposal unit and replaced the taps. Munro bagged the old ones and put them in an evidence box.

'There's something I must do,' Steadman said as he felt his way through to the kitchen. He went over to the sink and touched the taps.

'Ah! – you've replaced them with those lever type ones.'

Marco Lloyd had joined them, bringing with him a large tray of refreshments.

'I thought they might be easier, that is if…' His voice trailed away leaving the sentence hanging in the air.

John Steadman grasped both the levers and pulled them forward. Water gushed from the spout.

'What in heaven's name are you doing?' asked Linda.

'I'm proving to myself that the intended means for my execution failed. And,' he continued, 'I may make a point of doing it every day with wet hands and bare feet.'

Marco Lloyd was taken aback.

'I'm sorry – I just assumed that, after all that has happened here you would be leaving us as soon as you could.'

'No,' Steadman replied. 'Justice, in a rather odd way, has been delivered. I think I shall be very content staying here. You are all so kind to me. And the view is wonderful – at least, that's what everybody tells me.'

Printed in Great Britain
by Amazon